SCANDAL *at*
the HOUSE OF RUSSELL

Never Trust a Pirate

Also by Anne Stuart

Historicals

Scandal at the House of Russell

Never Kiss a Rake

The House of Rohan

The Wicked House of Rohan

Shameless

Breathless

Reckless

Ruthless

Stand-Alone Titles

The Devil's Waltz

Hidden Honor

Lady Fortune

Prince of Magic

Lord of Danger

Prince of Swords

To Love a Dark Lord

Shadow Dance

A Rose at Midnight

The Houseparty

The Spinster and the Rake

Lord Satan's Bride

Romantic Suspense

The Ice Series

On Thin Ice

Silver Falls

Fire and Ice

Ice Storm

Ice Blue

Cold As Ice

Black Ice

Stand-Alone Titles

Into the Fire

Still Lake

The Widow

Shadows at Sunset

Shadow Lover

Ritual Sins

Moonrise

Nightfall

Seen and Not Heard

At the Edge of the Sun

Darkness Before Dawn

Escape Out of Darkness

The Demon Count's Daughter

The Demon Count

Demonwood

Cameron's Landing

Barrett's Hill

Collaborations

Dogs & Goddesses

The Unfortunate Miss Fortunes

Anthologies

Burning Bright
Date with a Devil
What Lies Beneath
Night and Day
Valentine Babies
My Secret Admirer
Sisters and Secrets
Summer Love
New Year's Resolution: Baby
New Year's Resolution: Husband
One Night with a Rogue
Strangers in the Night
Highland Fling
To Love and To Honor
My Valentine
Silhouette Shadows

Category Romance

Wild Thing
The Right Man
A Dark and Stormy Night
The Soldier and the Baby
Cinderman
Falling Angel
One More Valentine
Rafe's Revenge
Heat Lightning
Chasing Trouble
Night of the Phantom
Lazarus Rising / reprint as *Here Come the Grooms*
Angel's Wings
Rancho Diablo / reprint as *Western Lovers*
Crazy Like a Fox / reprint as *Born in the USA*
Glass Houses / reprint as *Men at Work*
Cry for the Moon
Partners in Crime
Blue Sage / reprint as *Western Lovers*
Bewitching Hour
Rocky Road / reprint in *Men Made in America #19*
Banish Misfortune
Housebound
Museum Piece
Heart's Ease
Chain of Love
The Fall of Maggie Brown
Winter's Edge
Catspaw II
Hand in Glove
Catspaw
Tangled Lies / reprint in *Men Made in America #11*
Now You See Him
Special Gifts
Break the Night
Against the Wind

Novellas

The Wicked House of Rohan
Risk the Night
Married to It (prequel to *Fire and Ice*)

SCANDAL *at* *the* HOUSE OF RUSSELL

Never Trust a Pirate

ANNE STUART

The characters and events portrayed in this book are fictitious. Any similarity to real persons, living or dead, is coincidental and not intended by the author.

Published by Montlake Romance, Seattle

www.apub.com

ISBN-13: 9781477849118
ISBN-10: 1477849114

Cover design by Mumtaz Mustafa

Library of Congress Control Number: 2013911410

Printed in the United States of America.

For Sabra Jones and the Greensboro Art Alliance and Residency, with thanks for all the fun and sheer joy you've brought to my life

CHAPTER ONE

Somerset, 1869

MADDY RUSSELL CURLED UP on the window seat in Nanny Gruen's tiny, spotlessly clean cottage on the very edge of the former Russell estate in Somerset, looking at the drizzling mist of a spring day. Somewhere, a mile away, lay their country house, Renwick, a place of considerable beauty that had once been her haven when things were bad. Things were bad now, but the house was no longer theirs. It had reverted to the Dark Viscount, as her younger sister, Sophie, liked to call him, and if he knew that two of the daughters of the house's former owner were hiding at their old nanny's cottage he'd soon put a stop to it. In fact, he didn't even have to honor the gift of this small house to the Russells' retired retainer, but so far he had. He could always change his mind.

Nanny Gruen sat across from her on the faded sofa, her eyes focused on her needlework, but Maddy had no illusion that this was an easy silence.

"You're the most hardheaded girl I've ever known," Nanny Gruen said. "What happened to my sweet little Maddy?" she added plaintively, finally looking up at her former charge, all five foot seven of her.

Maddy grimaced. "Your sweet little Maddy had a father who absconded with a huge sum of money and then abandoned his three daughters, leaving us penniless, disgraced. I've been deserted by my worthless fiancé, my older sister, Bryony, has disappeared with only a cryptic note, my younger sister does nothing but complain, and I refuse to sit around and wait for things to happen, not any longer. Since Bryony's run off with the Earl of Kilmartyn, it's going to be up to us to find out who framed our father and murdered him, because that fall from the cliffs in Dartmoor was no accident. And right now it's going to be up to me."

"And what is it you're thinking of doing, missy?" her old nursemaid demanded. "Running off and getting into trouble, that's what I call it."

"We are already in trouble, Nanny," Maddy said in a deliberately calm voice. "And sitting around on my posterior isn't going to make things any better."

"Miss Madeleine!" Nanny said, shocked. "A lady doesn't talk about her . . . her limbs."

"My posterior is not a limb, Nanny. It's my backside."

Nanny shrieked, putting her hands over her ears. "Your sister will hear you."

"I did hear her, Nanny," Sophie called from the tiny kitchen where she was currently experimenting with scones. "And she's right."

"Don't you be using such language, Miss Sophia," Nanny said sharply.

Sophie appeared in the doorway. She was coated with flour—Sophie didn't consider her cooking adventures successful unless she ended up wearing half of her ingredients. "You don't really think you're going to follow Bryony."

"Of course not!" Maddy said. "We can assume the Earl of Kilmartyn had nothing to do with Father's disgrace and death since Bryony appears to have run off with him instead of finding proof of his guilt. That leaves Captain Morgan and Viscount Griffiths."

"So go up to the big house and investigate the usurper," Sophie said in dark tones.

"Viscount Griffith's not a usurper—Somerset was built by his family, and we only lived there because Father won the rights to it in a gaming club," Maddy pointed out fairly. "We were bound to give it up sooner or later if the mad viscount's heir had the money to redeem the deed."

"Well, apparently he did, thanks to the collapse of Russell Shipping," said Sophie tartly. "Which seems awfully suspicious, given the circumstances. I think you should go after him."

"Father had begun to distrust Captain Morgan. I don't know if he was even aware of Viscount Griffiths. I certainly wasn't," Maddy said, stretching out her legs and climbing from her cozy perch, restless as always.

"Oh, and if you didn't know, then no one must have," Sophie shot back. "You don't know as much as you think you do."

"I know more than you, that's a sure thing," Maddy snapped.

"Girls!" Nanny Gruen said, and Maddy felt a flush cover her face. She was being childish, scrapping with her nineteen-year-old sister when she needed to be cool and controlled if she was going to succeed in their investigation.

"Sorry, Nanny," she muttered.

"You should be apologizing to your sister." As Sophie began to smirk Nanny turned to her. "And you should apologize right back, missy! The two of you—I wonder if you remember anything I taught you."

Maddy crossed the small room and gave Nanny a kiss on her cheek. Sophie stuck her tongue out at her when Nanny couldn't see, but Maddy ignored it. "Sorry, baby sister," she said. "It's easy to forget you're a grown up." That was just barbed enough to satisfy her annoyance. "But neither of you are changing my mind. Remember the note Father left? It said 'never trust a pirate.'"

"Captain Morgan isn't a pirate," Sophie said, plopping herself down beside Nanny on the worn sofa. A cloud of flour billowed out from her peach-striped gown. "He was a privateer at one point in his long and checkered career, but he was hardly swinging a cutlass and making people walk the plank. You've read too many novels."

"You're the one who steals them from under my bed," Maddy retorted. "And I have no illusions about Captain Morgan. I've met other captains Father employed. They're old, weather-beaten, and have no use for women. Given what we know of Captain Morgan I expect he's ancient—at least forty, and dull and dry. But there was a reason Father distrusted him, and I intend to find out why. We need to look at the facts clearly, without emotion. It appears as if Father embezzled a fortune from Russell Shipping, the very company he founded, ran off with the money, and then conveniently died on Dartmoor, with no sign of the money left behind, no word to his daughters. But why would he be heading for Devonport? If he'd simply been trying to escape from England he would have left from Dover. The captain is the obvious one to investigate first. I don't know why Bryony decided to bother with Kilmartyn."

"Because Kilmartyn was right there in London, you ninny," Sophie said. "And the Dark Viscount is right here. It makes no sense to go haring off—"

"I'm not haring off. This is a well-thought-out plan, and I've even had Mr. Fulton's assistance."

"Our useless solicitor? What's he done besides tell us that we're penniless and disgraced and will never marry?"

Maddy could feel a nerve tick in her jaw. "We'll marry," she said grimly. "You'll have men falling at your feet and they won't care what our father did. But first I'm going to find someone titled and very wealthy, a baronet at the very least. Lord Eastham's been writing me letters, you know. He's got more than enough money to clean up our reputations."

"But he's so old! And what about Tarkington? Won't he come back once he thinks about it?" Sophie said in a worried voice.

Maddy kept her face expressionless, ignoring the pain in her heart. "Tarkington is gone forever, and Godspeed. I've decided if I have to marry for the good of my family, it might as well be someone with a title and a bit more money."

"I rather thought that was my job," Sophie said. "You're quite beautiful, Maddy, but you know I outshine you. People tend to prefer sweet, witless blondes to dark-haired viragoes."

"I am not a virago!" Maddy was outraged.

"Girls!" Nanny said again, this time in a pleading voice. "You're giving me a headache. Must you always bicker?"

"Things will be much more peaceful when I'm gone, Nanny, and by the time I return we can all leave and get out of your hair."

"Now, Miss Madeleine, you know perfectly well I don't want that!" Nanny Gruen said stoutly. "You can stay here as long as you like—for the rest of your lives if you wish."

"Don't worry—you won't be stuck with us that long. It's going to be fine. Mr. Fulton owes me a favor, after his total uselessness with Father's estate. He happens to be acquainted with Captain Morgan, and he heard he was in need of a maid of all work. So I had Mr. Fulton tell him he knew just the girl."

"You didn't!" Sophie breathed, her bright eyes round.

"I did. And I know I can trust Mr. Fulton not to betray who I am. He feels guilty."

"You could marry him and forget all this nonsense," Nanny Gruen said sternly. "He's a good-looking young man with prospects. A solicitor's a respectable profession, not like a shopkeeper or something."

"I have no intention of marrying anyone who has to work for a living," Maddy said firmly. "If I don't choose Lord Eastham then I'll find someone with at least twenty thousand pounds a year and a title to boot. I'm not throwing myself away on a penniless solicitor."

Sophie sighed dramatically. "Haven't I already told you I'm the logical one to marry a title? You're already twenty-two."

Maddy resisted the completely childish urge to pinch her sister hard. "Then we can both marry titles. The more, the merrier. And I'm hardly at my last prayers."

"Do you suppose Bryony really married Lord Kilmartyn?" Sophie said, clearly not realizing her imminent danger. "She always said she would never marry. And Kilmartyn could have anyone."

"Are you suggesting that anyone's more precious than our Bryony?" Maddy said in a dark tone. Sophie was going to end up black and blue at this rate.

"Of course your sister is suggesting no such thing. And shame on you, Miss Maddy, for even thinking your older sister would run off with a man without the benefit of matrimony. Miss Bryony isn't going to do anything she ought not to do," Nanny Gruen said with a determined tone they'd learned long ago not to thwart. "I know I can count on you not to do anything you shouldn't. There'll be a proper housekeeper there and all, won't there?"

Maddy managed to hide her astonishment. She'd girded her loins, metaphorically speaking, for a major battle full of dire threats and recriminations. Instead Nanny Gruen seemed to be surrendering at the first shot across her bow.

"Of course there is," she said soothingly. "Mrs. Crozier and her husband are in charge of the household, and there must be a boy for the heavy work. They just need extra help."

"I can't say that I like it, Miss Madeleine," Nanny said in a worried voice. "But if there's a respectable older woman in the house to look after the maids, and if young Mr. Fulton is going to be around, then I suppose I have no choice but to let you go. My mind won't be easy until you return, but at this rate if you two don't kill each other then I may very well drown you both."

"Thank you, Nanny!" Maddy said in a properly subdued voice,

but the look the woman sent her was far too wise. They both knew there was nothing she could do to stop her. In the end she was going, whether her old nanny liked it or not.

"Well, I expect it's going to be a dead bore," Sophie said with a yawn. "Some prosy old sea captain stomping around smelling of snuff. Do you suppose he has a wooden leg? If he does and he gives you too much trouble you could always steal it."

"Captain Morgan isn't going to give me any trouble," Maddy replied airily. "You forget—I'm used to seafaring men. Father used to let me accompany him to his office on occasion, and I met a fair number of the men who captained his vessels, though fortunately not Captain Morgan. He'll probably be just like all the rest of them. Old and gruff and boring. The man has no wife and apparently never bothered to marry. The ocean probably arouses his passions, not the female sex."

"Miss Maddy! Your language!" Nanny protested weakly, having given up the battle.

"Gender? Is that any better?" Maddy offered.

"A proper young lady wouldn't bring up such things in the first place."

"I don't think we're considered very proper anymore, Nanny," Sophie pointed out. "We're disgraced."

"All the more reason to be above reproach."

"I will be above reproach," Maddy said cheerfully. "It'll simply be in Captain Morgan's household rather than here. Don't worry—if the captain truly had something to do with destroying our father it won't take me long to find it out. I'll be back before you even know I'm gone. Trust me—one landlocked old man is no match for me."

The man currently calling himself Thomas Morgan walked down the sun-bright streets of the seaside town of Devonport, at peace with the world. It had been a long time since he'd been Luca, half-gypsy street rat, and while deep inside he knew he could never be anyone else, the role of Thomas Morgan suited him well enough. It was a clear spring day, though the weather was crisp, and the breeze blew the salty smell of the ocean straight to him, a taunt from his jealous true love. It had been too long since he'd been out to sea. Ever since that bastard Russell had pulled him off his ship he'd been landlocked, and he cursed the lying, thieving old man every chance he got. Not that he hadn't managed to profit in the end. He'd spent his twenty-nine years surviving one disaster after another, always coming out on top, as he had this time. With most of the assets of Russell Shipping disappearing into thin air the solicitors had had no choice but to put the few remaining resources, including the ships, up for sale, and he'd managed to buy two of them and was in negotiations for a third. It didn't hurt that his fiancée's father and his firm were in charge of settling Russell's disastrous estate.

And now negotiations were almost settled, and the *Maddy Rose* was almost his. All they had to do was find one of Russell's daughters to sign off on it. Every time he thought about the ship he felt a totally unaccustomed emotion swell inside him. The lines, the speed, the sheer beauty of the ship owned him as nothing else could. He'd sailed on many vessels, steam and sail, and commanded a large portion of them, but none of them moved him as the clipper ship did.

It was strange. He was used to lust stirring his privates, anger making his head pound, laughter in his belly. But his feelings for the *Maddy Rose* were in between, somewhere in the area that a heart was supposed to reside.

He didn't have one, of course. Oh, the thing still did its job, thumped obligingly in his chest, but he'd stripped that body part of any feelings when he was seven years old and his stepfather had sold him to Morris the Sweep, who'd run the chimney sweeps. Eight pence had been his worth, and the old man had starved him. Luca was no use as a climbing boy if he was too big to fit in the chimneys, and he spent endless years edging his way up and down the innards of the chimneys of rich, happy families in their rich, happy houses. By the time he was twelve he looked half his age, covered with burns and the mark of the lash.

He'd run away, of course, and kept trying till he succeeded. Tried to run back home but his family had already moved on, as the Travelers did. His gypsy heritage was in his face, his dark skin and eyes, curling black hair always filled with soot. His heritage was in his soul as well—rebellion and a determination to escape had always burned bright in him.

He should never have expected his mother to save him. He'd been born from a previous marriage to a non-gypsy, a *Gadjo*, an Englishman who'd given him his height and little else. His mother's second husband hated him and the reminder that he wasn't Anselina's first. Luca shouldn't have blamed her for letting him go—he knew how heavy his stepfather's fists could be. But he did.

He'd escaped Morris as soon as he was big enough to fight back, taking his friend Wart with him. Together they'd become the finest child pickpockets in London. They'd serviced gentlemen when they were starving and found their way into many a wealthy household in the middle of the night to relieve them of whatever silver they could carry. So the life of a pirate had been a natural move for him.

It hadn't started out that way. It had never been his idea to go to sea—the Rom had a natural aversion to it. But he'd been taken up one night when he hadn't run fast enough—coshed on the head, and when he'd woken up the next morning he was already in the middle of the ocean with no land in sight.

It still made him laugh to remember how sick he'd been those first weeks. He'd spewed all over himself, the sailor who had kidnapped him, and the burly captain whenever they got close. Eventually there was nothing left to spew, and he lay in the small hammock they'd rigged up for him, stinking of vomit, hoping he'd die.

Until he heard the captain and the quartermaster talking. "Might's well throw him overboard, sir," the quartermaster had said. "He won't last much longer and he's too much trouble."

He could feel eyes on his tiny, miserable body, and then the captain drawled, "Give him another day. See if he can hold down a bit of ale. He's a pretty lad, and a bright one, or I miss my guess. If he's no better tomorrow throw him overboard."

The quartermaster grunted, poking at him, and Luca wanted to hurl. Not a good idea, he decided, swallowing his bile. On land there were always a dozen places to escape to, particularly when you were small and wiry. He could fit almost anyplace. Here on the boat he was trapped.

It was another man who forced the ale down his throat, clamping his jaw shut so he had to keep it down or choke. A big man, with huge hands, the ugliest face in Christendom, and an unexpected kindness in his eyes.

And that was how he met William Quarrells.

Billy was going to approve of this day's work, he thought as he strode along the quayside. He'd loved the *Maddy Rose* as well, serving as Luca's first mate and the one man he trusted unequivocally.

Luca tossed his hat and coat on the dusty table in the narrow front hall of his house on Water Street and headed toward his office. It was a little past noon, time for a decent meal, but his very proper fiancée was trying to civilize him, and he was indulging her, at least for the time being. Gwendolyn Haviland had informed him archly that only the lower orders ate a full meal at midday. Proper people ate dinner in the evening, accompanied by wine and good conversation with one's equals. The very idea made him shudder.

His desk was as littered as the front table, though he rifled through things so often he didn't allow dust to settle. By the time Billy pushed open the door he'd already compiled a stack of bills for his business manager to attend to, and was just enjoying the reward for his labors—a small glass of Jamaican rum.

"Don't let Miss Haviland see you with that," Billy said in his rumbling, sea-dog voice. "She says rum is for lowborn limeys." He mimicked Gwendolyn's prissy accent.

Luca turned and poured him an even deeper glass—Billy was a larger man than he was and needed more rum. "I *am* a lowborn limey," he said, handing Billy his glass. "And a filthy gypsy as well."

"She expects you to rise above it. Cheers." He drained half the glass, made a face, and then fixed his deep-set, worried gaze on Luca. "You were able to get the *Maddy Rose*?"

"All taken care of. Just one little bit of business and then she's ours."

Billy sighed with satisfaction. "You know buying that ship makes no sense at all. The age of the clipper ship is over. It's all about steam nowadays. But the *Maddy Rose* is a thing of beauty, and it fair warms my heart that you were softheaded enough to buy her."

Luca grinned at him. "Even a man who's sold his soul to commerce has to be foolish every now and then."

"Ah, you're so rich you'll never miss it," Billy scoffed. "Now if you could only be sensible about the blasted woman you intend to marry."

"I may as well have respectability, Billy, since I'm about to have my own shipping company. You know that. Gwendolyn is my best way to achieve it. Besides, she's my solicitor's daughter. This way I know Haviland won't play me false."

"True enough. He dotes on the chit. Problem is, he expects you to dote on her too," Billy grumbled.

"I dote on her," Luca said cheerfully, draining his glass of rum and pouring another. "I proposed to her, didn't I?"

"You gave up," Billy said sourly. "That woman set her sights on you the moment she met you, and she's scarier than the . . . Lord, I can't think of who she's scarier than. I wonder you held out so long."

Luca stifled his momentary irritation. "Her plans happened to coincide with mine. She wants a wealthy sea captain for a husband; I want a society wife. I've a mind to turn respectable, and she's the way to do it."

"It's not your money she's after, laddie," Billy said dourly. "There's more than enough of that around, and Miss Gwendolyn Haviland could have just about anyone she pleases. It's your pretty face."

Luca snorted. "Then it's a great deal fortunate that she doesn't have an inkling what kind of dark soul lingers beneath it," he said lightly.

"She sees you as a project. You're like a doll—she can dress you up and teach you manners and trot you out like some trained monkey."

"You don't like women," Luca said unnecessarily.

"Aye. They're nothing but trouble and I've got no use for them."

"Tell me something I don't know. Like when am I going to get properly fed?"

"Miss Haviland told Mrs. Crozier you weren't to be served dinner until eight o'clock of an evening. You maybe have something light for luncheon, and tea and watercress sandwiches at teatime."

"And who hires Mrs. Crozier and pays her and her husband's wages?"

"You do. Which should give you a little hint that your sweet little fiancée isn't the angelic creature you think she is."

Luca laughed. "I don't believe in angelic creatures. If you think Gwendolyn's sweet ways fool me for one moment then you forget we've been together for twenty years. It's a business arrangement, whether she realizes it or not."

"Oh, aye," said Billy. "Then where's your food?"

Luca felt his stomach rumble. "In the kitchen, I expect." He rose, raising an eyebrow. "You coming?"

"Mrs. Crozier is a terrible housekeeper and her husband's a lazy drunk," Billy said, pushing his massive bulk to his feet. "And her cooking isn't much better, but at least it means I don't have to cook for myself. You're bloody well right I'm coming. Besides, I've got a word or two to say to the old witch about the state of this house."

"Wait till after we eat," Luca suggested. "Besides, I believe she's hired a new maid, so things should be improving."

"Another woman in the household," Billy said dourly. "Things can only get worse."

"You're prejudiced. In fact, let's not get in Mrs. Crozier's way. If she's been listening to Gwendolyn then there's no telling what she might serve us. I think the Crown and Rose near the docks would give us a much better meal."

"You're on, mate," Billy said. "It's too good a day to be indoors, though I'd rather be out at sea. When is the *Maddy Rose* coming?"

"Soon." It was nothing more than the truth. "Lunch today, and a long sail as soon as she gets here."

"She's a grand old boat," Billy said wistfully.

"Only five years old," Luca reminded him. "But you're right. She's the closest I ever intend to get to loving a woman. If I had a heart it would be pledged to the *Maddy Rose*."

"Amen," said Billy solemnly.

CHAPTER TWO

GETTING HERSELF READY FOR her new life as a maidservant cum spy was a bit more trouble than Maddy had expected. Mr. Fulton was aggrieved to be seen driving into the dockside town of Devonport with a servant by his side, particularly one he judged as far too pretty to be credible. Maddy knew better. People didn't actually look at their servants. As long as she kept her shoulders hunched and her face lowered the ancient captain would pay no attention to her at all.

Mr. Fulton hadn't liked dropping her off near High Street, but she was hardly going to show up at her new position in a fancy carriage, for all that Matthew was supposedly the source of the captain's new employee. She needed to do this alone, and she needed time to get in the proper state of mind. A nice long walk to Water Street would be just the thing, and Maddy planned to make good use of the time. It was astonishing how different a place was when you were walking on the streets, rather than viewing life from a carriage or the back of a horse. After their fall from grace six months ago, walking rather than riding in the poorer parts of London had come as quite a shock to her system, cushioned as she'd been.

Actually walking through the streets had been overwhelming and invigorating. In the past, while Bryony stayed secluded in the countryside and Sophie rollicked through the season, playing one beau against the other, Maddy had always had an unfortunate fascination with the real world, with the workings of her father's business, with politics, with investments. Unfeminine interests that she kept to herself, though her father had understood and even encouraged her. It was always accepted that she was destined for a great marriage—the value of her face and her dowry were indisputable, and her dead mother had been the daughter of a baronet, almost wiping out her father's less than stellar pedigree.

But everything had ended with her father's disgrace and death. At least, the easy part had ended, as well as her relationship with Jasper Tarkington, who was now as far away from her as he could manage, somewhere in the depths of South America. She hoped a jaguar ate him.

She was still planning on a great marriage, dowry or no. She was up to any challenge, and her goal was clear. A title and a fortune. Clearing her father's name was simply the first step toward achieving that goal. If, in the end she failed, Lord Eastham was always an option. But she didn't intend to fail.

She felt curious eyes on her, and she suddenly realized she'd been striding along, head up, shoulders back, her valise swinging in her hand. She resisted the impulse to look around her as she slowed her pace, almost imperceptibly. She should be nearing the quay by now, but instead she seemed to have wandered into a less prosperous area of town. The stink of garbage, horse dung, and dead fish was high on the midday air, and she wished she dared fumble in her reticule for a handkerchief to hold to her nose. Maids didn't hold their noses—they emptied slop jars and scrubbed the most disgusting things. Nanny Gruen had warned her there was no place for her so-called airs.

The streets had become darker, narrower, and she'd somehow lost her way. Up ahead she could see the brightness of sunlight, and she sped up, trying to force herself not to break into a run. She'd been careless while she'd been busy thinking. She couldn't afford to make mistakes like this.

She moved around the corner, into the sunlight, and froze. Despite the patch of light she now stood in, the rest of the alleyway was shrouded in shadows. The stench was even worse, and she realized with a sinking feeling that a new smell had joined the others. That of unwashed human flesh.

There were three of them blocking the other end of the narrow alley, and she blinked, staring at them. Nothing to be afraid of, she told herself. They were just sailors home on shore leave, out for a bit of fun. They'd leave her alone if she told them to.

"Look at 'er, will ya?" one of them said. "What a pretty little bit of fluff to come our way. What should we do with her, boys?"

They were an odd group, one of them huge and bear-like, his hands like hams as they hung loosely beside him. Another was small and wiry, with grizzled gray hair and beard and far too much interest in his faded eyes. But the third, the one who was doing the talking, was the worst. At some point in his life he'd suffered a cruel accident, and half his face was burned and scarred. He was barrel-chested, and his open, grinning mouth showed a handful of blackened, rotting teeth, the odor of decay so strong she could smell it from several feet away.

She had only a moment to react. The street she'd come from had been deserted—there would be no safety if she turned and ran back that way. It was the middle of the day in a solid British city—she had to be imagining her danger.

"You're going to let me pass and leave me alone." She raised her voice, sounding so calm it steadied her.

"Oh, I don't think so, lass. Anyone knows you don't wander around these parts if you're not looking for making a little money on the side."

"She's pretty," the big man said.

"That's the truth of it, Barney, old boy. Much too pretty for the likes of us, but who's to say we should look a gift horse in the mouth? She's here, we're looking for a bit of sport, and we all know no one interferes with what goes in these dockside alleys."

Dockside? They were near the harbor then, and there would be people nearby. "If you don't move aside I'll scream," she said sharply.

"No one will care." They were getting closer, and she could feel some of her self-assurance fade. "Pretty thing like you—you were asking for it, that's what we'd say. Or maybe we won't have to say anything at all, maybe you're just going to disappear. I know someone who'd pay good money to take you far away from here, sell you to some of them heathens who like white skin. Too bad you're not a blonde, but you'd still fetch a pretty price."

She started to back away from them. She could always hit one of them in the head with her valise, but it was far too light to do much damage. All right, so she'd miscalculated, and she hadn't been paying proper attention. She'd had instructions on how to get to Captain Morgan's house, instructions she'd merely glanced at and arrogantly assumed that had been enough. She was going to have to run for it, and while she could probably outpace the big one and the old one, the scarred one looked far too eager.

He was moving in on her, and one of his hands reached down and cupped the front of his filthy breeches suggestively. "You want to beg for mercy, little girl? I'm afraid I'm all out."

"I want her first," the big man said in a plaintive whine.

"You hurts 'em too much, Barney," the old man chided. "You get her last. Once you're done with them they aren't much good to anyone for a long time."

She was going to throw up. Right there in front of them. In any other circumstances it should have filled them with disgust, but these depraved creatures would probably enjoy it.

"Say 'please,' girly," the scarred man taunted.

She was almost at the corner of the alleyway. Just a few more feet and she could make a run for it. "Please," she said in a soft, breathless voice. "Please . . ."—her voice hardened—"go sod yourselves."

She spun on her heels, swallowing her fear. Something grabbed her sleeve, and she heard it rip as she yanked away. Her valise went flying. A moment later her arm was caught in a grip so painful she felt as if her bones were being crushed, and she was being dragged back into the alleyway. She opened her mouth to scream, but a filthy hand slapped over it, silencing her. She fought—kicking, hitting, clawing with her hands, though trapped in her cheap cotton gloves she couldn't do much damage. She managed to move her knee up sharply, hitting the big man in the groin, and he went down with a comically high-pitched scream of pain, writhing on the ground.

For a moment she was free, but she was so shocked that what her former maid had described to her had actually worked that she didn't move fast enough, and then another of them caught her, spinning her around and shoving her up against the side of a building, her face pushed against the crumbling brickwork as she felt someone fumble with her skirts.

"I think you'd better get your hands off her, boys."

The voice came from out of nowhere, and for a moment Maddy thought she'd dreamt it. Except that those crushing hands had immediately released her, and she pushed away from the brick wall, trying to catch her breath as she pulled her bonnet more tightly on her head.

"We weren't doing no harm," the talkative one wheedled. "You know that any woman comes around here is fair game. Only working girls walk these streets, and I'll grant you she's a lot prettier than most of them, but she ain't no better off. Some of them likes a bit of a fight."

"I don't think she did."

Taking a deep, calming breath, Maddy turned to face her rescuer, and for a moment everything froze within her.

She hadn't known a man could be beautiful. She was used to pale Englishmen—this man was bronzed by the sun, with long, curling black hair, high cheekbones, and faintly slanted eyes. He wasn't looking at her, he was concentrating on the miscreants, and when she was finally able to break the odd spell he'd cast over her she turned to look at them as well, now that it was safe.

The big man was struggling to his feet, groaning loudly, and the old man was fumbling with his breeches, presumably refastening them. She shuddered, just faintly, but it caught the stranger's attention. "You should know better than to walk alone in this area," he said coolly. He had a lovely deep voice with an odd accent that she couldn't quite identify. She could recognize a bit of the London streets, mixed with half a dozen other accents that made his voice indescribable.

He wasn't struck dumb with her beauty, a shock. In fact, he'd barely glanced at her, and what he'd seen didn't appear to impress him. It was a novel experience, and she wasn't sure she enjoyed it, particularly when faced with someone who could, in another life, have that same effect on her. "I got lost," she said, with no note of apology in her voice. "You would think a girl could walk through town without being molested, but then, I'm new here. I hadn't realized the scum of the earth lived in this city." She realized belatedly that she'd forgotten to use the accent she'd planned on. It didn't matter now, but she mustn't forget once she got to the captain's household.

"Real uppity, ain't she?" the old one said. "She needs to be taught a lesson."

The stranger's slightly tilted dark eyes crinkled in amusement. "I don't think she needs the kind of lesson you had in mind. Stupidity isn't a crime, rape is."

Maddy bristled. "I am not stupid, I simply don't know this wretched town. One can walk in London without being subjected to such vile behavior. Had I known Devonport was so depraved I would have looked for work elsewhere."

"Where do you work?" the stranger demanded, and she gave him a suspicious glance.

"I work for a milliner," she lied glibly. "And I'm already late. If you've finished discussing my stupidity then I'll be off."

"In what direction?" His voice was lazy.

Rats. She hadn't thought that far ahead. "I'm looking for North Water Street."

"And you were heading south," he observed.

It didn't matter how bewitching he was, he was thoroughly annoying. But she'd lost everything—her father, her comfortable living, the houses in London and Somerset. She at least still had her pride, and she had manners. "Thank you very much," she said stiffly. "I appreciate the rescue." She paused. "But I could have fought them off myself." The knee trick had worked so effectively that the big man was still hunched over, moaning slightly to his privates. She could have used it on the other two and then run for it.

"Oh, really?" he drawled.

She didn't want to look at him, but she kept her gaze at his shoulder. He was dressed in plain clothes of good quality—breeches, a white shirt, a dark blue superfine jacket that was loosely tailored, and no cravat whatsoever. She noticed a glint of gold beneath his black curls and recognized a hooped earring. She shouldn't have been so shocked—of course he was a sailor, with that bronzed skin and lean, wiry body, though he was definitely taller than most. "I don't need help from someone who's doubtless no better than the others. I've been warned about sailors on leave. Now if you'll excuse me," she said in icy tones. It wasn't the wisest thing to say, she realized, but she was furious, both with them and with herself. He was right—she'd been an idiot to get lost in this part of town. She should have paid closer attention to Mr. Fulton's directions.

"You gonna let her get away with that?" the talkative one said, outraged.

The man had been leaning against the brick wall, watching everything with casual interest. He straightened then, and for the first time she felt the full force of his attention. It was a disturbing feeling. "If you were warned you should have listened. But then, we've already established your stupidity."

At least she had the wit to bite back her instinctive retort. She glared at him instead. "I think I'll go now."

"I think not." He caught her arm, his strong hand surprisingly hard on her upper arm as he pulled her around. She lost her footing, and fell against him, or maybe he'd dragged her there, but suddenly she was plastered up against a warm, male body, her eyes at the level of his bare neck and gold hoop. "I think you need a taste of what you just escaped. That way you'll learn your lesson." To her shock he put his hand behind her neck, tilting her head up, and his mouth came down on hers.

It was hard against her lips, and to her astonishment he used his long fingers to push her jaw apart, enough for his tongue to thrust into her mouth, and she held still, motionless with shock.

It was disgusting. Foul. He tasted of fresh coffee and cinnamon, and she considered biting him. What was he doing to her? Whatever it was, it was wrong. And yet . . . how very odd . . . it was strangely enticing. She could feel the anger and outrage in her body begin to soften, and she tried to summon her fury back. It had disappeared. She heard fuzzy noises in the distance, and she realized it was the hooting of the men who'd attacked her.

He lifted his head, looking down at her out of hooded, dark eyes. "Open your mouth, my little idiot, and kiss me back."

She opened her mouth to tell him to go to the devil when he covered hers once more, holding her tight against his body as he continued with his shocking kiss, something she'd never experienced before. His tongue touched hers, coaxed, and for some reason she let hers drift against his, as he deepened the kiss, and she wondered idly if she was going to swoon.

That wouldn't be a good idea, not with the three sailors making loud sounds of approval. But lord, she'd been wrong about this kind of kissing. It was too intimate, too intense, too seductive. It made her want more, and for a moment she pictured his hands on her breasts, his hands pulling up her skirts and taking her in public up against a brick wall. She wanted to dissolve into the absolute splendor of his mouth, and she moaned in pleasure.

A moment later she was released, and she fell back, putting a hand on the side of the building for surreptitious support. Her rescuer had turned from her to the three men. "She'd be a waste of time, boys. She kisses like a virgin. You're better off paying for some companionship." He tossed them a handful of coins, and even the hulking one caught them deftly.

"Thank you, cap'n," they said cheerfully, backing away as if they hadn't been about to commit rape and kidnapping. "You knew we meant no harm. Just having a bit of fun, that's all."

"Next time find someone willing."

They ran off, and Maddy had finally managed to stand on her own two feet as anger washed through her, stiffening her. "You reward them for trying to rape me?" she demanded icily.

The man shrugged. "At least they'll be too busy to bother you again. And they'll have a much better time."

She was so furious she could barely speak. "How lovely of you," she said in a biting voice. "And now I suppose you're going to insist on accompanying me to my destination."

"No." He glanced down the empty alleyway. "In truth I was

more concerned about those boys getting in trouble with the law than your precious hide. Water Street's just two streets away—follow the smell of the sea and you'll find it. And turn right if you're looking for North Water Street." To her complete astonishment he started walking away, as if they'd had nothing but a casual encounter and not the searing kiss that she could still feel, still taste.

She wanted to throw something at him. He'd called her stupid, something she couldn't abide, and then he'd kissed her in that disgusting manner, as if she were some cheap doxy. Except in the end the kiss hadn't been disgusting at all, it had been . . . astonishing.

She reached up her gloved hand and rubbed her mouth, trying to scrub the feel of him, the taste of him, away. It didn't work—it only seemed to deepen the brand. She watched him go, his tall body striding through the alleyway as if he owned it, when he suddenly stopped, turning back to look at her.

His dark eyes seemed to bore into hers, and she felt her heart catch in her throat, a strange sensation washing over her skin as she stood motionless.

"Fuck it," he said succinctly, shocking her with the forbidden curse. He crossed the distance between them in a few long strides, and before she realized it he'd caught her up in his arms again, pushing her back into the shadows.

She ought to be afraid. He was a stranger, this place was deserted, and he could do what the others had threatened. Rape by a Greek god was still rape.

But he wasn't going to rape her. He wasn't going to hurt her. He kissed her again, hard at first, as if imprinting his claim on her, and then more slowly, brushing his mouth against hers, softly, back and forth, and she knew her lips were trembling beneath his. Her words were her best weapon, but they were locked in her throat as she felt his tongue, his outrageous, shocking tongue intrude into her mouth and the sensations moved through her body like fire. She knew she should protest, shove him away, use her knee again, give vent to the outrage that should have filled her. But she couldn't lift her knee when she was already standing on her toes, trying to get closer to him, when her arms had somehow found their way around his neck, her breasts pressed against the rough cloth of his coat. She felt his hand slide down her back, cupping her bum, pressing her hips against his.

She knew what that stiff ridge of flesh was, and it surprised her. How could he respond that fiercely to just a kiss, when it had taken Tarkington . . .

He lifted his head, and then flicked her chin with his long fingers. "Pay attention to the man who's kissing you," he said in a low voice. And his mouth descended again.

Oh, God. She'd never imagined it could be like this, the burning hunger that was racing through her body, making her knees weak, and she wanted to sink into him, dissolve into a molten puddle of forbidden longing.

He released her so abruptly she almost lost her footing. "That's more like it," he said, staring down at her from enigmatic eyes. "You'd better get going before I totally lose my mind. And watch yourself. Next time I won't be around to rescue you." And damned if the man didn't start whistling cheerfully as he strode away, forgetting about her entirely.

She stood very still. She was at a loss for words for perhaps the first time in her life, and then a clear, sharp, cleansing fury exploded within her. Spinning on her heel, she stalked away, following his directions, muttering imprecations beneath her breath, including the forbidden one he'd dared to use in her presence.

"Fuck it," she said succinctly, and then she picked up her discarded valise and she was out in the sunshine, feeling strangely better than she had in months.

CHAPTER THREE

THAT LITTLE ENCOUNTER, LUCA thought, had improved his mood tremendously. Who would have thought he'd run across such a tempting firecracker in the back alleys of Devonport? Too bad she was probably a virgin—they were always too much trouble. He kept away from the dockside girls—there were too many diseases floating around. When he needed a little distraction he used to visit a certain married woman, but he'd broken it off several weeks ago when he'd become engaged to Gwendolyn, and now, suddenly, he was thinking about sex.

Not that he wasn't entirely capable of doing without anything but his own hand for months on end, during the long voyages. But something about that girl, about the way she clung to him at the last minute, about her attempt to kiss him back, had aroused more than just his curiosity.

He hoped she found her place of employment without running into any more trouble. Though he couldn't remember any milliner's shop on North Water Street. That was a residential area, including his own house. Which meant she'd be walking by occasionally. Even if he managed to talk her into bed—and there was really no "if" about it—his fiancée would be a problem. No, now wasn't the time to pursue a bit of crumpet on the side, as Billy would put it. Though her mouth had been delicious.

Maybe Billy was right—Gwendolyn could be more trouble than she was worth. Yes, he wanted children, and he wanted a well-run household and a willing woman in his bed at night. But even though he fully intended to ignore most of the demands of marriage, there were bound to be inconveniences, like this current one, when he wanted nothing more than to follow the pert young miss to her place of employment and continue bickering with her. And then kissing her again.

Life was full of bad bargains. He'd made this one. If the lovely milliner was going to come into his life again he'd wait for it to happen. Otherwise he had better things to do. The smartest thing he could do was put her out of his mind.

He'd reached the quayside, and the girl was long gone. He looked out at the harbor, the sparkling blue sky, the nip of wind as it tossed the leaves on the trees. It was a perfect day for sailing, and he was stuck on land because of old man Russell's larceny, just as his new ship was stuck in London while solicitors wrangled over who actually owned her.

Apparently Russell had left a will, and he'd bequeathed the *Maddy Rose* to its namesake, his middle daughter, Madeleine Rose. Normally that would be of no consequence given that any assets of a thief were confiscated, but apparently the damned girl's name was on the legal papers, and one solicitor thought she needed to be found to sign off on it before he could take ownership.

And so he was stuck in limbo, with only a small ketch and a skiff to distract him. No wonder he was in a dangerous mood.

He really shouldn't blame old man Russell, Luca thought, breathing in the salty air. Luca had spent the first twelve years of his life stealing anything he could get his nimble hands on, and he still would, if the treasure was worth snatching. Who was he to pass judgment on another thief?

But this thief had stolen from *him*, and that was a different matter entirely. He'd trusted the old man, even when he'd showed up full of crazy accusations. Eustace Russell had died that very night, his carriage tumbling off the side of a cliff, and Luca had always wondered if some fever of the brain had afflicted the normally levelheaded man. But he'd been heading away from the port, dying somewhere in the vast expanse of Dartmoor, which didn't make it seem as if he was trying to escape.

It was no longer his concern, except for the missing signature to complete his ownership of the *Maddy Rose*. Until that happened he was temporarily landlocked, waiting for the solicitors to finish arguing among themselves, when he wanted nothing more to be out there away from responsibilities and nagging voices . . .

He stopped himself midthought. Being in command of a ship and God knew how many souls was hardly free of responsibility, and he'd never in his life listened to a nagging voice. Never heard one—no one had cared enough to prate on and on at him about things he found absolutely uninteresting, like the arrangement of a cravat or social conventions, the sort of thing Gwendolyn set such store by. Maybe Billy was right. Getting married to a woman like that could prove very tiresome.

Ah, but she was a gorgeous piece, like fine porcelain. He could dance to her tune gracefully enough, until they were married and bedded. Once she had a child or two to fill with such nonsense she'd leave off of him. And there was the sea. He didn't have to be home with her any longer than he wanted—he could tolerate marriage to almost anyone in those circumstances, and Gwendolyn would do.

So why did he feel so restless? This was what he'd decided upon. A proper wife to go with his proper life, a gypsy street rat and pickpocket pulling himself out of the gutter to almost laughable heights.

Gwendolyn was great-niece to a duke—his common, half-Rom blood would mingle with that of aristocracy. And he'd still be free to disappear on the ocean, with the sea breeze in his hair and the slap of salt spray against his skin, and Gwendolyn probably wouldn't notice. Oh, she was drawn to him, wanted him like a shiny new toy, but he suspected once it came down to the marriage bed she'd be happy enough to do without. The few kisses she'd allowed had been cold and close-mouthed, and he didn't think a parson's blessing was going to warm her. No, he'd find his pleasure elsewhere once he gave her enough children, and if she found out she'd pretend not to know.

So why wasn't he celebrating his good fortune? The problem with the *Maddy Rose* would be easily fixed, particularly since his solicitor was his future father-in-law. It was a little late to be changing his mind, about the ship, about his upcoming nuptials. Gwendolyn wouldn't be a problem, simply because he didn't care enough to let her be one. And he wanted children. He liked them—the cheeky little buggers.

So why did his mind keep going back to the milliner with her flashing, dark blue eyes, soft mouth, and fierce temper? His course was charted. He couldn't afford distractions, even one as tempting as the hatmaker.

CHAPTER FOUR

By the time Maddy arrived at the captain's house on North Water Street she had regained her composure, even if she couldn't quite forget what his mouth had been like. It wasn't like her to let any man fluster her, and unless she made the very foolish habit of wandering the back alleyways near the docks she was unlikely to run into him again. She couldn't quite place him socially. One of the men had referred to him as "captain," but it was more likely a generic term of respect for power, which the stranger clearly had. The ships' captains she'd met, and there had been many of them, were always impeccably dressed, whether in uniform or day clothes. Perhaps this man was a first mate or a quartermaster—something a little higher up than an ordinary seaman.

She shook herself. She had to hope her father's captains hadn't hired any foul creatures like the three who'd attacked her. But had her enigmatic rescuer ever sailed on her father's ships? It was a disturbing possibility.

It didn't matter. Her father had no ships—his empire was torn apart, the ships sold off one by one, including the one that bore her name. She needed to forget the rude stranger and his shocking kiss.

She would never see him again; no one would ever kiss her like that again. When she found her wealthy, titled husband she would never allow him such liberties.

But still . . .

She straightened her shoulders, determinedly dismissing the stranger and his mouth, and stared at her destination, the place she would call home for the next few weeks.

It was a narrow terrace house, painted blue, with a ship's flag flying from a post near the front door. She looked up at the windows and sighed. They were dirty, and she had a sinking feeling she knew who was going to be cleaning them. She shifted her valise to her other hand.

It was a blessing that *Mrs. Beeton's Guide to Household Management* had gone into its second edition. Inside that heavy tome was everything she ever needed to know about the duties of a maid and the arcane details of housekeeping. She knew how to clean a grate and set a fire, wash windows and sweep, make beds and iron sheets. Nanny Gruen had seen to it, at Maddy's insistence. She had no intention of living a life where these skills were required, but once she married her viscount or duke she would be a better mistress of the household if she understood the details of the tasks required.

The front steps needed scrubbing as well—wayward seagulls had left their calling card. She sighed, hefted her valise, and started down the basement stairs next to the front entrance. Maddy Russell was gone. Mary Greaves was now onstage, and she had no intention of fumbling her lines.

She knocked politely on the door, setting her bag down, and waited. It took less than a moment for a thin, sour-faced woman to swing the door open, eyeing her up and down.

"You must be Mr. Fulton's young lady," the woman said in dubious tones.

Maddy kept her head lowered just slightly. If they were dogs she'd be cringing at a lower level, letting the woman have dominance.

Unfortunately at five foot seven Maddy stood taller than most women and a great deal of men as well, so she was immediately at a disadvantage in the act of appearing humble.

"I'm Mary Greaves, missus," she said. She'd decided on a bit of a Northern accent. She'd never been terribly good at accents during their childhood theatrical endeavors, but a cross between Lancashire and Yorkshire would do her well. Irish would be easier, but that carried with it all sorts of trouble, and plain English kept things simpler.

"Well, come in, girl. No need to shilly-shally out there in the cold, and freeze us all," the old woman muttered.

Maddy walked in, standing in place when she longed to sit. It had been a longer walk than she'd expected, not to mention her unsettling encounter, and her feet hurt despite the comfortable shoes. She was going to have to build up her stamina, and fast, if she was going to succeed at this deception.

The kitchen, at least, seemed cleaner than the front of the house. The wide table in the center had only four chairs around it, and the stove was putting out vast, welcome amounts of heat. It had felt a great deal colder with the brisk wind off the ocean, and Maddy surreptitiously moved a little closer to it.

"I suppose you ought to sit down," the woman said grudgingly, and Maddy didn't wait for a second invitation.

The housekeeper was a thin woman with a beaky nose, sharp eyes, and a narrow mouth, but it took more than a crabby nature to intimidate Maddy.

"You're too pretty," the woman announced in a flat voice, taking the seat opposite her. "That's never a good thing in a household, but fortunately my Wilf is the only other male here and he's too old to even notice."

Maddy was about to ask about the aging sea captain, then realized he must be even older than Mrs. Crozier's husband. That, or in the world of the serving classes the master wasn't considered a viable male.

She ducked her head, trying to shield her face. "I'm a hard worker, Mrs. Crozier."

"You'd best be, or you'll have no place here," Mrs. Crozier warned. "We've been understaffed for too long, and there's only so much I can keep up with in a place this size. Captain Morgan doesn't pay attention to the household—he'd rather be at sea, and he looks at this place like a hotel. But he's getting married and the new mistress isn't going to accept such slovenly lack of attention to details."

"Yes, Mrs. Crozier." It seemed the most likely response, instead of the "indeed?" that almost popped out.

"There are four rooms on the ground floor—the kitchen, scullery, laundry room, and Wilf's and my quarters. On the first floor are Captain Morgan's study, a large salon, and a dining room. On the second are four bedrooms, one for the captain and the other three unoccupied. There's also a modern bathing room. You'll be sleeping in the attics. No one's been up there in a while so you'd best allow yourself enough time to make a habitable space for yourself."

"So the only members of the household are the captain and the three servants?"

"Oh, we have another member of the household: Mr. Quarrells. He was at sea with the captain, and he serves as his secretary, best friend, and business partner. He lives in the apartments over the stables, back in the mews. He's a formidable man, is Mr. Quarrells, but you shouldn't have any trouble with him as long as you do your duty and don't ask too many questions."

That was a direct answer to her previous, impertinent question. If Mrs. Crozier thought she'd ended up with a complacent, well-behaved servant she was due for an unhappy surprise. Asking questions was one of Maddy's main occupations in this dank old house, in between searching every space she could find.

"Yes, ma'am," she said politely. "And when is the captain planning to marry?"

"I imagine by summer. I suppose it's possible Miss Haviland will insist he sell this place and buy something fancier. A very pretty, very determined young woman is Miss Haviland, and she's used to getting what she wants. They haven't called the banns yet, so I imagine there's still time."

"Time for what?"

Mrs. Crozier eyed her grimly. "You're just full of questions, aren't you? That doesn't concern you. All you need to know is I'm in charge, and you're to keep out of the captain's way. In fact, don't even go into the captain's study without me. I don't know where the term *shipshape* came from, but it certainly don't apply to Captain Morgan. He says he has his own way of organizing but many the times I've heard him cursing and throwing things while he searches for something. Looks like a rat's nest to me, but he says he knows where everything is, and if I so much as dusted it would disturb his careful arrangements."

Clearly getting into the captain's study should be her first order of business. "Yes, Mrs. Crozier," she said meekly. That seemed to be the obvious response to most things. She was a servant, she reminded herself, and at the bottom of the pecking order, just one step above the boots. Which reminded her . . . "What are my duties?" she asked, trying to keep her voice humble.

Mrs. Crozier bristled. All right, not humble enough. "Anything I tell you to do. You've been hired, against my will, I might add, as a maid of all work, which means you'll do exactly that. All that I can think of."

"Against your will? Didn't you want more help?" Another question, but this time Mrs. Crozier's flat black eyes met hers straight on.

"Of course I want help. Any fool would. But I'm the housekeeper here, and I prefer to hire my own staff, not have someone forced upon me by the captain's solicitor."

"Beg pardon, Mrs. Crozier," she said again. "I was that desperate for a job, and Mr. Fulton kindly offered to help. I'm sure no one meant to overstep your authority."

"I can imagine how desperate you were, and just how you repaid Mr. Fulton for his favor," Mrs. Crozier said waspishly.

"No!" Maddy said a little more sharply than she meant to, and the older woman gave her a suspicious look. "I worked for Mr. Fulton's mother, and she asked him to find me a post away from the city."

"Why?"

She'd worked this out ahead of time—she'd always had a fevered imagination. Not as impressive as Sophie or Bryony, but serviceable enough. "There was a gentleman," she said. "A friend of the family. It seemed wisest that I simply disappear, move to a new place."

"Ah, that face of yours," Mrs. Crozier said knowingly, and it took all Maddy's concentration not to grimace.

"I can't help what I look like, Mrs. Crozier," she said with only a trace of asperity. "I just need someplace quiet-like where I can work and not be bothered by anyone. This household should suit me fine."

"Not even by Mr. Fulton?"

"Certainly not!"

Mrs. Crozier didn't look entirely satisfied, but she nodded. "Then you may as well start. You won't be getting any coddling from me. I'll show you the attics and you can spend some time making a place for yourself before you start in on the public rooms."

"Yes, Mrs. Crozier." She was going to get extremely bored if the entirety of her conversational opportunities consisted of "yes, Mrs. Crozier," and "no, Mrs. Crozier."

"The post doesn't come with uniforms—it's too small a household, but it looks as if what you're wearing will do. I'll have fresh aprons and a cap for you." She tilted her head sideways, like an old crow. "I don't suppose there's anything we can do about your face, is there?"

Not short of throwing lye on it. "No, Mrs. Crozier."

"Well, keep your head down."

Blast it; she needed to remember that anyway. She was a serf, a drudge, a maidservant, for heaven's sake! If she had absorbed the information correctly, the more servants a household maintained, the more pride a servant might have in her employment. Which, given that she was the only maid, pretty well put her at the very bottom of the domestic social ladder.

"Yes, Mrs. Crozier."

The housekeeper eyed her warily, as if expecting open rebellion, but Maddy simply plastered a docile expression on her face, waiting for her next set of instructions.

"You can put your shawl on the peg there and follow me."

Hunch your shoulders, Maddy Rose, she reminded herself.

If the windows of the captain's house had been grimy, the trip to the attic was even more depressing. Some effort had been made to keep the stairs and hallways clean, but she could see dust lurking in the corners, and the walls needed a good scrubbing. Once Mrs. Crozier opened the narrow door leading to the attic stairs, it took all her determination not to flinch.

"What's that?" Maddy said, pointing to a moldering lump on the shadowy third step.

Mrs. Crozier moved closer, not touching it. "Probably a dead bat. You know what attics are like, having been in service. Bats are always a problem." Climbing the first two steps, she prodded the lump with her foot and a noxious smell emanated from it.

"Bats?" She tried very hard not to stammer, but there was a small, nervous hitch in her voice. She wasn't afraid of hard work, filth, or facing the man who might have murdered her father. Bats were another issue entirely.

Mrs. Crozier was watching her closely. "You don't have a problem with bats, now do you? A strong Northern lass like you?"

At least her accent had worked, Mattie thought dimly. And there was no doubt at all that Mrs. Crozier was enjoying her discomfiture. "Of course not," she said, her voice stronger. "Do you have rats as well?"

"The rat catcher comes in every month. The nasty creatures don't come up here that much. They're after the food stores."

"The rats get into the food?" She couldn't quite hide her horror.

"Hoity-toity, miss," Mrs. Crozier snapped. "What kind of household do you think I run? There's no way any kind of vermin can get into my kitchen. That doesn't mean they won't try." She kicked the malodorous corpse again. "Are you going to clean it up?"

It was a test, but Maddy had no intention of being bullied. "Of course. But dead animals breed disease. I'll use a rag. And where shall I put it?" *In your bed*, she thought, wistfully rebellious.

"Out the window, of course."

"Onto the street?" Maddy said, horrified.

Mrs. Crozier looked at her with contempt. "Of course not. What were they thinking, sending me a useless git as a maid? I thought you had years in service."

For a moment Maddy was affronted. She hardly looked her twenty-two years—how old did the woman think she was? And then she remembered some of the younger girls in service and she swallowed her outrage.

"I served in large households—removing animal carcasses was left to the footman." Too late she realized she was casting aspersions on the current domestic arrangements and she struggled to find a way to lessen her implied criticism. "Really, those large households are so tedious. You just do the same thing over and over again. I expect I'll be much happier in a smaller household with a greater variety of tasks."

For a long time Mrs. Crozier said nothing, clearly not mollified. "Tedious, is it?" she said finally with awful majesty. "And your enjoyment is, of course, my main concern. Let me tell you, young miss, that I may not have hired you but I can most certainly fire you."

All right, so far her impersonation of a maid was pathetically inept. She had no doubts that Mrs. Crozier could get rid of her quite easily, and she swallowed her irritation. "I'm a hard worker, I am," she said, pleased with the added "I am." "You won't find any cause for complaint with me."

"Hmmph," Mrs. Crozier said derisively, pulling her voluminous black skirts aside as she started up the stairs. Maddy gathered her own skirts and followed suit.

The attics could have been worse, she supposed. At one point the household must have supported a larger complement of servants. There were two long, narrow rooms on each side with four beds each buried beneath boxes and broken furniture. She glanced nervously up at the ceiling, but there were no ominous figures hanging from the eaves.

At one end the attics were simply an open space, now crowded with the same castoffs that filled the bedrooms. At the other end was a closed door, and she felt a faint moment of hope.

"Is that the water closet?"

Mrs. Crozier's laugh was downright cruel. "You think we have a water closet up here? You'll use a slops jar, and carry your own bathing water up here like any decent Christian."

Maddy had no idea what Christ had to do with slops and carrying water up three flights of stairs, unless Mrs. Crozier was thinking that cleanliness was next to godliness, but she doubted it. Not considering the state of the windows.

"Yes, Mrs. Crozier," she muttered.

"That room is more storage, things of the captain's. It's locked, and we're not to touch it. Even I don't know what's in there."

Bluebeard's nine wives, or however many he had? Maddy looked at the very solid padlock that had been set in place. She was going to have to brush up on her lock-picking skills.

"Take whichever room you want. If you need help hauling things I can send my Wilf up to help you." The offer was definitely grudging.

"I'll be fine. Where can I find water and cleaning supplies?"

"I'll have them ready when you're finished up here."

Maddy took a calming breath. "I'll need them to clean my room. This place is covered with dust and what I presume are . . . are you sure there aren't rats up here?"

Mrs. Crozier surveyed the obvious droppings littering the floor, the chewed up mattresses, then shrugged her skinny shoulders. "Rodents do what they want to do. In the meantime you've got duties downstairs. Pick a room, find a bed and a mattress that suits your highness, and put your clothes away. You can do your personal cleaning on your own time. Be downstairs in half an hour—I'll need help with dinner and you need to dust and sweep the dining room and salon. You don't have time to dawdle."

"Yes, Mrs. Crozier." She stuck her tongue out at the housekeeper's ramrod-straight back as the woman departed. Well, no one said this was going to be easy.

She removed her hat and turned to look at the rooms on either side of her. The one on the left had broken furniture stacked to the ceiling and only a small window. The one on the right was less jumbled and it had a huge dormer, but it smelled very strongly of mouse and at least two of the four mattresses had been chewed.

She glanced back to her left, about to attack it when she noticed some ominous shapes in the eaves, the kind that belonged in dark caves. She slammed the door shut and turned back to the rat room. She could fight rodents with the help of an imported cat—she couldn't fight bats.

The thin, mouse-shredded sheets on the beds ripped as she pulled them off, and she placed them at the head of the stairs very carefully, not wanting to drop any more mouse dung on the floors. She held back a piece of the fabric, and her first act was to descend the stairs and retrieve the dead bat. Flinging the rag over it to hide it from her view, she then gingerly scooped it up, trying not to breathe.

The dormer window looked out over the tangled garden behind the house, and she tried to toss the foul thing as far as she could, letting the rag go with it. The scrap of cloth floated down slowly and gracefully, and she suddenly noticed the figure of a big burly man watching her. He had grizzled gray hair but he was too far away for her to see his face. Obviously the captain, and he looked much as she'd imagined him to be. She resisted the impulse to wave at him, pulling back inside the room.

One bed held a mattress that seemed to have avoided the predatory mice, and she chose that one, dragging the other mattresses out of the room and dumping them in the open space as well as the rusted bed frames, broken chairs, and accumulated detritus of a once larger staff. When she was finished, the large room held a single bed with a mattress that didn't sag too badly, a small dresser with a washbowl and pitcher, a three-legged table she propped in the corner, and a decent chair. Once she was able to give it a good scrubbing, it would do very well.

Maddy glanced out the window. She'd left her watch behind—no simple maid would possess anything so valuable—so she had no idea what time it was. If she had to guess by the waning light it was likely close to six o'clock, and Mrs. Crozier was probably on the verge of coming after her. Maddy's feet hurt, her lower back had a crick in it, and she wanted more than anything to sit on that bed, even lie down for a few moments. She hadn't even started her day's work and already she was exhausted.

Tant pis, as Bryony would say. Too bad. She was the one who'd decided to do this, and she'd reap the consequences. A little hard work never killed anyone.

CHAPTER FIVE

By dinnertime Maddy was convinced she was going to die. Her feet were past hurting—they were numb. She hadn't sat down in three hours, and now was washing what seemed to be three weeks' worth of dishes, shifting from one foot to the other, trying to find some sort of ease. Her shoulders ached, the small of her back was screaming, her arms felt rubbery and weak. She was a naturally energetic creature—there was no reason she should be so tired.

She had merely cleaned out eight fireplaces and reset the fires, hauling out the ashes and hauling in the coal since the so-called boy seemed to be nonexistent, and Wilf, Mrs. Crozier's elderly, slightly inebriated husband, seemed to be glued to a chair in their quarters, appearing every now and then to fetch a mug of ale and then disappearing again. Maddy swept the salon and dining room furiously, letting loose a cloud of dust that settled over every surface, astonishing given the amount she was able to shovel into a dustbin. She then dusted every possible surface, shaking the rag out the windows at constant intervals. At first she paid no attention to the wind, and the dust simply blew back in, accompanied by a selection of street dirt. After dusting everything once more, she carefully chose a back window where the wind off the ocean couldn't enter and undo her hard work.

The captain's residence was a terrace, bound on each side by other houses, and occasionally a word or a thump emanated from the other side, startling her. The Russells had always lived in the best of the best—while townhouses like this one and the ones in London were perfectly acceptable, Eustace Russell had had expensive tastes that he'd unfortunately passed on to his two younger daughters. Maddy had always enjoyed the luxuries money could buy, and she'd spent it lavishly when her father had given it to her. Now her extravagance shamed her. The cost of one of her ball gowns could have provided better lodgings for her sisters while they'd lived in London, and she'd worn that dress only once before discarding it.

Tarkington had particularly enjoyed all the trappings of wealth. His own family had been prosperous, though not anywhere near the level of the Russells with their nouveau wealth, but his family went back to the Domesday Book, and her father had encouraged the match, wanting to work his way further up the social ladder. And she'd been a damned fool.

"What are you doing, Mary?" Mrs. Crozier's whip-sharp voice broke through her abstraction, and she looked up from the sink dazedly, wondering whom the housekeeper was talking to.

A moment later she knew. "Are you deaf, Mary Greaves?" Mrs. Crozier moved closer, trying to loom over her. Since the housekeeper was shorter than she was, the effort failed, but she made up for it in her voice. "Because if you are, then you're on your way. I can't deal with someone who's deaf. For all I know you might be slow-witted as well. Most people don't stand leaning against the sink, their hands in the water, staring into space."

"I'm not slow-witted, Mrs. Crozier," Maddy said, determinedly standing on both feet. "I'm sorry—I was thinking of something else."

Mrs. Crozier sniffed. "Most like your last placement, and how much better it was."

"Actually I was thinking how I like the size of this household." Which was true—the house, upon reflection, was just right. Like the story of the three bears, the Russell houses were too big, Nanny Gruen's and the cheap flat in London were too small, but the captain's house was just right.

In a perfect world Tarkington would come back from South America, throw himself at her feet, begging for forgiveness. The aging captain would die and they would buy this house and live happily ever after, away from the craziness of London. There was plenty of room for children here, and the view of the ocean was tantalizing.

But Tarkington would never beg forgiveness, and besides, she wouldn't want him if he did. She didn't love him, had never loved him, and she wanted half a dozen estates and a titled, preferably dead husband . . .

"Are you certain you're not moon-brained?" Mrs. Crozier was staring at her, gimlet-eyed.

Maddy didn't dignify this with an answer. "I'm almost done here."

"And it's taken you twice the time it should have done. Leave it for now—you need to set the table for the captain and his guests. There'll be six for dinner—very *intime*." Mrs. Crozier gave the word an English pronunciation instead of the French, confusing Maddy for a moment until she realized it was simply the housekeeper trying to sound sophisticated. "The captain is having his fiancée, Miss Gwendolyn Haviland, and her parents, as well as Mr. Quarrells and his particular friend, Duncan."

"But the numbers are uneven," she blurted out before she realized what she was saying.

"You think we should go out and find two more women to even things out?" Her tone was derisive. "You'll find that Mr. Quarrells and Mr. Duncan have no interest in the fairer sex. At all." There was something meaningful in her voice, but Maddy had no idea what she was hinting at. "You ask too many questions, and you have too many suggestions. You need to learn your place. You may have been an upstairs maid at your previous employer's mansion but here you're just a slavey, and you need to remember that."

"Yes, Mrs. Crozier." Eventually she was going to get her revenge on this old witch. When Tarkington returned . . . no, she didn't want him to return. And she'd forgotten, she wanted money and a title, and she'd make someone like Lord Eastham buy this house and toss Mrs. Crozier onto the street before whisking her off to his country estate.

Except she liked this house more than the thought of some mansion. And she didn't want Lord Eastham, who had liver spots and smelled of camphor. She wanted someone like that outrageous stranger who'd kissed her in the alleyway after paying off her attackers, the swine. She couldn't afford to let herself fantasize about him—he was rude and not what she wanted at all. Except for his kisses . . .

"I assume you know how to set a table after all your superior positions?"

That was one thing that had been drilled into her at the Swiss finishing school her father had insisted on sending her to. Not the setting so much as the proper order in which to use things, but it worked for the job at hand. "Of course. What's on the menu?"

Mrs. Crozier's eyes narrowed. "Why do you care?"

"Because I need to know whether we need spoons for a cream soup or a broth, if seafood forks are necessary, teaspoons or demi-tasse spoons . . ." Her words came to an abrupt halt at the expression on Mrs. Crozier's thin face.

"Jayzus, girl, do you think this is Buckingham Palace? Two forks, one knife, two spoons, one small, one for soup, and who cares if it's a cream soup or a broth? I've told you, the captain doesn't care for folderol. Besides, Wilf has the key to the silver—you don't think I'm about to entrust it to you, do you? He'll get the cutlery out for you."

"But what does Miss Haviland think about all this?"

Mrs. Crozier snorted. "It'll be up to her to train the captain, not me, thank God. He'd be a right handful, the captain would."

Old men were always difficult and set in their ways, Maddy thought.

"Go on, then. Wilf will serve when he gets his uniform on, but you'd best put on a clean apron and tidy that ridiculous hair in case you're seen by any of them."

Maddy put a hand to her hair and felt it drifting out of its tight knot and floating down around her face, escaping the cap entirely. "Yes, Mrs. Crozier."

"There's a mirror in the back hallway, and fresh aprons are piled in the cupboard just beyond it. Make yourself presentable. You look like a slattern."

Mrs. Crozier wasn't far off. Maddy's dark hair was falling in loose waves from the tidy white hat that looked just a bit like a nightcap, and she was flushed from toiling over the hot sink. Of course her arms were red up to her elbows, and she quickly rolled down the sleeves of her dress, thankful she wouldn't have to pull those blasted sleeve covers over it. That was for heavy work, and with luck her heavy work for the night was done.

Exchanging her wet apron, she scurried back up to the dining room. The linen tablecloth had already been set out, as well as the cutlery, and she went to work, ignoring the pain in her feet as she set six places with a shocking minimum of flatware. The tablecloth was excellent quality, the glassware all crystal from Ireland, the china a politically questionable Limoges. Exquisite, all of it, she thought, looking around her.

The disgruntled Wilf had appeared, uniformed this time, though the livery was ill-fitting. "Watcher looking for?" he demanded, surveying the table with a reluctant sniff of approval.

She turned. "A centerpiece of some kind. An epergne, perhaps?"

"What's an epergne?"

Rats! That wasn't that uncommon a piece, was it? "A silver or gold centerpiece? With little baskets or bowls or candleholders?" she said hopefully.

"Naaah," he said after much consideration. "Don't think so. Happen the captain doesn't like things in the middle of the table. He says it gets in the way of seeing people."

Good point, Maddy thought grudgingly, remembering all the dinner parties when she was closed in by flowers and candles and unable to see anyone across the table. And the ones across the table tended to be the most interesting, even if you were supposed to confine your conversation to the guests flanking you. "Surely there's something low we can use. The table looks too . . . austere."

Wilf just looked at her, and she had the sneaking suspicion he didn't understand the word. And then she remembered dusting a beautiful ceramic bowl in the salon, one done in shades of blue and red by an artist from a foreign country. The signature was Asian, and she suspected the bowl was Japanese, but not the common stuff that flooded the market. This was something particularly beautiful.

"Don't worry—I've got an idea."

Fortunately no one had arrived in the salon as yet, though she thought she could hear voices from the front hallway. She snatched up the bowl and dashed back into the servant's quarters, to the butler's pantry just beyond the dining room.

Filling the bowl with fresh water, she racked her brains for the sight of the back garden. She'd noticed at least some flowers blooming in the back. She would have to make do.

The spring air was cool and crisp, and something seemed to have dragged the bat's corpse away, thank God. It was early in the year, but there were daffodils and tulips in bloom, and she cut a handful, hurrying back in to avoid Mrs. Crozier's evil eye. She arranged the flowers, swiftly and perfectly, so that they floated softly. If there was one thing she excelled at in the so-called feminine arts, it was arranging flowers. She was ghastly at needlework, hopeless at cooking, but give her a container and flowers and she could create a masterpiece.

They were already in the salon. She could hear an elderly male voice, slightly loud, slightly bombastic, and immediately decided he must be the captain. She set her creation down in the middle of the table and dashed back to the kitchen and Mrs. Crozier's unnecessary demands.

All should have gone perfectly. Wilf carried course after course up to the dining room while Mrs. Crozier cooked and Maddy scrubbed at the pots and pans and dishes as they were returned to the kitchen. The waste was extraordinary—apparently Mrs. Crozier's cooking skills matched her sunny temperament, and Maddy dutifully scraped everything into the slop pail.

"We'll keep that inside for the night, until the farmer comes to get it for his pigs."

"Why?" she said, looking down at the unappealing mass of foods mixed together. "Are you afraid it will draw wild animals?"

"It'll draw children, and they're worse," said Mrs. Crozier. "Once they know they can find food here they'll be loitering about all the time, hunting for scraps."

"You'd rather feed pigs than starving children?" There was no way Maddy could keep the outrage from her voice.

"You can eat pigs once you fatten them up."

Maddy was, quite fortunately, speechless, or she would have been fired on the spot, never having set eyes on the suspicious captain. Before she could regain her ability to speak and therefore blast Mrs. Crozier with her rage, a loud crash was heard from the dining room.

"Oh, gawd, what's Wilfrid done now?" Starving, inedible children were forgotten as Mrs. Crozier spun around. "That fool man is always dropping things. You'll have to go out and help him clean up. And keep your face down—I know what men are like, and even though the captain wouldn't dare to trifle with his own maidservant with his fiancée looking on, that face of yours could change a man's mind. Go along, now."

Maddy could barely contain her excitement. She was finally coming face to face with her nemesis. Quickly rolling down her sleeves, she dashed up the stairs, heading for the green baize door that led to the butler's pantry and on to the dining room, with Mrs. Crozier chasing after her holding a fresh apron. "And tuck that hair under your cap again. Or you'll have to cut it all off."

There was no way in hell that was going to happen, Maddy thought mutinously, taking a deep breath. A moment later she found herself pushed through the door into the narrow butler's pantry, and then on out into the dining room.

Her eyes first went to Wilf, who was on his knees trying to scoop up broken dishes onto the heavy silver tray. He looked up at her and rose, pulling his ill-fitting uniform down with affronted dignity, as if she was the one who'd made the mess. "Clean that up, girl," he said dismissively.

She didn't hesitate, dropping to her knees and picking up the shattered pieces of Limoges. It had been beautiful china, and she wanted to weep at Wilf's clumsiness as shard after shard of destroyed beauty was laid to rest on the silver tray with appropriate gravity.

"Beg pardon, captain," he was saying. "The girl is new and she obviously didn't polish the tray correctly. The handles were slippery."

Maddy's back stiffened in outrage, her mouth open to protest, but she shut it again, keeping her head down. Maybe, just maybe if she took all the abuse the Croziers felt like dishing out they'd stop trying to sabotage her. She'd always assumed servants stood up for each other, though Bryony had mentioned dealing with arguments and conflict even in the harmonious Russell households.

"Fire the girl." The elderly, pompous voice, the one she'd heard earlier, came from the dinner table, and she looked up in horror, certain she was finished before she'd even begun if the captain himself was firing her.

But the man who'd spoken had been to her left, and she glanced up to find he was sitting on one side, a choleric-looking gentleman who'd probably never been to sea in his life. Beside him was a beautiful young woman, with hair so blond it was almost white, pale skin, and blue eyes that hadn't even bothered to glance at the troublesome servants. The man she'd spied through the window was at the foot of the table, so he was clearly not the captain, and her eyes swung immediately to the far end, for her first glance at her elderly employer.

She almost dropped the shard of glass she was holding, and she clutched it instinctively, barely feeling it bite into her skin.

She knew that face, even though he was talking with the beautiful woman beside him, not even looking down at the mess his servants had made. Knew that mouth, had felt that mouth on hers what seemed like a lifetime ago, but in fact had only been a few hours ago. He still hadn't bothered with a proper neckcloth, but he had something draped around his neck as a nod to propriety, and his dark, curling hair had been pushed back, probably another sop to decency, though it only exposed the barbaric gold earring. He had a strong profile—a long nose, flashing eyes, his dark brows slanting upward and his cheekbones high and sharp. She already knew too much about that wicked mouth of his.

He must have felt her eyes on him, and he turned, but she was fast enough to duck her head and finish cleaning up the broken dishes. There was blood dripping onto the tray, and she realized she'd cut herself more deeply than she thought. With the last bit of food scooped onto the tray, she rose, lifting the wretchedly heavy thing with her, and it was all she could do not to stagger, her legs and arms ridiculously weak. Keeping her face glued to the tray, she backed out of the room, while Wilf was continuing on with his convoluted tale of how it had been all her fault, when she heard his voice again.

"I really don't give a bloody damn how it happened," her employer said irritably.

"Captain!" the old man huffed. "There are ladies present. Moderate your language."

There was no apology. "How it happened doesn't matter," the captain continued after a weighted moment. "Just get it cleaned up and see to the girl. She's cut herself on the broken glass."

So he'd noticed that, had he? What else had he noticed?

But Wilf, the idiot, didn't get the message. "She's unbearably clumsy, Captain. We'll see she's bandaged before she leaves."

"She's not going anywhere. This house is a disaster, and you and your wife have been complaining that you need help for months. This is her first day and she's allowed a few mistakes."

Defending her again, she thought dazedly. But did he even get that good a look at her? He didn't strike her as a knight errant by nature. His smile was too wicked.

By that time she'd backed out of the room, setting the heavy tray on the counter in the pantry, and she was trembling slightly as the door swung shut behind her, hiding her from view.

"Well, I for one do not tolerate shoddy service," an older woman's voice broke in. The pirate's future mother-in-law. "And I would hope my daughter would follow my standards in all things."

"Not in all things, I hope," the captain said lazily, and Maddy wondered if she were the only one who caught his subtle, sexual hint in that statement.

There was a laugh from the far end of the table, and Maddy knew she wasn't alone.

"Of course I shall, Mama," came a meek voice. Poor girl. She was bullied by her parents, for doubtless that blustery old man was just as controlling, and she was about to marry an indiscreet lecher who kissed strange girls on the street. Though he also rescued them from rape, she had to admit fairly. So despite his thoroughly bad behavior in claiming her mouth she ought to put that out of her mind and concentrate on the fact that his act had been essentially noble.

Of course, putting that kiss from her mind was far from an easy task. When she thought about it, a strange tightness caught beneath her breasts, and heat bloomed where it shouldn't. Would her husband kiss her like that? She could teach him to.

Except maybe she wouldn't be wanting to kiss her husband like that, depending on whom she landed. She was going to be practical and hardheaded, and the unfortunate fact was that titles and large incomes tended to come with elderly, pockmarked, overfed men like Lord Eastham with too much hair on their faces and not enough on their heads. The captain's smooth-shaven face was another sign of his disdain for society. How would it feel to kiss someone like that when they had a moustache, and perhaps side-whiskers? Tarkington had had a luxuriant mustache, but he'd never kissed her like that, even when they . . .

Maybe she should stop thinking about kisses, but at least it kept her mind off her sore feet and aching muscles.

"Pssst."

It took Maddy a moment to realize Mrs. Crozier was signaling her. With a sigh she hoisted the tray once more and carried it down into the kitchen.

"Set it on the table, you stupid girl," the woman snapped. "At least you had the sense to keep your mouth shut. And stop bleeding all over my clean kitchen. There are supplies in the cupboard where you found your aprons. Clean yourself up."

Easier said than done, and by the time she'd managed to wash the blood away and wrap a crude bandage around her hand the bleeding seemed to have stopped. She'd allowed herself a moment to sit while she tried to bandage herself, and it would have been so easy simply to close her eyes and sleep, just for a few seconds.

Life had suddenly become a great deal more complicated. Instead of an elderly sea captain full of bluster she found herself in the household of a . . . a gypsy king. With those long, black curls and a golden hoop, he was a far cry from anything she'd ever dealt with. He was more like something from her childhood dreams, when she'd wanted nothing more than to run off and live in a gypsy caravan, traveling the country.

She'd even done so for three days. She'd been ten years old. Her father had disciplined her for shoving Sophie in the pond at Somerset, which was ridiculous because Sophie had always been a great swimmer, and in affront Maddy had decided to run away. She'd gotten as far as the neighboring Gorton Woods, only to run across an encampment of Travelers.

She'd been dirty, wet, hungry, and miserable, and the grandmother, who seemed to be in charge of the group rather than the old man, took her in, bathed her and fed her and tucked her up inside her own *vardo*. And Maddy had immediately decided right then that she would marry a gypsy and live in one of those wonderful caravans and travel the world.

Of course, she had been so young. And the grandmother had returned her to her father three days later, a brave act since she could have been accused of kidnapping. But her father had always been a fair man, and he knew his rebellious middle daughter well, so he'd simply thanked the grandmother, gave her a gift of wine and foodstuffs, and told her they would always be welcome to camp on his land.

But it wasn't his land anymore. She hadn't seen them for years, but she hoped they wouldn't return to be faced with the new viscount.

Now here she was in the household of someone who looked like her adolescent dream of romance, with that honey gold skin and flashing eyes. And he'd kissed her! So much for her plan to slip through the household unnoticed. Most people never even gave housemaids a second glance, and despite Mrs. Crozier's complaints Maddy had made herself as plain as possible. An elderly sea captain might not notice her, but the man who'd accosted her this afternoon certainly would.

She should have paid more attention when her father spoke of him. She'd known he was a far cry from the other men who commanded Eustace Russell's ships, with his mysterious background, a stint at piracy in the Far East, and a gift for getting a cargo where it needed to be faster and safer than anyone else. Sailors fought to be on his ships. Her father had trusted him implicitly as one of the most valued of his employees, or so she thought, until they'd found that scribbled note after he died. *Never trust a pirate*, he'd written. Why couldn't he have said more?

This was going to be a great deal more difficult than she'd expected, starting out, but then, she had no choice. She'd committed herself to this path and she would see it through. If the captain made unwelcome advances she would scream her head off. But she'd seen his fiancée—her own complete opposite. Gwendolyn Haviland was skinny, flat as a board, Maddy added uncharitably, with watery blue eyes and pale skin and colorless hair. . .

She stopped herself, astonished at her own cattiness. Gwendolyn Haviland was a beauty. She was slender rather than thin, with porcelain skin, pale blue eyes, and the blond hair that her sister Sophie assured her was so much more à la mode. She was like some exquisite doll, and she made Maddy feel like an overblown peony, with her dark hair and dark blue eyes and admittedly voluptuous figure. Clearly she wasn't the captain's type—that kiss had been just what he'd said it had been—a salutary lesson. She just wasn't used to lessons feeling so disturbingly . . . good.

"Greaves!" Mrs. Crozier's carping voice came from the kitchen, and she couldn't dawdle any longer. She'd find some way to coexist with the captain, perhaps pretend it hadn't even happened. Pushing herself out of the seat with her one good hand, she returned to the kitchen and her two taskmasters.

Wilf was busy shoveling food into his mouth, and he didn't even bother to look at her. She'd been a fool to expect him to thank her for taking the blame for his own ineptitude, but of course he ignored her completely, as he'd ignored her before. Which suited her fine—she didn't want his rheumy old eyes on her.

"You'd best go up to bed, girl," Mrs. Crozier said, and Maddy ground her teeth. Answering to the name of "Greaves" had been bad enough—the convenient "girl" was impossibly demeaning. "The captain will probably want to see you, and I don't think you'll be wanting to face him tonight. He'd probably fire you on the spot. I'll tell him I've sent you to bed."

She was ready to put off seeing him for as long as she possibly could. "That won't be a problem?"

Mrs. Crozier shrugged her thin shoulders. "You'll simply have to prove yourself, same as anyone. If you do your job and keep out of his way the captain won't have anything to say to you. But if you're lazy or nosy you'll be blistered with words, you will. I hear tell they don't use the lash on his boats—all he has to do is use his tongue."

It was a sudden, disturbing image. He'd used his tongue with her, in an entirely different manner from what Mrs. Crozier was describing, and it had demoralized her completely. She sincerely doubted he kissed his erring crewmembers, though there were stories about long trips . . .

No, not the man who'd put his mouth on hers. And she wasn't even supposed to know that men did such things, but she'd always had a great curiosity and one of her father's retired captains had explained things to her. She still couldn't quite fathom what men did together, and she certainly couldn't imagine the captain, but then, she was hopelessly naïve in some matters and preferred it that way.

"There you go again," Mrs. Crozier snapped. "That faraway look in your eyes fair gives me the chills, it does. Like you're seeing ghosts or something."

Well, that was at least one form of defense against the old biddy, Maddy thought. "Beg pardon, Mrs. Crozier," she said meekly. "I was just thinking of something."

"Don't you go be thinking about the captain! He doesn't have any interest in a pert housemaid, not when he's got a beauty like Miss Haviland, so you can put it right out of your mind. If you were a doxy he'd pay the price easily enough, I imagine, but he doesn't soil his own nest, if you know what I mean."

"I'm a good girl, I am," she said immediately, putting just the trace of a whine in it. "I left London because my employer was trying to take advantage of me. If I'm not going to lift my skirts for a lord I'm for certain not about to lift them for a sea captain."

Mrs. Crozier was not impressed. "I'm thinking your lord didn't look like Captain Morgan. For all that he's part gypsy the women fall all over him, and I expect you will too. Just don't make a pest of yourself."

"Yes, Mrs. Crozier." She'd make a pest of herself, all right, just not in the way Mrs. Crozier imagined. Things had suddenly become a great deal more difficult. An elderly sea captain, no matter how larcenous, seemed a lot easier to deal with than someone like the man who . . .

No, she couldn't think about it, not tonight. Tonight she had to find her way up three flights of stairs to her attic, lugging water to wash in and sheets for the bed, and she had to pray there were no bats to greet her.

It was the least she deserved after such an exhausting day.

She wasn't counting on it.

CHAPTER SIX

LUCA WAS NOT A happy man. With Vincent Haviland's rheumy eyes on him, he had danced attendance on Gwendolyn and was rewarded with the beautiful smile that lit her blue eyes, her slight, restraining touch on his arm, a mild flirtation that hardly suited their engaged status. Mrs. Haviland was looking at him as if he'd crawled out of a sewer, and he would have given almost anything to lean over and inform her that's exactly where he'd come from.

Ah, but he had a role to play, a brand-new reputation, hard-won and relatively honest. His thieving, pirating days were behind him, as well as his whoring and brawling. He'd decided to marry a very beautiful, very proper young lady, and he needed to ignore his rebellious second thoughts. From now on, when at home, he was going to be the perfect model of a captain and a budding industrialist. He knew Gwendolyn—she would revel in her role as leader of Devonport society. She'd assured him she had no aspirations toward London, and he believed her. In London she'd be nothing, the daughter of a country solicitor. Dukes' nieces were thick on the ground already, and her tenuous claim to aristocracy would be ignored for the greater scandal of whom she'd married. Here in Devonport, where shipping lines were more important than bloodlines, she could queen it over everyone, because there was simply no one better than he was at running a ship, be she powered by sails or steam.

He understood the ocean and the vessels that plied it. While his heart would always love the beauty of the clipper ships, his practical side responded to the power and speed of steam and steel. Fools had tried to race him, and they always lost. Other fools had tried to lure his best men from him—they lost as well. Now, with a burgeoning fleet of two ships, soon to be three, he was unstoppable.

So why was he suddenly troubled by the young woman who'd entered his household this very day?

He seldom noticed maids—this house and living on land was a tedious and always temporary necessity, and he paid little attention to the disreputable state the house was in until Gwendolyn gently brought his attention to it. It had to be sheer coincidence that he'd run into the girl earlier, trying to fight off three drunken sailors, the silly cow.

Except she was no cow. She was a rare beauty, with a fire inside that was carefully banked but still glowing, a fire that made Gwendolyn seem pale and lifeless in comparison. He'd been a fool to kiss her, but he'd taken the excuse, simply because he wanted to be bad, be outrageous, do something that would horrify his fiancée had she ever found out. Kissing a beautiful woman in the rough neighborhoods of Devonport had been as good a way as any to vent his frustration, and if the girl had been willing he would have pulled her deeper into the alleyway and taken her up against a wall like a sailor just home from the sea. There'd been something about her, about her soft, unskilled mouth, her flashing eyes, her brave fury, that had called to him, and it wouldn't have taken him long to show her just how to use that mouth.

He'd thought better of it, of course, and it had only taken the second kiss to realize she wasn't someone you fucked in an alley on a bright spring day. At least he'd thought he'd scared her off from wandering around the docks alone. So why had he gone back to kiss her one more time?

He couldn't get her face out of his mind. When he first looked over and saw her kneeling on the floor he thought he was imagining things, so caught up in her memory that he was dreaming she'd appeared.

But damned if it wasn't her after all, and one sharp glance was even more unsettling. He knew the girl, and not just from the encounter in the alleyway. He couldn't remember where he'd seen her before today, but he most certainly had. And what the hell was she doing in his household, picking up after that sotted Crozier's mistakes?

It wasn't as if she was fair game. Even if he weren't engaged, he wouldn't touch a woman in his employ. That was what the toffs did—seduce and discard people like him without a second thought. Though who was he fooling—maids were a step up from where he'd come from. He'd seen them on the streets, following their mistresses when he was a cutpurse, seen them in the houses when he was a climbing boy. Superior they were, clean and starched and prim, looking at him like the dirt he was. No, he'd dealt with the upper crust in the last few years while in Russell's employ, and he hadn't been impressed. The only one he'd liked and trusted had been Russell himself, and that had proven to be a mistake. He was hardly going to start aping their bad behavior. Russell. Why was he suddenly thinking of Eustace Russell so much? That part of his life was over.

Of course, if he hired the new maid for bed sport rather than cleaning his house, that would be a different matter, but it was already too late. And that wretched old woman who'd served as his housekeeper since he'd bought this place would keep her at a distance as well. Prunella Crozier tended to drive off maids and cooks with surprising speed, leaving him living in a state of chaos—the only mitigating factor being her acceptable cooking skills. The house didn't matter—as long as the ships he commanded were spotless and the food on his table edible, he didn't care.

He would have to apologize to the girl, he supposed, but not until he remembered where he'd seen her before. His solicitor's junior partner had recommended her, so perhaps he might have seen her in Fulton's house. But she'd supposedly worked for his mother, and he'd certainly never been welcome in Mrs. Fulton's august presence, so he couldn't have seen her there. There were too many unacceptable things about him: his gypsy blood, his refusal to conform to society's demands, his past. The impressive amount of money he'd amassed over the years, both from legitimate and questionable sources, would only take him so far.

No, he wouldn't deal with the girl tonight—the day had been too long, and tomorrow would be soon enough.

It seemed as if his guests lingered forever. Billy wouldn't abandon him to the Havilands, and old Haviland didn't seem in any hurry to leave his fine cognac. By the time he'd gotten rid of them he was bone weary, and he sat staring at the fire, knowing he should go to bed, but he was still feeling restless. It was the damned girl beneath his roof that was making him edgy, and he knew it.

Wilf Crozier couldn't be trusted to properly damp a fire, so Luca kicked the blaze down and set the grate in front of the coals. Fortunately warm weather was coming, and maybe his delectable new maid would be better at laying fires. Though he could think of other things she might be good at laying.

He shook his head, both to toss off the effects of the whiskey and to negate the temporarily lustful thought. Not for him.

He started up the stairs, turning down the gaslight as he went, moving through the shadowy hallways, silent as the thief he'd once been. He'd just reached his room when a bloodcurdling scream tore through the quiet house.

He could come to full attention no matter what state he was in, and he immediately knew where the scream had come from and who had made such a hideous sound. He slammed open the hidden door to the attics and bounded up the stairs in the darkness. There was only a faint glow at the top to guide him, but he had eyes like a cat, and he could see when there was no light at all but the faint pinprick of the stars above an ink-black sea. The screaming had stopped, and he wondered if someone had cut the idiot girl's throat when he heard the panicked whimpers coming from the room on the left.

He charged in, only to be brought up short, frozen.

She was sitting up in bed, her long, silky dark hair loose around her shoulders, though one side was partly braided, as if she'd been disturbed in the act. She was wearing a soft white nightdress of some sort, too thin for the chill in the attics, her eyes were wide in fear, and she'd stuck a small fist in her mouth to silence the noise she'd been making.

He had a knife drawn, and he whirled around, looking for a possible assailant. There was no one there but the two of them, and as she stared up at him she looked, if possible, even more frightened.

"What the bloody hell is going on?" he roared, his heart beginning to fall back to normal.

She opened her mouth to say something, but only a tiny whimper came out. She cleared her throat, stammering something he couldn't understand.

He shoved the knife back into the narrow sheath, glowering down at her. "What?"

"B-b-bats," she stammered.

"Oh, sweet Neptune's briny pants," he swore. "Is that all? I thought you were being murdered."

Belatedly she seemed to realize her compromising position. She leapt out of her narrow, sagging little bed and quickly took the threadbare cover off it, wrapping it around her. A shame, too, as the moonlight coming in the window had outlined her silhouette quite nicely, and spending time with Gwendolyn always made him randy as a goat.

"Beg pardon, sir," she said, and her voice had changed subtly, sounding a little more like the rough North and less cultured than her original tones. Granted, one stammered word wasn't enough to be sure, but she'd done the same thing that afternoon when the sailors had been pestering her. Moved between Mayfair and Lancastershire with suspicious ease. "I'm mortal feared of bats."

No, it wasn't quite right. He could see her eyes, and while he had no doubt she was honestly frightened, he could see a tiny hint of calculation in their depths, as if she wanted to be certain to say the right thing. *Too late for that, my girl,* he thought grimly.

"I'm afraid, Miss . . ."

"Greaves, sir," she said, going for a little more North-country in her voice. "M-M-Mary Greaves."

And his name was William Kidd. Then again, his name certainly wasn't Thomas Morgan, though he'd taken the last name in honor of one of England's most famous pirates. But what reason would the girl have for giving the wrong name?

"Is your stammer permanent, or simply as a result of flying rodents?" He saw her inadvertent shiver, and knew that at least her fear of bats was very real.

"I'm that sorry, Captain. I didn't mean to disturb you. They surprised me, is all. The moon came out from behind a cloud and one flew across the room . . ."

"You'll have to get used to them until I can get someone in. I can hardly have you sleeping on the second floor."

"Of course not, sir." She sounded even more panicked at the thought. Jesus, the girl was afraid of her own shadow. Except she hadn't been afraid this afternoon, when she ought to have been. She'd been defiant and outraged. "It just startled me. I'm all right now."

"I'm delighted to hear it," he said dryly. "Is this your first day here?" He knew perfectly well it was—he never would have kissed her if she'd been in his house previously.

She blinked, obviously disconcerted. So she'd expected him to recognize her? Far be it from him to fulfill expectations. "Y-yes, sir." The stammer again, he thought. She hadn't stammered earlier in the day.

"Well, Mary Greaves, I hope you don't make a habit of screaming in the middle of the night and waking me from sleep. I'm a lenient employer but there are limits."

"Were you asleep, sir?"

He cocked an eyebrow. "Is that any particular business of yours?"

She was gaining back some of that steel he'd detected beneath her cool exterior earlier today. Now she was more like the young virago who'd kneed a man in his privates without hesitation. Perhaps it was a good thing he didn't poach the staff for his bed—he valued his privates too much. But who the hell was she?

"No, sir. Beg pardon, sir."

He knew his expression showed nothing of his thoughts—another talent earned young. "I presume Mrs. Crozier has already filled you in on my particular preferences. I drink coffee, not tea, in the morning, and I like it strong and sweet. Do not wake me up unless I request it, never think to enter my library or touch my papers. In all, do what Mrs. Crozier tells you and stay out of my way and we'll get along fine."

"Is there any reason we shouldn't, sir?" she asked, another inappropriate question. If this girl had been a maid before, then he was a landlubbing pig farmer.

He looked at her with complete indifference. "I see no reason." He could recognize it, even in the shadows, that glimmer of confusion in her eyes. She had been certain that he'd recognize her, but now she was unsure, which was exactly how he wanted it. As far as she knew he was in the habit of kissing any pretty girl he met, and one was much like the next. Except for this one, his truthful self admitted, but he ignored the notion. No, he would play it this way for both their sakes. He'd never met her, never tasted her virginal mouth, and he damned well never would again. At least, not until he remembered where he'd seen her before.

"Very good, sir." Her voice was drifting into Mayfair territory again. There was a perfectly acceptable reason for that, of course. Anyone in service with ambitions would work toward bettering herself, and the first step would be her accent. Voices placed you in society, and the girl would want to ape her so-called betters, not sound like a country lass.

He had an ear for accents—he could take and discard any of them at his pleasure, and every now and then he liked to let the sound of the London docks into his voice to shake up the Havilands. They wanted his money, of course—old man Haviland had lost a fortune when Eustace Russell had decamped, and Luca had no doubt he wouldn't have gotten within ten feet of his precious Gwendolyn if he hadn't come equipped with a relatively staggering amount of money. Haviland knew to a penny what he was worth, and probably did daily calculations, and that wasn't counting the priceless items he kept hidden. It didn't matter—if money could buy an exquisite porcelain doll like Gwendolyn, he'd decided he was willing to pay the price. And the smartest thing he could do was ignore his present doubts.

He moved into the hallway, heading toward the pile of rubbish at one end, and he heard her start after him. She was just about to close her door in his face when he turned, presenting his offering.

She looked down at the broken tennis racket that had belonged to some indolent creature who'd lived here long ago. "Did you want me to mend this, sir?" she asked blankly.

"No, I want you to play tennis with me," he drawled. Her hair had come free from her half braid now, and it was truly glorious hair, the moonlight sending a warm glow into its rich depths, and he wondered what it would smell like. Bleach and carbolic? Or the heady scent of flowers?

Not now, he reminded himself. "It's to drive any stray visitors away," he said casually. "Just open a window and knock them outside."

"If I open the window, won't more bats come in?" It was stuffy up here, despite the damp chill. That explained it then.

"You close the window, in between dispatching them. Who knows, you might develop an impressive backhand in time."

She shouldn't know what he meant, but apparently she did and she wasn't amused. Interesting, when most women found him irresistibly witty. "Yes, sir," she said in not much more than a disgruntled mumble. "Will that be all, sir?"

She was dismissing him. He found the thought so amusing he almost moved back toward her, crowding her, pushing up against her . . . no. Not now, he reminded himself.

"Yes, M-Mary." If she truly had a stammer that was unconscionably cruel of him, but he knew she didn't. She simply wasn't sure which name she'd chosen to use. He was almost at the top of the open stairs when she spoke, halting him.

"Sir, you look a bit familiar. Have we met before?"

He turned to look at her. So she was going to go there, was she? He needed to set her mind at ease. "I don't think so. But then, I meet so very many people. Too many, in fact. Part of your job will be to lie and tell people I'm not at home."

"Yes, sir." She didn't bob a curtsey, which was just as well. She looked ridiculous clutching that thin blanket around her, her bare feet just peeping under the hem of her nightgown. Her feet were going to get cold. They were very pretty feet.

"Get back in bed, Mary. Morning will be here sooner than you think."

"Yes, sir," she said again, but he could see the relief in her eyes. So she didn't want him to remember that kiss any more than she wanted to remember it. *Easier said than done, my girl,* he thought, clattering down the narrow staircase. It was going to be a long time before he forgot her taste.

Maddy looked at the battered tennis racket in her hand. She hadn't held one in years, not since she'd started spending so much time in London with her father, learning the business. Oh, not that he'd expected her to take over. She was only a female, after all—not a fit heir to the empire he'd built so carefully, she thought with that trace of bitterness she'd never been able to stifle completely.

Bryony had chosen to retire from life—she'd insisted she was never going to marry—so their father been looking to Maddy to find a husband and produce a suitable heir to the business. There'd been no particular hurry—Eustace Russell had intended to live forever, and he could wait until her offspring grew up. In fact, he'd only been in his late forties when he'd died, far too young.

Her father hadn't particularly cared for Tarkington, but apart from a word of warning he'd said nothing. Jasper Tarkington had been charming, devoted, and Maddy thought she'd loved him. Oh, she'd been reasonable about it—she was an heiress and he was a younger son of an ancient family. He needed her money, but he loved her, he truly did.

Or so she thought. What would have happened if things hadn't changed so dramatically? Would their marriage, because it had been inevitable, have been a happy one? Unlikely. He'd proven himself untrustworthy, abandoning her the moment the scandal became known. Taking just enough time to relieve her of her virginity before heading for South America, out of her reach and any consequences of that awful night.

There'd been no consequences, thank God. She'd gone to him, alone, desperate, needing proof that he wasn't going to abandon her, that he truly loved her no matter what her father had done. And she'd been so determined to prove her own devotion she'd let him have what he'd been trying to get from the very beginning. She'd gone with him to his bed, willingly, certain it would cement their relationship. In the morning he'd been gone, with nothing but a note expressing polite regret that their relationship was at an end.

Cowardly bastard that he was. She'd wept private, bitter tears of shame and regret and yes, longing, until she'd finally grown disgusted with her own weakness. She moved on to berating herself, thinking she'd somehow been found wanting, but common sense told her otherwise. He'd used her body and enjoyed himself, so thoroughly that while she took little pleasure in the act, holding him afterwards, stroking his damp hair had given her a wonderful sense of fulfillment. Until he left.

She wasn't going to make that mistake again. Her lack of virginity might prove an issue in the impressive marriage she was determined to make, but there were ways around that particular problem. Tarkington had hurt her, but according to her outspoken married friends the amount of pain had more to do with the skill of the lover. Not that she'd told anyone about her fall from grace, not even her sisters, but she'd quietly gathered information. It would be easy enough to pretend discomfort and then leave behind a bit of chicken's blood on the linen sheets. And if worse came to worst, Eastham was so determined he probably wouldn't mind.

And why was she thinking of Tarkington again? Was it something about the captain that reminded her of those unpleasant hours in Tarkington's bed? And would it be the same with someone like the captain? No, she wasn't going to think of him in those terms.

He was so unlike the other captains she had met—gruff, bluff men who strode through life as if the entire world was their ship and under their command. They were like English bulldogs—straightforward and forceful.

This man was more like a cat, some great jungle cat, sleek and graceful, secretive and prowling. He unnerved her, made her think of things she shouldn't be thinking of . . .

She had to stop that right now, she thought, hefting the racket in her hand. It could be used to fight off libidinous desires as easily as winged rodents . . . She shuddered, amending her term. Bats.

It was a good thing he didn't even remember her. Apart from the moment when he kissed her all his attention had been on the three sailors. And he'd finally walked away from her without a glance back.

She wanted to laugh at herself. She was so used to being the toast, the exquisite heiress, Miss Madeleine Russell. Men would fight to dance with her. She had dismissed half a dozen suitors for Jasper Tarkington, tall and blond and arrogant. Would any of them have stayed the course after the scandal broke? If she'd already been engaged, any one of them would have had a hard time crying off without looking like a total cad. With Tarkington it had been an understanding, not an actual engagement, making it easy for him to disappear. Damn him to hell, she thought, savoring the curses. Her father had always deplored her language, but right now she was glad of it. Tarkington deserved her most profane sentiments.

How much of that devotion had been the result of her father's money? She had a mirror and clear vision—she knew what she saw in her reflection: a perfect oval face, the dark blue eyes of her father, rich, wavy hair. Nose—small. Mouth—generous. Skin and teeth—tediously perfect. It was a fact, not vanity, to say she was a beauty, and that was more of a liability than a gift in this particular endeavor. Surely there must be less attractive things to do with her hair. Even braiding it tightly and poking it into the cap Mrs. Crozier insisted she wear didn't do much to dampen her appearance.

She tried to remember her and her sisters' amateur theatricals. She had played Richard the Third once, with her sisters taking the other roles, and Richard was certainly heinous, though Maddy had always had her doubts about the real man. He probably wasn't any worse than the rest of them, he just ended up on the losing side, and winners were the ones who wrote the history.

Perhaps she could use some of her Richard traits. Hunch one shoulder, squint, or develop a useful limp. Mrs. Crozier already thought of her as half mad because of her habit of getting lost in her thoughts—if she could use that, it might make people steer clear of her. She'd played ghosts as well—she could try a breathy, eerie voice.

She closed the door to her room, still clutching the tennis racket in one hand. She swung it back and forth tentatively—she'd played tennis with Bryony in the court at Somerset, back when life was simpler. She swung it through the air again, trying to imagine whom she wanted to smack with it. For some reason the captain's exotic, wicked face came into view.

Clearly she wasn't made for being in service—she didn't take orders well, either from Mrs. Crozier or the captain. Something inside her wanted to rebel, and she wanted to charge downstairs, go into his office, and toss his precious papers all over the place.

If this didn't work out she'd best not seek work as a governess but rather find the rich, titled husband immediately. They grew on trees in London, didn't they?

And imagine that Bryony had ended up with one. Beautiful Bryony with her scarred face and her determined soul was now a countess. Granted, she was a countess in exile, but still and all, she'd done what neither of her conventionally beautiful younger sisters had managed.

In fact, it had been Bryony's idea to go into service in the first place, though she hadn't imagined Maddy would go haring off on her own. Bryony had gone after their first and most-likely suspect, their father's business partner and the one man who'd emerged unscathed from the collapse of the company, the notorious Earl of Kilmartyn, and instead of proving him guilty of their father's destruction she'd gone and married him, despite rumors that he murdered his first wife.

Right now they were on the continent, well out of the way of the law while Kilmartyn's men tried to prove his innocence.

Apparently the Earl of Kilmartyn had enough money to support them all, a lovely thought, but Maddy intended to take care of herself, and Sophie besides. Maddy had no intention of going into exile, despite her longing to travel. She wanted the truth, she wanted justice, and she'd do just about anything to get them.

Including being a maid in the household of the most disturbing man she ever met. He made her feel strange, uneasy, with a clawing feeling inside that wasn't completely unpleasant. It wasn't just because he kissed her. She'd been kissed before, but never like that. But he was unlike anyone she'd ever known, he was a conundrum, and at another time, in another life, she'd be fascinated, even tempted. She couldn't afford to let that happen.

No, she'd stay the course. He didn't even remember her, and no one ever looked at maids. She could ferret her way around things and find the truth. And maybe, in the end, if he turned out to be innocent and she was ready to leave, she might just grab him by his open white shirt and kiss him good-bye.

She laughed, sliding under the threadbare covers again, the racket still tight in one hand. She could just imagine the expression on his face. It would make all the hard work worth it.

But in the meantime she needed to concentrate on the job at hand, not Captain Morgan. His guilt or innocence would come to light soon enough. She just couldn't afford to get distracted.

CHAPTER SEVEN

LUCA HADN'T BEEN PLANNING to leave for London the next morning. He usually slept well, deep and undisturbed by dreams or any of the things that should plague his nonexistent conscience unless there was some emergency on board ship.

Last night had been different. Last night he'd woken over and over again, the taste of the girl on his tongue. She'd looked so delicious, sitting there in bed, pulling the covers up to her chin like a terrified virgin. Terrified by the bats, not by him.

Hell, he was a lot more terrifying than a few harmless bats, and he was offended that she considered him the least of her worries, particularly since she remembered the one time she'd seen him before. She knew as well as he did that he was twice as strong as she was, and she didn't know that he wouldn't use that superior strength to hurt her.

It was the unsolved mystery that was plaguing him, he told himself, not the girl herself. That elusive, hidden memory that was driving him mad and yet no matter how hard he tried to remember, the answer remained out of reach.

He hadn't spoken to her that long ago time—he knew that much. They'd been separated and he'd seen her from a distance. But where and when? In which lifetime? His time on the streets of London had been so long ago that it could scarcely be then. She was young; she probably hadn't even been born by the time he went to sea.

Russell's ships had never carried many passengers, though there'd always been a few, and Luca had made it his practice to keep the hell away from them. His job was running the boat, not flattering the upper crust. Besides, they were much happier with Lindholm, his bland and charming first officer, than a raffish former pirate who didn't have time for polite chitchat.

But still, nothing came to mind. He couldn't picture her anywhere near the ocean, and his life was the water.

He had no intention of spending another sleepless night. There was one person he could count on for information, even the most impossible to find, and once he got to London he would be easy enough to locate. Even the endless train ride would be worth it, much as he hated the things. Travel should be on the ocean, not trapped in a steel cage with smoke and soot belching all around him.

It was late when he reached London, but he didn't hesitate. The warrens of the West End were well-known to him—it didn't take him long to track down the Wart in their old hunting grounds. He leaned against a lamppost, surveying the world he had once known so well, and waited.

"Well, look at the toff, wandering down in the gutter with us lowlifes." The rough voice came from just behind him, but Luca didn't jump. He and the Wart had perfected the art of silent movement, and he would have expected nothing less. "Why no, I think it's nothing but a gyppo, come amongst us city dwellers." Wart moved around to the front, and Luca didn't give a damn, he pulled the man into his arms for a heartfelt embrace. It had been too long since he'd seen him, but Wart liked to keep his distance. Luca had grown up with him, picked pockets, and serviced gentlemen with him, but

Wart had been faster than he was when the press gangs had come, and Luca had found the sea.

"Lemme alone," Wart said, shoving him back a moment after returning the embrace. "I've got me reputation to consider. They'll think I'm a nancy boy, and I'm done with that lay." He spat into the filthy street. The sky over London was thick with greasy smoke from the manufactories, and the soot had covered everything in the Seven Dials area, including Wart, who was half Luca's size nowadays. "So how does it feel to be a contributing member of society?"

He grinned, giving Wart a punch to his thick shoulder. "Smothering."

Wart laughed. "I should think so. Too bad the gangs caught you and made an upstanding citizen of you."

"Not quite. I was a pirate before I turned honest."

Wart rolled his eyes. "Never say it, mate! The very word *honest* makes me shudder."

"Don't worry, I won't torment you with it."

Wart settled one haunch on the remains of a broken wagon. They were deep in the back alleys near the notorious Dials, where filth and despair were taken for granted and the police never showed their faces, and the air smelled of refuse and human waste and the stench of life rotting. At one time it had smelled like home, and Luca could still feel a faint tugging.

"So what are you wanting from me, Luca, me boy? It won't come cheap, not when you have the blunt to spare," Wart said amiably. "And don't be expecting me to change me ways—I ain't leaving the Dials to be your bloody pensioner. I like me life here."

"I've given up offering," Luca said. "But I've got a job for you."

"That's different then," Wart said. They both knew that Wart would do anything he could for his old pal, free of charge, and Luca would give him the shirt off his back, but it was a game they played.

"It's about a woman," Luca said.

Wart shook his head. "It always is. Though not so much with you. Women have always been besotted by that pretty face of yours; I can't believe you've finally found one who's immune to it. More power to her."

"What makes you think it's a woman I want?"

"What else could it be? You wouldn't be looking for your mother—that gypsy trull was long gone after her old man sold you to Morris the Sweep. No, you're wanting to get between someone's legs, and I can't imagine anyone saying no to you."

"Ah, Wart, I didn't know you felt that way about me," he shot back, unruffled by the slight against his mother. It was a fair enough description.

"I don't care how pretty you are, you're not my type," Wart shot back. "Only if you paid me."

"I thought you said you'd given that up. How about I pay you not to?"

Wart laughed. "I miss the old days, I do. We were a devilish pair around here, weren't we? No pocket was safe. Too bad you couldn't run as fast you could talk."

Luca shrugged. "It all worked out for the best. We both know it's a waste of time to think about 'what ifs.' Do you want to hear about this woman or are we going to keep talking about the good old days of sodomy for hire?"

Wart grinned at him. He still looked like a boy in the dim light of the Dials, a very bad boy. "You think I'm going to weep over it? We did what we had to do to survive, neither of us are squeamish, and we don't complain. Unless you developed a taste for it?"

"Sod off," Luca said amiably.

"Tell me about the woman then. What do you need from me? I can always kidnap and tie her down for you, but if I remember rightly you were never much for rape."

"No," he said shortly. Not when he'd had to endure it himself. He'd take no one by force. Of course, despite Wart's jibes he had little doubt he could talk anyone he wanted into his bed, including his lying maidservant.

And that was definitely where he wanted her. Soft and naked beneath him. Though she wouldn't be a sweet, gentle fuck. There was something about her, something beneath her meek exterior that was so fiery that he expected she'd almost be able to keep up with his unexpectedly fierce hunger for her.

"There's a young woman who's just come to work for me down in Devonport," he said, leaning against the broken wagon with a complete disregard for the state of his clothes. "She calls herself Mary Greaves, and she's been hired as a maidservant. Recommended by one of my solicitors, Matthew Fulton. But she's not who she says she is. She tries for a Northern accent but half the time she sounds like Mayfair."

"That's what comes from soft living, me boy," Wart said with a contemptuous sniff that was only half playful. "Maidservants and solicitors! Next thing we know you'll be getting leg shackled to some virgin and making up to the bloody queen."

"Victoria's not my type," he said, deliberately not mentioning Gwendolyn. Indeed, he was beginning to wonder why'd he'd thought respectability had been such a good idea.

"Maybe the girl saw you on the street and followed you home for your beautiful eyes?"

"And who could blame her?" Luca retorted. "But no, it's something else. I need to find out who she is and what she's doing in my house. She's not trying to seduce me, more's the pity, so we can rule that out."

"Might be part of a gang of thieves. We've done that in our time—gone in as climbing boys, checked out the lay of the land, so to speak, and passed along the information for a cut of the proceeds. She might be running the same game."

"It's possible. But then, why would she have a more cultured voice than she's showing? And it would take an educated eye to find the things of value in my house. They're not your ordinary booty—not much silver or fancy china. It's in books and artifacts from distant countries that most people wouldn't even recognize."

"But you said she sounds like she's from the upper classes. She's the type most likely to recognize rare things."

"Maybe," he said doubtfully. "But I don't think that's it. I've seen her before, I know it. I just can't place her."

"Never tell me you've been pining after some unattainable goddess all these years!" Wart begged.

"Hardly. She's not a goddess, though I admit she's beautiful. But then, beauty's an easy commodity. And no one is unattainable."

Wart laughed. "Tell me what she looks like. Mebbe that will jog your memory."

"Brown hair. Very dark, long and curling."

"Every woman has long hair," Wart scoffed. "Tell me something I wouldn't know. And when did you see her with her hair down? I thought you said she'd just started to work there?"

"None of your business."

"It's my business if you want me to find out who she is. If she's an easy piece that makes a difference."

"She's not. She's either a virgin or close to it."

"Hmmm. Not too many of them in my line of work."

"And what exactly is your line of work?"

Wart grinned at him. "Purveyor of information. But a pretty dark-haired semi-virgin isn't giving me enough to go on. You got anything else?"

"She's got interesting eyes," he said slowly, suddenly remembering them. "A very dark blue. I think I've seen those eyes before, in another . . . hell and damnation!" Memory flooded back, and with it a powerful fury that swept over him, rendering him almost speechless.

"You've remembered?"

"I'm going to kill her," Luca said grimly. How had she managed to trick him? How had she thought she could get away with it? They knew enough people in common that she would have been recognized sooner or later. And why the hell was she doing it?

"Not your lay, laddie." Wart shook his head. "You've never been one for murder unless it was necessary, and I don't see you killing a woman. You don't even hit 'em when they deserve it. Who is she?"

"Eustace Russell's daughter," he said bitterly. "I saw her a few years ago at the christening of one of his ships. I don't know which one she was—he had several of them."

"Ships? Or daughters?"

"Both," Luca said in a dark voice. "But what the hell would she be doing pretending to be a maid? And in my household?"

"Leave that part up to me. It'll be dead easy to get the rest now that you've remembered. I'm guessing she didn't see you at the time?"

He shook his head. "I was too far away, and she was too busy being Russell's little princess." He made an effort to tamp down the anger that suffused him. "I remember that he used to bring one of his daughters with him on occasion, though he never brought her around me."

Wart snorted with laughter. "That surprises you? He wouldn't want his precious cargo in the hands of a bad 'un like you. She'd take one look and fall madly in love."

"Not that I noticed," he said drily. "She wasn't cut out for docility or domestic work. No wonder I had the feeling she'd just as soon stick a knife in my back as look at me. Though she did kiss me back," he added, more to himself than to Wart.

"Kissed you back? You told me the girl had just arrived. You work fast, laddie."

He wished he could find the humor in it. "I always have. Faster 'n you, in the old days."

"Yeah, but I didn't let the press gangs get me," Wart shot back. "So what are you going to do about this?"

"Kick her out on her arse," he said darkly.

"Before you know why she's there?"

"I know why she's there. His daughters insisted their sainted father could never have done such a terrible thing."

"Remind me—what terrible thing did he do?"

"Embezzled all the cash from the company he started and ran off. Died in a carriage accident a little too close to Plymouth and Devonport for my piece of mind. They must think I had something to do with the old man's death."

"Did you?"

He gave Wart a look. "You just said it—I've never been much for unnecessary killing." He frowned, thinking back to that night.

"So are the daughters right? Not about you, but their father? You think the man was set up?"

He was remembering it far too well, now. Russell's appearance at his door, the flood of crazy accusations. He'd thought it was a brain fever, particularly when he'd heard the old man had driven his coach off a cliff. And then he'd forgotten about it, putting all his focus on getting his hands on the ships. "I have no idea."

Wart shrugged his narrow shoulders. "I'll see what else I can find out for you. Seems to me there was some scandal about one of his daughters running off with some lord who murdered his wife. Can't be that one, I wouldn't think. If I were you I wouldn't say anything for the time being. Wait and see what I can find out before you go turfing her out. Might be interesting."

Luca thought back to her, sitting in the bed, her eyes wide and her soft mouth trembling. Damn her. Kicking her out immediately would be the smartest thing he could do, before she fouled up his life completely.

But he knew he wasn't going to do it, and Wart had given him the perfect excuse. "I don't know," he said grudgingly. "She's already proved to be a thorn in my side and I don't think she's going to make things any easier."

"Since when have you cared about easy? Not the Luca I've always known. You sure you didn't have anything to do with her father's death and the disappearance of all that lovely money? I'm thinking it would have been easy pickings."

"No," Luca replied flatly.

"Too bad. I'd think better of you if you had," Wart said cheerfully. "So what's it going to be? Give her a kick in the bum and send her on her way, or pretend to believe her?"

"I can think of much better uses for her bum."

"Must be nice to have servants," Wart mused, counting the fat stack of paper money Luca had handed him.

"You aren't the kind of man to pay for something when you can do it yourself or steal it."

"True enough. And for servants you need a home, and I prefer to move around." He peered up at Luca. "You want to tell me what you're going to do with the lass?"

"I think you're better off not knowing."

Wart snorted. "How's that going to go down with that fancy lady you got yourself engaged to?"

He didn't bother to ask how Wart knew about Gwendolyn. Wart could find out anything he wanted to know, the main reason Luca had come to him. "I think the fancy lady is going to be a thing of the past once I figure out how to get rid of her. I'm better off with my own kind."

"And what about the Russell chit?"

"She's a liar and a cheat. I think that qualifies her as my kind, don't you?" he said calmly.

Wart grinned. "That's the bad man I've known and loved. Let me know how things work out."

"What do you mean by that? She's pretty enough—I'll shag her a few times and then get rid of her. I don't need a female hanging around."

"You've never gone to this much trouble for a female before. I don't think you're going to be getting rid of her that quickly."

"Ten quid she's gone in a week."

"A hundred quid she never leaves," Wart countered.

Luca stared at him in shock. "Are you out of your mind? She's Russell's daughter, and a liar to boot. I don't need that kind of trouble."

"A hundred quid," Wart repeated. "Unless you know you're going to lose the bet."

"Make it a thousand," Luca said grimly. "Except you won't be able to pay up."

"I can pay my debts of honor," Wart said with comic dignity, "just like any toff. But you're the one who'll be paying up, me lad. And I haven't even seen the girl. You say she's pretty?"

"No."

"No?" Wart repeated.

"Beautiful," he said reluctantly.

Wart hooted with laughter. "The money's already in my hands."

A weaker soul might regret her determination to follow the life of a housemaid, Maddy thought three days later as she swayed slightly on the last rung of circular stairs. She sat down and leaned her head against the wall, waiting for the dizziness to pass. It wasn't simply the few hours of sleep she managed to claim in her attic bedroom. Mrs. Crozier didn't allow her upstairs until she'd washed all the dishes and put them away, cleaned the downstairs fireplaces, and laid the morning fires. It didn't matter if the previous day had been warm and no fire had been needed—she was still required to empty the grates, sweep them out, and relay the fires.

Every morning she was yanked from sleep by Mrs. Crozier's nasal voice from the bottom of the stairs before it grew light, giving Maddy about five hours in her bedroom, she figured. Five hours she spent clutching the tennis racket, determined to stay awake to guard against the bats, not sleeping until her poor weary body took over and insisted. The only bright spot in all this was that the captain had disappeared.

Every muscle, every inch of her skin felt flayed. She was too tired to do anything but put one foot ahead of the next, fulfilling Mrs. Crozier's unending demands. It made her furious to have to sweep already clean floors, polish already bright silver, but she hadn't dared complain. The captain's study remained off-limits, but he, fortunately, was nowhere to be seen. When she'd been bold enough to ask Mrs. Crozier, she'd been told he'd gone to sea, and you never knew when he might return.

She would celebrate that fact if she weren't too exhausted to take advantage of it. Either Wilf or Mrs. Crozier was always awake, always watching her, so even if she'd been able to summon the energy it wouldn't have done her any good.

She could hear voices in the basement kitchen, new voices that she didn't recognize. Taking a deep breath, she rose and continued down the last section of the circular staircase to find the large room surprisingly full. Wilf was standing at attention, his uniform impeccable for a change. If that weren't strange enough, Mrs. Crozier was wearing a fresh apron and her behavior was almost . . . obsequious. All due to the expensively costumed Dresden doll in the middle of the room. The glorious Miss Gwendolyn Haviland had condescended to the kitchens, bringing with her two very proper-looking female servants, already dressed for work in apron and cap and sleeves rolled up, and an officious-looking gentleman with fierce moustaches and the mien of a chef.

"What the . . ." she began, but the girl closest to the door, a plump young lady with bright red hair, hushed her.

"It doesn't do to interrupt her ladyship when she's on a rant," the girl whispered, her voice almost soundless, and yet Maddy understood her completely. She nodded, hoping to blend into the woodwork, as Gwendolyn Haviland continued on.

"This house is disgraceful, of course," she was saying, "but I intend to do something about that. Even though we haven't set the date for our wedding there's no reason why I can't start preparing this wretched place for the short time I'll have to live here."

"You don't intend to stay here for long, Miss Haviland?" Mrs. Crozier was positively cringing with servility, totally ignoring the insults being flung her way.

Gwendolyn tossed her pretty head with a light laugh. "Of course not. The captain is a very wealthy man, and I expect he'll make a great deal more money as time goes on, and a house this small will hardly suit his consequence. In the meantime, I must make do, and I've planned a small dinner party for tonight to welcome him home from London. There will be six of us." She made a little face that the captain probably found delightful, Maddy thought sourly, keeping behind her red-headed compatriot. Damn it all anyway! She hadn't even had time to try his study, and he was already coming home. "Unfortunately he refuses to accept the fact that there must be an even number of females and males at a dinner party, and alas, I shall be the only female in attendance."

"And don't think she don't like that," her new friend whispered silently. "She don't like competition, she don't." The girl's frank green eyes swept over her. "Best keep out of her way or you'll be out on the street in a trice."

"There'll be the captain and myself, of course," Gwendolyn went on, oblivious, "and my father's business partner, Matthew Fulton, and my dear new friend Mr. Brown, and of course the captain insists on Mr. Quarrells and his . . . his companion." She made the word sound like something revolting. "Mr. Brown has recently been in an accident and he uses a cane, so we shall do our best to make him comfortable. The one good thing about such an unfashionably tiny house is that the dining room is on the first floor, and dear Mr. Brown won't have as far to walk. I've brought my own chef, Monsieur Jacques, since, as even you must agree, Mrs. Crozier, your culinary skills leave something to be desired, as well as Polly and Nan, two of my maids, since yours has shown herself to be so clumsy and inadequate." Her sharp blue eyes speared the room, narrowing in on Maddy. "You there, girl. Step forward." Her tone was peremptory, and Maddy ground her teeth. She could do this. She had to do this—no one said it would be easy.

She moved forward at a carefully controlled shambling walk, her shoulders slightly hunched, and the others moved to make room for her.

"I've complained to the captain about her," Mrs. Crozier was saying helpfully, "but since Mr. Fulton arranged things he said we're to give her a full month." She cast Maddy an ugly glance.

"I would have hoped she'd provide some assistance in your day-to-day duties," Gwendolyn said, looking her up and down while Maddy determinedly kept her face lowered. The ugly cap neatly hid her hair, and if Gwendolyn Haviland followed the pattern of others she wouldn't look more closely.

"She does work hard," Mrs. Crozier said quickly, and Maddy suspected that she suddenly realized if she were gone there'd be no one to do Mrs. Crozier's dirty work. As far as she could tell the only work Mrs. Crozier did was her abysmal cooking, and when the captain was gone that deteriorated into almost nothing.

"We have no choice," Gwendolyn said. "Lift your head, girl, and look at me when I'm speaking to you."

She hoped the flash of pure rage that went through her didn't show on her limpid face when she lifted her head, but there was a swift, shocked intake of breath from Miss Haviland, and Maddy was afraid the woman had seen her fury.

But that wasn't it. There was a long, charged silence. "Turn around, girl," Miss Haviland said, her voice icy with dislike.

"My name is Mary, miss," she said, knowing she'd kick Miss Haviland if she said *girl* one more time. "Mary Greaves."

"I don't care what your name is—you'll be gone by the time I take over this household. Now turn around." She made a little twirling gesture with one delicate, gloved hand, as if Maddy were too slow-witted to understand her orders.

It was tempting, so tempting to give Miss Gwendolyn Haviland what she expected, but Maddy resisted, turning slowly, ending up back in her original position despite the fact that she'd desperately wanted to end with her backside to the intrusive witch.

"This is outrageous," Gwendolyn said under her breath. "How dare he?"

How dare he what, Maddy wondered. How dare he hire someone with a relatively pretty face? One could hardly advertise for household help with the caveat "only the disfigured may apply."

"You," Gwendolyn said, and Maddy held still while she pointed a long, thin finger at her. "You will stay in the kitchen. I don't care if the dining room catches on fire, you are not to appear. Nor will you bring the captain any nighttime beverage he may require or his morning coffee, is that understood? You are to stay out of his way. Mr. Crozier is more than capable of taking care of the captain, and there's far too much cleaning that needs to be done to keep you busy."

"I'll be needing some help," Wilf said in a suddenly quavering voice, sounding twice his age. "It's too much for one man . . ."

"Then I'll leave one of my footmen here to help out, though the captain must be billed for his work."

"Skinflint," her red-haired friend whispered.

Miss Haviland was already sweeping out of the kitchen when she paused, looking back at Maddy. If she were superstitious she would think the delicate blond woman had no soul. She certainly looked as if she could happily drop Maddy in the harbor and watch her drown.

Ah, but I can swim, Maddy thought. *And I don't let pampered, self-important young women get away with treating me like dirt.* She smiled back at Gwendolyn, raising her chin, and Gwendolyn's eyes went dark with anger. She opened her sweet little mouth to say something, and then shut it again with such a decided gesture that Maddy almost thought she heard the snap of her jaw, like some errant crocodile.

And then she realized why Gwendolyn had stopped her attack. The captain had returned—his deep, slightly husky voice came from above in the butler's pantry. At the sound Maddy felt a strange, tingling sort of relief, which was ridiculous. This was far from a good thing—he was the enemy returned to the fold, before she had a chance to even get inside his library or the locked room in the attics. She was much better off with him gone. And yet the sound of his deep voice sent delicious, troubling little shivers through her.

Before Gwendolyn could manage her sweeping exit, the door at the bottom of the stairs opened. Maddy's nemesis walked in, and her stomach clenched. She tried to disappear behind the redhead so she could watch him covertly. He really was a beautiful man, with that unfashionably gilded skin, the black curls, the dark, implacable gaze.

"Dear Thomas," Gwendolyn said immediately, going up to him and practically trying to physically bar him from entering the room, "don't you know the master of the house never enters the kitchens? Only the mistress does. If you have a question for the servants you summon them."

For a moment Maddy was so distracted by his smile that she missed the words that accompanied it. "Ah, but dear Gwendolyn," he said in his husky drawl, "you aren't the mistress of this house."

For a moment Gwendolyn's sweet exterior seemed to crack, but she quickly regained her composure with an airy laugh. "Not yet, my darling. Just you wait until I get my hands on this place."

"I tremble in my boots," he said lightly.

And he was wearing boots, not a proper suit and street shoes as a businessman or even a ship's captain ought. He wore a loose-fitting, blue jacket and white shirt, and the lack of a cravat exposed too much of his throat and even his chest. Bronzed. Smooth. She had almost forgotten how . . . different he looked. An outsider, a stranger. She wouldn't have thought a stuck-up priss like Gwendolyn would want to ally herself to someone so out of the ordinary, but then, no woman could deny that he was devastatingly handsome. Not even his in-house spy.

"You should," Gwendolyn said archly, and Maddy wanted to smack her. "You need a cravat for dinner." She turned, and her cold, china-blue eyes focused directly on Maddy. "Girl," she said in her dismissive tone, "repair to the captain's chambers and retrieve a number of cravats, and be quick about it."

Maddy bristled, trying not to show it. What was the idiot woman up to? Apparently entering the captain's rooms was acceptable if he wasn't in them. She turned, only to be stopped by the captain's lazy voice. "Her name's Mary," he said, "and she doesn't need to go anywhere. I'm not wearing a cravat."

Gwendolyn had frozen, and the look she cast Maddy was of such intense hatred that Maddy was shocked. Life would be wonderful indeed if only Gwendolyn Haviland were responsible for the evil that had befallen the House of Russell, and if Maddy could prove it, but alas, the woman had absolutely no reason and no opportunity. Life could be singularly unfair at times.

"Since when do you know the names of your servants?" Gwendolyn asked in a dangerously cool voice.

"I only have three—it's not that great a task. I know the names of every man jack under my command at sea. It's the least I could do on land."

Gwendolyn's frozen expression had vanished, and she batted at the captain's arm in a playful gesture. "Then when we have a full complement of at least forty-five servants I'll expect you to know all their names as well."

"Why the hell should we have forty-five servants?" he demanded, looking slightly horrified.

"When we buy our house in the country, of course. You don't want our children growing up in this filthy city, do you? And of course you would want me to have the proper setting. And trust me, forty-five is a conservative number for the size of house I want."

There had been more than that at Somerset when the Russells had been in residence, including, of course, the stable hands and gardeners, laundry workers and dairymaids, gamekeepers and governesses. She couldn't quite see the pirate captain in such an ornate setting, but she wasn't about to underestimate the determined Miss Haviland.

Maddy had managed to slide behind her red-haired friend, trying to be less conspicuous, and she watched carefully as the captain slid his dark eyes over his fiancée, slowly, consideringly. And then, to her shock, his eyes turned her way before she could sensibly lower them, and she felt an unaccustomed heat flush her cheeks. Absurd, when the most determined flirts in London society couldn't make her blush.

"We shall see," said the captain, but he didn't move his gaze from Maddy's, and she was unable to look away. For a frozen moment it seemed as if they were alone in the kitchen, and everyone else had faded away.

And then he broke the spell, taking Miss Haviland's arm and moving her toward the door. "Gwendolyn, your admirers have arrived, and while I can hold a decent conversation with Fulton I think Mr. Brown is far more interested in you."

"Mr. Brown is absolutely charming," Gwendolyn said as they moved away. "We were introduced at the Mortons' ball, but of course the poor man cannot dance due to his unfortunate accident, and I . . ." Her voice faded away as the green baize door closed behind them.

It was as if everyone in the room had been frozen, holding their breaths. Suddenly they began to move, to speak, a hushed comment here, a nervous giggle there. The gentleman with the moustaches quickly clapped his hands, demanding attention. "You heard Mademoiselle 'aviland," he said in a thick, almost impenetrable French accent. "She wants a meal *magnifique*, and it is our duty to provide it for her. Polly, clear away some of this clutter so I may have some workspace, and Nan, you will work with Madame Crozier to set a table worthy of my art."

Mrs. Crozier drew herself up to her full, skinny height. "I believe this is my kitchen, Monsieur Jacques, and I am in charge of this household. I will be the one giving the orders."

The small man marched up to Mrs. Crozier, his beady gaze focusing on her own slightly protuberant eyes. "And I believe you are wrong, madame. Any kitchen I enter is under *my* direction, including anything to do with the meal. You may either assist me as sous chef or you may retire to your rooms."

Mrs. Crozier looked torn, and Maddy could read her conflicting emotions. On the one hand, she certainly didn't want to surrender the playing field to this French upstart, but on the other, she had a tendency to avoid work like the plague, and Monsieur Jacques was likely to work her like a slavey. The housekeeper drew herself up.

"I have better things to do than be insulted in my own kitchen," she said, but Monsieur Jacques had already dismissed her, turning to the imported maidservants.

"You heard me, girls." He rolled the "r" extravagantly. "And the pretty one, Mary, is it? You are slow-witted, *hein*?"

"No, monsieur, I am not slow-witted at all," she replied in French.

He beamed at her. "And a perfect accent. Not like the rest of these English canailles," he replied in the same language. "Mademoiselle Haviland hates your liver, and I can see why. Next to you she looks like a pale stick."

"*Merci du compliment, monsieur.*" She shouldn't be so pleased, but she'd developed a real dislike for Miss Gwendolyn Haviland. "What would you like me to do?"

He switched to English. "Polly will show you. She is English and therefore will never be a cook, but she 'as some talent," he said grudgingly, and the red-haired girl beamed at him. He looked back at Mrs. Crozier, who was glued to her spot, ready to explode with outrage. "You," he said. "Get out."

Oh, dear. Maddy hadn't been able to resist showing off her almost perfect French with the chef, but she'd forgotten that the evil harpy was still in the room. A simple maid shouldn't be able to speak French so well, though most likely Mrs. Crozier wouldn't know the difference between a finishing school accent from Switzerland and a dockside whore's.

The housekeeper stormed out of the room, and Maddy felt almost limp with relief, until she remembered the look in the captain's eyes. The seemingly endless moment when she felt her heart catch in her throat as they looked at each other. It had felt as physical as a touch.

"That Mrs. Crozier's a real corker, ain't she?" Polly murmured. "Must be living hell to work for. Our housekeeper, Mrs. Simmons, is a treat, but we still have to put up with her highness out there." She jerked her head in the direction of the front rooms, where Gwendolyn's arch voice could be heard above the lower rumble of male tones.

Maddy pulled herself out of her abstraction. "Not much of a choice."

"It's not. But those of us in service don't tend to have choices."

Maddy thought about it. If she was ever in a position to have servants again she would go out of her way to treat them fairly. Not that she hadn't in the past, but she'd been brought up to think of servants as little more than furniture. "No, we don't," she agreed.

Polly snorted with laughter. "And you've been in service such a long time, then?"

Maddy wracked her brain, trying to remember her lies. "Most of my life," she said. "From thirteen a least."

"I believe you. Thousands wouldn't," she said flatly, and Maddy blinked at the sarcastic comment.

"I beg your pardon?"

"That's all right, Mary, is it? You keep on with whatever you're doing and I'll cover for you. I don't know what game you're playing, but I don't care one way or t'other about the captain, though he's handsome enough to make me bones melt if you like that mysterious, foreign look."

"Do you?" Maddy asked, deciding to ignore her cryptic statements.

"Oh, I've got a young man, I do, been calling on me for three years now. He's trying to earn enough money so we can both leave service and have our own little farm, but it's mortal hard to save money. But if I didn't have my Dickie I might find the captain tempting. If it weren't for his eyes."

"His eyes?" Maddy echoed, remembering his intense black gaze with a feeling of warmth stealing beneath her skin.

"They scare me. Just a bit. He's got gypsy blood in him, or I miss my guess. Though the Rom don't usually like the water, and the captain can't keep away from it. Anyway, he's not for the likes of us girls in service. He leaves the maids strictly alone. He'll most likely have his own piece of fluff on the side, set up all nice and cozy in a place of her own. And won't her highness have a fit when she hears about it!"

"Mary!" Mrs. Crozier had reappeared in the kitchen, a flush on her cheekbones that was either rage or a quick nip of gin. Everyone looked at her, and no one moved. And then Maddy started, remembering the stupid name she'd chosen.

"Yes, Mrs. Crozier," she said belatedly, moving from behind the kitchen table.

"You're not needed here. Monsieur Jacques may have claimed ownership of my kitchen, but he hardly has any say over my staff since he seems to have brought his own. Go upstairs, lay the fires, and turn the beds down."

"Will anyone else be spending the night here besides the captain?"

"That's none of your business! When a gentleman throws a dinner party one must be prepared for any possibility. And the floors need scrubbing—you did a terrible job the first time."

Maddy kept her face blank—any sign of rebellion would simply add to her duties. The floors were spotless—she'd been on her knees for hours that day, and as long as she was a maid she was determined to be the best damned maid in the history of the world. Besides, in the gaslight there would be no way Mrs. Crozier could see any imperfections. "Yes, Mrs. Crozier." She needed to keep track of how many times she said those damned words, she thought, trudging over to the scullery to fill a bucket of hot water. When she married her fabulously wealthy, titled old man she would buy herself a piece of jewelry for every time she'd said "yes, Mrs. Crozier." Her collection would rival the crown jewels.

CHAPTER EIGHT

THE ADVENT OF GWENDOLYN Haviland and the kitchen crew, including her friendly Polly, had given Maddy new energy, energy that vanished before she was halfway up the narrow, winding stairs. The pail of steaming water was abominably heavy, and in the tension of the captain's return she'd forgotten how tired she was. She'd forgotten how much he disturbed her. What was behind that look he'd given her? Maybe it was simply that he finally remembered kissing her, though she had her doubts whether he'd actually forgotten in the first place. Granted, he hadn't expected to see her in his household, but it had only been a few hours earlier. And it had been quite a kiss. Kisses.

At least for her. It may have, probably had, meant absolutely nothing to him. A salutary lesson for a stupid girl. But why? A married friend of hers, one who had never been at home to her once her father's scandal hit, had confided to her that men didn't really enjoy kissing. It was simply the price they paid for deeper intimacies, and most of them would prefer to do without it entirely.

But the captain had seemed to enjoy it, and there certainly hadn't been any question of further intimacies.

What had that look, in front of the watchful, jealous gaze of his fiancée, signified? Did he suspect she might not be who she said she was? No, that was impossible. She'd done everything right. Maybe she was imagining things—after all, there was no denying that the man unnerved her in a particularly intimate way.

She expected she would have reacted the same way to him whether she'd met him in that alleyway or not. A great number of men had stolen kisses from her during her social season, stolen them or been graciously granted them. Some of them she'd enjoyed immensely. But none of them had ever caused her to look at the giver of those kisses with such a feeling of dread and excitement and, yes, longing.

A longing she had every intention of ignoring. This had nothing to do with the way she'd felt about Tarkington. The giddy excitement of his attention, the soothing pleasure of his compliments, the mild thrill of their secretive flirtations. Nothing to do with the stupid tenderness she'd felt for Tarkington when he lay spent in her arms.

No, the captain was clearly a dangerous man. She didn't need to be anywhere around him to find out whether he'd been involved in her father's death. All she had to do was get into his library and the locked room. She already knew enough of him to realize he was a far cry from the usual men her father had hired to captain his ships. Never trust a pirate, he'd said, words so obvious she should have them emblazoned on her heart.

She scrubbed the floor first, while the water was still hot. It scalded her hands, but she was getting used to it, and no amount of salve and kid gloves were going to fix the ruination of her skin overnight. It was one more thing that she could deal with later. It was amusing—when Eastham asked for her hand in marriage he wouldn't know the state of the appendage he was requesting. At least she was relatively sure it would take more than chapped hands to discourage the libidinous aristocrat.

"There you are." The words made her jump, and she almost spilled the bucket of water. She sat back on her knees, drawing an arm across her damp brow, and looked up at Matthew Fulton.

"What are you doing up here?" she demanded in a whisper.

"Told him I needed to use the water closet."

"There's one downstairs. What do you want, Matthew? You're putting me in jeopardy."

"While you're indulging in this little bit of playacting the world goes on," he said in a tight voice. "There are some papers you need to sign."

She looked up at him warily. "What kind of papers?"

"You were left certain commodities that the courts have taken away from you in order to satisfy the people your father cheated."

"He didn't . . ."

"I know, I know," Matthew said hastily. "And if by any rare chance you manage to prove it, the ensuing legal mess will provide us with work to last the rest of my natural life. But in the meantime it's no longer yours and you need to sign off on it."

"It?"

"The *Maddy Rose.*"

"No," she said mutinously.

"You can say 'no' all you want and it won't make a difference. If you can't be found, the courts will simply make an arbitrary decision and terminate any rights you might still have."

"But if I still have rights . . ."

"You don't. It's all merely a technicality. I need you to come to the office when, or if, you get a day off from this ridiculous drudgery. I don't suppose you've come to your senses? Surely by now you realize that Thomas Morgan could have had nothing to do with your father's debacle, both legal and otherwise. I can spirit you away tonight—just give me the word."

"I have no intention of signing any bloody paper." The muscles in her arms were quivering from overuse, her legs were numb, and she didn't dare sit still for long. "Or leaving this place until I'm damned well ready. I haven't had a chance to get into his library."

"You look worn to the bone, Maddy," he said earnestly. "And your language is appalling for a well-bred young lady."

She grimaced. "I'm afraid it always has been. I was the despair of my father. And I'm all right. Russells are built strong—I'm no frail society lass to drop at the sight of hard work. Not like your Miss Haviland."

He stiffened. "Miss Haviland is a very fine young lady."

"Miss Haviland is a bitch in sheep's clothing!"

"Miss Russell! You're being corrupted by the company you've been keeping!" he said in horror.

She grinned up at him. His stiff-rumped reaction was one of the few cheery things that had happened during this long day. "I'd recognize Miss Haviland as a bitch if I were Queen Victoria herself. Now go away and let me finish my work."

"You're impossible," he said, his frustration clear.

"True enough. And you're endangering me. Go away."

He turned on his heel and stalked, actually stalked, toward the stairs. She watched him go with real affection. If she could do anything in the area of matchmaking she'd make certain the captain ended up with that malignant harpy who was so intent on changing everything about him and making his life miserable. If Fulton nourished a tendre for that young lady then he could deal with a broken heart—such things were temporary. A marriage with the diabolically wicked Miss Haviland would last the rest of his life.

She paused with one hand in the bucket of hot water, not even noticing its scalding heat. Broken hearts were temporary, she'd been told, and for the first time she realized that was true. Her longing, her pain and sorrow at Tarkington's betrayal were gone, leaving her with nothing but a coolly murderous rage that she'd never be able to indulge. At least, not on him. But let one other specimen of the male gender attempt to cozen her, trick her, treat her with deceptive tenderness, and what she'd done with the sailor would be mild in comparison.

She rose, staggering slightly, and wondering what she would do with the bucket of water. She should take it down and dump it, but any unnecessary trip up and down those damned stairs was out of the question. Despite Mrs. Crozier's orders she wasn't about to throw it out of the window on some poor passerby. Not unless she could time it for Gwendolyn's departure.

Assuming she planned to depart. Gwendolyn had had a determined look on her face, and it wouldn't surprise Maddy if she didn't intend to cement the captain's commitment to her by having him ruin her.

It hadn't worked in Maddy's case—it probably wouldn't work with Morgan either. Shame washed through her again, the shame that was a constant companion, and she shook it away, concentrating on the captain and his betrothed. Truly, there was no need for the woman to trap him further—once an engagement was announced there was no way a gentleman could back down.

But pirates weren't gentlemen, no matter how much they tried to be. And if the captain didn't want to marry someone, she could scarcely imagine him doing so. He wouldn't think twice about leaving someone at the altar—the man seemed to have absolutely no concern for social mores. Mixed numbers at dinner, not the right cutlery, kissing strange women on the street. What next?

She moved back to the three other bedrooms on the floor, lugging the bucket with her, resetting the unused fire that was laid in each grate, carefully folding back the bed coverings for whatever fantasy guest Mrs. Crozier might think would appear. She'd left the captain's room for last.

Which was foolish—it was always the first one she finished in the mornings, eager to get it out of the way. It smelled like him. Like the sea, and sun-bleached cloth, and herb-scented soap. She'd first smelled that enticing scent when he'd kissed her, and every time she went into his room she was forcibly reminded of those shattering moments on a public street.

The gaslight had been turned low. He didn't bother with a valet, and why should he, when he seldom wore cravats and cared not one whit about what a proper gentleman should wear. Gwendolyn would change that, Maddy thought, moving toward the bed. Sooner rather than later—she wouldn't want her wedding ceremony tainted by the slightest lapse in proper etiquette.

Not that it mattered—Maddy would be gone well before then. *Soon, please God*, she thought, staring at the high, wide bed in a dazed stupor. She could still hear the laughing voices downstairs, and she wanted to crawl onto that bed, for just a few minutes, and sleep. Wanted it so badly she could have wept.

She folded down the covers, her hands lingering for a moment on the tight weave of the starched linen sheets. She loved linen sheets—the feel of them on her skin. There were times, when no one was around, when she would sleep naked beneath them, simply to enjoy the sensation.

She couldn't reach the far side of the big bed, and instead of going around she climbed up, pulling the rest of the coverlet up. She was so tired. She closed her eyes, swaying slightly, then gave in to just a flash of temptation, stretching out on the soft, lovely bed. Just for a moment, and then she'd get up. Just for a moment.

* * *

Luca was in an odd, discontented mood tonight, and he couldn't shake it.

It might have been the company. He liked Fulton well enough, but Rufus Brown was exactly the sort he usually wanted to throttle. Sly and shallow and full of gossip, a little bit of the man would last a long while. Gwendolyn seemed to have adopted him as her new pet, which meant he'd be seeing far too much of him before he figured out how to drive his fiancée away.

If he were still a street rat he'd have Billy knock Mr. Brown into the bay, just so he wouldn't have to deal with his snide comments and mincing ways. Fifteen years ago he would have happily done it himself.

But the years at sea had changed him. Death came too swiftly and capriciously on board ship, and it had given him a new respect for life. He might not care for Mr. Brown, but he was hardly going to arrange his murder.

A small accident that might leave him housebound was another matter, however. Though considering the extent of the injuries the man had recently suffered in a carriage accident, there didn't appear to be much that could slow him down.

But Brown was the least of his problems. He knew exactly what was bothering him, and both Billy and Wart would have laughed at being right. It was women. One particular woman.

He'd seen the fury in her dark blue eyes when Gwendolyn had called her "girl," and it had been one of the few entertaining moments of an endless evening. That "girl" would cut Gwendolyn's throat as soon as look at her. If she'd been born on the streets as he had been.

But she hadn't been. She'd been born with a silver spoon in her mouth—that accent of hers that kept slipping, that was the upper-class one, when she forgot she was supposed to be a maid.

His eyes had gone to hers unerringly as she tried to hide behind the red-headed girl, who was a half a foot shorter than she was. Seeing her again, he was astonished that he hadn't recognized her right off. Back when the *Maddy Rose* had been christened, he hadn't been able to keep his eyes off her, and while he had the good sense not to consider interfering with his employer's daughter, the thought of her had provided him with many a pleasant fantasy.

And now she was here, under his roof, and fair game. He wasn't the kind of man to trifle with gently bred virgins, but this girl, virgin or not, was a liar and a cheat. He didn't give a damn if she was doing this for her father—he allowed for no excuses. She'd declared herself his enemy by coming into his household under false pretenses, and when it came to his enemies he was ruthless. If they were on board ship he would have had her flogged.

No he wouldn't, he reminded himself. He didn't have anyone flogged—there were better ways to get cooperation and mete out punishment. Locking her in the brig for a week would have put the fear of God in her.

But there was no brig in his house on Water Street, and much as he liked the idea of having her locked up and totally at his mercy, it would be very unwise on his part. No, his anger was fading, but his determination was growing. He was going to get what he wanted from the interloper. He was going to get the truth, and anything else he wanted. And he wanted a great deal.

In fact, her presence in his house was the most interesting thing that had happened in a long time. He knew little about her except that she was beautiful, angry, and afraid of bats. And her name, of course. Madeleine Rose, Maddy Rose, the name of the ship she'd christened. The woman who needed to sign off before he could claim ownership of the ship he loved.

He stopped outside his door, glancing toward the end of the dark hallway and the door to the attics. It was open a crack, but there was no shaft of light coming down. She must be asleep. The bats would be less likely to bother her if she kept the gaslight going. Though come to think of it, the gas hadn't been piped up to the attics—she must have had to make do with oil lamps or candles, both a great deal more dangerous than the gaslight. Miss Madeleine Rose Russell had had to come down quite a bit to effect this particular masquerade. He felt a renewed trace of annoyance, and then forced it back. She deserved everything Mrs. Crozier heaped on her. If it were bad enough, maybe she'd decide to make a clean breast of it. God, he didn't want to be thinking about her breasts.

He moved to the end of the hallway, silently, opening the attic's door and glancing upward. He'd been gone for three days—had she had any more screaming bat encounters, or had she made her peace with them? He ought to go up and check on her.

No, he most certainly shouldn't. Because the taste of her mouth had haunted him, the feel of her body against his, rigid with fury and then softening. Gwendolyn hadn't allowed him much in the way of kisses, and when she did she always had her hands up between them, as if to ward him off. This girl had done the same thing, but the second time he kissed her mouth, her body had begun to shape to his and her hands to cling, and he knew her experience in kissing had been limited to closed-mouth pecks, the kind that his fiancée allowed. By the third, most dangerous kiss, he'd known he could have her. Would have her, sooner or later.

And if he went up there he wouldn't simply check on her, and he wasn't about to confront her with the truth. Once he did, she'd leave, and he wasn't quite ready to let her go. He could tell himself that he wanted to wait until he received more information from Wart, made sure there wasn't something unpleasant that might trap him. He'd had a life full of adventures, most of them illegal, and there was always the chance something might come back to haunt him. It was a convincing argument, but his prodigious skill at lying didn't extend to lying to himself.

As tempting as it would be to go up there and confront her with the truth, it was more interesting to see what lengths she might go to keep her place here. To accomplish whatever it was she was hoping to accomplish.

He shut the door to the attics very quietly, turning away from temptation, heading back to his own rooms.

The gaslight was turned down low, and he didn't bother to turn it up. There was no fire burning in the grate, but it had been warm the last few days, and the heat rose in this old house, making the second floor faintly stuffy. The attics must be stifling, he thought, and wondered if she'd opened the windows. And whether the bats had flown at her head when she did.

There'd been no bloodcurdling screams from above, so he had to assume not. He closed his door behind him and pulled off his jacket, tossing it across a chair. Gwendolyn was always on him to get a valet, but he couldn't see the use of it since he was at sea more often than not. Wilf Crozier managed to keep his clothes in order, though if things were as he suspected, the new maid was probably doing that work as well. The Croziers were possibly the worst servants in the world, and he hadn't cared enough to do anything about it. If they were working Eustace Russell's highborn daughter half to death then that was her problem.

He moved to the window, pulling his shirt free from his breeches. There was a quarter moon, casting enough light that he could look out over the harbor, see his sloop lying at anchor, see the dark outlines of the two he'd bought from Russell Shipping. He was still waiting for the *Maddy Rose*, the one he wanted with a fierce possessiveness. He'd known from the start that she was his ship, built sleek and trim, the last of the clipper ships as Russell Shipping turned completely to steam, and he wanted her beneath him. He wanted her namesake beneath him as well, he thought with a wicked grin. It was no wonder the solicitors were having trouble getting Russell's daughter to sign off on the deed of ownership. They didn't know where she was.

No, that wasn't true, was it? She had entered his household under the auspices of Matthew Fulton, who had to know exactly who she was. Not something to endear the solicitor to him, Luca thought.

Once he managed to convince Gwendolyn that she didn't want to marry him he was doubtless going to be in need of new solicitors. It had made sense to use the same solicitor as Russell had, and once the old man had died there'd been no reason to change. Moving his business over to Haviland's young associate, Fulton, was no longer an option.

He yanked off his shirt, stretching, then turned, suddenly aware that he wasn't alone in the room. She was so slight he hadn't even noticed the small lump on his bed. His new housemaid was curled up on the counterpane, sound asleep.

He moved across the room, taking care to be silent on his stocking feet, though he knew he made little noise when he moved, an old habit from his pickpocket days

Oh, bloody fucking hell. She'd undone the front of her dress, and he could see the hollow of her throat, the creamy swell of her breasts as they rose and fell with the softness of her breath, and damned if he didn't feel his cock stir. He normally kept his parts under control—his cock got hard when it needed to and stayed quiet the rest of the time. In fact, he didn't think Gwendolyn had managed to stir him in the slightest. But looking down at his treacherous intruder seemed to be another matter entirely, and he could feel himself start to react.

A better man would have hesitated, but he'd never had any illusions about himself. A woman he couldn't stop thinking about was lying asleep on his bed, as sure an invitation as he'd ever known. It didn't matter that she was clearly exhausted, shadows beneath her eyes. Her dress was open, and he wanted her.

She didn't stir when he got on the bed. He sat back and calmly began to finish releasing the buttons on her bodice, one by one, his fingers sure and practiced. He wanted to bury his face in her sweet, pale breasts, he wanted to bury his cock between her sweet, pale thighs. He wasn't going to think twice—she was there and he wanted her. Levering his body over hers, barely touching her, he let his lips brush against her with just the lightest of pressure. She sighed against his mouth, and he groaned softly, moving his mouth against hers. He touched her soft lips with his tongue, wetting them, and then slowly sealed his mouth over hers, sliding his tongue inside to claim her, as he lowered his body to hers.

She woke instantly, and any illusions he might have had about her arranging this vanished as she began to struggle. It took only a moment to subdue her flailing hands, her kicking legs, and he lifted his head to look down into her furious gaze.

"I'm presuming your presence in my bed wasn't the blatant invitation it appeared to be?" he said mildly.

"Of course not!" she said. "Get off me!"

"No."

It was a simple answer, but she stared at him in momentary confusion. "No?" she echoed.

"Don't pretend to be stupid. You know what 'no' means."

"Do you?" she shot back.

He gave her a lazy grin. "I'm not sure. I haven't heard it very often."

Her blue eyes darkened even further. "You are an insufferable popinjay!"

"Is that any way to talk to your employer?"

There was no missing the dawning horror on her face. Miss Madeleine Rose Russell suddenly remembered who she was supposed to be.

He took advantage of her momentary hesitation, lowering his mouth again to take her. Her struggles had ended up with him lying between her legs, her skirts rucked partway up her thighs, and he pressed his erection again her, feeling the shock vibrate through her body. He could feel her reluctant response, a shimmer of reaction dancing through her, and he wanted her, needed her so badly that his hands shook slightly as they slid down her legs, caught the heavy skirt and drew it up, feeling the silken warmth of her thighs. Suddenly he wanted to taste her, push her back on the bed, tie her up if need be, and teach her about sex. He wanted her to take him in her mouth, he wanted to watch her as she did it, cradle her head with his hands as she took him, sucked him. He wanted her damned clothes off, and he reached for the tapes of her drawers, ready to rip them, when a last, damnable bit of conscience hit him, and he hesitated, only for a moment, but it was a moment too long.

She shoved him, pushing him off her, and he went easily enough. He was more than strong enough to stay just where he was, but the idea of force took all the pleasure out of it. He fell back on the mattress with a groan as she scrambled off the bed, knocking against the bucket of water and sending the contents spilling over the floor.

"Oh, bloody hell!" she snapped in patrician tones. And then slammed her hand across her mouth as her eyes met his in the darkness.

CHAPTER NINE

Oh dear God in heaven, Maddy thought in sudden horror. What had she almost done? One moment longer, lying beneath him, and she would have been tupped before she knew it. She did her best to temper her instinctive glare. "Beg pardon, sir," she said. "I don't know what got into me. I'll clean this up . . ."

Something white flew through the air at her, and she managed to catch it. "Use my shirt," he said in his deep, distinctive voice. "There wasn't that much water, and you can clean the rest up tomorrow."

It was then she realized he wasn't wearing a shirt. In fact, he was half-naked. Those short, yet somehow timeless moments she lay beneath him she hadn't even realized it had been his bare skin pressing down on her sensitive breasts.

She stared at him, momentarily stunned. She had only Tarkington to compare him to, Tarkington and the sight of an occasional farmhand. Tarkington had been pale, almost white, and his skin had been surprisingly soft, she remembered in sudden dismay. There was nothing soft or pale about the captain. Even in the dim gaslight she could see the hardness of muscle and bone beneath his bronzed skin.

Muscle and bone that had been pressed against her, and she realized her heart was still hammering, her breathing strangled.

"I suppose I ought to put a new shirt on," he said in a lazy voice, as if he hadn't been about to strip her of her clothing and what little remained of her self-respect. "You'd best soak that up before it leaks through into the room below. You don't want to deal with Mrs. Crozier."

She tore her eyes away for a moment, then dropped to her knees, pressing the fine cambric to the puddle of dark, dirty water. There hadn't been much in the bucket, though she hated to ruin his shirt, a shirt that was still warm from his body and smelled like cinnamon and the sea. And then she looked up again to see his back as he was reaching for a new shirt, and she froze.

He was scarred. Not whip scars, as many sailors bore, but other, myriad wounds, some deep, some shallow, but bad enough to have left the marks of abuse on his strong, wiry body. But those were commonplace next to the strange picture that covered his left shoulder and snaked down his side.

A tattoo. She knew sailors often got them, just small blue marks on their arms or shoulders, but this was something very different. It seemed to be a cross between a snake and a dragon, and it was full of colors she'd never seen before. The scales seemed to glow in the gaslight, reds and blues and greens, moving as he moved, a sinuous dance across his muscles. She simply knelt there and stared at him in mingled awe and astonishment. And something else, something she refused to recognize. If he touched her again she wasn't sure she could summon her moral outrage.

She scrambled to her feet. He must have felt her eyes on him, or maybe she'd made some involuntary sound. He turned around without putting on his shirt, and she could see that the tattoo reached over the top of his shoulder, one scaly, beautiful claw pulling at his skin. Oh, God, he had nipples, she suddenly realized. She'd forgotten that men had them as well, though in their case they were useless.

Useless, but fascinating. It had been too dark to see Tarkington, but his cool skin had been covered with pale fur, whereas Captain Morgan had nothing but a faint trace of dark hair disappearing beneath his breeches, and he looked warm enough to . . .

"That's Ren," he said in a conversational tone.

She knew she must look like an idiot as she stared at him blankly. "I beg your pardon?" She knew it sounded too upper-class once the words were out, but she had to hope he hadn't noticed. Even though she suspected the captain noticed everything.

"My tattoo," he said. "Her name is Ren. She comes from the Japan Islands. Their dragons are a bit different from ours." He moved marginally closer to her. "Ren is an elegant specimen, but I should warn you; she eats little girls for breakfast."

Good God, why should that start a strange warmth in her belly? She rallied herself, belatedly, trying to draw her gaze away from the mesmerizing dragon. "Then it's a good thing there are no little girls in this household."

His smile could almost be called predatory, and he still held his fresh shirt in his large, capable hands. "I'm not sure Ren knows the difference. Though she does like being petted."

All right, this was getting to be too unnerving. "I didn't realize we were trading with Japan."

"England wasn't at the time. When we sailed there we weren't under the flag of any country."

"You mean you were a pirate."

His mouth curved up in a faint grin. "I prefer *privateer*. You're very knowledgeable about my career. Did you have any other questions?"

He was close, too close. If she turned to run he could simply reach out with his long, strong arms and stop her. But if she backed away from him he'd know she was scared. "When were you there?" she said, then realized a maid didn't ask such questions. Nor stand there like an idiot staring at him. Remembering that when she was young she'd wanted to run away with pirates or the gypsies, and here she had both in one irresistible package. But she didn't have those daydreams any longer, she reminded herself.

The captain didn't appear shocked at her impertinent question. "Five years ago. Just before I took up with Russell Shipping."

He made it sound as if he'd been her father's partner, not his employee. Though indeed, she remembered her father's particular affection for this one captain of his. At least until the end, when he'd suddenly withdrawn his command and left that cryptic note. "Never trust a pirate . . ."

He came closer, so close that she backed away without thinking about it, almost knocking over the bucket again. "Aren't you going to ask me the next question?"

"What next question?" she said dazedly. There was no place she could move, except forward, toward him, toward the warm, seductive length of him. She was so tempted. When he kissed her she forgot everything, her rage, her sorrow, her doubts. All that existed was him, and God help her, she wanted him.

What was wrong with her?

He leaned forward, his mouth almost brushing her ear, and her entire body felt as if it were on fire. "Did it hurt," he whispered. For a moment she thought he was asking her a question, and then she realized his meaning. She jerked away from him, trying to pull her scattered brain together, and she met his hooded gaze with the best version of limpid interest she could summon. Not this man, she reminded herself.

"Well, did it?" she asked. "They do tattoos with needles, don't they?"

There was just the faintest light of amusement in his dark eyes. "It hurt like bloody hell."

"Then why did you do it?" She should stop this conversation immediately, grab the bucket, beg his pardon, and run like the wind. Instead her feet were frozen to the floor.

"Pain isn't something to be avoided at all costs, Mary—that's the name you're using, isn't it? In fact, there are those who can find a certain pleasure in pain."

"I cannot imagine it. Sir," she added. What did he mean, *that's the name you're using*? What did he think she was?

His smile was fleeting, disturbing, a flash of white teeth in his dark face. "If you're a good girl sometime I might show you," he said softly.

Good luck to that, she thought grimly. She had to get away from him, as quickly as she could. She'd always been able to put importunate young men in their place—she certainly should have been able to handle a retired pirate.

But this man was different from the London beaus, and he was about as easy to handle as one of the wild jungle cats she'd seen in the London Zoological Society. He fascinated her, drew her, frightened her, when she was a woman who refused to be frightened. But she couldn't make herself leave him. Maybe it was that unsatisfactory time in Tarkington's bed that was suddenly making her think about things she shouldn't be thinking about. Such as whether he would feel the same between her legs, if he'd be harder, if he'd be larger, if he'd know how to awaken her longings instead of driving them away as Tarkington had done. She already knew the answers to those questions. He'd pressed against her, that hard, rigid part of him, so very different from her limited experience. And she'd felt more pleasure from his mouth than she'd received from all of Tarkington's fumblings. She could suddenly see why some women sought out the degrading experience. For the sake of kisses like that it would almost be worth it. Almost.

She could feel her face flush.

"Whatever are you thinking about?" he said with a soft laugh. "Whatever it is, it must be quite decadent to make you blush like that. Would you rather I put on my shirt?"

He was so close she could see the tattoo perfectly, stretched across his golden skin with gold-tipped scales. So close she could feel the heat from his body, so close she could simply sway toward him and she'd be in his arms. She wanted him to kiss her again, she wanted him to touch her again.

She was crazy, she told herself. Tarkington's efforts shouldn't make her think of the captain in the same light. There'd be no reason she'd ever want to do that again unless she had to. Marital relations were just the faintest bit unpleasant if not for the snuggling before and after, and there hadn't been enough of either. She was hardly eager to try with someone new. The captain didn't look like a man who snuggled.

In fact, he was a man who might very well have betrayed and murdered her father, a man who was disturbingly shirtless in a bedroom in the middle of the night, watching her with unreadable dark eyes.

She started forward, but he was too close, his eyes glittering and wary in the darkness. "Beg pardon, sir," she said breathlessly, reaching for her accent and knowing she fell short. "I don't know what got into me. I didn't meant to fall asleep. I was tired—I just closed my eyes for a moment. Please don't tell Mrs. Crozier."

"Mrs. Crozier answers to me," he said, not moving. "You may come to my bed any time you please."

She took a deep breath. "I'm a good girl, sir."

"And I do prefer bad girls," he said with a sigh. "But good girls don't lie. And they don't move into a man's house and pretend to be a maid."

A moment of shocked silence in the darkness, and her irrational longing vanished into cold fear. "What makes you think I'm pretending anything?"

"A maid doesn't speak like a toff sometimes, a Geordie the next, and a Cockney for good measure. A maid doesn't have your lack of stamina or your dull but expensive clothes or your dislike of being told what to do. And a maid would know how to kiss. I could teach you."

"Why?" The question came out before she could stop herself.

He laughed. "Don't be ingenuous, my sweet. I don't kiss strange women on the docks of Devonport unless I want to fuck them."

Her cheeks flamed at the crude word, at the image. He remembered. Of course he did! *Steady on, girl,* she told herself. This was a tricky game she was playing, and she had to watch her step. "I told you, sir, I'm a good girl. And why would I pretend to be something I'm not?"

"I have no idea. That's why I'm asking you."

She took a deep breath. She'd thought this through ahead of time, prepared for questions. "It's simple enough, sir," she said, favoring her Northern tones. "My mother was from Lancashire and me father was from Shepherd's Bush, and I worked for a lady who gave me some of her cast-off clothes and was helping me learn to better meself, including my way of talking. If it weren't for her husband sniffing around me skirts I would be well on my way to being a lady's maid by now."

"Maybe he recognized his wife's skirts." He was entertaining himself, she thought, irritated. This was a game to him. The odd, sensual languor in the air was simply part of his entertainment, the bastard. He continued, "You don't like it when Mrs. Crozier or Miss Haviland tell you what to do."

"I don't like Mrs. Crozier or Miss Haviland," she said, then could have bit her tongue, but he simply looked amused. He moved back, and suddenly Maddy could breathe again, though the strange tension inside her still held.

"I'm not sure I blame you. But being in service means being told what to do."

"That's what me mother said," she replied pertly. "I've always been a bit impertinent. I need to work on it."

For a moment he was silent as he considered her. "I don't tend to sleep with my servants," he said in a soft voice, out of the blue, and she could feel her face flame.

"Then why did you kiss me?"

"Some temptations are too difficult to resist, and I don't tend to resist even the easy ones. Come to my bed and we can pretend you're exactly what you say you are."

For a moment she was struck dumb, a rare occurrence. He was appalling, bewitching. She should slap his face, but she didn't dare touch him.

He was watching her, and she would have given almost anything to see what lay behind his enigmatic expression. Was he going to let her go or take her back to that soft, enticing bed, cover her with his strong body, push that hard part of him between her legs, kiss her into senselessness . . . ? Her entire body tensed at the thought, flooding with heat rather than ice, which made no sense. She wanted it. She wanted him to kiss her again, to touch her, take her, to give her no choice.

Had he read her mind? Could he see in her eyes the need that plagued her? He reached out one hand to cradle her face, his thumb gently caressing her skin, and she wanted to turn her face into that hand, to bury herself in his body, lose herself, forget everything. She held very still, unwilling to pull away, unwilling to go forward.

Finally he spoke. "If you won't come to my bed then go to your own," he said, dropping his hand and moving out of the way.

That wasn't disappointment flooding her, she thought. It was relief, though she didn't make the mistake of thinking she was safe yet. She picked up the bucket, tossing his ruined shirt inside. She edged toward the door, carefully, and now there was real amusement on his face, his eyes glinting in the darkness.

"Are you afraid of me, little girl?" he murmured. "The big bad pirate, plundering and pillaging? I've given that all up for Lent."

She didn't smile. He hadn't truly dismissed her, and she was uncertain what to do. There was a long silence, and then he stepped back. "I'm going to bed," he said, reaching for the fastening on his breeches. "You can stay there and watch me disrobe if you like. You're no housemaid, and sooner or later you're going to tell me who you are, and you're going to be naked with me. Beneath me. Or above me, in front of me, any position I can think of. But for now you'd better run like hell."

Finally, *finally* common sense hit her. And Maddy ran.

Shit. Shite. Shit. Shite. The words went round in her head, a litany of obscenity that would have pleased her no end if she weren't so disgusted with herself. She'd never been sure which term she liked more, *shit* or *shite*. The stable hands had used *shite* with abandon, the sailors seemed to prefer *shit*, and Nanny Gruen had washed Maddy's mouth out with soap the first time she'd dared utter it when she'd dropped a rock on her foot. In fact, she could still taste the nasty, almond-scented stuff, and she'd hated almonds ever since.

But it was a damned fine word, particularly when she'd made such a mess of things. And here she'd been so cocky, thinking she was doing such a brilliant job of her masquerade, when all she had to show for it was blistered feet and hands, a suspicious employer, and not a damned bit closer to the truth than she'd been when she'd left Somerset.

Not to mention the fact that she'd been ready to forget everything for the touch of those sure hands. Shit!

Nanny had warned her when she'd used the word *damn* or *blast*. She knew other words as well—her education had been very thorough—and there were worse ones she kept for special occasions, like the one the captain had used. But that word was dangerous, it conjured up physical intimacies, not anger, and she couldn't use it. She really shouldn't use any of those words. In fact Bryony, whose own language could get a bit salty, would often berate Maddy for her ability to curse, and she'd tried to behave herself, particularly when she was traipsing through society in search of a proper husband. Things had changed with her father's death, and she'd been confused, hurt, and above all, angry. She was beginning to cherish those words she'd heard and hardly begun to use.

"Shit," she said again, remembering the captain's hands on her. How could she have been so stupid as to fall asleep on the captain's bed, of all places? She had been so weary, and yet right now she was wide awake, tense and shivering with all sorts of conflicting emotions. Why couldn't she remember what she was supposed to be? A maid never criticized the housekeeper or her employer's friends and acquaintances. And lovers. The beautiful Gwendolyn Haviland must be his lover—after all, they were engaged, and how in the name of God could she resist such a devastating man?

How could anyone? Except that Maddy had resisted him, a small triumph in a debacle of a night. Obviously he was the center of her thoughts at all times—that was what she was here for. She needed to know what he did, what he thought, what he hid. He'd been a privateer, which was simply a socially acceptable term for a pirate. He would have killed when necessary, just as a soldier would. He would have faced death, and he would have laughed at it.

He didn't believe she was a maid, despite her working so hard she'd fallen sound asleep in the midst of her duties. She'd let something slip, at some point, probably more than once. The problem was, she'd always been inherently honest, even to the point of tactlessness. She'd never been one to keep her opinion to herself, not unless it caused pain to others, in which case she could lie with the best of them. If there was something wrong, she dealt with it. She didn't sweep it under the rug.

There was nothing she wanted more than to slam the seductive, sarcastic captain up against a wall and demand answers. She might not lie well herself, but she was very good at reading other people, and she would know if he told the truth.

She laughed, only slightly amused at the thought of her taking the tall, muscled captain in her smaller hands and forcing him anywhere, much less up against a wall. And if she had her hands on him, what would she do? She knew what would happen. He would turn her, push her up against the wall, and take her that way. It would give him the excuse, and she suspected that was all he needed.

He could be everything she hated in this world. A man so devoid of conscience he'd betray and murder a man who'd befriended him, and the devil take the hindmost. He was a reprobate through and through, the complete opposite of what she wanted in this life.

And the wretched truth was, she was drawn to him. Her honesty extended to herself. In the quiet of her room, away from his unsettling presence, she could admit it. His dark, intense eyes, his laughing mouth, the indecent gold of his skin, and yes, the strange, tattooed creature embedded in his flesh. She could still feel the weight of him atop her, the overpowering strength of him that was both comforting and terrifying. She also knew why her father had never described his favorite among the captains of his ships, never allowed her to meet him as she'd met so many of the others. Her father had known her better than anyone, known the wild streak that she tried to keep hidden. He knew she'd be fascinated.

This was a devastating weakness, and she could fight it, as she fought everything, but the sooner she found answers and left this house the better. She needed to get this over and done with. Yanking off her clothes, pulling at her corset, she fell onto the bed in her shift, too tired to search for her nightdress. She was going to find her way into the captain's study tomorrow, by hook or by crook. At this rate she wasn't going to last here much longer, and once she was sent packing there'd be nothing she could do, and a murderer might go free. No, she couldn't afford to let things go any longer. Tomorrow she was going hunting.

Luca found he was smiling when his door slammed shut behind his supposed maid-of-all-work. He could have finished what he'd started on the bed—he knew women well enough to know he could have her, soft and willing beneath him, with just a trace more perseverance. She liked his kisses as much as he liked kissing her, which was a great deal, and he wanted her so badly his very bones ached with it. He unsettled her, disturbed and aroused her, just as she did to him, and the resultant bed play might be quite remarkable. She was a spy, and a proper lady, for God's sake, and he really shouldn't keep her in his house.

But he was going to, at least for now. A game of cat and mouse could prove quite entertaining, and he'd been so bloody bored recently. His unwanted interloper was the best thing that had happened to him in months. In fact, since Russell had taken his command away and then shown up accusing him of thievery.

Now Russell's daughter was here, at Luca's mercy, and he couldn't resist her. It was the fire in her dark blue eyes, the secrets she hid, the fierceness that drew him. She could have faced down the dreaded pirates of Madagascar without blinking—she was more than up to handling him even in his worst temper. According to rumor, she wasn't even a virgin—why did he hesitate?

He wanted to teach her how to kiss him back properly, how to do other things with that lush, remarkable mouth. He wanted her secrets, her body, her heart and soul.

What the hell was wrong with him? How had one smallish female upset his carefully arranged plans?

He'd have Crozier get rid of her tomorrow. That was the smart thing to do.

Just dump her and find some strapping lass with no secrets to take her place.

Tomorrow. Miss Madeleine Rose Russell would be on her way. Absolutely. Tomorrow.

CHAPTER TEN

RUFUS GRIFFITHS SETTLED HIMSELF very carefully into the overstuffed chair in his rooms on George Street, his new manservant assisting him. He missed Collins—the Irishman had known his little ways, and been smart enough to be afraid of him. But he was a lost cause, along with the Earl of Kilmartyn, at least for now. Collins was back in London with his beloved cook and that filthy but very pretty little street urchin, and as far as he was concerned the man he'd known as Rufus Brown was dead.

Collins should have known better. Never trust that anyone was truly dead unless you see the body yourself, but Collins hadn't had the chance. For a short while Rufus had considered sending for him—he'd proven useful, after all, reporting on the happenings in the Kilmartyn household. And while Rufus had temporarily given up on ensnaring Kilmartyn and the Russell chit he'd married, sooner or later they'd have to return home, and Rufus could take his time finishing what he started.

But in the meantime he had better things to do. Eustace Russell had had not one but three daughters, and the second one was pretending to be a maid, ferreting around in the house of Russell's favorite captain.

He couldn't imagine there'd be anything to find—Morgan would have no idea what was behind Eustace Russell's disgrace and death. No matter how hard the middle daughter searched, she wouldn't find anything. Too bad he couldn't arrange things so that she did, but it felt like too much effort. He despised the captain, with his arrogance and his gypsy blood, but he had to concentrate on the matter at hand. The daughters were the problem, and they needed to be dealt with.

For a while he'd considered not even bothering. After all, the middle one was safe on the coast, away from London and Somerset, busy chasing villains who didn't exist. But he was annoyed that Bryony Russell and Kilmartyn had temporarily gotten the better of him, annoyed that he'd almost been crushed by the collapse of the burnt remains of the Russell house on Curzon Street and yet Kilmartyn and his doxy had emerged unscathed.

He'd been so certain success had been at his fingertips that he'd gotten cocky. Kilmartyn and the Russell bitch were supposed to die in the burnt-out hulk, but instead the back stairs had collapsed beneath him, and the two of them had escaped, out of his reach.

There was always the chance that even from France, or wherever they'd gone off to, they'd be able to get a letter to the sisters, warning them. Ah, but what could the new Lady Kilmartyn say? She didn't know his name, she didn't even know what he really looked like. If she saw him in the streets today she wouldn't recognize him, with his jet-black hair and elegant beard and side-whiskers, not to mention his recent frailty. He'd embraced it, rather enjoying his languishing air, but he'd learned to take nothing for granted. As long as the middle one . . . Sophia? Madeleine? That was it! As long as Madeleine Russell was on her own she could run into something unexpected. And it would make everything so much neater if that unexpected something was his humble self.

It wasn't that he particularly enjoyed killing, he mused, taking a sip of the cognac his man handed him before Parsons knelt to remove his shoes. But he was a tidy man, dedicatedly so, and he despised the idea of loose ends. Loose ends could unravel, destroying the carefully woven plans of even the smartest men, and Rufus counted himself in that group. In truth, it annoyed him to do things out of order, but in the end he'd been forced to let go of his overwhelming need for perfection. It mattered not who died first—Lady Kilmartyn, Madeleine, or pretty little Sophia. What mattered was getting rid of them, the only possible claimants to everything he'd ever wanted.

If he'd underestimated their importance initially, it hadn't taken him long to adjust his plans accordingly.

"Parsons," he said lazily, "is there a storm coming?"

"So I've been told, sir."

"I gather Captain Morgan enjoys the challenge of riding out a storm."

"So I've heard, sir." Parsons was an excellent gatherer of information, and while news of the captain was sparse, there'd been enough to be useful.

"I think he should be encouraged to take his boat out into the bad weather."

"Which boat, sir? He has several, not to mention the steamships."

"Oh, I have no doubt about his ability to control one of Russell's steamships, as long he has a full complement of sailors. He has smaller boats of his own, does he not?"

"Yes, sir. A skiff and a smaller boat."

"I think the skiff would be his most obvious choice. I trust you can arrange things? You're a man of experience and discretion."

"I can take care of the boat, sir. No one will notice."

That was the lovely thing about hiring a certain class of criminals. Not the thugs—they were boring. But the smarter ones, who'd almost gotten away with it. They came from prison with rage and imagination at full boil, and he knew just how to use them.

"Very good," he purred. "We'll ensure he takes the boat out. It would be lovely if he'd take his new housemaid with him, but they'd most likely argue the entire time. I do not see a happy wedding in their future, Parsons."

"Assuming I understand you correctly, sir, I don't see any future at all for the captain."

Rufus smiled benevolently. "We are in accord," he murmured. "Now why don't you fetch me another glass of brandy before you remove my trousers?"

Maddy woke early the next morning, even before Mrs. Crozier's shrill bellow could tear her from her well-earned rest. Though come to think of it, Mrs. Crozier probably couldn't shriek through the house if the owner was in residence. The housekeeping standards here might be appallingly lax but she doubted Captain Morgan would tolerate Mrs. Crozier's screeching voice.

Which meant that the captain was still here. Of course he was—he'd only just returned from London. Sooner or later she was going to have to face him, unless she could somehow manage to keep one step ahead of him.

She wouldn't have thought she'd sleep at all, given what had happened last night. The fiery, almost undeniable arousal of lying beneath him, the heartbreaking gentleness when he'd cupped her face with his rough, calloused hands. Why had he taunted her and then let her go? He didn't believe she was a maid, he'd found her asleep in his bed, and yet he'd said nothing about dismissing her. But his eyes, as they'd looked into hers last night, were disturbing, drawing her to him. She had expected them to haunt her.

Instead she'd slept like the dead, thank God, and after six hours she was able to drag her aching body out of bed and head for the ewer of water she'd brought up yesterday. It was cool, and she splashed her face with it, then stripped off her shift and proceeded to wash herself so thoroughly her skin hurt. There was so much dirt in this life; she felt she'd never get clean enough. Odd, when spending your days cleaning things ended up with all the dirt on you. She looked over at the dull brown day dress that was her only uniform—the navy blue dress she'd arrived in was ripped from her encounter with the sailors, and stained, though she hadn't yet figured out how to wash it properly and how to get Mrs. Crozier to give her the time to do so. The brown was at least wearable, though probably filled with dust, and she carried it over to the back window, pushing open the casement and leaning out, shaking it fiercely in early morning air. Dust flew, and she shook it again, over and over until nothing more came out of it. The air smelled fresh and clean, and she had the suddenly brilliant idea of hanging it outside during the night. The night air would freshen it, make it almost feel clean.

Or clammy with dew. Maybe not such a brilliant idea after all. She began to gather the bulky garment into her arms, pulling it back through the window when she stopped, feeling eyes on her. She looked down, into the weedy garden, and her momentary shock was just enough. She lost hold of her gown, and it went sailing downward, three stories down, to land in the garden at the very feet of the captain.

Oh, God, as if things weren't bad enough! She was leaning out the window wearing nothing but her shift, which was damp from her morning ablutions, her hair loose around her shoulders, and he'd been watching her, not saying a word. He probably thought she'd tossed her dress at him on purpose. Why wouldn't he, when he'd found her curled up on his bed the night before, like a midnight snack?

She knew her face was scarlet with mortification, and she drew back, slamming the casement window behind her. Why was it that she lost her composure around that man? She was no missish creature and never had been. She'd had men dancing attendance on her during her seasons in London, and she'd never been flustered around any of them. Not even Jasper Tarkington, the man she thought she'd loved, had been able to unsettle her like one glance from the captain's dark eyes.

She was going to have to go out and fetch the stupid dress, but first she'd have to put on the blue one. She picked up her corset, one of Madame Mimi's finest creations. Thank God she'd had her design one with the hooks and laces on the front. She'd had Gertie as a maid at the time, but she hated being at the mercy of anyone, and she wanted to be able to get dressed and undressed on her own if need be. She'd had no idea how soon that would be the case.

She cinched herself in, so angry with herself that she tightened it past the point of pain, so that she had to catch her breath. While working she'd been leaving a little space to breathe, but not today. She yanked at the ribbons and fastened them, then moved over to fetch the bunched up blue dress from its ignominious heap in the corner with the other laundry. She hated the dress—she and Bryony had retailored it so she could put it on by herself, but it required squirming and shifting to get it to sit right. She started to pull it over her head when she heard the sound of footsteps on the narrow attic stairs and she panicked, the hooks from the dress caught in her hair. She struggled desperately, making the tangle only worse, when she felt strong hands catch her wrists over head. Strong hands, with rough skin, and she knew who it was. Of course. Life couldn't get much worse.

It had been quite a way to start a morning, Luca had thought, leaning against the brick wall that enclosed the garden. He'd been talking with Billy, about to ask his opinion of the cuckoo in his nest, when the attic window had opened and she herself had appeared, some dark cloth in her hand.

She was wearing absolutely nothing. Or close to it. A thin cotton shift that was damp in places, and he could clearly see her breasts beneath it, the darkness of her nipples, and he groaned softly.

"What's she doing?" Billy had asked, unmoved by this glorious display of feminine treasures.

It didn't matter that Billy had no interest in the female form—for some reason Luca didn't like him looking. "Go back inside," he said. "I'll come by and talk to you later."

Billy had looked from him to the girl and back again, and Luca expected some ribald joke. The fact that Billy said nothing was even more disturbing. Billy was always ready to mock the women who tended to cluster around Luca, but for some reason Miss Madeleine Russell seemed off-limits.

So Luca had leaned back against the wall and enjoyed the view. She had no idea she was being watched, and her long, dark hair hung down around her as she shook the dark object. It was an inspiring display for the first thing in the morning, watching the movement of her breasts beneath the thin cloth, the way her dark hair rippled in the morning breeze. How would she look aboard a ship, her hair long and loose and tossed in the sea wind? A ridiculous thought—he never brought women on board with him.

When she finally realized she had an audience he was almost disappointed, until she dropped what she'd been holding and it had floated down, landing at his feet. It was unmistakably a dress. She'd already retreated, slamming the window behind her, and he laughed. Life was hard, full of bad luck and challenges, but on rare occasions things just fell his way. Like the dress of the woman he couldn't stop thinking about, the woman who had invaded his household in some misguided attempt to blame him for her father's crimes.

He picked it up and shook it. It smelled like her. Odd, that he would know her scent already. It was lavender, mixed with lemon wax and lye soap. If she weren't working hard for doubtless the first time in her life, she'd probably smell of perfumes and powder. He preferred this scent.

He folded the dress over his arm and started back toward the house. The sunrise had been a glorious thing, in shades of red and pink, a clear warning of stormy weather on the horizon. He'd never been afraid of a little bad weather—in fact, he loved the challenge of it. A perfect day to go sailing.

There was no sign of the Croziers in the kitchen. Gwendolyn would be shocked he'd entered that way, but it was the most direct route to the servants' staircase. He took the narrow steps two at a time, hoping to reach her while she was still in her shift. What he found at the top of the stairs was even better.

Maddy Rose was trapped in a dusty blue dress, her arms overhead as she tried to wriggle into it. He could pull her into his arms; he could do anything he wanted to her. It was tempting, but he'd much rather have her be a willing participant if she were going to be tied up.

He caught her wrists as she flailed. "Stop struggling," he said. "You're only making it worse."

"What the hell are you doing in my room?" she demanded furiously, her voice muffled by the folds of cloth.

"That's 'what the hell are you doing in my room, *sir*,'" he corrected her. "Since you were dangling out the window in your undergarments and flinging your clothes at me I presumed you wanted me to visit."

The sounds she was making from inside the dress were unintelligible, which was a shame. They were sounding impressively profane, and he wondered just how far her bad language went. That was one of the things he liked about her, he thought. Her very unlady-like cursing was almost as delectable as those soft breasts that had been on partial display this morning.

"Just hold still," he said, tightening his grip as she kept fighting him. "You've got your hair caught on the fastenings, and the dress is twisted around backwards. Behave yourself and I'll get you out of it."

Her response was derisive and unintelligible, and he was glad she couldn't see his grin. Her dark, silky hair was wrapped around the jet buttons, and he carefully unwound it, the curls slipping through his fingers. He'd forgotten how much he loved dark hair. Cats were all gray in the dark, but he preferred women you could see in the daylight as well, talk with, banter with. Gwendolyn wasn't much for banter, and he knew women well enough—too well, Billy would say—to know that her hair would be fine and straight when let out of its elaborate arrangements, not this luxuriant mass of curls.

Madeleine Russell couldn't keep her thick dark hair under control, no matter how hard she tried. He released one strand, and then another.

"Just tear the hair," she muttered from within her fabric prison.

"Now that would be a tragedy," he said lightly. The last piece was free, and before she could realize what he was doing he'd grasped the heavy dress at the sides and pulled it down. He was holding her at the waist, the dress open down the front so that all he could see was a combination of ribbon and lace, until she shoved him away, stepped back, and pulled the dress around her. It was a mess, he realized belatedly. There was mud along the hem, splotches of dirt all over it, and a tear in one sleeve. He remembered how that sleeve had gotten torn—the brute who'd been holding onto her in the alleyway had done it.

He'd viewed that encounter with detachment at the time, and he'd kissed her because he'd been in such a foul, frustrated mood. He wasn't nearly as sanguine looking back on it, and some illogical part of him wanted to track down the three men who'd tried to hurt her and beat them bloody. Which was simply madness on his part.

But then, Miss Madeleine Rose Russell, his own Maddy Rose, tended to make him completely insane.

He wanted to kiss her again. She was watching warily, as if she fully expected him to, but he'd never enjoyed doing the expected.

He stepped back, releasing her, and had to resist smiling as he saw the crestfallen expression flash in her eyes.

She started busily buttoning the front of her dress, a damned shame. "Thank you, sir. You're very kind. I should be down in five minutes."

"Are you dismissing me, Mary?" he drawled.

Faint color stained her cheeks. "I can think of no reason why you'd wish to stay in the servants' quarters," she said primly.

Ah, she opened herself up for that one. "Can't you? You show an alarming lack of imagination. Have you forgotten last night so quickly?"

The flush deepened, but she remained obdurate. She really was practically fearless, he thought. She would have made an excellent pirate queen, one of those legendary creatures who no longer existed.

"Sir, it pleases you to tease me, but I need to be in the kitchen or Mrs. Crozier will be very angry."

"Mrs. Crozier scares you about as much as she scares me." He needed to leave her. She was breathing deeply, from her struggle with the heavy dress, or from stress. He wanted to rip that ugly dress right off her again, carry her over to that narrow, sagging bed, and . . .

He had to stop thinking like that. He wasn't going to take her with lies between them, not if he could wait. "I think we should talk," he said abruptly.

The bright color on her cheeks had faded at that. "Now?" It was almost a squeak of dismay.

He shook his head. "There's a storm coming up, and I've been on land for too long. I'll be taking a boat out before things get bad. We'll talk this evening or tomorrow morning."

"Yes, sir." She sounded docile enough, and he wondered if she would try to run. He could find her, of course, if she did. Fulton was her partner in crime, and he didn't trust the solicitor to keep a secret. No, he'd find her wherever she went.

For a moment he just stood and looked at her. The light was dull in the attics, both from the early hour and the coming storm, but she looked beautiful, even in the ugly dress, with her hair down to her wrists and her face in a mulish expression. Damn. Why did she have to be who she was? He'd give ten years off his life if she was an ordinary girl, the milliner's assistant she'd said she was, or even a solicitor's daughter. He wouldn't have to rush things. There could be a slow, delicious build-up to finally taking her, in a bed with clean sheets and all the time in the world.

Not now. Not until she came to him with the truth.

But soon.

CHAPTER ELEVEN

It was fully an awful day, starting with the disaster of losing her dress out the window, followed by the captain's appearance in her room, his hands on her, holding her. He wanted to talk with her, did he? How was she going to avoid that? Oh, she could put off just about anyone, and nothing could make her say anything she didn't want to say, but she still felt edgy.

So far she'd found next to nothing to explain how the captain would have profited from killing her father. The locked closet had proven stubbornly resistant to her lock-picking efforts. Granted, she'd had little time, daylight, or energy to give it her full attention—it was all she could do to wash herself and tumble into the hard, narrow bed. And Mrs. Crozier hadn't let her get anywhere near the study. She needed some kind of proof, either of guilt or innocence, before she ran from this place and never looked back.

Admit it, Maddy, she told herself. *You're running from the man, not the place.*

It wasn't that she was a coward. She was simply wise enough to know when she was out of her depths, and with Captain Thomas Morgan she was floundering, weakening. Longing.

It was hard to think of him that way. He wasn't a Thomas—it felt artificial, and she wondered if he had a pirate name, like the Dread Captain Morgan or Morgan the Black. In fact, she wasn't even sure he was a Morgan—wasn't that already the name of a famous pirate from centuries ago? Of course it was probably her own guilty conscience—she was the one with a false name, not the captain. But she really couldn't think of him using that name.

She didn't have to think of him using any name at all, except as a possible thief and murderer. Supposedly her father had driven the carriage to the edge of the cliff—he'd been found at the bottom, his neck broken, the carriage and horses abandoned. The one thing the solicitors had been able to do was quash any suggestion of suicide, and Maddy knew it was an impossibility, because Eustace Russell didn't know how to drive. He always hired a driver. And there had been no one else out there on the windswept heart of Dartmoor. Had he died alone? Or at the hands of a killer?

She couldn't afford to brood; she'd been brooding for too long. That was why she'd come here. She could take action, and that was exactly what she'd do, she thought, moving down the narrow staircase to Mrs. Crozier's kitchen lair.

By late afternoon the sky was dark with clouds. The housekeeper had been at her, all day, criticizing, making her do things over and over again, which, Maddy well knew, was entirely unnecessary. Nanny Gruen had believed that a lady should know how to accomplish any household task in order to properly direct the raft of servants she would one day employ, and Maddy never did anything halfway. When she scrubbed a floor it was spotless, when she polished something it gleamed. Mrs. Crozier was simply venting her spleen, and clearly she had a great deal of it to vent.

The captain had been right—there was most definitely a storm coming. Maddy could practically feel the electricity in the air. The sun was nowhere to be seen—all day the sky had been dark and threatening, and she'd heard the rumble of distant thunder as an ominous accompaniment to the wind that rattled the windows and shook the trees in the back garden. Out front the waters of the harbor foamed, rocking the ships on their moorings, and Maddy tried not to think about the captain. He was already gone by the time she reached the kitchens, barely ten minutes after he'd left her. Her first thought had been a devout hope that he'd be on his boat for the entire day. Her second had been a fear that he'd do just that. This was no sort of day to be out on the open water, though admittedly she was no judge of the matter, having never set one foot on a boat. She might think the captain capable of heinous crimes, but she didn't want him dead.

Was it possible that there might be more than one man behind their father's destruction? What if the captain was merely a part of some larger scheme? There was only one problem with all this—what possible reason could anyone have to destroy the House of Russell? Stealing the money was one thing—why did they have to steal her father as well?

The Earl of Kilmartyn had managed to survive the debacle with his fortune intact, and he had seemed a logical villain. But Bryony was too smart to be tricked by some wealthy Irish rakehell, and she'd married him out of hand, despite the fact that he was suspected of murdering his wife.

So he was out of the question—she trusted her older sister's judgment too much. But what possible reason could the captain have for killing his employer? To be sure, her father suspected him of something, had even relieved him of his command. But what could her father have done to him that would have justified murder? And what had her father suspected him of? Morgan could hardly have embezzled all that money from across the country.

Their third possibility, Viscount Griffiths, the man who now owned their country estate, Somerset, was an even less likely villain. But that scrap of paper and common sense were all that they had to go on.

"Why have you got the lass down on her knees all the time?" A deep, rumbling voice broke through her abstraction as she rubbed the scrub brush back and forth, back and forth beneath Mrs. Crozier's direction. At least all the endless, mindless work gave her plenty of time for introspection. She looked up, way up, into the craggy, sea-worn face of the man who lived in the mews.

"Work must be done, Mr. Quarrells," Mrs. Crozier said. "I'll thank you not to interfere with my arrangements."

Mr. Quarrells snorted in contempt. "I'd like to see you do a bit of work for a change. I don't know why he puts up with you."

"My husband and I are devoted to the captain and this household," she said sharply, but Maddy could hear the trace of fear in Mrs. Crozier's voice. She longed to sit back on her heels, rest her aching arms during this argument, but she didn't dare. Mrs. Crozier had taken to giving her sharp little kicks when she thought Maddy was slacking off, and she already had bruises.

"Ah, it's his business and none of mine," Quarrells said, disappointing Maddy, and she ducked her head. "And speaking of himself, where is he? Isn't he back yet? He knows better than to stay out when a storm like this is brewing."

"I have no idea, Mr. Quarrells. He didn't tell me when he expected to return."

The man shook his shaggy head. "I hope the lad had sense not to take the small boat out on his own. He's going to run into trouble if he went too far."

"Jesus and Mary protect him," Mrs. Crozier said devoutly, and Maddy would have given a silent snort if she hadn't been filled with her own irrational worry. It was bad enough when she thought he'd gone out to sea in a large ship. If he were in a smaller vessel he'd be that much more vulnerable.

"More like the devil," Quarrells said with a heartless laugh, and Maddy tried to feel encouraged. Surely a friend wouldn't laugh if he were in any real danger. "Tell him I need a word with him when he gets back, Mrs. C."

"Surely not about my household arrangements?" Mrs. Crozier said sharply.

The man laughed. "Not really worth my time, is it? I've got more important things on my mind. Just don't kill the lass. You don't find such hard workers every day."

The housekeeper made a harrumphing sound, and Maddy kept scrubbing, not slowing her efforts as she heard the kitchen door close behind Quarrells. She half-expected Mrs. Crozier to deliver another sharp kick, but the woman didn't move.

"Looks like you've got yourself a champion," Mrs. Crozier said with a sniff. "If I were you I wouldn't get your hopes up. He's not going to be much help to you. You're not his type." The woman cackled to herself. "Have you got that floor clean yet? You're taking forever."

There was revenge and there was revenge, Maddy thought, plastering a sweet smile on her face. Mrs. Crozier was trying to defeat her, and the best possible response was sweetness and light. "I believe I've done it right this time, Mrs. Crozier."

"Then clean it up, girl. I've got dinner to prepare, and that miserable Mon-sewer turned my kitchen upside down. I don't know whether the captain is lying at the bottom of the sea in this storm or not, but if he gets back safely he'll need his dinner."

Maddy's smile didn't falter. "What would you like me to do next, Mrs. Crozier?" She was so weary she could fall asleep where she knelt, but she couldn't afford to show it. She was never going to fall asleep in the wrong place again—it was much too dangerous for her peace of mind.

There was a crack of thunder, followed by pelting rain, and a shiver ran down Maddy's back. What would it be like to be on the ocean in a storm? The very thought was terrifying.

Mrs. Crozier eyed her skeptically. "Are the fires laid?"

"Yes, Mrs. Crozier."

"Everything dusted and swept?"

"Yes, Mrs. Crozier."

"Floors waxed and polished?"

"Yes, Mrs. Crozier."

"Windows. How are the windows?"

"I washed them yesterday and the day before."

"You didn't do a good enough job. There were streaks."

There hadn't been a single streak on any pane. "Would you like me to do them again?"

She could see the thoughts tumbling in the woman's brains—she could send her out into the thunderstorm to wash the outside of the windows and court death, even though the outside was ostensibly Wilf Crozier's bailiwick. Finally Mrs. Crozier made a disgusted sound. "Go on then and do something about the disaster the attics are in. I'm astonished you can live in such squalor."

Maddy forbore to mention that Mrs. Crozier had refused to allow her any time to deal with the mess in the attics. The only problem with going up there in the storm-shrouded afternoon was the chance she might disturb the bats. "When would you like me back downstairs?"

"If I need you again I'll call you. And don't be thinking you'll steal a nap. You're not being paid to sleep on the job."

For a moment Maddy wondered whether the captain had said anything to his housekeeper about finding her asleep in his bed. He couldn't have—Mrs. Crozier wouldn't have let her hear the end of it. "Yes, Mrs. Crozier."

She might not have dared sleep when she climbed the endless flights of stairs to the attics, but at least the bats did. She brought up a broom and a bucket of hot water, and what had been an unending chore downstairs was surprisingly pleasant in her own space. The clean windows looked out over the storm, and she peered through the thick clouds to the harbor, looking for any signs of a boat foundering on the rough waves. Which was patently ridiculous—if the captain was out there she had no idea what his vessel looked like. And why would an experienced sailor go out on the water when he wasn't working? It would be like a cobbler making shoes in his spare time, wouldn't it?

By the time she was finished, the sky was full-on dark, and the captain hadn't returned, at least, not by way of the front door. She'd planned to attack the locked closet again, but she couldn't concentrate. She'd deliberately left the window open, returning time and again when she thought she heard someone outside. The wind-driven rain soaked the floor in front of her, but Maddy didn't care. Her stomach was tied in knots, and all the rationalizations couldn't stop her anxiety. She needed him home, safe and sound, and then she could worry about whether he needed to hang for her father's murder.

Finally she dragged a sagging, mouse-chewed old chair in front of the window, covered it with a quilt, and sat down, waiting. The rain blew in on her face and she closed her eyes, breathing in the smell of the sea and the freshness of the storm, and she let her body become still and quiet. She hadn't been to church since her father died, and before then it had been more of a social obligation than an act of religious observance, but this undercurrent of thought couldn't really be called prayer. She closed her eyes and pictured the captain, the wicked, laughing captain, alive and well. Any port in a storm, the captains would say. And he would be more than adept at saving his own neck. He'd be fine. But still she let the vision move inside her, to quiet the unbearable fear.

She would have thought she'd fall asleep, but despite her exhaustion she stayed awake, alert, waiting for the sound of him outside. Every time a carriage rolled by she leaned out the window, but there was almost no traffic during the powerful storm, and not one of the few vehicles stopped at the house. There was no sight of a tall, strong figure striding through the rain, just a few hardy souls scuttling by. She leaned out once more, then looked down at the front door beneath her. That was when she noticed the open windows on the first floor.

Open windows that would allow the rain to soak whatever room lay two flights beneath her, windows that she hadn't touched, and wouldn't have dared open. Windows, she suddenly realized, that were in the one room she hadn't been allowed in. The captain's study.

Before she stopped to think she was racing down the stairs, calling to Mrs. Crozier. There was no sound from the kitchen, no smell of food, and Maddy realized it was well past nine o'clock. The Croziers had probably retired for the night.

She spun on her heels and ran to the forbidden door, jiggling the locked doorknob she'd polished so assiduously the day before. To her shock and relief it turned, and she pushed open the door, only to freeze with shock.

The wind was still blowing fiercely through the three open windows that faced the front of the street and the ocean, and the curtains were flapping wetly in the breeze as papers danced around the room like leaves in autumn. The gaslight was turned low, enough that she could make her way across the littered floor to the windows to slam them down, one after another, though they were harder than she would have thought. The third was jammed open, a stick holding it, and once she discovered and removed it the panel slammed down so hard two of the panes shattered.

She turned to look at the disaster. The water had sprayed halfway into the room, the papers were everywhere, and she could see the tread of her cheap shoes on some of the white foolscap. She slipped them off, then moved in her stocking feet to turn up the gaslight.

It was a disaster of almost biblical proportions. She was going to be blamed for this; she knew it as surely as she knew her own name. This debacle would be laid at her feet, and she was going to be out of the house the moment the captain returned and discovered it. Unless, of course, he'd drowned, which would certainly make life easier, she told herself, looking for some black humor in the dire situation. That way she wouldn't have to endure whatever questions he had waiting for her.

She couldn't even summon up a smile. She was well and truly buggered, and there was nothing she could do about it. Except try to find out what she could during the short time she had left.

She started with the wettest of the papers. The ink was running, but not so badly that they were unreadable, and she picked them up, one after another, very carefully spreading them out on the sofa at the far end of the room so they could begin to dry. She moved outward, the drier of the storm-tossed papers making another semicircle, until she had all the pieces picked up. She looked around her. The wet curtains were flapping in the breeze from the broken windows, the desk itself had been soaked, and Maddy had no rags to clean things up. The last thing she wanted to do was alert Mrs. Crozier, so she simply slipped off her petticoat and used it to blot up the water on the desk, the leather chair, the windowsills, and the floors.

Propriety and Nanny Gruen had insisted she always wear at least two petticoats—one sensible one next to her skin and any number of decorative ones on top, depending on her costume. She'd already used the sensible one, and the papers were still wet, the ink still bleeding off some of them. With a sigh she reached under her skirts and released the tapes to her good petticoat, letting it drop to the floor. The ink would stain it, but it was for a good cause, and she folded it up and began patting it against the wet papers, soaking up water so the ink wouldn't bleed anymore. Of course it was necessary to make sure each page was readable, and they were all boring. Many were simply copies of statements sent to Russell Shipping, lists of crewmen, bills of lading, and the like. There were details of repairs, bills of sale, bank statements . . .

She became very still, as she heard the clock over the mantel strike midnight. It was cold in the room, and she'd been rushing around so much she hadn't noticed, but suddenly a shiver ran through her. She shouldn't light the fire—that would be an act of gross impropriety for a servant. Except that it would help dry things out, wouldn't it? And she was going to be summarily dismissed the moment the captain came home. If he came home.

She didn't hesitate any longer. The fire was already properly laid, and it took one taper to start it. It flamed into life, the heat spreading into the room, and she started to sit back on her heels, then groaned in pain. She'd spent far too much time on her knees and her legs were protesting. She shifted onto her bum, spreading her legs out in front of her, and looked at the damning evidence she had found.

Bills of sale. She recognized the names of what the captain was buying, and his motive was now obvious. The best ships owned by Russell Shipping had been purchased by one Thomas Morgan, including her own namesake, the *Maddy Rose*. Matthew Fulton had neglected that salient point when he asked her to sign the papers to make the sale final. The bank statements made it very clear that not only could he afford the ships he had bought and several more as well, but that he was far wealthier than any sea captain should have a right to be. Wealthier than this relatively modest house on the waterfront suggested, money that must have been embezzled from her father's company in order for the captain to steal his ships, his business, his life. And for a while, perhaps even his daughter.

That was a stupid, wicked thought, and she had no idea where it had come from. She didn't like handsome men, she didn't like young ones, or men who wore earrings and had bronzed skin and wicked smiles. She liked old, wealthy, titled men who'd marry her, give her an heir, and then die, leaving her a rich dowager with no damned man to worry about. And that was exactly what she'd get, because if she set her mind to something she always achieved it. If she wanted the captain to pay for what he'd done to her family then she would do everything she could to find proof, real proof and not just these hints, suggestions, clues. She'd found her villain.

And she wouldn't give a bloody damn if he ended up climbing the execution block. She'd be there, dancing . . .

She burst into tears, feeling like a total idiot. She was so tired she was afraid she was going to pass out. She hadn't eaten anything since that morning, and while her sleep last night had been surprisingly deep, it hadn't been that long between leaving the captain's chambers and waking up at the crack of dawn, waking up with the memory of his mouth, his hands on her. And then this morning, when she'd been so sure he would kiss her again. She'd been all prepared, determined to show him how unmoved she was.

But he'd stepped back, and she'd felt . . . cheated. Since then she'd been on the run, following Mrs. Crozier's orders, working until she'd been ready to drop.

It probably didn't matter. The fool man had gone out in a boat, alone, according to Mr. Quarrells, and he hadn't returned. The storm that was still lashing the harbor would be more than any one man could survive. He was dead, she knew it, she could see him now, at the bottom of the sea . . .

Stop it! She mentally slapped herself. She was being a fool. She wiped her tears with the skirt of her dress, the only dry piece of material left, and probably transferred more dirt onto her face. She had to stop imagining disasters. Besides, what did it matter to her if the captain drowned or not? He was the enemy—she had proof. She had to stop being such a blubbering baby and be glad of some sort of resolution. It wasn't really proof, of course, but it was a glaring reason for the captain to have committed such crimes. After all, he had been a pirate.

She moved to pick up some of the now-dry papers near the fireplace when she heard the sounds of Mrs. Crozier's sharp voice, the tread of a man's footsteps, and she knew a sudden moment of panic before she took a deep breath. Had someone come to tell them the captain's body had been found?

The door opened, and she looked up, way up, into the captain's tight, expressionless face, as Mrs. Crozier followed him into the room, talking nonstop. "I told her never to come into this room, sir, but she's a willful, sneaky sort, and I was afraid she'd do something like this. It's a disaster, plain as day, and the wretched girl is trying to cover up her carelessness."

Maddy couldn't move, stunned into silence. He was alive, and a fierce joy filled her. But he was most likely the villain she'd been seeking, and the conflicted emotions left her paralyzed, mute.

The captain said nothing, surveying the mess around him, and Maddy pulled herself together. She was a Russell, she could get through this. He was probably going to explode at the sight of his sanctuary, invaded, destroyed. Though in truth, it wasn't that bad a mess anymore. She'd sorted things into piles—one for his private business transactions, another for Russell Shipping. A pile for notices and statements for Bartlett's Bank and Trust, and the damning deeds of ownership for the ships that had once been the pride of her father's fleet. If there had been secrets in this untidy room then they were secrets no more. She'd read everything, tidied things up, and he looked as if he was so furious that words failed him. It was a good thing he had no idea who she really was.

He was alive, though, and she felt an irrational joy in that fact. His clothes were soaked, clinging to his lean frame, hugging his body, his ink-black hair curlier than ever, the gold hoop gleaming in the gaslight. He looked more like a gypsy or a pirate than a budding industrialist. Like some wild, romantic creature that she was too old and wise to believe in. But not like a man who'd arrange the cowardly acts that had destroyed her father.

"Aren't you going to say something, Captain Morgan?" Mrs. Crozier was growing impatient, clearly wanting her pound of flesh.

"This girl disobeyed both you and me, her thoughtlessness has turned your library into chaos that will take weeks to recover from."

He moved into the room, past Maddy, who was still sitting on the floor, her petticoats wet and wadded up against the wall, her best one now stained with ink and the tracings of the captain's financial arrangements on the delicate fabric. She ought to get up, but she was feeling dizzy, and her corset was so tight around her it was cutting off her breath. No wonder she was going through such a shifting mass of conflicting emotions. She was exhausted, starving, and she just realized she could scarcely breathe.

He moved to the sofa and picked up a pile of papers, shuffling through them carefully. Setting them down, he picked up the next one, skimming the contents. He turned and looked back at Maddy, then at Mrs. Crozier. "Did you help her clean this up and put things in order, Mrs. Crozier?" His voice was rough, slightly raw.

"Of course not, sir! I know better than to come into your library—you've told me often enough that I wasn't to touch anything, not even to dust. If I'd had any idea the girl was in here I would have sent her on her way." She glared at Maddy with triumph.

He set the next pile of papers down carefully, and then looked up. "Explain this to me, Mrs. Crozier. It appears that my struggles with the storm have rendered me a bit witless. If you didn't know she was in here then how were you able to inform me of that fact?"

Mrs. Crozier's face colored. "I . . . I heard her footsteps overhead," she stammered. "And the wind howling through the house. I knew the windows must have been left open, either by accident or design. I don't trust the girl—she's like no maid I've ever seen."

But the captain wasn't about to be distracted, focusing all his attention on Mrs. Crozier and ignoring Maddy entirely. "If the wind was howling through the house and you realized the windows were open then why didn't you do something about it?" His voice was very gentle, and it sent a cold chill down Maddy's spine, even though she was still sitting close to the fire. He must use that voice when he was at sea to make the rough and rowdy sailors do what he wanted.

Mrs. Crozier's complexion had gone from ruddy to pale. "She . . . she locked the door. I couldn't get in."

"Then why was it unlocked when you dragged me up here? Where did she find the key when the room is always kept locked?"

"I . . . I . . ." *The dimwitted housekeeper hadn't thought that far ahead,* Maddy realized with a certain vague relish. *Served the old crone right.*

"I tell you what I think, Mrs. Crozier," he said softly. "I think that even though our unlikely maid does all your work for you and you barely have to lift a finger, you don't like her, and you set this up to get rid of her. Your lies are contradicting your lies, and I'm a very hard man to fool. Some of the best liars and tricksters in the country have tried, and they've failed. You're a schoolgirl compared to them, though I hesitate to use such a term for you. I think it's past time for you and your husband to leave. You'll be gone by morning, and presuming you don't run off with the silver or any more of my very best whiskey, you'll be paid an extra month and have decent references. I want you gone with the least amount of fuss. Annoy me further and that money will disappear, as well as any possible recommendation."

"But . . . but, sir!" Mrs. Crozier protested. "We've worked for you for over six years."

"That's about five and a half years too long. Go away, Mrs. Crozier. I'm tired of you."

"And what about the girl?"

"I don't think that's any of your concern," he said softly, and another chill ran down Maddy's back. He'd been ignoring her completely while he dealt with the housekeeper, something that made Maddy perfectly happy. She didn't want that quiet fury turned on her, but once Mrs. Crozier left she'd be the object of his wrath.

She should get up, Maddy thought dazedly, exhaustion and an empty stomach sapping the last amount of energy she possessed. If she tried to stand she'd probably fall over.

She could feel his eyes on her now, and automatically she turned to look up, way up the length of him to meet his dark eyes. His rough trousers were wet, clinging to his legs, to his . . .

She knew she should lower her own gaze, but she couldn't seem to summon the energy. She just sat there, frozen, staring up at him. She'd thought he was dead; she'd seen him at the bottom of the sea. And yet here he was, vibrating with equal parts energy and fury. "Did you leave the windows open?"

"No, sir," she said, sounding perfectly meek and servile.

"And you're going to believe her?" Mrs. Crozier shrieked. "She's no more a maid than Queen Victoria."

The captain shrugged, never taking his eyes from Maddy's. "True enough," he said. "But she didn't leave the windows open, you did. I suggest you leave before I lose what little of my temper I have left. You wouldn't like to see me when I'm truly angry."

Maddy could thoroughly agree with that sentiment. She heard the door slam as Mrs. Crozier departed, and the captain continued to stare at her for a long moment before moving to the fireplace. There was no reading his dark, enigmatic gaze, and she didn't want to try. "You did a good job of organizing my papers," he said mildly enough. "You seem to have a talent for understanding the shipping business. Did you learn anything interesting?"

She was on a slippery slope, and she wasn't sure she had enough of her wits about her to play this particular game. "Beg pardon, sir," she said. It wasn't much of an effort to sound faintly dull-witted—she was feeling slow and clumsy. "I just tried to put things together that talked about the same things. I'm not a great reader, but I tried my best."

Again that shuttered look. "Where did you learn to read, Mary?"

Mary? Who was Mary? She felt as if she were trying to fight her way through spider webs—nothing was making sense. And then she remembered. *She* was Mary. "I learned in the parish schools, sir."

She couldn't tell whether he believed her or not, and desperately she glanced around her, trying to think of something to say. It was a study much like her father's, filled with books that no one ever read, bought in bundles from the warehouses. Except these books looked different. Not the same perfect, uniform rows, everything matching, the shiny leather bindings uncracked. This was a room full of books that people had read. She glanced behind him, and saw a pile of them on the floor, one left open as if someone had set it down in the midst of reading it, and she could see it held charts of the ocean depths. Her father had taught her to read such charts, even if he himself had never opened a book if he could help it. Clearly the captain was a very different sort of man. "Where did *you* learn to read?" The moment the impertinent question was out of her mouth she followed it with a silent moan of dismay.

Fortunately he didn't appear to notice how inappropriate such a question was. "Billy Quarrells taught me the basics, and for the rest I learned myself. Sea voyages can be very long, and you need some way to spend the time. I prefer reading."

She wanted to know what kind of books he read. She hadn't had time to even glance at the shelves—they had been out of the path of the rain and she'd concentrated on the papers. Did he read scientific treatises? Philosophy? Novels? She looked around her, fascinated, but he forestalled her next question.

"We can discuss literature another time. Do you have any idea why Mrs. Crozier hates you so much?"

"No, sir."

"That, at least, I believe."

"Sir?"

"I think you'd better go to bed," he said, suddenly sounding weary. "It's been a damned long day for me, and I'm not in the mood to deal with you."

She should be alarmed. He knew she was lying, and yet he'd dismissed Mrs. Crozier, not her. She could think of only one reason he let her stay, and she should have found it terrifying. He was her enemy, a villain, he'd killed her father and stolen his ships, and if he put his hands on her she wasn't sure she could tell him no. At least, not right now, when she felt so abysmally weak.

"Go on, then," he said when she didn't move. "Before I change my mind."

Escape was a good thing, she thought, gathering her strength. There was nothing to hold on to, but she managed to pull her legs underneath her and rise unsteadily.

And suddenly he was there, in front of her, looming over her, smelling of the sea that had drenched his clothes and his hair, so close she could feel him, and she looked up, way up at him in mute despair.

"And are you ready to tell me exactly who you are, Mary Greaves?"

There were times when you fought. And times when you took the easy way out. Maddy opened her mouth to come up with a plausible lie, when it was suddenly all too much. She felt the swirling darkness come over her, the floor rushed up to meet her, and she collapsed in a perfectly gothic faint.

CHAPTER TWELVE

LUCA WAS SO STARTLED by her sudden descent that he barely had time to catch her before she hit the floor. He wasn't used to women swooning, and the one time Gwendolyn had tried it he'd caught her, dumped her on a nearby settee, and called her mother to deal with it, taking his leave. She hadn't tried it again.

But the girl in his arms was a different matter. She was a dead weight, though not a heavy one, and he could feel her ribs beneath his hands. And then he realized the fool girl was wearing a corset, and he let out a particularly vile curse. He looked around him, but every spare inch of furniture was covered with piles of his papers. He would have no secrets left from her prying eyes, he thought grimly. Not that he gave a damn. He didn't have any particular secrets for her to find.

He carried her from the study, kicking the door shut behind him. He'd deal with that later—first he had to get this surprisingly lightweight creature in his arms settled.

"What have you got there, Sonny Jim?" Billy Quarrells loomed up out of the darkness, and Luca didn't know whether to be relieved or annoyed. "Been bothering the servants again?"

"Mrs. Crozier and her useless husband are leaving."

"Best watch the silver," Quarrells advised. "What did they do, beat the poor little thing?"

"Starved her and worked her half to death, more like," he said.

Billy laughed. "And you such a noble gentleman!" he mocked. "I never figured you much the sort for rescuing damsels in distress." He came closer, looking down at the girl. "Damn, but she's a pretty one. If you like that sort of thing. You sure she's not faking to play on your sympathies?"

Luca snorted. "The fool girl is wearing a tight corset."

"Not familiar with the contraptions. I thought all ladies wore tight corsets."

"Ladies do. Maids don't. Not if they need to breathe."

Quarrells said nothing for a long moment. "And which one is she, a lady or a maid?"

Luca looked at her. He had no idea just how deep the girl's faint was. "Look at her hands. I doubt she's done a day's work in her life before she got here."

Quarrells picked up one of her limp hands, staring at the red, blistered palm. "And I suppose you're going to be a gentleman and carry her up to bed and remove her corset? I don't think your darling Gwendolyn is going to like that much."

"I'm going to loosen her corset and leave her to recover. In fact, I think I'm going to ask Gwendolyn for help. She's offered to send some of her staff over, and she's always disliked Mrs. Crozier."

"She'll be rabid if she finds this one still here," Billy pointed out.

"I can only hope so."

"Seen the light, have you? Glad to hear it. So exactly who is this one?"

Luca looked down at the girl in his arms. Her face was pale, her eyelashes long and sooty against her smooth skin. "Heaven only knows," he said. He usually shared everything with Billy, but for some reason he'd kept this particular truth to himself. For one thing, he didn't want Miss Madeleine Russell to realize he knew who she was. He wanted her to tell him.

"And you've not got much acquaintance with heaven, now do you?" Billy said amiably. "What are you going to do with her?"

Luca shifted her in his arms. She was just beginning to come around, and he wasn't about to tip his hand. "Put her to bed." He could feel the faint tension in her body. She was awake, all right.

"You watch out, Luca. You don't want to get free of one woman just to get tied up with another. And this one a liar to boot. Then again, all women lie."

"Everybody lies, Billy." He started toward the stairs, then said over his shoulder, "Pour me a glass of whiskey, will you? This shouldn't take long."

Billy made a noise of mock disapproval. "Shouldn't take you long? And here I'd always thought you were such a gift to the ladies."

"Stuff it, old man."

Billy's laugh followed him up the winding stairs. He was tempted, so very tempted to carry her to his own bed, to stretch her out there and finish what he'd started, remove her clothes, slowly. Ah, but he was a wiser man than that. This woman was his enemy, and the last thing he wanted to do was bed her before he knew exactly what she wanted from him.

He was going to need her to volunteer that information, and it didn't appear that she was going to do it anytime soon.

He headed for the narrow stairs to the attic, then changed his mind. He'd lost track of what time it was, he was bone weary from his exhilarating fight with the storm that day, and he wasn't in the mood to rescue her from bats if they decided to dive at her.

He pushed open one of the unoccupied bedrooms, half expecting it to be a disastrous dustheap. Apparently his upper-class maid had already been in there—even in the light from the hall he could see no dust, the curtains looked fresh, and the bed was turned down for the next guest to arrive.

He managed to pull back the covers before setting her down carefully, then went to turn up the gaslight just enough to see her. He sat down on the bed beside her. His trousers were crusted with dry saltwater, and he would have liked nothing more than to get out of them, but now wasn't the time.

"It seems I have a habit of dressing and undressing you," he said softly, reaching for the row of buttons that ran up the front her dress. "You know, this is a very ugly dress. You should have thrown this one at me this morning."

She didn't move, but he knew she was awake now and doing her best to pretend she wasn't. He smiled to himself, continuing his gentle litany. "Not that that one's much better. But then, maids don't usually have Worth gowns and diamond pendants." She gave a little start, and he knew he'd been right about that. Not that she probably still owned the diamonds. He'd gotten word from Wart, who'd reported that Russell's three daughters had been stripped of almost everything, including most of their wardrobes. God only knew how they'd managed to survive the last few months.

By becoming domestic servants? Not likely—why would she just happen to end up at his house? No, she was here for a reason and he intended to find out why.

He pushed open the dress, exposing the very expensive corset. The laces were knotted, so tightly that his fingers, a bit clumsy after clutching at lines and sails in the lashing rain, couldn't untie it. He reached in his pocket and pulled out the small knife he always carried when he went to sea and simply ran it up front of the corset, cutting through the laces so that it fell apart.

Her eyes flew open at that, and she took in a deep, desperate breath. "What did you do?" she demanded in a hoarse voice.

"Destroyed your corset." Her skin looked crushed from the punishing contraption, and now that it was open he simply yanked it out from under her and tossed it on the floor.

"Do you know how much that thing cost?" she demanded in outrage.

"No. Do you?"

It silenced her. She lay there, dragging in deep lungsful of air. Good God, how long had the girl been struggling to breathe? All day, since she'd first fastened that instrument of torture? Finally she managed to speak. "My former mistress . . ." she began, but he cut her off.

"Supposedly your former mistress was Fulton's mother, and she weighs fifteen stone at least. Come up with a better one, Mary Greaves."

"It was her daughter's."

She was game, he had to give her credit for that. "Matthew doesn't have any sisters."

"It was . . ."

"Stop lying." And he slid his hand behind her neck, pulling her up to meet his mouth.

She tasted sweet and warm, so sweet after the cold seawater he'd swallowed during his ignominious dunking. He put his other arm around her, pulling her up against him, and she felt so good, slight but solid, not a creature who would blow away in the first strong gale. For a moment she didn't move, and then she opened her mouth for him, and he deepened the kiss, tasting everything, using his tongue, using his teeth, drowning in the sweetness of her mouth. He lowered her back onto the bed, slowly, following her down so that he could kiss her leisurely, leaving his hands free to catch her wrists as she tried to push him away.

But instead her hands turned in his, her fingers entwining with his own, and for a brief moment she kissed him back, thoroughly, with that lack of expertise he found somehow devastating.

He caught her knee seconds before it slammed into his privates.

He was fast, damn it, Maddy thought, as he flipped her over onto her stomach on the bed, covering her, holding her down. No matter how she struggled, he had her trapped, and she wanted to scream in frustration. It had been so hard to fight the drugging lassitude of his mouth on hers when she'd been thinking about it all day. But she had fought, refusing to give in to the sudden, carnal nature she'd never known she possessed, and with anyone else she would have managed to cripple him long enough to escape.

But she wouldn't have kissed any other man, she thought. He was on top of her, holding her down, but she didn't want to think about that, think about the various parts of his strong, hard body and what was pressing where. He moved his head down, so that his voice was at her ear. "Dirty tricks, my little liar. You're just damned lucky I've already seen you in action. If you'd connected you'd be very sorry."

"I'd be gone," she said, her voice muffled against the pillow.

"No, you wouldn't," he said flatly. "And I wouldn't be in a very forgiving mood. Now why don't you tell me who you really are?"

His breath was soft, damp against her ear, and she wanted that soft damp breath in her mouth. She was just as glad she was lying on her stomach on the bed, because everything in the front of her wanted to be touched—her breasts, her stomach, between her legs. Pressing against the mattress was at least some relief. She tried to lift her head to look at him, but it was too difficult, so she dropped it back down again, closing her eyes. "I told you who I am. Mary Greaves, a maidservant."

"And I'm Benjamin Disraeli."

"No, you're Luca," she shot back, then realized that wasn't the wisest move on her part. She had no idea what that name meant, only that it was secret, and secrets were dangerous.

"You heard that, did you?" He sounded unconcerned. "So why don't you return the favor and tell me your real name?"

"Mary Greaves," she said between clenched teeth.

"You know you're very frustrating, don't you?" Before she realized what he was doing he'd turned her beneath him once more, and he was covering her, his much larger body stretched over hers. "I don't like to be frustrated."

His hips were against hers, and she knew what she felt, knew what that hard ridge of flesh was. "Are you going to rape me?" she demanded in a furious voice. "Are you going to use your fantasy about who I am as an excuse to assault me?"

"No," he said, and there was a light in his dark eyes. From the tone of his voice it sounded like a ridiculous accusation, but she was still lying pinned beneath him, and he was most definitely aroused.

"Then let me go."

"Tell me who you are."

"Mary Greaves."

"Look at me, Mary Greaves." His voice didn't allow for disobedience, and she glared up at him. "When we go to bed together it will be because you want it. And it will be when I know your real name. Now if you promise not to try to unman me again I'll leave you to get a good night's sleep."

Ha! she thought. Not bloody likely. Then again, he was a stubborn man, and he wasn't going to move until she did so. "Just get off me," she said, and that note in her voice was only tinged with resignation. "I promise I won't hurt the big bad pirate captain."

He laughed then, and the vibration in his chest danced against hers, against her breasts, and she couldn't even begin to understand her treacherous body. She knew she was damp between her legs, embarrassingly so, and Jasper had done nothing but complain about how dry she was. It made no sense.

A moment later she was free. The captain . . . Luca . . . was standing above her, looking down at her with an unreadable expression in his eyes. "I think you need a good night's sleep. Mrs. Crozier's been wearing you to the bone. Stay in bed as late as you want—Miss

Haviland will be sending some servants over to help until I can replace the Croziers."

Of course she would. That mean, skinny creature was his fiancée, his beloved, and he had no damned right to kiss her when he was engaged to someone else. To kiss her as if he meant it.

She said nothing, lying perfectly still in the bed, as if she were a corpse in a coffin or a mummy in its case. He reached over and turned down the gaslight, then left, closing the door softly behind him.

A second later she was out of the bed and across the room, reaching for the key to lock it, when the door opened again and he caught her, pushing her up against the wall. "I don't think I want you locking any doors, my sweet."

"I don't care what you . . ."

He kissed her again. Long and hard and deep, holding her against the firm surface of the wall, taking his time with it. One arm around her waist held her still, the other slid up between them and cupped her breast, the sensitive, hardened nipple sending sparks through her body, all leading down to that place between her legs, and this time she couldn't fight it. She'd tried, but he'd been too fast, too smart. If he was going to kiss her, touch her, she may as well give in and do what she'd wanted to do all the time.

She slid her arms around his neck, pulling him closer to her, and she kissed him back, using her tongue as he had, biting him just a little bit, nibbling on his lower lip, sucking on his upper one, letting herself dissolve into a world of touch and taste and scent. He pushed her fully back against the wall, both hands on her breasts now, and there was only a thin bit of cloth between them, a thin bit of cloth he pulled down, so that she felt the rough texture of his calloused hands on her sensitized skin and she let out a helpless moan of pleasure against his mouth. His knee was between her legs, and somehow she'd ended up straddling it, so that it was pushing up against that damp, most sensitive part of her, and she wanted . . . she wanted . . .

His mouth left hers, and she dragged in her breath, not realizing she'd been holding it. "You need something to think about," he said in a husky voice, moving his mouth down the side of her neck, his teeth nipping slightly against her skin. It was strange, erotic, the feel of his tongue against her skin, until she realized he'd pulled her thin skirt up. She'd left her petticoats behind in the library, and she was acutely aware of how vulnerable she was, and she tried to stop him, but he simply held her wrists in one strong hand as he slid the other beneath her skirt, beneath the thin delicate cotton of her knickers, to . . . oh, my God, he was touching her there. Even Tarkington had only used his . . . his thing, not his hands, his fingers . . .

"You're wet." He moved his head to whisper in her ear, and a frisson of desire ran through her. Desire for what? "I knew that you would be. You're so damned tempting, little liar."

She could feel his fingers moving against her, sliding between her legs, into her most secret places, and she felt a jolt of pure pleasure that forced a shocked cry from her. "Don't," she choked, hoping she sounded like she meant it.

"Don't what? Don't do this?" He slid one finger inside her, the invasion shocking, terrible, not enough. "Or don't do this?" She felt the pad of his thumb brush higher, and a shaft of wicked delight had her closing her eyes, her head falling back against the paneling. "Oh, you like that, don't you, my sweet?" His voice was no more than a low, carnal whisper. "I could show you so much more. All you have to do is tell me your name."

She wanted to. She wanted to do everything he asked of her, and more, just for the sweet, drugging pleasure. She opened her mouth to betray all her secrets, only to gasp in shock as he bent down and put his mouth on one hardened nipple. He made a soft growl as his mouth tugged at her, but it was nothing compared to the heat that flashed through her, and her fingers dug into his shoulders, savoring the exquisite sensation. *More*, she thought. *Please, I need more.*

It took every ounce of strength, of determination she possessed, to bite her lip, hard, and say, "My name is Mary Greaves."

He pulled away, his mouth releasing her breast, and it took all her self-control not to cry out in protest as he moved out of her reach. "Bloody hell, woman," he growled. "There's only so much a man can stand. Get back in bed and stay there, or damned if I won't join you to keep you there."

She didn't need to be warned twice. She flew across the room and burrowed beneath the cover, belatedly realizing that her breasts had been bared, the loose shift shoved beneath them. "Don't move," he said from the doorway. "I'll hear you if you do, and I don't think you're ready for the repercussions."

She said nothing, pulling the blankets up higher and turning her back on him. And a moment later she heard the door close, and she waited, breathless, expecting to hear the lock in the door.

She didn't. So he trusted her, at least that far. Even though he somehow knew she'd been lying to him, knew she was no housemaid.

She should leave, now. But he seemed to have almost preternatural hearing, and he moved with such silent grace he could catch her before she even realized he was close. Besides, she was so tired she could barely move. If he came back in the room he'd be able to do anything he wanted to her—she was too exhausted to put up even the faintest protest.

Particularly when she didn't want to protest. She wanted to take him, to hold him in her arms as she'd held Tarkington, to let him lie spent against her, his golden skin hot against hers. It didn't matter if it was uncomfortable, undignified, she wanted it anyway.

She wanted him to touch her again, in that shameful, intimate manner, with his mouth on her breast. She wanted . . . she wanted everything. Everything she couldn't have.

It had been too long a day. She would sleep, and tomorrow she would figure out a way to deal with . . . Luca. His real name was Luca.

Now that fit him, not the sober Thomas Morgan. He was Luca, a gypsy pirate with the face of an angel and the soul of a devil.

And she was trapped. Trapped by her fascination with him. Trapped by her longing for him. Trapped by her suspicions and doubts.

She couldn't fix it, not tonight. She couldn't fix anything.

All she could do was close her eyes and sleep.

CHAPTER THIRTEEN

Billy was still waiting for him in the library when he came down. He sat in one of the leather chairs, well out of the way of the piles of rescued papers, a glass of whiskey in one huge hand, with another glass waiting for Luca. "You back already?" he chided. "And here I thought you were such a gift to the ladies. If it only takes you that long . . ."

"Shut up, Billy," he said wearily, dropping into his chair and reaching for his drink. "I didn't fuck her."

"I don't believe it. You've always had a weakness for pretty ones, and I know you well enough to know you've been thinking about this girl since the day she arrived. For which I say, God bless, because anything that distracts you from that skinny witch you got yourself engaged to is a good thing."

"I'll be getting rid of the skinny witch as soon as I think of a way to do it." The whiskey had a lovely, soft burn, and he leaned back in his chair. "That was a mistake. I just wish I'd had the sense to realize it weeks ago, before I went to her father."

"I can give you the answer to that," said Billy. "Your pretty little housemaid hadn't appeared on the scene. Once she did, Miss Gwendolyn Haviland was done for."

"She's not a housemaid," Luca said grimly.

"Tell me something I don't know. Any idea who she is or what she wants from you?" Billy drained his glass of whiskey, then looked up at Luca from beneath shaggy eyebrows.

"I know exactly who she is. Old man Russell's middle daughter."

"Maddy Rose herself?" Billy whistled, clearly impressed. "How did you happen to get your hands on her?"

"How did she happen to get her hands on me, more like?" Luca asked. "And how did you know the boat was named after a daughter?"

"I pay attention. So what's she doing here?" Billy asked, settling in comfortably.

"I don't know. As far as she's concerned I haven't twigged to who she is."

"Why not? Why not tell her you know and ask her what the hell she's doing, scrubbing your floors?" Billy reached for the decanter and poured himself another splash.

"I'm enjoying myself."

"You heartless bastard." Billy grinned. "You're like a cat with a mouse."

"More like a cat with a baby tiger. She's got claws and she spits. I'm waiting to see how long it takes her to tell me the truth."

"Why?"

Luca shrugged. "I'm not sure. A sign of trust, maybe. She must know her father thought I was stealing from him. Maybe she thinks I killed him as well. I know his daughters were trying to convince the police he'd been murdered, and she must be snooping around looking for proof."

"That's ridiculous! Russell stole his company blind and then died in a stupid accident," Billy said with a huff.

"Maybe. Or maybe she's right, and someone else was behind it all. We know that someone wasn't me, but she doesn't. I'm waiting for her to ask me."

"You're wanting the moon. I think you should throw her out on her arse. You don't need the kind of trouble a girl like that brings."

Luca snorted. "Have you ever known me to run from trouble, Billy?"

The older man laughed. "Not once in all the years I've known you. But sooner or later you're going to wish you'd thought better of things. Though on the other hand that coldhearted bitch you're marrying isn't going to like it one tiny bit, so you have my encouragement."

"Gwendolyn's not going to be a problem for much longer. All I have to do is put my hand between her legs and she'll run screaming home to papa."

"And what about Maddy Rose?"

"She has no papa to run screaming home to."

Billy snorted. "Oh, that sounds right heartless, it does, coming from the pirate captain. But you and I both know you're not going to hurt some defenseless girl."

"She's not a defenseless girl. She's a liar and a cheat and a spy, and that makes her fair game." He thought he sounded properly ruthless, but Billy still wasn't buying it.

"You keep telling yourself that, Luca, me boy," he said. "Though if she's fair game, why didn't you take her to your bed and join her? It's not as if you don't want her—you can try to convince me of a lot of things but don't even bother with that one. "

"I'm not taking her to bed until I know what I'm getting into," Luca said stubbornly, trying to forget the taste of her, the feel of her, the hard nub of her breast in his hungry mouth, her sound of pleasure . . .

"I can tell you exactly what you'd be getting into, and if you've forgotten, it's been too long since you've had a piece."

"It's been a long night, Billy," he said wearily. He glanced toward the window. He could tell himself he'd been a fool to take the skiff out in such threatening weather, but he knew the sea too well. He'd relished the battle against the elements, never in doubt that he would win, and the icy dunking he'd taken had merely added to the zest. "I need to wash the sea salt off me, change, and get some sleep. I've got things to do tomorrow."

"You keep pitting yourself against the sea and one day the sea will win," Billy warned him.

Luca grinned slowly. "You really think I can't take it on and win?"

"I think you shouldn't keep taking stupid chances to prove you're alive. You need to find a good woman and settle down."

Luca clutched his heart, staggering backwards. "Never would I have thought to hear such words from you, Billy! Don't tell me you're changing your ways after all these years."

"I said you, not me. And don't tell me Gwendolyn Haviland is a good woman—you know as well as I do what a piece of work she is."

"A piece of work who's the niece of a duke," he pointed out lazily.

"And when have you ever cared about such things?"

"Maybe I liked the idea of a street rat bedding an aristocrat."

Billy snorted. "You've bedded plenty of aristocrats in your time. Even a princess or two if I remember correctly. You don't need to be risking yourself in that woman's icy grip."

It was an old argument, and he was tired of it. "I tell you what, Billy. You don't tell me where to stick my cock and I won't tell you."

"Get on with you," Billy grumbled. "But I'll tell you one last thing. You'd be better off with a cheat and liar like that girl than someone like your bloody fiancée. At least she knows how to earn a living."

Maddy could hear her sisters whispering outside her bedroom, but she didn't move, too deliciously comfortable. Her maid hadn't come with her morning tea yet, but the room was warm, and Gertie must have already stoked the fire without waking her. She ought to get up, Maddy thought. She couldn't remember the last time she'd slept later than Bryony or Sophie. She must have had a very busy day. Had she gone into work with Father? That was always tiring in the most pleasant way—walking through the shipyards, talking with the workers, going through the books with her father leaning over her shoulder, explaining things to her. Or was she going in today? She almost thought she could smell the ocean on the air, but that was impossible. They were in London, near the foul-smelling Thames, a long distance from the sea.

She stretched out her legs beneath the fine linen sheets, reveling in the softness of the bed as it cradled her. Had she come back to Somerset without realizing it? She was in that curious state between sleeping and waking, where she couldn't be sure of anything, but she knew her father had challenged her with a very difficult task, and she had promised him she would take care of it

Her eyes flew open as reality came crashing back, and she bolted upright in bed, looking around her wildly. She didn't recognize the room—it was too dark, and someone was moving in the shadows. The fear that spiked through her was inexplicable, and then the curtains were pulled open and sunlight spilled in, revealing the red-haired maid from the dinner party, Polly.

"There you are," the girl said cheerfully. "I was thinking you were going to sleep forever. They told me not to wake you, and I figger it's not often a girl gets a good bed without having to pay for it, if you know what I mean, so I let you sleep, but I'm thinking you're going to want to get moving before my mistress gets here."

It took a moment for things to shuffle back into place. Maddy blinked. "Your mistress?" she said, confused.

"Well, since the captain fired the housekeeper and her husband, that leaves just you in the household, and even if you were doing all the work you were fair worn to the bone, or so I was told. Not that I've ever noticed any of them worrying about how much work we do, but I figger the captain comes from a different world, and if he wants to let you sleep in one of the fancy bedrooms and use the real bathing tub then more power to you, I sez."

"The bathing tub?" Maddy echoed. She must be dreaming.

"But we'd better get to it fast. Miss Haviland said she was coming over to check up on me and the others and she won't be any too pleased if she finds you out of uniform." Polly moved closer.

"Mrs. Crozier doesn't have me wear a uniform," Maddy said, then looked down in horror at her body. She was wearing nothing but her thin shift. "Where are my clothes?" she gasped. She couldn't remember anything about last night. She'd been sitting on the floor in the captain's study, he'd been there, yelling at Mrs. Crozier . . .

No, he hadn't been yelling. He'd been deathly quiet, and she could still remember the chill that had washed over her. And then he'd turned to her and . . . She'd fainted. Good God, she'd actually swooned! It was her own stupid fault for wearing her corset beneath her heavy dress, but she could hardly go around without one.

"Miss Haviland's sent over extra uniforms from her house. I'm to stay here and manage some of the cooking, and there'll be a couple of footmen, including that cheeky Baxter. You'll have to keep an eye on him—he'll have your skirts over your head in five minutes flat if he's a mind to it."

Maddy blinked. "What am I to do? Not about Baxter—I can handle him. I mean, what am I supposed to do in the house?"

Polly surveyed her critically. "I guess that depends on Miss Haviland and why you're in this bed?"

"I fainted. Presumably someone carried me up here, but no one wanted to go all the way up to the attics. There are bats," she said darkly.

"Of course there are. There are always bats in the attics. The footmen will get rid of them."

Maddy brightened. "Will they be staying here too? There's not much room up there—it's full of broken furniture."

"They'll get rid of that as well. Miss Haviland says she's coming to inspect things and she'll decide who sleeps where. So if you're wanting to get the bath they said you could have then I'd get a move on."

"Who said I could use the bathing room?"

"That Mr. Quarrells did. I like him, even if he's a deviate. Never did me no harm, and he always has a kind word for the servants." Polly gave her an impatient glance. "And I have to put this bedroom back in order or my mistress will have the kind of questions I don't want to be answering."

Maddy scrambled out of bed, swaying for a moment when her bare feet hit the floor and then memory flooded through her. He'd carried her up here, the captain had, with his gentle, calloused hands and his hard, warm body. He'd kissed her—oh, God, he'd kissed her, again and again, and then he . . .

Her breasts grew tight, hot with the almost physical memory of his hands on them, his mouth on them. His hand between her legs. He knew she was lying, and yet he'd let her go last night, when she wasn't even sure she'd wanted him to.

Luca. His name was Luca, a Romany name to go with his gypsy looks. No wonder thinking of him as Thomas Morgan had felt so wrong. He was Luca.

"I've already drawn you a bath, and your new uniform is in there as well. Best hurry."

There were some things worth any kind of risk, and a bath was one of them. She wasn't going to waste another minute. At Nanny Gruen's cottage bathing had been a laborious experience, and during the time the three sisters let rooms in London they'd had to make do with sponge baths.

It took her a moment to yank off her shift and slip into the warm, rose-scented water. She slid down, feeling her long hair flow around her, and closed her eyes, giving herself just long enough to embrace the warmth and calm. And then she went to work, scrubbing and rinsing her hair, washing every part of her body twice. She leaned her back against the cooling copper of the tub, ready to steal another short moment of peace, when she heard the unmistakable sounds of Gwendolyn Haviland approaching the end of the hallway.

"I 'aven't gotten to the back bedrooms and the bathing room, miss," Polly was saying.

"That's all right—if I'm going to be mistress of this house I need to observe the amenities."

Maddy was already out of the tub, as silent as she could be, wrapping herself in one of the heavy pieces of Turkish toweling that had been provided. She couldn't decide which was worse, standing there naked with her hair braided or dressed with a curtain of wet hair dampening the ugly new uniform that had been provided.

It wouldn't matter. If Gwendolyn Haviland opened that door she was ruined, and there'd be no chance of finding out the truth. To be sure, despite his wickedness, the longer she was around the captain the less sure she was. He didn't seem like the kind of man for betrayal and murder. But she needed proof.

"There's been a bit of damage back here, Miss Haviland." Polly was doing her best to distract her mistress, but Gwendolyn was single-minded. "The bathing room's a mess."

"Then I need to see that as well, so that I can make arrangements for its repair."

"Certainly, miss," Polly said stoutly. "As long as the rats don't trouble you."

She could practically hear Miss Haviland come to a sharp halt. "Rats?" she said in horror. "This house is infested with rats?"

"Oh, no, miss. Just the bathing room. The little buggers crawled up the pipes and they've been trapped in there, chewing away at everything." Polly was clearly getting into her tale of rodent invasion. "There are bats as well," she added helpfully.

"Good God," Miss Haviland said. There was a long pause. "Still, I think I should see it . . ."

Unfortunately Maddy had instinctively pulled the plug when she'd climbed out of the tub, and as the last of the water began to swirl down the drain it made a loud, rasping, sucking noise.

"What's that noise?" Miss Haviland demanded.

"The rats," Polly replied. "They're bigger'n cats, Mr. Quarrells told me."

Maddy had fallen back against the wall, the towel clutched to her naked body in a useless effort to hide herself. If Miss Haviland took one step farther, opened the door, then there'd be no saving the situation, and Polly might very well pay the price as well.

"I don't think . . ."

"Gwendolyn." It was the captain's voice, and the cold chill that had covered Maddy's body was immediately replaced with a rush of heat. "What are you doing up here?"

She hadn't heard him approach, of course. How long had he been in the hallway, listening to Polly's tales of unusually sized rodents? Next she'd be saying the bats were the size of ravens, a horrifying thought.

"Since my servants are taking over the care of your house, and it will soon be my house as well, I thought it was only natural that I inspect the premises, only to be told that you have an infestation of rats."

Maddy held her breath. It was all going to come out now, and she didn't even dare tiptoe across the room and turn the key in the lock. No matter how big the rats were purported to be it was unlikely they could accomplish that little trick.

"So I've been told," he said mildly, to Maddy's surprise. "You don't particularly mind them, do you?"

"Everybody minds rats, Thomas," she snapped. "I still wish to see . . ."

She heard a shuffle, and she sank back farther against the wall, prepared for the worst.

The worst was what she got. "I'll just check first to make certain you're safe," the captain said, and a moment later the door opened.

She was out of the direct line of sight, but she should have known he wouldn't have any trouble finding her. She stood frozen, her wet hair falling to her hips, the towel covering her from the tops of her breasts to the tops of her thighs and not much more, when even the sight of an ankle was considered indecent. He let his eyes drift down her body, slowly, reflectively, and then move back up, meeting hers. For a long moment she was caught, breathless, her heart pounding with something other than fear as she stared back into the dark, dangerous promise of his eyes.

"I'm afraid the rats have made quite a mess, my dear," he said in a perfectly calm tone, never moving his intense gaze away from hers. "I have workmen coming to deal with it. By the end of the day it should be ready for inspection."

"I still don't . . ."

"Rats have the unfortunate ability to climb up the inside of a lady's petticoats," he observed mildly.

"Thomas!" Miss Haviland's tones were shrill. "How many times have I told you that you must not refer to anything so personal in regards to a lady!"

"They could run up the petticoats of a maid, then," he said with just the faintest hint of a smile. The damned man was still looking at her, tilting his head to one side as if she were a tasty confection and he was considering where he was going to start nibbling. She half expected him to walk into the bathing room, lock the door behind him, and begin to pull away her bit of toweling. And she half wanted him to. "You never know when they might have to tear them off and deposit them in strange places."

Oh, God, her petticoats! She'd been using them to mop up the rainwater, and he must have found them.

"Don't be ridiculous, Thomas. Maids don't remove their . . . their undergarments. At least, not for any acceptable reason." She was sounding suspicious again.

Luca gave Maddy an annoyingly sweet smile and withdrew, closing the door carefully behind him, and she silently released her pent-up breath. "Gwendolyn, I expect we're going to need to have a conversation about our nuptials."

"Are we?" Maddy could practically hear the simper in her voice. Their voices trailed off, as he led her away, and Maddy immediately began to towel-dry her hair, then yanked on the rough, scratchy underclothing that appeared to be a part of the uniform of the Haviland staff. By the time the door opened again she was fully dressed in a dowdy gown the color of rotten apples, her hair braided and tucked under an even uglier cap.

She stiffened, but it was only Polly. "That was a close thing," she said breathlessly. "Lucky the master seems to want to protect you. Want to tell me why?"

"Maybe he's just afraid of his fiancée. Thank you for lying for me."

Polly shrugged off her thanks. "With a witch like Miss Haviland we all have to look out for each other. She's enough to put the fear of God into anyone. It's a rare treat to be here, out from under her watchful eye. But the captain doesn't strike me as a man who's afraid of anyone. I've seen the way he looks at you when he thinks no one will notice."

"I've barely exchanged two words with the man," Maddy lied, shivering slightly. The storm had brought in a stream of cold weather, and the wind came directly off the water, rattling the windows in their frames and reaching into her bones.

"Sometimes talking's not what gets you into trouble," Polly observed wisely. "Go on, then. I've gotten word that you're to be staying in the housekeeper's quarters below stairs, while the footmen and the maids will be in the attics."

Maddy opened her mouth to protest until Polly added, "with the bats," and she shut her mouth. Why were they putting her downstairs? She could see absolutely no good reason for it. "Perhaps I should speak to the captain . . ." she said reluctantly, the last thing she wanted to do, but Polly shook her head.

"He's headed off to London to pick up his new boat. Ship, I guess I should call it. Miss Haviland wanted to go along with him but he told her she couldn't, so she's in a rare taking. She'll still be working her wiles on him, and you mark my words, she'll end up on the boat or drown trying. She doesn't take no for an answer."

"New ship?" The man was buying up her father's ships—she'd seen proof of it in his rain-soaked library. Which one was he bringing back this time? It couldn't be the *Maddy Rose*—she hadn't signed the papers that Fulton had wanted her to.

Polly shrugged. "None of my business. None of yours either, if you got any sense. You may be beautiful, and clearly you're no maid-servant, but even so, the likes of us don't end up with sea captains and we both know it. Come on with you. I'll help you take your things down to the housekeeper's rooms. They were in a fair mess when the Croziers left, but Lucy and me have been working on them, given them a good scrub and an airing out, and you should be just fine."

"Thank you," Maddy said, hiding her mixed feelings about her unexpected move. *At least there were no bats.*

The apartment was a great deal better than that, she discovered when she followed Polly down the back staircase, careful to avoid the captain's . . . no, Luca's fiancée in case she lingered. She might very well be counting the dinnerware she was going to end up with or something equally intrusive. If she was, she was going to be very disappointed with the silver.

The Croziers had used two adjoining rooms, the front room containing a table and chairs and a settee that should surely belong in one of the upper rooms. Doubtless the Croziers had brought it down for their own use, as well as the large bed with the carved, rococo headboard with cavorting angels and nymphs doing things that were far from celestial. It wasn't to her taste, and the thought of what the dour Mrs. Crozier and her unnerving husband did beneath that headboard gave her pause, when Polly seemed to read her mind.

"That bed was in storage—the one the Croziers used was past saving. The captain said to bring anything down you might need, and I thought you might like this one." She cocked her head, looking at the carvings. "Maybe not such a good idea after all."

"It has a certain charm," Maddy said mendaciously, wondering if she could find a blanket to throw over it while she slept. If she slept.

At least the two rooms were spotless, even the small, high windows that looked out into the street, and she was certain she knew she could thank Polly for that. She hated to think what kind of shape the rooms had been in.

"I'll be making us all some tea and scones," Polly said. "And getting an early start on supper. While the captain's gone we'll have simple food, Miss Haviland said, but I imagine she'll send Monsieur Henri over when the captain returns and she starts haunting the place. Good country cooking is a bit too rough for her refined palate."

Maddy'd be gone by then—the longer she stayed the deeper she sank. She'd always been able to trust her instincts, and the longer she spent around Luca the more certain she was that her father had been wrong. Luca might have been a pirate and pirates were, by definition, thieves, but he would never sneak around, embezzle, murder. She knew he was innocent in her father's death, her foolish heart told her so, and she could force her sisters to take her word for it.

She should leave. She just wasn't sure what she should do next. There was always Lord Eversham. His love letters had grown more effusive, and it had become clear that she could be Lady Eversham the moment she snapped her fingers.

But would Eversham be enough? Was it simply a cruel trick of fate that she should suddenly start feeling the things she should have felt for Tarkington, the man she had supposedly loved? He'd touched her bare breasts and she'd felt nothing. He'd put his . . . thing inside her and it had been painful and messy.

So why was she longing for Luca? Had giving herself to Tarkington turned her into a harlot?

No, not if she looked at handsome, earnest Matthew Fulton and felt nothing at all. The idea of marriage and conjugal relations with him was as unpleasant as the thought of sharing Eversham's bed. At least in Eversham's case he wouldn't live as long—the man was sixty if he was a day.

Perhaps she was now ready to face it. Eversham. Was it an even trade? Because the wretched, stupid, heartbreaking truth was that she wanted the captain, her captain, Luca, to be innocent. Well, he could hardly be innocent, she thought fairly, but at least not guilty in her father's so-called crimes.

She couldn't decide what to wish for. In the end it didn't matter—it was clear fate or God or whoever wasn't paying the slightest bit of attention to her interests. It would play out as it was meant to, and all she could do was act her part.

Miss Haviland's housekeeper had apparently been over the house while Maddy lay sleeping and come up with a surprisingly short list of chores, assigning tasks to the makeshift staff now in residence. Oddly enough, none of those tasks were allotted to her, a fact she found disturbing. Most likely she was out the door the moment the captain returned, and she'd best redouble her efforts before she was on the streets. She needed to wipe out any last question in her mind before she could leave here.

She needed proof.

CHAPTER FOURTEEN

IT WAS LATE AFTERNOON the same day, and Maddy was in the midst of arguing with Polly about whether she could help with the preparation for dinner, when one of the new footmen appeared in the kitchens. "You have a caller, Miss Greaves."

For a moment she didn't react, both at the unfamiliar name and that she would be addressed with a title. Momentary panic swamped her, before she realized it simply had to be Matthew Fulton, trying once more to pry her away. For a man who didn't care for her he seemed most eager to make her leave. Of course, she'd gotten in under his aegis, and there were bound to be repercussions if the truth came out. Which it never would. She sighed. "I'll be there in a moment. Did you offer the gentleman tea, Mr. . . ." She didn't even know his last name, she realized in sudden embarrassment.

"Just Curtis, Miss Greaves. I did, but the gentleman said he preferred brandy, so I served him some of the captain's best, seeing as he's already been a guest in this house."

How odd of Matthew to drink in the middle of the day. He'd seemed like such a straight-laced sort of fellow, Maddy thought, moving through the hallways. The door to the salon was closed, but there was no other room Curtis would have taken him.

She pushed open the door without knocking. "What in God's name are you doing here, Matthew . . . ?" The words trailed off into horrified silence as she realized the man in the room was a complete stranger. The midday light illuminated him perfectly as he sat in one of the comfortable, slightly shabby chairs that the captain favored and Miss Haviland would doubtless get rid of, and he made no effort to rise upon her entrance. She was about to give him an affronted look when she remembered she was a maid, not a lady, and gentlemen certainly didn't rise when maids entered the room, they ignored them.

She pulled herself together with an effort. "Begging your pardon, sir," she said, not having to make any effort to appear flustered. "I thought you were someone else."

"Mr. Fulton, I presume? I don't think Captain Morgan realizes you're on first name terms with him."

A very slight shiver ran down Maddy's spine. Just what she needed—an observant stranger to cause her trouble. "Oh, no, sir, I'm not," she said blithely, not giving an inch. "I was thinking it might be a lad I've been seeing recently."

"And Curtis would show him in the front door and offer him brandy?"

She gave him a cheeky smile. "Curtis is very fond of me." It was a calculated risk, but she was tired of scrambling. Might as well be hanged for a sheep as a lamb.

"I imagine he is, and rightly so." He smiled at her, a singularly charming smile. He was a very handsome man, with longish, coal black hair that fell in a single curl in the midst of his high forehead. He had a close-trimmed beard and mustache, pale skin suggesting a recent illness, a supposition borne out by the cane by his outstretched leg. Another handsome man who left her cold. Perhaps she wasn't a harlot after all. Or merely a harlot for Luca. For some reason that was even more disturbing.

"Please sit down, Miss Greaves," he continued, surveying her. "It hurts my neck to look up at you."

She didn't move. She didn't trust charming men—in truth, she didn't trust men at all. Some instinct told her to leave, but curiosity, always her besetting sin, overruled her seldom-utilized sense of caution. "How may I help you, sir?"

"Sit."

Why hadn't she realized just how difficult obeying orders would turn out to be, she thought, sinking gingerly onto a chair opposite him. A maid's life was to take orders, bob and curtsey, and swallow back any retort. Clearly this was a far greater challenge than she ever imagined.

The elegant young man nodded approvingly. "That's right. We haven't met yet, but I'm a close friend of your employer and his fiancée. My name is Rufus Brown." He paused, watching her.

Was the name supposed to mean something? Because she'd never heard it, never seen the man in her life. "Good afternoon, Mr. Brown," she said with automatic courtesy, then realized it was more the response of a lady than a maid. "What may I do for you?"

"Oh, a great deal, my dear Miss Greaves. I have a small, rather charming house in the countryside near Avebury, and we're dreadfully short staffed. I promised my housekeeper I'd rectify the problem while I was in town, and I've been told you're a prodigiously hard worker, not to mention the fact that you're very ornamental. I'd like you to come back with me, and I promise I won't be ungenerous."

She didn't blink, despite her surprise. "And exactly what position were you thinking of, Mr. Brown?" she said finally, unable to keep a slightly caustic note out of her voice.

He laughed, a light sound that should have put her suspicions to rest. "Oh, my dear, acquit me of designs upon your person! I must confess I tend to share Mr. Quarrells's preferences, though doubtless I would be at your feet if I were differently inclined. I promise, there's nothing untoward. We need a new parlor maid, one who could assist my housekeeper, and I promise she's the salt of the earth, by the way, not an old bitch like Mrs. Crozier."

She blinked at the language, but said nothing, waiting for him to continue.

"And there's always room for advancement. My sister lives with me, and while she's only just leaving the schoolroom she'll be needing a personal maid, and she's a sweet, undemanding child." He sighed affectionately. "My only sibling, and we're quite close. Or if you prefer to have control of minions, my housekeeper is elderly and will be wanting to retire before long. I expect she'd be delighted to train you to take her place. There's no question how high you might rise."

He was watching her too closely beneath those half-closed lids, trying to gauge her reaction to his odd proposition. She had no intention of giving him one. "You're very kind to think of me, Mr. Brown," she said, "but as you know I already have employment, and I find I like being here. I have a great fondness for the sea." She was surprised to realize it was the truth. The captain aside, she loved looking out the front windows of the house to the harbor, the boats and ships bobbing up and down on the swell, the noise and confusion of the docks. The idea of actually stepping onto the deck of a ship might terrify her, but that didn't mean she didn't love watching the world of shipping, a world she knew so well. She realized with a shock that she'd missed it. Sorting through the captain's rain-soaked papers, she'd felt more at home than she had since her father had died.

"Ah, but Miss Greaves . . . may I call you Mary?" he said, leaning forward, holding his elegant malacca cane with its gold head in both hands. "Well, Mary, the truth of it is, in a very short time you'll be out of a job and we both know it. Miss Haviland is a close friend, but she's plagued by the green-eyed devil."

Maddy blinked, momentarily confused. "She drinks absinthe?"

He let out a short bark of laughter. "No, my dear. That's the green fairy. She's jealous, whether she'd admit it or not. She doesn't like the idea of a beautiful woman swanning around her fiancé's house, and who can blame her? She's a lovely young woman, but she looks just a bit faded next to you. She'll boot you out the first chance she gets, and if she doesn't have a reason I have no doubt she'll manufacture one. Why don't you save her the trouble and accept my generous offer?"

Odd, how it didn't sound the slightest bit flattering. "I've told you, sir. I have a job, and I signed papers promising to stay for at least six months." That was a complete lie. She'd heard of people insisting on such contracts, to offset the expense of training a new employee and ordering uniforms, but the Russells had never insisted on such a thing and neither had the captain. Luca. "And besides, I like it here."

Mr. Brown was not looking as benevolent as he had, though the smile was unwavering. "Ah, Mary, I was so hoping you'd want to come with me on a permanent basis. But the truth of the matter is that Captain Morgan offered me your services for the next few months, just to help me out; a great kindness on his part. I was hoping you might be interested in a permanent change, and once you're at Highfields you may find you like it very much indeed, but if, once I find the right person for the job, you wish to return then I would hardly detain you. It was very thoughtful of Morgan to lend you to me, and I think you'll find you enjoy the change of scene."

Maddy blinked. "But I don't wish to go."

The benevolence was slipping a bit. "My dear, you're a servant. You go where your employer sends you, do what he tells you to do, if you wish to retain your job. Indeed, if you have no wish to continue on here you may refuse Captain Morgan's orders, but I think that would be a mistake, since I believe it's your fondness for your employer's . . . house that makes you reluctant to come to my aid."

Maddy lowered her eyes to her lap, glad she'd hidden her hands, which were now clenched in impotent fury. How much did the man know? What had she given away in this short conversation? How could he know what she wouldn't admit to herself?

Gwendolyn Haviland! The woman was so possessive she would think everyone wanted her fiancé. It was no great perception on Mr. Brown's side, though she had hardly been as circumspect as she ought to be. But why was she worrying about giving away emotions that she was doing an excellent job of resisting? Wasn't she?

Now what was she going to do? Was a servant really at her employer's beck and call to this extent that she had to go wherever she was sent? It seemed grossly unfair, but then, life in service was hardly a world of equality. She suspected Mr. Brown was right—she either had to go with him or lose her position entirely.

Going with him would ruin her plans anyway, but perhaps she could put him off for a bit. After all, her time was rapidly running out here anyway, and if she couldn't find anything incriminating she had no choice but to return to Nanny Gruen's, a failure.

The one good thing was that she'd never have to see him, Luca, again. Never feel his dark, flashing eyes running over her, never risk the touch of his hands, the taste of his mouth. Her future was set—Lord Eastham would do what Tarkington had done, she would have a baby, and the old man would eventually die, leaving her a complacent widow with no need for a man like the unsettling captain.

She lifted her eyes, perfecting shy deference. "Very good, sir," she said meekly. "And when would we be leaving?"

For a moment he looked slightly taken aback, as if he hadn't expected her to agree, but he rallied immediately. "Excellent. Why not now?"

Oh, hell no, she thought, looking demure. "I'm so sorry, sir, but if it's immediate help you'll be needing then Lucy might suit you better."

He frowned. "But why can't you come now?" He brushed aside the notion of taking Lucy, one of the new maids, as inconsequential.

"Well, sir," she said in a low, confidential voice, "I'm afraid I have certain . . . er . . . difficulties with my health, which can make things a bit . . . complicated."

Most of the affability had vanished from Mr. Brown's handsome face, which was just fine with Maddy. She'd never believed it in the first place. "Enlighten me," he said with a bit of a snap.

You asked for it, she thought. "Well, it's me women's parts," she said in a confiding tone. "When I get me monthlies, which have just started, I expect, because I saw some blood on my pantalets, I find I have to take to me bed for three days at least, and nothing gives me ease."

He had been pale already, but now it was faintly tinged with green. But he wasn't ready to give up, no matter how graphic she was being. "That's no problem. A bit of morphine should take the edge off your pain, and you may ride in the good carriage with a warm brick to your stomach."

"Ah, sir, it sounds lovely, it does, but I'm afraid that won't do. You see . . ." she leaned forward, "I bleed too much, and then something happens and it stops for a while, and then bursts through and the blood runs down my legs and makes a fair mess. I'd be ready to go in less than a week's time, but I'm really not fit to be around when I have my monthlies. I tend to cast up my accounts as well, plus there's the problem of needing a water closet without any warning, and . . ."

"I understand," he said swiftly, shutting down her graphic details just as she was about to get even more colorful. She'd seen someone with the flux, and a full description of the symptoms would be enough to disgust a man as fainthearted as Mr. Brown. She was astonished he'd held out as long as he did. "We will leave Monday week. You should be more than recovered by then. I am not well acquainted with women's maladies, but I gather your courses last no more than a week." His voice was icy with disdain, as if the way a woman's body functioned was a personal affront to him.

A week would do it. She'd be gone before he came to collect her, back to Nanny Gruen with some kind of truth about Luca. No, she shouldn't think of him that way. It was too intimate. He needed to remain the captain. The captain, who had kissed her, touched her, intimately, his mouth on her breasts, his hand between her legs.

Nanny Gruen would have had a heart attack if she heard about Maddy's discussion of the forbidden. It had been such an effective weapon she almost wanted to laugh. Poor, squeamish Mr. Brown. Served him right for trying to force her.

"Yes, sir. I'll be ready." She couldn't control her color, but she could certainly simulate a frail constitution. "Would you mind if I got back to me rooms, sir? I find one of me little fits coming on."

"Little fits?" he echoed, sounding horrified. "No, don't tell me. I trust the other servants will be able to assist you. They'll be near enough in the servants' quarters to hear you if you call?"

Now that was a peculiar question, one that deserved an outright lie. "Oh, yes sir. I'll be sharing a room with Polly up in the attics, and Caitlin and Lucy will be next door, not to mention the footmen down the hall." She couldn't imagine how they'd all fit into the crowded attic, but fortunately that wasn't her problem. And the anxious Mr. Brown didn't need to know she was going to be sleeping three flights below in the basement apartments once allotted to the Croziers. He was up to something.

She rose, and he automatically started to rise as well, then covered up the movement by reaching for his cane. He'd already deliberately refused to rise for a maid—why was he about to make the mistake of doing so? Either she was failing in her impersonation of a servant or he knew far more than he was letting on.

She could think of no reason for him to be so determined to get her away from the captain, unless he was doing it for his jealous friend. That was a reasonable enough explanation, given that he said he was very close with Gwendolyn Haviland. Reasonable, but her instincts told her it was much more than that.

"I'll return in a week, Miss . . . Mary," he said, stumbling over the words, another troubling thing. She thought she'd done a good job of the accent, but then why was he reacting to her with the automatic courtesy of a gentleman confronted by a lady of quality? "You may, of course, let me know if you find you recover sooner. And I would think it might be wise to leave Captain Morgan's household as soon as possible."

She was already at the door, one hand on her stomach in a dramatic gesture, when his words stopped her. "Why?" she said bluntly.

"Captain Morgan is not exactly who or what he says he is," Mr. Brown murmured.

Hell and damnation. Maybe Mr. Brown was a better source of information about the captain than all her attempts at detective work. She might have found out more, faster, if she'd simply agreed to go with him.

Too late for that, and her instincts agreed. There was more to Mr. Brown than met the eye, and she had no intention of going anywhere with him, no matter what enticement he might dangle in front of her.

So she gave him a slight smile as she clenched her stomach. "No one is."

The bitch. The filthy little slut had outfoxed him, and he wanted to strangle her. Rufus settled back into his carriage, necessary for even the short distance to his lodgings, given the condition of his leg, and cursed Madeleine Russell to hell and back again. He could almost be impressed with her acting abilities and her quick wit, except there wasn't any room in his fury for such emotions. He was going to take a great deal of pleasure in ending her life. This would have been so much simpler if the sisters had been in residence when he'd set fire to their house on Curzon Street, but unbeknownst to him they'd left that morning for the countryside. For Somerset, where they had no business being.

He'd made sure they were tossed out of there soon enough, but poverty and shame weren't enough to render them harmless. Now he had to go to a great deal of trouble to silence each of them, and the first one, the easiest one, the scarred, shy, eldest sister, had managed to get away entirely.

He wasn't about to let this one escape. He could employ his old favorite, fire, and burn down the captain's house with the people inside. He wasn't sure if he wanted Morgan alive to be a scapegoat, or whether he might serve that purpose just as well if he were burnt to a cinder. And there was Morgan's damned watchdog in the mews. If he were to kill Morgan he would have to kill William Quarrells as well, or he'd never have any peace again. Quarrells was the kind of man who held grudges and suspected everyone, and he would scarcely believe in a convenient accidental fire. If he could figure some way to get Quarrells into the house as well it would be convenient, but right now he was too weak to manage such a feat with Quarrells's large body, and he wasn't completely sure of his man. Parsons seemed to have very few moral qualms, but people were surprisingly squeamish when it came to murdering pretty young women. He was good enough and lucky enough to have managed the sabotage of Morgan's boat with no one, not even the captain, realizing it, though the bloody man was too good a sailor to die. Parsons could carry off the girl's death with no problem whatsoever.

Rufus would need to consider things carefully. He'd let his fury get in the way in London, and he'd ended up suffering a major setback. Not a defeat—never that. But matters were much more complicated with Bryony Russell and her new husband somewhere on the continent, and he preferred elegant simplicity.

He had no intention of waiting. He had no idea how long it would take Morgan to return to Devonport—he gathered the man usually spent a week or more in London when he traveled to the city, but he doubted he'd have that luxury.

He had no idea whether Morgan suspected his housemaid was anything other than what she pretended to be, but he didn't need Gwendolyn's jealous whining or his man's spying to know the captain was going to bed her sooner or later. Not yet—Rufus was a good enough observer to know she hadn't been whoring around yet.

But she would. And Morgan would be in a hurry to make it happen. He wouldn't be gone long.

No, Rufus was going to have to deal with the girl promptly and efficiently, and if that involved strangling her with his bare hands then so much the better.

CHAPTER FIFTEEN

It seemed to Maddy as if she'd slept for days. Leaving Mr. Brown and his very suspicious demands, she'd gone back to her room and lain down beneath the disgraceful headboard. She'd fallen into a deep sleep, and hadn't woken up until close to dawn, ravenous. She'd raided the kitchen, making herself a plate of cold lamb, crusty rolls with butter, and a mélange of root vegetables seasoned with nutmeg, and seated herself at the wooden table where she'd eaten before under the scornful eye of Mrs. Crozier. There was something almost blissful about the silence of the predawn kitchen, the light just coming in through the windows. Polly and the others would probably be up soon enough—a servant's day started early, particularly for a cook, but for the moment Maddy savored the stillness, simply happy not to have to rush and do anything.

There were five new servants in the household: Polly, two other maids, and two footmen, and somehow they'd managed to all cram into the attics. Her own meager belongings had been transferred to her new rooms, but she wondered how they'd dealt with all the broken furniture and detritus of an old house. Had they finally managed to rid the place of bats?

And what about the locked cupboard? She'd forgotten all about that in the last few days—she'd been too tired at night to do anything more than collapse in bed, and she hadn't had time to do more than try to pick the lock with a hairpin. She was going to have to get up there again, though preferably when the new servants were out and about. Though perhaps they'd already opened it—after all, the space up there wasn't vast. Three beds in one room, two in another would leave things crowded, and what would they do with the leftover furniture? She moved to the window and looked out past the garden into the mews. The pile of broken chairs and rat-chewed mattresses created an almost sinister bulk near the back gate, and she wondered what else had found itself onto that pile. Had they come across anything interesting?

She went back to the table and her meal, thoughtful. She had no idea how long the captain intended to be gone, but once he was back she would have the devil to face. Literally. The devil with the face of a fallen angel, which was far more tempting. If he stayed away longer than a week she'd have to deal with Mr. Brown, and she certainly wasn't about to take off into the unknown countryside with the man.

She couldn't imagine why Mr. Brown was so determined to have her. She believed him when he said he had no interest in her body, but as handsome footmen were a symbol of status in the world she had once lived in, pretty maidservants were probably almost as valuable, and Maddy had no delusions. She was pretty—it was one of the few weapons she possessed along with her intellect and pure determination, and she had every intention of using what a perverse God had given her.

She didn't trust Mr. Brown. Didn't trust his determination to remove her, though it might simply be a favor to Gwendolyn Haviland. The woman viewed Maddy as some major rival, which was absurd. Luca would hardly trade a solicitor's daughter for a housemaid, and while he might be interested in bedding her, that was most likely a normal male reaction and meant nothing. He would have kissed any marginally pretty woman.

No, his relationship with his fiancée would rise or fall on its own merits, and Maddy had the strong feeling that it was descending rapidly. The captain was too wise to chain himself to a harpy like Gwendolyn Haviland, and Maddy expected the woman would be gone soon after she herself left Devonport, if not sooner.

Of course, that was assuming that the captain wasn't guilty of conspiring against Eustace Russell. That kind of scandal would send Gwendolyn packing at the first hint—she wasn't a woman to stand by her man in the face of adversity. Even if Maddy was wrong, and they were married before she found proof, Miss Haviland would be out the door if the captain was accused of murder.

Except if that were the case, she'd be Mrs. Morgan by then. Mrs. Thomas Morgan. Which wasn't even his name—would the marriage be legal if he used an alias? And wouldn't the additional scandal be delicious, if Gwendolyn found she'd been living in sin?

Maddy leaned back. She never would have thought she'd be so petty, but the captain's fiancée had declared her enmity the moment they met. She deserved anything she got. Maddy and her sisters had had disaster rain down on their heads through no fault of their own. At least Gwendolyn might get a taste of it.

Except, of course, she was coming to the reluctant conclusion that Luca was innocent, and perhaps she was wrong and he truly adored Gwendolyn and they would marry, have herds of children, and live happily ever after. Maddy heard an odd noise, and realized it had come from her. She'd made a growling sound.

She shook her head, rising and taking her plate into the scullery to wash it. Far be it from her to add to her fellow servants' duties. The sun was almost up, she could hear the faint stirrings above stairs, and her stomach knotted.

Not Luca, she reminded herself. He had disappeared again—it was simply the new servants. She wasn't quite ready to face anyone, though she wasn't sure why, and she quickly slipped back into her rooms, closing the door just as the first footsteps reached the kitchen.

She leaned her forehead against the panel, listening to the cheerful voices. This wasn't her life. Neither was cozying up to the captain, chatting with him about his books. She didn't really belong anywhere. Finding the proof about her father wouldn't fix everything. Even if she managed to get his name cleared and the money back, the hint of scandal would always attach to their name. The House of Russell was no more, and assuming they all married, even their name itself would disappear. Probably just as well, but it would have broken her father's heart. He'd almost convinced Tarkington to change his name to Russell, just to keep the name alive. And instead the bastard had deflowered her and run off to South America, leaving her brokenhearted.

Or close enough to brokenhearted that it didn't matter.

She wasn't going to think about that. In fact, she hadn't thought about it in days. And when she did, there was no lingering pain—just a righteous anger that was deliciously liberating. She was over it. She was free.

At least, if she could talk herself out of her ridiculous fascination with the captain. Blast him. And blast her, for being such a cotton-headed romantic, that his gypsy beauty and his dark eyes set off ridiculous longings inside her. She was a practical woman, and she had no proof he wasn't a villain. She had to remember that.

She would use her time wisely while he was gone. If she were lucky, she'd find what she needed before he returned, and never have to see him again. Never have to risk temptation.

The door to the library was no longer locked—in fact, now that warmer weather was upon them the door was wide open a few hours later when Maddy wandered by with a deliberately casual air. No one was there to see her, so her affected languor was unnecessary. The two new maids had scoured everything Maddy hadn't gotten to, but in fact Mrs. Crozier had worked Maddy so hard that there wasn't much left to work on. Apparently even the formerly sacrosanct library had been put in order.

She slipped inside, then hesitated. If she closed the door then there was no risk of anyone seeing her as they passed by on their various duties. If she closed it, though, it might rouse curiosity. The day was sunny, though the sky over the harbor was hazy, and a light wind was stirring the trees. On impulse she closed the door, turning the key in the lock. If anyone tried to get in she would explain she'd been looking for a book to read, and the door had locked by accident. It was a thin enough excuse, but at least for now there was no one on the premises who would suspect her of anything. Just to make sure she had her excuse in hand, she went straight for the first section of bookshelves.

And was promptly lost. He had everything—the latest Charles Dickens serials now bound in volumes, older books by Jane Austen and the Brontë sisters. George Eliot and William Thackeray were there, as well as whole shelves of what looked like novels in French, Italian, and Spanish. Even odder, the books looked as if they'd been read fairly recently—their placement on the shelves slightly uneven. Did the captain really speak and read those languages? She wouldn't put it past him.

Hadn't he said something about the long voyages? Perhaps that's when he learned the other languages as well. She plucked a slim volume of one of her favorite French writers and tucked it under her arm before moving on to the next set of shelves.

Good Lord, the man had books on everything! Geology, history, maps and sea charts, plant characteristics and gardening tomes, astronomy and mathematics, and some sciences that Maddy, who had always preferred novels, had never even heard of. The idea of the fascinating, dangerous captain being a reader of such complicated and arcane subjects made him even more mysterious. And even more compelling.

On impulse she pulled out a book on trade routes in South America—she knew a bit about them already, having been at her father's side, but she'd only heard his views. An expert opinion on them might be fascinating.

Putting the books down, she turned to the desk. The sheaves of rain-splattered papers had disappeared, but they didn't matter—she'd read every one of them while she'd endeavored to save them. She half expected the drawers of his desk to be locked, but they slid open easily enough, revealing any number of fascinating things, including a small gun that was clearly loaded. Who did he think was going to accost him in his library, for heaven's sake? What kind of enemies did he have, and why?

Three hours later she was hot, sweaty, and dusty—the new staff hadn't been as thorough as downtrodden Mary Greaves had been—and she had absolutely nothing to show for it but the two books. No mysterious communications—the letters she found written by her father were reasonable and even vaguely affectionate, and she remembered that the man calling himself Thomas Morgan had always been her father's favorite among his captains. He once explained he liked the man's sheer effrontery, a pirate, someone with gypsy blood, living as a prosperous seafarer. She should have realized that the man he was talking about was no ancient salt but a far younger man.

His affection for the captain had made the possibility of his betrayal all the more heinous. What exactly had the note said?

Don't trust any of them. Someone's stealing money, and it looks like Kilmartyn's in league with them, no matter what excuses he makes. Don't trust Morgan either. Never trust a pirate. Something's going on, and I'll get to the bottom of it, or . . .

If only they knew what in heaven's name he meant. Couldn't he have written something a little more detailed? Like names, dates, reasons? Dealing with a scrap of paper and a half-finished, almost illegible note was almost worse than nothing. If there'd been no clue to their father's innocence they might have accepted the inevitable.

No, they wouldn't. They were Russells, in the end, and they wouldn't allow their father to be calumnized without proof.

Could Luca have done it? Could he have somehow managed to embezzle half the assets of Russell Shipping and then arranged for her father's murder? The longer she stayed here the less she thought it possible, but maybe she was being blinded by her attraction to him. She needed to pull back, view all this with an impartial eye, or she'd never find the truth.

There was nothing, *nothing* in the library to give her any kind of hint. Where else would he keep papers? Up in the locked closet? Might he have an office down by the docks—that was a reasonable supposition, and a good place to hide anything. Or even the less-than-forthcoming Fulton might hold some secrets that he hadn't mentioned.

She sat at the desk, frustrated. On impulse she pulled a piece of paper and wrote a note with her exquisite hand, one that her Swiss instructors had insisted upon before she was deemed ready to make her debut in the world. She couldn't exactly summon Fulton, but she could ask him a question about Luca and his acquisition of the ships and hope he found a way to see her, or at least answer her. Not that it mattered. In the end the captain had figured out a way to take possession of the *Maddy Rose*, her ship, without her agreeing to it. Fulton had said it was pro forma, and apparently he was right. And the very thought infuriated her.

What right did he have to the *Maddy Rose*? He'd taken everything else—the cream of her father's steamers, possibly his reputation, and his life. Not to mention casting some kind of romantic spell over his stupid, vulnerable daughter and making her a total nitwit.

Not that she'd ever thought of herself as vulnerable. Nor had she thought herself a nitwit, until now. She ripped up the note and pushed away from the desk. She went over to drop it in the fireplace and paused, admiring the neatly swept hearth. She doubted if she'd take a clean surface for granted ever again, not since her own intimate acquaintance with scrubbing everything in this house.

Instead she shoved the wadded up pieces of paper in one pocket, went over, and unlocked the door.

The halls were silent. It was early afternoon—usually a quiet time in any household, once the morning duties were finished. The borrowed servants were probably downstairs in the kitchen, having tea or helping Polly with dinner. The only reason she'd need help would be if the captain was due home tonight, and the last thing Maddy wanted was to run into him without fair warning. She'd better ask, in case she wanted to disappear.

The kitchen was empty. Very odd—the stove wasn't even warm. Polly hadn't said anything to her that morning about going out, but perhaps she'd needed some last minute ingredient. Or more likely Gwendolyn had called everyone home in a fit of pique.

She headed up the narrow, winding stairs, all the way to the attics, calling out when she reached the bottom of the stairs. There was no answer.

She could only hope there were no bats as well. She climbed up the final flight of stairs into the shadowy depths of the attic, only slightly out of breath from her rapid ascent, to find the place deserted as well. The bedroom doors on either side were open, and each now held a row of narrow beds and small dressers. The front space, where she'd sat and waited for Luca just a few short days ago, had been transformed, with a couple of desks, a loveseat, and several chairs. The rest of the broken furniture had disappeared, along with the ripped mattresses and bits of trash.

There were only two questions left. Were the bats still in residence, and was the back closet still locked?

It appeared the bats were gone. There were no ominous shapes in the corners of the room, at least, as far as she could tell in the dim light. And the closet door at the end of the hallway still boasted a heavy chain and lock.

She sank to her knees in front of it, pulling a steel hairpin from her tightly coiled hair. It would probably all come tumbling down, she thought ruefully as she stared at the lock, but it would be easy enough to fix, and there would be no one to see her with her hair halfway down her back, in particular the captain. Even the servants were oddly absent, and she should be able to get back to her room and fix her hair before anyone noticed.

It wasn't the first lock she'd picked. Sophie had a drawer where she kept her journal, billets-doux from inappropriate suitors, and anything she happened to steal from Maddy, such as her emerald earrings or her diamond pendant, and Maddy had learned to override a simple lock, not just to retrieve her possessions, but to gain an advantage over her younger sister as well. This one was twice the size and weight of the one Sophie had used, but the function was basically the same. Grasping it in her hand, she bent the hairpin straight and set to work.

It was a long and arduous task. Her knees and legs still hadn't quite recovered from all that time spent scrubbing, and within moments they were aching again. Every now and then she thought she heard a sound from beyond the staircase, but she steadfastly ignored it. If anyone ascended the last flight of stairs she would hear them, and she had an excuse ready. She would claim that her valise had been stored there, and the Croziers had taken the key to the cupboard, which was more than likely true.

But she heard no one on the stairs, and she concentrated on the metal contraption with single-minded ferocity, until finally, finally she heard the blessed click, and the bar of the lock fell free. She rose, stretched with a quiet moan, and then listened again for the sound of servants below. It was still oddly quiet, but she could only be grateful for it.

She slipped the lock off the door, reached for the handle, and pulled it open, not quite sure what she suspected.

The bats dove at her with shrieks of rage, and she screamed, ducking, covering her head with her arms as they exploded around her, squeaking and flapping their leathery wings, and she crouched on the floor, her eyes tightly shut, just waiting for them to disappear.

Eventually all was silent, though she had no idea whether they'd simply perched nearby and were waiting for her to emerge from her panicked crouch so they could attack again, or whether they'd found some handy eaves to continue their somnolent daytime activities. And then she heard the sound of someone moving nearby. Not on the stairs. But on the worn wooden flooring behind her.

It was an undignified position to be found in, but Maddy wasn't quite ready to move. She listened to the steady footsteps, and knew it wasn't the captain. Luca's tread was almost silent, with a catlike grace. This was someone who weighed more and walked with a swagger. Luca didn't need to swagger.

"Coo," came a cockney voice from behind her. "So here's where he keeps the goodies."

She sat up at that, about to turn and face the newcomer, when she looked into the closet she'd gone to such pains to open, and she was momentarily stunned.

Pirates had treasure—it was a given. Even a tamer privateer would have booty somewhere, though she'd assumed he'd simply sold everything. Not everything. The closet was neatly arranged, and filled with such wondrous possessions that she, unlike the man behind her back, was momentarily silenced. There were paintings with the jewellike tones of the old masters, there were gold figures that had to come from South America and were far too indecent to be seen in mixed company, presumably some kind of fertility gods. There were heavy chests, and whether they were filled with jewels, pieces of eight, or dead men's bones she had no idea, she only knew there was enough money in this simple closet to buy and sell her father's fleet twice over. He had no reason to kill Eustace Russell or steal his money—he had more than enough of his own.

She rose as gracefully as she could, given that she'd been caught snooping and her hair was already coming down, prepared to face one of the new footmen with one of her ready excuses. It died on her tongue.

"Weren't expecting me, missy?" the stranger demanded. He was a big man, in a gaudy striped suit with rings on his thick fingers, and the coldest, emptiest eyes she'd ever seen. One of his heavy, bludgeoning hands held a ridiculously small pistol. "No one ever is."

"I beg your pardon?" Unfortunately her attempt at calm disdain failed utterly, and she sounded exactly like what she was—a terrified girl.

"No need to beg anything. It won't do you no good." He leaned past her and opened one of the boxes. The gleam of gold and precious stones would have blinded her if she weren't already stiff with fear. The man pulled out a handful and tucked it in the pocket of the loud suit. "I'll come back for more after I've dealt with you, that is, if I can. Cap'n Morgan's supposed to be returning today, and I wouldn't be wanting to run into him, not if I can help it."

"Dealt with me?" she said. Her brain had kicked back into working order and it was racing. Her immediate thought was Mr. Brown—for some reason he'd seemed obsessed with having her travel with him to his house near Avebury. Apparently he didn't take "no" or even "wait" for an answer. "You work for Mr. Brown, don't you?"

There was no amusement, no emotion whatsoever in the man's stolid face. "I do, miss."

She took a deep breath. "Well, if he's that eager to have me come to him right now then I suppose I have no choice. If you give me a moment I'll assemble my things."

"You've got it wrong, miss," the man said with exquisite politeness. "He don't want to take you away from here."

"He don't? Er . . . doesn't?" *Now was not the time to give grammar lessons, Maddy,* she reminded herself. *The man held a gun.* "Then what does he want?"

The man didn't answer. He didn't need to, but Maddy had never been one to simply accept the inevitable, particularly when this time it seemed to concern her very existence.

She looked past him. He was big, and therefore probably slower than she was, but her legs were shaking so much she wasn't sure she could manage her usual speed. *Buck up,* she snapped to herself. *Just because he's holding a gun on you and planning to kill you doesn't mean you should fall apart.*

"Don't even try it, miss," the man said, reading her mind. "I'm a good shot, and I'd splatter your brains all over the floor if you ran. You don't want to leave that kind of mess for the other servants, now do you? Let's do this right and tidy, just you and me. No need to make a fuss."

"You really think I'm willing to die without making a fuss?" she demanded, perhaps unwisely.

"Most people do. They accept it, and I makes it as painless as possible. You annoy me and I'll make it hurt." And he meant it—there was no mercy in his small, soulless eyes, only practicality.

"Fair enough," she said after a moment. There was no way she could escape up here—he'd have a clear shot if she tried to get to the stairs. But there would be other chances as he took her down the flights of stairs, unless he was planning to toss her out the window.

No, people would see her. "Where are you going to take me?" The sooner she knew what his actual plans were the sooner she could come up with an alternative.

"Somewheres nice and quiet-like. We'll go out the back way and there'll be a carriage waiting for us. With luck we won't run into anyone. You ask for help and they're dead too. You wouldn't want to go to your grave with that on your conscience, now would you?"

"I'd rather not go to my grave at all," she said frankly. "I don't suppose you feel like telling me why you're going to kill me?"

He gestured toward the stairs with the gun. "Twenty pounds."

"What?" she almost shrieked, and at the last minute quieted her exclamation. "I'm only worth twenty pounds?"

He shrugged his heavy shoulders. "I do most for ten. I got offered more for this one because my employer don't want any more mistakes. Come along then. My associate is waiting in the mews for us."

The mews, she thought. There was a good chance Mr. Quarrells might see them and rescue her.

"No one's here, miss. The servants have all been summoned back to the house they came from, the man who stays in the cottage at the back has gone to London with the captain. It would be a waste of time to struggle."

Personally she couldn't think of a better way to spend her few remaining minutes or hours. But she was an actress. She might not have been able to convince the denizens of this house that she was a maid, but she could surely convince this hired brute that she was cowed and frightened, particularly because a good part of her truly was terrified. "All right," she said, though the words were bitter on her tongue and she started down the narrow staircase, the man with the gun directly behind her.

CHAPTER SIXTEEN

Being on board the *Maddy Rose* should have filled Luca with the same inner peace that always settled over him when he was out at sea, whether it was smooth sailing or fighting a fierce storm. If it weren't for the cuckoo in his nest he'd be tempted to take his favorite ship out into the open waters, simply disappear for a week as he'd done so many times before.

But life had changed. He had a burgeoning business to deal with—two of Russell's finest steamships to ferry cargo and passengers around the world, and now this beautiful indulgence. He'd been a fool to spend the money on the *Maddy Rose*—the age of the clipper ship was over, steam was replacing everything, and he had no quarrel with that. He was in the business of making money, and the profits from steam far outstripped what could be made from the smaller, lighter clipper ships.

Ah, but running with the wind was something he would never tire of. He could keep the *Maddy Rose* simply because he wanted to. He had more money than Croesus at this point, and he could spend it as he pleased. Besides, there were still certain runs that were best accomplished by the smaller clipper ships.

It had been easy enough to put pressure to bear on Matthew Fulton, simply by confronting him with the truth about the so-called maidservant he'd sent into Luca's household. Matthew had managed to free up the title to the *Maddy Rose*, and he wouldn't dare talk to its namesake or risk losing Luca's very substantial business.

And now he was returning to Miss Madeleine Rose Russell with every intention of forcing her to admit the truth. He wanted the words from her, and he had every intention of getting them.

He was half tempted to simply throw her over his shoulder and carry her off, as his gypsy ancestors had done. He hadn't lived within a tribe long enough to have learned the ways of the Travelers, but he remembered a surprising number of things, including the language and philosophy. His gypsy side abhorred the wealth and property he'd accumulated over the years, though it lauded his stint at privateering. His *Gadjo* side relished it.

Of course, it was the Romany way to carry a young girl off, but it was for respectable reasons. For marriage and children, and God knew he didn't want to marry anyone. Gwendolyn was hanging on by a string, but he would sever that last bit today. The harbor was already in sight, and even with a smaller crew they'd have no trouble docking.

He still hadn't decided what he was going to do with Russell's daughter. Wart had been full of information. She'd been engaged until her father's disgrace, and there were rumors that she'd lost what little reputation she had left by spending the night with her fiancé before he took off for parts unknown. Luca found the thought annoyed him. When a woman was as beautiful as Maddy it would only make sense that other men would have touched her, tasted her. Virgins tended to be more trouble than they were worth. But for some reason he didn't like the idea of another man seeing her, touching her. And one night wasn't going to make much of a difference in her bed skills—it would have simply dispensed with her virginity but left her essentially unmoved, unless her fiancé had taken a lot of time and trouble. And since he'd left her the next day, according to the omniscient Wart, Luca doubted it.

He watched the docks as they approached, Billy handling the wheel. He found he was impatient, eager, when he'd never been eager to get off a ship in his life, particularly one like this one. His maiden voyage as her owner, and all he'd done was rush back to the Plymouth area, rush back to Miss Madeleine Rose Russell.

He'd wasted enough time with her. What he'd do next was a conundrum. What he *ought* to do was send her away. What he wanted to do was . . . well, there were so many things he wanted to do to her that he could spend an hour just fantasizing and be in no condition to walk down the streets of Devonport.

He would deal with things as they unfolded. First, he needed the truth from her own mouth. What he'd do next with that mouth was another matter entirely.

He disembarked as Billy went through the paper work. The boat was fully stocked for a longer voyage—Luca had promised Billy a proper sail—but at the last minute he'd changed his mind. Simply abandoning Gwendolyn wouldn't be enough to make her break the engagement—he needed to do something a little more outrageous. And while he was totally capable of simply breaking it himself, he had enough sympathy for her pride to give her an excuse. She cared so much for appearances and reputations, while he couldn't give a tinker's damn. But he'd led her on, and he was a man who believed in fairness if it were at all possible.

The sky was darker than it should be as he strode toward North Water Street, leaving Billy behind, and he felt a foreboding inside him that might or might not have something to do with the weather. That was another curse of his gypsy blood—he sensed things before they happened. It had always aided him in his life—that split second of foreknowledge had saved him any number of times and greatly increased his substantial assets. And right now he was sensing some very bad things.

He sped up, his long legs eating up the distance to the narrow terrace house on Water Street. He was about to bound up the front steps when something stopped him. The house was dark. With the coming of the storm someone should have turned on the gaslight—it was bright in the homes on either side of his. But his was dark and abandoned.

He kept walking, down to the end of the block and around the corner to where the mews lay, the stables and storage for the various town houses. He saw the carriage at once, tethered to the side of a back gate. It was small, black curtains shielding everything, and he knew he'd never seen a carriage like that anywhere near his house or his neighbors. He looked ahead, through the gathering shadows, and saw them on the narrow platform at the top of the back staircase, and he froze.

She was struggling, of course. Maddy would never be forced to do anything without a struggle, and the huge man holding on to her was having a difficult time managing her and the gun in his hand. It was a small pistol, adequately lethal if he put it to the side of her head and pulled the trigger, and yet the stupid girl was squirming, kicking, as he hauled her downstairs. He had the arm with the gun around her waist, lifting her, the other over her mouth to silence her, and he was so busy with the struggle that he didn't even notice Luca's stealthy approach.

It was a good thing he hadn't rushed in—the man had an accomplice waiting at the end of the garden, his hands full of ropes and bonds of various sorts. The idiots should have gone in together and bound her there, he thought with a professional's eye. Much smarter way to go about it. They could have used chloroform or a knock on the head to make her behave, but these men had made two grave mistakes. They'd underestimated their quarry. His Maddy wouldn't go quietly with anyone.

And they'd forgotten whose household she resided in, and therefore who she could call on for a protector. Though he couldn't imagine why anyone would want to abduct her. Well, apart from him.

He was calm, cool, and deadly. It took him the work of a few seconds to break the neck of the furious accomplice, dragging him out of the way so his body wouldn't alert the bully holding Maddy. He could hear the man now, cursing and threatening.

"Bite me again and I'll blow your fucking brains out," the man growled. "I told you I can hurt you real bad if you fight, and you're heading for the slowest, painfulest death I can think of, the way you're carrying on."

Maddy didn't seem to think much of this, because she kept fighting as the man dragged her down the stairs. "Damn if I won't shoot you in the head and leave you here and to hell with what Parsons said." He peered into the gathering gloom, but Luca had hidden himself just beyond the gate. "Parsons, where the hell are you? I can't hold her much longer."

Apparently Maddy didn't believe in paying any attention to the fact that the man could easily kill her—she bit down hard again, and he let out a howl, dropping the pistol as he whirled her around and slapped her, so hard her head jerked back. A second later he'd grabbed her again, one burly arm around her neck, and Luca knew the man was about to kill her, was about to snap the slender, beautiful neck with one swift jerk.

He had no weapon but his knife, and it had been a long time since he'd used it on another human being. He stepped into the light. "Let her go," he called out.

The man froze, looking up and peering into the shadows. "Now you know that's not going to happen, guv'nor. Even if I weren't getting paid I'd do this one for free, for all the trouble she's caused me."

"I can pay more." Not that he would—he'd kill the man as soon as he released her.

The man shook his head. "Sorry, Captain Morgan. I know your reputation, but trust me, my employer's far worse. I wouldn't go foul of him for love nor money. Now you just step away and Parsons and I will clean up this mess."

"I'm afraid Parsons is unavailable."

Silence for a moment, as the big man considered it. Maddy was looking at him, her eyes wide and staring, and he could see both the fear and fury in them. It took a lot to frighten his Maddy, and . . .

And why the hell was he thinking of her as "his" Maddy? No one had ever been "his" anything.

"Then I think, cap'n, that you'd best just turn around and go back the way you came. Because there's no way you can stop me, and I've been around a time or two, and I've seen men in love before. Trust me, you won't be wanting to see this." And he positioned his arms, about to snap her neck, when Luca called out.

"Kick him." The sound of his barked order startled the kidnapper for almost a fraction of a second, but it was enough. For probably the first time in her life Maddy followed an order without questioning. She kicked, and Luca threw the knife, hard and true.

The big man went down immediately, dead before he hit the ground, and he took Maddy with him, so that she was trapped beneath his suffocating body. There wasn't much blood—Luca had aimed for the man's eye, the force of the throw would have driven it directly into his brain, and thank God he hadn't lost his touch. Leaping across the weed-choked garden, he grabbed the man's arm and dragged the dead weight off her, and she scrambled away from him, from both of them, struggling to catch her breath.

"You killed him," she said after a long moment, crouching against the railing.

"I did. He was about to snap your neck like a twig." He was waiting for hysteria. He got none.

"My neck isn't like a twig," she said absently in a dazed voice, clearly trying for composure. "I'm accounted to have a beautiful neck."

He could agree with that accounting, though he could see the marks from the man's rough fingers color the pale skin of that beautiful neck, not to mention the beginning bruise on her cheekbone where the man had struck her. If Luca had carried a gun he would have shot the man in the face just . . . just because. "You would have made a lovely corpse," he managed to say wryly.

She struggled to her feet, and he didn't make the mistake of going forward to help her. She was shaky but doing her damnedest to hide it, to hide any sign of weakness from him. Her enemy.

"I gather a friend of yours hired him. Did you have anything to do with it?" she asked, brushing off her ugly dress with careful hands. Damn, he hated those dresses of hers. The sooner he got her out of them the better. And he'd made up his mind. Get her out of them he would.

And then her words sank in. "What friend?" he demanded. "And if I had anything to do with it why would I rescue you? Besides, if I ever decide to kill you I'll do it myself."

"Lovely," she said. She looked up at him. "And if you decide to kill me I'll stop you by any means I can."

He didn't bother to tell her that wasn't humanly possible. If he wanted to kill someone then they were dead. He recognized the man now—a bullyboy who went by the name of Dorrit the Cleaner, and he'd been responsible for a great number of private executions like the one planned for Maddy. The police, as well as some of the best criminals in the country, had tried to defeat Dorrit and failed. The fact that Luca had succeeded was only one of his sudden pleasures at the way things were unfolding.

"What friend?" he said again, impatient.

"Your Mr. Brown. He told me you were lending me to him to work at his family estate, and I told him I didn't want to go."

He gave her a dubious look. "That makes no sense on any level. You're not my property, to lend to other people. And Rufus Brown is a ridiculous, harmless fribble. On top of that, wouldn't that be rather an extreme reaction to someone refusing a job?"

"I asked the man who was trying to kill me if Mr. Brown sent him. He said yes."

He still wasn't convinced. "He might have been lying to you."

"Why? He told me he was going to kill me—what difference would it make?" she argued.

"I have no idea. That's Dorrit the Cleaner, one of our most notorious denizens. He probably never told the truth in his short, misbegotten life."

Maddy looked down at the corpse and shuddered. "None of it makes any sense. Who would want to kill me?"

"Gwendolyn Haviland, for one, though that would be quite a gesture of friendship for Brown to make, considering they only met."

Her brow furrowed. Her color seemed to be returning, though she still seemed a little unsteady. "Why in God's name would your fiancée want me dead?"

He didn't bother informing her he'd sent a note to inform Gwendolyn that she was no longer his affianced. Unspeakably rude, of course, which would make her view her broken engagement with relief. "When you figure it out, let me know."

Maddy was strongly considering throwing up. She had a stomach of cast iron, Nanny Gruen had always told her, and every time her sisters contracted some kind of stomach ailment she'd always proved resistant, but there was a knife sticking out of the man's eye, and apparently there was another corpse nearby, and Luca looked completely undisturbed.

It was no surprise she was shaken, but Maddy wasn't about to let that defeat her. "Did you kill the other man as well?"

"I did," Luca said, apparently unmoved by that fact. "I could have asked him to go away in my nicest voice but he had a knife as well, and I prefer being alive. What's your real name?"

Damn the man! Why was he doing this to her, now, while she was clearly vulnerable? There weren't many times when she needed comfort, but right now she wanted nothing more than Nanny Gruen's arms around her, a warm blanket, and a hot cup of tea.

She'd get none of those things from the captain, and his arms weren't made for comfort. She really couldn't stay here any longer—the masquerade was over, whether she was willing to admit it or not.

She should tell him who she was, she thought, trying to keep from swaying slightly as blood began to pool beneath the dead man at her feet. If Mr. Brown had really sent him to kill her it was more likely that he was the villain, not Luca. He'd saved her life. So why couldn't she melt in gratitude the way she foolishly wanted to? Why couldn't he put his arms around her, damn it?

But how could she say, "I'm Madeleine Russell," and not expect that cool, disdainful rage to turn on her? He killed without hesitation, and he was watching her out of unreadable eyes. No, the man wasn't going to get anything from her. She was going to run, as soon as she could coerce her shaky muscles into obeying.

"My name is Mary Greaves," she said stubbornly. He had moved closer, but there was a clear enough path to dart around him once she got her strength back.

For a moment he said nothing. "So be it," he said flatly. "I'm afraid you can't stay here. I can't keep fighting off marauders, and whoever sent these men won't stop. He'll send more, or come himself."

She lifted her chin, determined not to show her fear. In truth, she'd come to the same conclusion. "How do you know that?"

"That's what I would do."

"Then I'll leave," she said promptly.

"And where will you go, Mary Greaves?" The light mockery in his voice when he said her false name was maddening. She'd go to her grave before she told him the truth, damn it. "Back to Lancashire?" He even mocked her on-again, off-again accent.

"Of course," she said, not even bothering to sound as if she were anyone but Miss Madeleine Russell, toast of the 1868 season. Last year was so long ago.

"You aren't going anywhere except with me. And don't even try to run. It'll be a waste of time and it's growing dark." He turned his back to look up at the night sky.

Arrogant bastard, she thought fiercely, the anger bringing strength back to her limbs. *He was so wrong about that!* "I don't think so," she said sweetly, and before she could think twice she darted to the side, leapt over the corpse with every intention of running down the pathway.

And she would have, if he hadn't suddenly whirled around and caught her midair, so that she landed hard against his body with an "oomph," his hands closing around her arms, and she was trapped once more.

Her feet were off the ground, and he was holding her against him, his dark, gypsy eyes level with hers. "You really are too easy. What's your name?"

"Mary Greaves," she said between clenched teeth. "Put me down."

To her surprise he did, slowly, letting her body slide down his, and some weak, inner creature wanted to moan. She glared at him—right now impassivity was beyond her.

He didn't release his hold on her. "Let go of me," she said. "I think I've had quite enough of being manhandled for one day."

"At least I have no plans to kill you. I think the smartest thing I can do right now is to take you away from here until the police find out what's going on."

"I'm not going anywhere with you," she said affably. "But don't worry—I won't linger. I'll be heading to the coaching inn or the train station."

He laughed. "You don't have any money, my sweet liar. I haven't paid you, and it would be a rare maidservant indeed who had enough to move on."

"I'm a very rare female," she shot back, squirming. She could bring up her knee when he didn't expect it, but she really, really didn't want to do that. Not to him. "Now let me go."

"Let go of such a treasure?" he mocked her. "Not likely. You're coming with me."

"Oh, Jesus Christ, I'm not going to be abducted twice in one day!" she burst out, knowing Nanny Gruen would do more than wash her mouth out for the uncontrolled blasphemy.

Luca laughed, damn him. "I'm afraid you are. I'm taking you on board my new ship and we'll get away from everything for a while. You'll like her—she's the prettiest little clipper ship that ever sailed the oceans."

She had frozen. "No," she said in a choked voice.

"Yes."

"I . . . I can't get on a boat."

"Ship," he corrected.

"I don't give a bloody damn what you call it, I won't get on one. You can't make me."

"You have the most atrocious language for a maidservant, did you know that? And I'm afraid I most certainly can. I'm much bigger and stronger than you, and if I leave you behind someone will kill you. I can't in good conscience allow that to happen."

"You don't have a conscience, good or not," she said wildly. "And you can't make me. I'll scream, I'll tell people you're kidnapping me, I'll do anything I can to stop you."

"I was afraid of that, sweetheart," he said, and he loosened his grip on one arm. "I'm so sorry."

"About what?" she said, just moments before everything went black.

Luca caught her deftly before she landed on top of the big man's corpse. He realized with distant shock that he'd never hit a woman before. He hoisted her up and moved away, cradling her against him. He felt guilty. That was very odd—he wasn't used to remorse. He did what he had to do. Life handed you choices and you made them and you didn't waste your time worrying about it.

He'd had no choice but to clip Maddy Russell across the jaw, or she would have raised enough fuss to get half the people of Devonport down on him. He was tolerated in the dockside community because of his sailing skills and his wealth, but no one really liked a half-gypsy living in a house next to theirs.

He knew how to clock a man, to put them on the deck with a solid hit to the chin. He had to tone it down for a female, even one with as stubborn a jaw as Maddy had, and when she dropped bonelessly he even knew a moment's fear that he had hit her too hard.

But she was breathing easily, her pulse felt strong, and a woman like Maddy Russell could withstand more than a very gentle knockout punch. Besides, he was saving her life, wasn't he?

In the name of expediency he shifted her, tossing her over his shoulder like a sack of grain, and headed back down the walkway. It was almost full dark now, the streetlamps were being lit, and he paused long enough by the body of the first man to borrow his ropes and gag. He had no idea how long Maddy would be out—for the sake of his supposedly nonexistent conscience he hoped not for long—and he needed to get her trussed up enough so that he could get her aboard her namesake without her making a fuss. He needed to sail by the next tide, and he couldn't afford to waste time subduing her.

He took the waiting carriage, simply because it was there, dumping her in the back before he jumped into the driver's seat. There was nothing to tell him who had sent the men—it was a simple coach for hire. The notion that it might be Rufus Brown was absurd, but just to be on the safe side he'd send a note to the police before they set sail, informing them of the dead bodies and suggesting they might question Gwendolyn's "dearest friend." Stranger things had happened.

He drove through the streets of Devonport at a maddeningly slow pace. He was easily recognizable by most of the citizens, both for his height and his clear ancestry, but no one could see how tall he was in the driver's seat of a brougham, and he kept his head down. Besides, he never drove anywhere in the city—no one would expect to see him there.

It was teatime, and the docks were deserted. Maddy was still and silent in the back as he pulled the carriage into the narrow lane near the dockside office of what had once been Russell Shipping.

Carrying her aboard ship was a risk, but he took it, not wanting to wait any longer. People down at the docks knew to mind their own business, particularly the few who were around at this time of day, and he bounded up the walkway with his precious parcel over his shoulder, looking neither right nor left.

Billy was still on deck, watching the stowing of gear, and he didn't even raise an eyebrow at his unexpected return or the bundle over his shoulder. "I take it we're setting sail again?" he said evenly enough.

"Next tide." Luca disappeared down the passageway without another word, carrying her directly to his cabin. She was just beginning to stir, and while no one on his ship would blink if he had a screaming, struggling female on board, he'd just as soon not risk it.

In fact, it was only an assumption that none of the hardened men he sailed with would blink—he'd never had a screaming, struggling female aboard before. Kicking open his door, he dumped her on the berth, then glanced around the cabin. There was nothing she could break, nothing she could hurt herself with. She'd be safe enough, locked in, until they were well out to sea. He locked the door behind him, heading back on deck. Thinking back to her fury the moment before he clipped her, he wondered just how safe he'd be when she came to.

"Pull the gangplank," he said as he came into the cool air.

"All the men aren't back yet. This may be a small ship but you know we'll need men to sail her, even if you're only planning to go as far as France or Spain. You weren't thinking of heading across the Atlantic, were you?"

"If I do we'll pick up more crew. Why are you looking at me like that?"

Billy was smoking a clay pipe, looking so relaxed Luca wanted to hit him as well. Billy shrugged. "So, you've taken to your gypsy ways, have you? Carting off the girl of your fancy when no one else is looking? I knew you were an idiot for the girl, but I didn't think you'd go this far."

"I was never an idiot for her," Luca said, controlling his irritation with an effort. "She's a cheat and liar."

"But a pretty one," Billy pointed out. "She's also an upper-class lady, no matter what her father may or may not have done. What makes you think you can carry her off like this without someone raising a fuss?"

"Such as?"

"Hasn't she got a family?"

"Not close enough to keep proper reins on her. If they knew where she'd been the last few weeks they never would have let her do it."

Billy scratched his head. "Seems to me that she's not a female who's easily stopped, once she sets her mind to something."

Luca finally laughed, some of the tension draining out of him. "You're right about that. And she has a couple of sisters, but one's run off with a man who probably murdered his wife and no one knows where the other one is. Our Maddy Rose hasn't corresponded with anyone since she's been here. It'll be a while before she's missed."

"And what do you intend to do with her? Apart from the usual, that is," Billy added with only the trace of a smirk.

"Maybe you ought to ask me why I brought her here. I don't bring women on my ships, at least not my own women. Not if I can help it," he said, looking out over the inky dark sea as the ship rocked gently on the harbor waters.

"And is she? Your woman, that is? I don't know if I've ever met one before."

"Don't be ridiculous—I've had so many women I've lost count of them," Luca shot back, annoyed and uneasy.

"You've had women, Sonny Jim. They've just never been 'your woman' before. Not even that piece of work you said you were going to marry. What about her?"

"I sent her a note breaking it off, and by now she's rejoicing in her reprieve from marrying an uncivilized gypsy."

"Which brings me back to the question. Why this one? Because of her father? You figure you owe the old man something?"

"I owe him kidnapping his daughter and having my wicked way with her?" Luca drawled. "I don't think he'd be thanking me for that."

"Is that why you're doing it? You wouldn't have to take her anywhere to get it done—I've seen the way she looks at you when she doesn't think anyone will notice."

He hated the fact that that pleased him. He knew full well she was attracted to him, no matter how much she didn't want to be. "I killed two men tonight, Billy."

Billy didn't bat an eye at the change of subject. "Did you have a reason, or was it just spur of the moment?"

Luca managed to laugh at that. "It was Dorrit the Cleaner and some man who hired him. Probably not the man with the money, I expect—he wasn't dressed well enough to afford someone like Dorrit. The man behind all this would have been waiting at home for a report."

"Dorrit the Cleaner? I'm impressed, boy-o. Many the man's tried to take him and lost their lives in the trying. Where did you run across that one?"

"Trying to snap her neck," he said, nodding toward the cabin.

"Hmmph," Billy said, considering this information. "Dorrit don't come cheap. Someone must have really wanted her dead. Got any ideas who it might be?"

"She insists it's Rufus Brown," Luca said.

Billy hooted with laughter. "Did Dorrit tell her that? That's a good one."

Luca frowned. "Yes, but why would Dorrit lie if he was planning to kill her?" he said, repeating Maddy's argument.

"Who knows how a madman thinks?" Billy dismissed him. "Does she know you've figured out who she is?"

Luca leaned over the side of the boat, watching the waves ripple along the surface of the water. "No. She knows I don't believe her. Who would? I'm waiting for her to tell me her name and she's still refusing and I'm not going to do a thing until she decides to trust me enough to tell me the truth."

"That'll keep you busy during the journey," Billy observed wryly. "And would you mind telling me just where we're headed?"

Luca shrugged. "The continent somewhere. The destination is unimportant for now, just getting away from whoever hired Dorrit is what matters. The police will find the bodies and go from there. Even if they know I killed him I'm not likely to be brought up on charges, given Dorrit's reputation. And if they can identify the body of the second man it might give them an idea who sent them in the first place."

"All right. What're you going to do with the girl? You going back in there before we set sail?"

"Not if I can help it. She's all trussed up for now, but she's going to be furious when she wakes up, and I think we need to be well out to sea before I take the gag off."

"Speaking of which, what put her out. Dorrit use chloroform? That's not his lay."

"I hit her."

Billy looked at him in astonishment. "Jayzus," he said with a whistle. "You really must love her."

Luca stalked away.

CHAPTER SEVENTEEN

Rufus sat back, considering the situation. Failure had never been an option. Parsons was dead—an inconvenience and nothing more. No, he'd been very helpful with the police when they'd come to inform him that his man's body had been found in an alley off Water Street. He had no idea what the man had been doing—in fact, he'd dispensed with his services earlier that day for dishonesty. He must have tried something desperate.

No, he'd never mentioned a man named Dorrit. Did he know Captain Morgan—yes, he'd had dinner with him one evening with his dear friend, Miss Haviland, the solicitor's daughter. He was certain Captain Morgan would be just as horrified at the carnage.

Captain Morgan had been a privateer? He'd had no idea! Well, perhaps horrified was too strong a word. And where was Captain Morgan at the moment? They didn't know? Ah well, it didn't matter. He was only curious. No one else was hurt, were they? None of the servants?

Ah, good news that they were all gone from the house. So what did the police suppose the men wanted? To rob the house? No, of course they could only guess.

And certainly he would inform the police if any new information came to his attention. After dismissing Parsons he'd discovered the man's references had been forged. He wished he could help further, and if there was any way he could be of assistance they mustn't hesitate to let him know.

Rufus waited until they left, still reclining in his chair with his cane clutched in one thin hand, looking wan and interesting. He had expressed all the right emotions—sorrow, concern, anger—and the slow-witted police of the dockside town had believed everything. He waited until the door closed behind them, sitting very still as he felt the rage sweep through him. That fury was a pure, powerful entity of its own, and it made him strong, stronger than mortal men. He was coming to realize he had a gift, a task to complete, a holy calling if you like, and each setback only made the eventual triumph sweeter.

He pushed out of the chair, and his weak leg faltered for a moment, then he straightened it. Nothing would hold him back, not the temporary frailty of his too-human body, not the stupidity of his hirelings, nor the bunglings of the police. And that a gypsy half-breed would dare to interfere . . .

Again the rage washed over him, filling him with power. He had no choice then. He would take care of it himself. First he would find out where she was, but he had little doubt she was with that Rom bastard. And he would kill them both if it was the last thing he did.

But it wouldn't be. He still had the youngest, and he had complete faith in his own invincibility. He was on a mission, and lesser warriors had fallen along the way. He would finally have a chance to finish with the elder one as well—he couldn't afford to leave anything to chance. And then Rufus Brown could safely disappear, and Rufus Griffiths could re-emerge, full of charm and conviviality. He would prevail, and all would fall before him.

They sailed with the midnight tide. Navigating the crowded harbor of Devonport was no easy task, but Billy could do it blindfolded, and

Luca could hear pounding from down below, pounding he expected came from his unwilling guest. "I'll leave you then," Luca told his old friend. "It appears someone wants to see me. Come get me if I'm needed."

Billy chuckled. "The day I can't handle a ship like this is the day I give up the sea. Go see if you can calm the girl."

Luca slid down the companionway as he heard the voices overhead, the men calling back and forth to each other as sails were unfurled and the boat rocked on its mooring with the weight of the anchor being pulled. The pounding from his cabin was thunderous, the walls shaking, and he wondered what she was using. He unlocked the door, carefully, in case she'd managed to get free of her bonds, but she was still on the bunk, gagged and trussed, slamming her feet against the wall in impotent fury.

He'd brought a lamp with him, and he turned it up before setting it onto its hook so it could swing freely with the rocking of the ship. She'd stopped kicking moments after she heard him come in, and as he approached the berth she somehow managed to squirm around and launch herself at him in frantic rage. He staggered back for a moment, catching her, and set her squirming, thrashing body back on the mattress. Her eyes were wild, and she tried to scratch him with her bound hands, but he kept out of the way of those fingernails, holding her down against the bed.

It was then he realized it wasn't anger in her dark blue eyes, it was terror. Her body was shaking with it, and her desperate struggles were born of fear, not justifiable outrage. Maddy, who wasn't afraid of anything, not hired killers or pirate captains or vicious society women like his erstwhile fiancée. No, she was afraid of bats, but the only bats aboard his ship would be down in the hold along with the rats and whatever cargo Billy had managed to pick up.

He glanced around the ceiling, looking for intruders. "There are no bats here, my sweet," he said calmly.

She shook her head, so fiercely he worried that she might hurt herself.

"I'm going to regret this," he said with a sigh, reaching for her gag. "If you start screaming I'll simply gag you again. So behave yourself." He slipped the gag free from her mouth, and he could see it took all her formidable strength to keep from shrieking.

"I have to get off this boat," she managed to choke out after a long, desperate struggle. Her voice was raspy, maybe from muffled screams; he could clearly see the fear coursing through her.

"Ship," he corrected absently. "And you're not going anywhere."

"You don't understand. I can't be on a boat . . . ship. I can't be on water."

"Don't be ridiculous. This ship is as solid as any I've ever sailed on. There's no danger."

"I can't," she repeated breathlessly. "Please. I'll do anything. Just get me off this thing."

He looked down at her. "Tell me your name and I'll consider it." It was cruel of him, particularly since he was looking at the bruise on her chin. His blow actually hadn't left that much of a mark—Dorrit's backhand across her face was a much more telling bruise, as were the places where his fingers had pressed into her neck. Her beautiful, non-twiglike neck, he reminded himself with distant amusement.

She was glaring at him with absolute hatred, something that might disturb him if he didn't understand what lay beneath it far better than she did. "Mary Greaves," she spat. "Now let me go or I'll have the police after you."

The ship lurched, then smoothed out, and he knew by the feel of it that they'd left the harbor. Any experienced sailor would recognize the signs, but the daughter of Russell Shipping had never been on a ship before, a fact that astonished him. He couldn't very well task her with it, though, without giving away that he already knew her name.

"I'm afraid the police are most likely busy trying to solve the death of Mr. Dorrit and his accomplice to worry about you. If they'd found your body it would be a different matter, but I did, in fact, rescue you. Saved your life, and I have yet to hear a word of thanks from your dulcet voice."

"If you don't let me off this boat you'll hear screaming from this dulcet voice."

"If you start screaming I'll throw you overboard."

"Fine," she snapped. "I'll swim to shore."

He shook his head. "I'd say we're too far out by now, and the night wind is picking up. Even a strong swimmer would have a hard time against the tides, and you'd be encumbered by all those clothes. If you tried it naked you'd probably freeze to death in ten minutes—the waters are cold off Plymouth this time of year. I'd say you're not going anywhere but where the ship—not boat—takes us, at least for the time being."

She grew very still, her eyes impossibly wide and her entire body vibrating with fear. "We've set sail?" Her voice was little more than a croak.

"We've set sail," he verified. "Someone was intent on killing you back there, either Rufus Brown or someone else, and the only way to make certain you're safe is to take you out of the reach of casual marauders. Why don't you like to sail?"

"I *don't* sail," she corrected him fiercely. "I know I'm going to drown. I nearly did when I was a child and the little dinghy my father gave us capsized, trapping me underneath. I haven't been in a boat since, and I don't intend to . . ."

"This has nothing to do with your intentions, my sweet, it was decided for you. And I'm not going to let anything happen to you or this ship." Her fear made no sense to him, but he knew it was nothing she could be reasoned out of.

She was trapped, and she knew it, and he watched in fascination as she exerted sheer will over her trembling body. The shaking slowly ceased, and she turned her back on him, her hands and ankles still trussed with the ropes from Dorrit's companion. "I'm going to throw up," she muttered.

It was a possibility, but she was showing no signs of mal de mer, just impotent fury. "I'll bring you a basin," he replied. "Do I dare untie you, or will you try to strangle me with your ropes?"

"I'll kill you the first chance I get," she said grimly, and he wanted to laugh. That would have been a grave mistake—she was holding on to her self-possession with the desperate grip of a drowning woman, and it wasn't wise to anger her further.

"Then I'll leave you as you are. Try to sleep—it's a long time until morning. I'll bring you something to eat when I come to bed and I'll untie you then. You're less likely to get seasick if you have a little in your stomach."

That was enough to make her flounce around again, staring at him with new horror. "You're not sleeping here." It was a statement, not a question.

"It's my cabin," he said mildly. "Where else would I sleep?"

"Not with me!"

"Your chastity is safe," he said, and saw the flush mount to her cheeks briefly. So the rumors were true and she had given herself to her faithless lover. So much the better. He didn't have to worry about hurting her—all he had to do was give her pleasure, and he was very good at giving pleasure. "Tell me your name and I'll untie you and give you your own cabin."

She didn't even hesitate. "Mary Greaves."

In that case, she'd literally made her own bed for the night. He was simply going to have to up the stakes.

He locked the door behind him as he headed for the galley. The sea was smooth, just a light wind filling the sails as they headed south toward France, and he reveled in the rightness of it. Billy was out of his mind, talking about love, for God's sake. Luca knew nothing of love, and he preferred it that way. Women were for pleasure, not for a lifetime, not for a wanderer like he was. A woman terrified of setting foot on the deck of a ship with a man who couldn't breathe when he wasn't near the water was no possible match . . .

Not that he was thinking of matches. He simply needed her to admit to who she was. He needed that sign of trust from her, and until he had it he wasn't giving her a thing. Once she told him then maybe he'd drop her off somewhere safe with enough money to get her home again. After all, Russell had been good to him up until almost the very end, and he owed him the safety of his daughter. She was just an annoyance to deal with and then dispose of. If he managed to get between her legs before that, so much the better, but in the end it didn't matter. One woman was the same as the next.

He slammed his fist into the wood planked wall in sudden frustration. Who the hell was he trying to fool? Himself? That was an idiot's trick. He could lie to anyone, deny anything, but when he couldn't face his own truth it was time to worry.

So Billy knew him well enough to be partly right. He was a bit too . . . interested in Maddy Russell. In fact, he was almost obsessed with her. During the trip back from London she was all he could think of, her stubborn mouth, her fierce eyes, the soft, lovely curves of her body beneath all those ugly layers. So he wanted her. There was nothing wrong with that—she was a beautiful woman. He should be more disturbed if he didn't want her.

Except. He couldn't picture being without her. Before he slept with a woman he always had an exit strategy. He knew the ones who could be bought off with jewels, the ones who needed to be convinced they were too good for him, as in Gwendolyn's case. Of course, he hadn't even managed to bed his fiancée, mainly because he'd never really wanted to. She was a classic blond beauty, and she'd always left him cold. At least she'd now consider herself well-rid of such a ruffian, and it hadn't cost him a thing.

He had no idea what Maddy's price would be, any more than he could imagine sending her away. It was simply because he hadn't had her yet, he told himself. The longer the anticipation, the greater the reward. A week or so in the confines of his quarters and he'd grow tired of her very quickly.

She'd probably make the fool mistake of thinking she was in love with him. Women were like that—they didn't know how to enjoy their bodies just for the fun of it, and in order to assuage their consciences they had to tell themselves they were "in love."

He didn't believe in it, at least, not for him. He'd seen it occasionally, and always wondered at its strength and elasticity. No matter how far Billy roamed, Duncan was always waiting for him. Russell had mourned his wife for his entire widowhood, and Luca's gypsy grandmother and grandfather had seemed blissfully happy.

But love wasn't for anyone like him. He was a gyppo half-breed, and there were many doors closed to him, many societies shut off. He didn't mind the troubles he'd gone through, but he'd be damned if he'd submit his wife or his children to that kind of vicious, casual cruelty.

And God, what was he doing thinking about marriage? Another ridiculous supposition. Except that he'd stolen her from her house, even if it was technically his, just as his family had done for centuries, and she lay in his bed now, mutinous and angry and just ready for him to walk over and change her mind.

He should tell Billy to turn the ship northeast, sail up to Victoria Dock in London, and dump her there. She was possibly the most dangerous female he'd ever met—the most dangerous to his piece of mind, to his carefully ordered way of life. His gypsy blood had nothing to do with his life, except to mark him as one of the unwanted. So why couldn't he stop thinking that he'd ended up stealing his bride after all?

The galley was deserted, and Luca began searching through the stores for food for Maddy. She'd probably throw the tray at his head, but it was worth a try.

"What are you doing?" Billy appeared in the entryway. "Mooning over the lass?"

Luca made an extremely rude suggestion. "Why are you down here?"

"I'm looking for you. I left Jeffries at the helm—he'll be good enough for the time being."

Luca leaned back against the wooden table that was bolted to the deck. "What do you want? If you feel like punching me it might be a good idea. Might knock some sense into me."

"Ah, don't tempt me." Billy grinned. "Your romantic troubles aren't at the forefront of my worries right now. There's a storm brewing."

"I saw no sign of it."

"You're too busy thinking with your John Thomas instead of your brain. It's a few days out, and I'm thinking we can avoid it if we head west for a bit."

"Do what you have to do." Billy had always had a sixth sense about the weather, something Luca envied. Then again, he always knew trouble when it was on the horizon, giving them the choice to dive in or avoid a brawl. So why hadn't he recognized trouble in the form of Madeleine Russell?

Ah, but he had. And he'd ignored it.

"What's that you got there?" Billy demanded. "Bread, cheese, wine? You thinking food will do it? I thought she had a problem with sailing. You don't want to waste good food on a tricky stomach."

"It's not her stomach that's the problem, it's her mind."

"I could have told you that," Billy shot back.

Luca managed a reluctant grin. "She's afraid of sailing."

"Russell's daughter?" Billy didn't bother to hide his amazement. "Is she a changeling or what? I heard she used to hang around his office all the time and visit the docks with him."

"She did. She just never got on a ship."

"Well, you're already broadening her horizons," Billy said with a heartless laugh. "Give her enough of that wine and you'll broaden them some more."

"Go to hell, Billy. I'm sending in one of the cooks. Maddy would probably try to kill me."

"Maddy, is it now?" Billy shook his head. "Well, who can blame the girl if she wants you dead? Many's the time even I wanted you dead. You need to forget about her. Come on out on deck and I'll see if I can finally teach you the signs."

"There aren't any signs, Billy," Luca growled. "You've got a fortune-teller's magic powers when it comes to weather, and if I haven't learned in fifteen years I'm not going to start now."

"Just get it over with and you can get your mind back on business."

"I'll get it over with when I can dump her on solid land, as far away from Plymouth and all its ports as I can get." He picked up the tray from the table and started past Billy. "Get around that storm and get us somewhere safe."

"Aye aye, cap'n," Billy said, grinning.

Maddy hurt. Everything in her body hurt—the ropes around her wrists weren't tight enough to cause pain but she'd struggled so long she had rope burns. Her feet ached from kicking the wall, her neck felt as if someone had crushed it, and her throat was raw from screaming behind the gag. At least he'd left her alone in here, but it was a mixed blessing. It gave her too much time to think.

Her face was tender, her chin hurt, and she couldn't remember why. The stranger had knocked her across the face—that explained her painful cheekbone, but why did her jaw . . . ?

He'd hit her! That goddamned, bloody, no good whoreson of a bastard had hit her, knocking her unconscious so he could carry her off. For a moment she bordered on apoplectic rage. It was one thing when a hired killer slapped you—that was at least expected. But when the man who rescued you socked you then enough was enough. She was going to kill him.

On top of that colossal insult he'd brought her onboard a ship, refusing to release her despite her pleas, and the gentle rise and fall of the deck beneath them was still sending shards of terror through her.

She only wished she were seasick, so she could spew all over Luca when he came back. Unfortunately her stomach wasn't responding to the power of suggestion; even conjuring up the vision of the dead man with the knife in his eye couldn't make her stomach lurch.

All right, she was trapped, at least for the moment, and she seemed to have survived her first few hours on the ocean. If she wasn't going to die then her next step was to ensure Luca wished he would. She struggled once more with the ropes around her wrists, but even using her teeth to try to untie them hadn't done any good, and they were beginning to bleed. She sank back, panting. Damn him, damn him, damn him.

He expected her to thank him for saving her life? He was going to have a good long wait for that impossibility. He wanted her to tell him who she was? She'd be burned at the stake before she gave in. Revenge was a dish best served cold. It didn't matter if it seemed as if Luca hadn't had anything to do with her father's death, he'd done enough to her to earn her lifetime enmity. She'd find a way to repay him for hitting her and then dragging her on board this ship. She'd make him rue the day he met her.

Though in truth he probably already did, she thought, sinking back on the bunk, trying to relax her tense muscles. But if there were any room for doubt she'd take care of it. Luca was going to be very sorry indeed.

Luca was bloody tired. They were five hours out from Devonport and Plymouth, there'd been no thumping from the cabin, but he couldn't bring himself to go back down there. It had nothing to do with the fact that she'd bitten the cook's assistant when he'd tried to feed her. Nothing to do with the fact that his entire crew was going to think it extremely odd that he had a woman locked in his cabin and he wasn't doing a thing about it.

In fact, he wasn't sure what was stopping him at that point. They'd been out at sea long enough that she would have had to make peace with the fact. In fact, if she were going to be prey to seasickness it would have started by now, and she might be lying in his bunk, covered in her own vomit.

Which gave him a good excuse to go down there, and a good way to tone down his hunger for her. Nothing like a little seasickness to dowse the flame, he thought cynically. If she tried to bite him he could always gag her again, but he'd taken the rag off her face for a reason. If she did cast up her accounts she would choke to death with a gag covering her mouth.

So he'd deal with her fury and her teeth. In fact, the idea of her biting him was unexpectedly arousing, though he didn't think the cook's lad had thought so. He'd reported she was a rabid dog who ought to be tossed overboard, and Billy had seconded the notion, just to cause trouble.

Luca was tired, and he wanted to sleep. Which was ridiculous—he could go days without sleep, and had, often enough, when the weather was bad. If he was really tired he could go bunk in Billy's cabin while his old friend manned the helm, and to hell with what the sailors said. No, he had only one reason to go back to his cabin. Because he wanted to see her.

The sun was just beginning to appear on the distant horizon, the bright, pinky-red glow verifying Billy's concerns. Red skies at night, sailor's delight, red skies at morning, sailors take warning. The sky was blood-red in the east, and a storm was brewing. If Maddy wasn't frightened of sailing before, this would probably put the fear of God into her.

He'd never made an unwanted sound in the last twenty years of his life, and the key turned silently in the lock as he let himself into his cabin. The predawn light was filling the place with a rosy glow that would have been pretty if he hadn't known what was coming. She lay curled up on the berth, her bound hands in front of her, her long hair loose and tangled. She was sound asleep, and she looked like a slightly battered angel, with her bruised face and her thick eyelashes against her creamy skin. She wasn't an exquisitely pale English beauty like Gwendolyn—there was fire in her, warmth to her skin, flames in her heart. She'd probably stab him the first chance she got. His kind of woman.

He walked to the edge of the bed. "Move over," he said.

She jerked, startled awake, and opened her eyes, staring up at him dazedly. And then her gaze sharpened.

It was all the warning he needed. Before she could move he was on the bunk, wrapping his arms around her body, rolling onto his side so that she lay between him and the wall. It took surprisingly little effort to keep her contained—her struggles weakened and then stopped, and she rested her head against his shoulder, breathing heavily.

He didn't move, didn't loosen the encompassing circle of his arms, not trusting her, but as the minutes passed and her breathing deepened once more, her body flowing against his, he realized she had actually fallen back asleep. He started to release her, slowly in case she'd managed to trick him, but instead she made a sound that was a cross between a moan and a purr, snuggling closer.

In the shadowy light he rolled his eyes at the entire ridiculousness of the situation. He was her worst enemy, or so she believed, and she was curling up against him like a kitten. He wondered what would happen if he licked her.

Christ! He was already hard as a rock, just lying up close against her; he didn't have to make it worse by envisioning all the things he'd like to do with his tongue. He let his chin rest on top of her head. It was surprisingly comfortable. He never slept with a woman in his arms—if they shared a bed for a night they kept to their own sides when they weren't busy. For some reason Maddy just seemed to fit against him, around him, perfectly.

He closed his eyes. He'd never been a fool, and he recognized the signs. So had everyone else, apparently. He wasn't going to dump the lying, treacherous, devious Madeleine Rose Russell off at the nearest port. He wasn't going to let go of her ever again.

The problem would be to convince her, but at least when she was mostly asleep she trusted him. That was a good enough beginning. He slid his hand up her back, urging her closer, and she came to him, sweet and warm, as the ship rocked beneath them, and he fell asleep in the arms of the ocean and the woman he loved.

CHAPTER EIGHTEEN

MADDY HADN'T FELT THIS safe in years. Maybe ever. She was warm, protected, loved, and she refused to surface from the drugging depths of sleep to examine why. It felt too good to examine—all she wanted to do was experience it. She couldn't see anything—it was pitch black wherever she was, and she knew she wasn't alone. She took a deep breath and recognized the intoxicating scent of his skin, the feel of his arms around her, the steady beat of his heart beneath her ear.

She waited for the familiar rage to fill her, empower her. She waited for anger, so that she could take him unaware, shove him off the bed, bring her knees up first. All those thoughts flitted through her brain like the shreds of clouds disappearing in the wake of a storm. She was so tired of being angry, and if felt so good lying in his arms. Even the gentle, almost imperceptible rock of the ocean was a benison, comforting her like a mother's arms.

She hadn't mourned her father—she'd responded with fury, first at him, then at whoever had destroyed him. Her anger had extended to everyone around her, until she was consumed by it, and there was nothing left but a hard, cold cinder of regret. She didn't want to be that cinder. She wanted to be a woman, whole and lush and alive, not lost in a cyclone of anger and death. She wanted to be a woman in the arms of a man, a man who held her gently and kissed her hard. She wanted to be in Luca's arms, right where she was, and it was too late for her. She had made her choices, and now she would pay for them. Once he knew who she was he would hate her.

Her face felt wet, and she realized to her horror that she was crying. Tears were for private moments, when no one could see or hear her, not even her sisters. She had to stop this, immediately. She couldn't show weakness, she couldn't feel weakness, tenderness, longing. She tried to move her hands, to wipe the tears away, but her wrists were still bound and trapped between their bodies, and the knowledge only made her cry more. In the darkness she knew that Luca was wearing only a light linen shirt, and if she didn't stop the tears would soak through. She could bite him, tell him she drooled in her sleep, and she tried one more time to summon up her constant companion, vengeful fury. There was none to spare.

Very well. He might not notice the dampness—after all, how much water did tears make? As long as she was very silent it would pass soon enough. It always did. These bouts of tears didn't last long, and when it was done perhaps she might reclaim her anger. This was just a way to release the treacherous, weakening sorrow so that she might fight again.

She couldn't be angry with him for her father's sake, but hitting her, kidnapping her, forcing her on board a ship was more than enough reason on her own.

But then, if he hadn't, there would be no saving her life, kissing her like a fallen angel, holding her while she slept. How could she hate him?

To her horror her breath hiccupped, just a small, infinitesimal hitch in her breathing. She had cried much more forcefully than this after Tarkington had fallen into a heavy stupor, and he hadn't stirred. Luca would never notice . . .

His hand brushed her cheek, so gently, taking the tears with him, and she waited for her body to freeze, in anger or in fear. Instead she turned her face into his hand, rubbing against it, as the tears kept flowing.

He pulled her closer, then seemed to realize her bound hands were still between them. Without a word he reached down and untied them, in a quick, skillful act that should have infuriated her. All her struggles, even using her teeth, had availed her nothing, and yet a few twists with his clever hands in the darkness and she was free.

Her wrists stung from the abrasions of the rope, and she tried to concentrate on that, but as she lifted her hands to shove him away she found that his arms had slid around her. She was pressed up against him, and now she was sobbing, her entire body shaking with the fury of her grief, for her father, for her sisters, for her lost innocence and hope. And for the man in whose arms she lay, the one she could never have, the one it seemed she had always wanted.

He held her, tightly, letting her weep. His hand rubbed her back, a soothing, gentle gesture, and through her sobs she could hear his soft voice, hear the gentle, comforting murmur of words she didn't understand, didn't need to understand. He wasn't telling her to stop crying, to calm down. He was giving her the freedom to grieve, to mourn, telling her she could let go and he would be there to catch her.

But even she couldn't cry forever, no matter how many tears she had stored up. Eventually they slowed as he held her, stroked her, and then there was nothing but the occasional dry hiccup as she hid her face against his soaked shoulder. And yes, there was a surprising amount of water in tears, she thought, moving her hand to grasp the wet linen.

She'd hoped for anger to follow even such a storm of weeping, but there was nothing but a peaceful exhaustion. She couldn't fight, didn't want to fight, no matter how much he deserved it.

"I've drenched you," she whispered in a raw, resigned voice.

He pushed her hair away from her face. That was wet too—it felt like everything was covered in her tears. "So you have, *monisha.* Lie back for a moment."

She did as he said without question, and felt him sit up and move in the darkness. And then he slid down beside her again, and she realized without shock that he'd removed the damp shirt, and he was using it to dry her own tears and strands of hair, imprinting the scent of him on her. He tossed it to the floor and pulled her back into his arms, back against the shock of his warm, hard chest, her face up against his skin, and she closed her eyes, breathing him in, wanting to inhale him, take everything inside of her. She couldn't fight anymore.

Why him? Why now? She needed a title and a fortune to restore the House of Russell. Running off with a gypsy would be a considered an even greater breach of society than her father's so-called crimes, at least by some people.

And why should she suppose he'd want anything from her? Oh, he wanted what Tarkington had wanted—that much was clear. In truth, she hadn't met many men who didn't want her in their beds, with the exception of Mr. Quarrells and his singular taste. And Mr. Brown. There was something about Mr. Brown, something important, but she was so tired and worn out from crying that she couldn't remember, didn't want to remember.

She would tell Luca her real name, and he would hate her. That would simplify everything. He would pull away, leave her, and she could curl up into a ball and not think about anything for a while.

His long fingers were stroking her face, very gently touching the painful bruises. "I wanted to kill the man when he hit you," he said in a low voice, "and then I had no choice but to do the same thing. I'm sorry, love." She felt his lips brush against her cheek, and her jaw, and she wanted to weep again.

She tried to speak, but the words caught in her throat for a moment, as his lips brushed against hers, softly, back and forth. She caught his shoulders in her hands, and he felt so strong, so alive, that she wanted to pretend it was another time, another place. But she couldn't.

"Ask me my name again," she said in a hoarse voice. This time she would tell him. This time it would end it.

He brushed his mouth against her eyelids. But he didn't ask her the question. "Do you know what ship we're on?"

She should have felt irritation, but even that was denied her in her weary acceptance. "I don't care. Ask me my name."

"We're on the *Maddy Rose*," he said, and before she could react his mouth covered hers.

This was different than the other kisses. There had always been an element of control, of command, the other times he'd kissed her, a command she'd responded to despite her better judgment. This kiss was gentle, wooing, teasing her mouth into opening beneath him, teasing her tongue into a shy response. This was the kiss of a lover, not an enemy, and she had nothing left to fight him with.

She no longer had the protection of a corset—he'd already destroyed that, and someone, probably Luca, had loosened her clothes, so that the bodice was open against the cool night air, and the hand that had brushed her face was now cradling it, his fingers gentle on her bruised neck, splaying across her shoulder and pushing the fabric out of the way.

She wanted it gone. She wanted to be skin to skin with him, she was willing to pay the price and have him inside her if she could give him that pleasure and hold him afterwards. It was an intoxicating feeling, and she wanted it with him.

"How long have you known?" she said, trying to keep her voice steady as his fingers moved down the front of her bodice, unhooking button after button. She felt like a fool, thinking she'd been so clever, but his hands, his mouth kept distracting her.

"From the first day." His mouth followed, kissing the tops of her breasts.

"No."

"Yes," he said. "I saw you when you christened this ship. It was five years ago but I remembered."

She closed her eyes. "I thought . . . I thought . . ."

"You thought I'd killed your father," he said, not sounding offended. "I'm guessing you were convinced I somehow managed to embezzle the assets of Russell Shipping and then lure your father to his doom. I didn't, you know. I was a pirate, not a bookkeeper."

"I know," she said miserably, her voice quiet. "But we found a note from my father. It said 'never trust a pirate.' "

"Well, that's obvious enough. And your father came to see me just before he died, accusing me of all sorts of crazy things, and I'd done nothing. I thought I managed to convince him, but he died that night after he left me."

Maddy tried to stifle the ever-present pain at the memory of her father's death. "I'm so stupid," she said miserably.

"For infiltrating my house and trying such a thing? Yes," he said equably. "For the way you carried it off? Not at all. You just picked the wrong man."

Those words were like a death knell, whether he realized it or not. She had picked the wrong man. A Traveler, a sailor, a man who never settled down when she needed permanence so badly. A man not made for the kind of commitment she needed, a man who hadn't picked her. She'd simply thrust herself upon him.

"Lift your hips, Maddy," he whispered. "I have to get this damned dress off of you."

Her name sounded so right in his voice. She could have argued, but she didn't, lifting her hips as he tugged the voluminous dress over her head and tossed it somewhere in the darkened cabin, then unfastened her petticoats and tossed them as well, leaving her in her shift and drawers. His hand moved down her side, not touching her breast, to end up holding one hip with a possessive gesture, kneading it gently. But he didn't pull up the thin fabric and untie her drawers. He just held her.

"Why did you stop?" she asked finally. Maybe he'd thought better of it. Maybe Tarkington had left because she was so unsatisfactory, maybe Luca didn't want her either, maybe she was . . .

"This has been inevitable from the first time I kissed you, and we both know it. I need you to show me. I need you to finish taking off your clothes."

A dance of icy fear raced across her skin. He was asking for everything. This way she couldn't pretend the wicked gypsy was seducing her and it was out of her control. This way she had to own it.

What would he do if she refused? Would he then cajole and seduce her? Would he tear off her remaining clothes in a frenzy of lust? Or would he leave her?

"I need you to show me," he'd said. It was the one honest thing she could do, after so many lies. She moved back, away from him, and he didn't move, didn't try to pull her back. She sat up, and yanked the shift over her head, then sent it sailing into the darkness. It felt strange, her breasts free in the night air, even if it was too dark to see, and then she reached for the tapes to her drawers and untied them, shimmying out of them so that she lay beside him in the bunk, absolutely naked with a man for the first time in her life.

She heard his deep, fierce intake of breath. "Your turn," he said.

"I already took the rest of my clothes off."

"I mean it's your turn to undress me."

Oh, bloody hell, she thought, suddenly panic-stricken. "I . . . I can't."

She'd been afraid of anger. Instead he laughed softly. "Of course you can. You can build up to it." He caught her hand and brought it to his, palm to palm, *like holy palmer's touch*, Maddy thought, suddenly remembering her Shakespeare. But they were no Romeo and Juliet and she refused to end in tragedy.

His hand was so much bigger than hers. His fingers were long, elegant, and his warm palm enveloped hers. Bringing her hand to his chest, he let it rest against him. She could feel the delineation of his muscles beneath the taut firmness of his skin. It would be honey gold, she knew, and the thought made her want to run her fingers over him, feel the tough, tensile strength of him. He lay back, letting her explore, and eventually her fingers slid down to the flatness of his stomach, the hollow of his navel, and the first faint touch of hair leading down into his breeches. She started to draw her hand back in sudden shyness when he caught it, pulling it downward to the row of buttons. He didn't bother with them, instead he cupped her hand around the insistent ridge of flesh behind those buttons, holding her there when she tried to pull away.

He was big. And she was ready to change her mind. "Nothing's inevitable," she said in a panicked voice, and he released her hand, letting her roll back to her side of the bunk.

She expected anger. "Chicken," he taunted her. "Here I thought you were afraid of nothing, and now I find out a simple body part has you cowering in terror."

He was manipulating her, they both knew it, but she rose to the bait anyway, because that was who she was. "It's not my body part," she said in a stiff voice.

"Oh, yes, it is. I'm not going to hurt you, Maddy. You know that."

She wanted to touch him. She wanted him to wrap his arms around her again. She was cold, so cold, even though the cabin was surprisingly warm. She needed his heat. She said nothing, not moving, and he turned to her, putting his mouth against her temple, moving it down her bruised cheek to her ear. "Put your hands on me, love." It was a soft request, not a command, but she wasn't quite sure she could do it. Instead she reached up and put her hand in his again, silently asking him. His fingers entwined with hers for a moment, and she felt the last of her nervousness, the last of her doubts leave, as he moved it to rest lightly against his erection.

This time she didn't jerk away. She let her fingers trace the outline beneath his rough cotton trousers, the breadth, the length of it, straining against the buttons. He was right, there was nothing to be afraid of. It was just a body part. Just a body part that would push inside her and hurt her, but then he would be happy and she could hold him.

She slid her fingers down, cupping him, and he made a low, growling sound of pleasure. She liked that. She moved closer, letting her head rest on his flat stomach so she could experiment, brushing against the top, sliding down the length of him. She could feel tension running through him now, and she knew he was going to take her at any moment, but she let herself drift, slipping her fingers inside the placket of the trousers to the tiny buttons. The fabric was taut against his erection, and unfastening the first button was more difficult than she expected. But she wanted to touch him, touch that part of him without the barrier of rough cloth in the way. And he seemed to want her to.

There were seven buttons, and she undid them, one after another, moving upward as he seemed to grow even bigger against her hand. The last button, the top one, defeated her.

She loved the inky darkness, the safety of it. It was as if they were both blind—they could feel each other but they could see nothing, and if it couldn't be seen then maybe it hadn't happened. He reached down and unfastened the last button, freeing himself.

This time she didn't hesitate. She put her hand on him, tentatively, and then drew back, surprised. It was the oddest sensation, the skin so velvety soft encasing something that seemed hard as iron. This wasn't what she remembered at all. She let her fingers move down, tracing the thick veins that ran along his cock, up to touch the flanged head of it. He was damp, there, and she realized suddenly that she was damp as well. Was it supposed to be like that?

She remembered what she was supposed to do. She encircled his cock with her fingers, sliding up and down, but to her surprise this time he drew her hand away. "Wasn't I doing it right?" she asked, nervous.

His voice was low and delicious in the darkness. "I'm already about to explode, love. Too much of that and you'll be very disappointed."

Disappointed by what? She didn't ask the question out loud, though, instead saying, "Then you don't want me to put my mouth on you?"

There was a long silence. And then he swore. "Do you want to?"

"No."

"You don't have to do anything you don't want to do. If you want to get out of this bed and get dressed, you can do that. I don't force women."

"You don't have to." There was no disguising the trace of resentment in her voice. She didn't want to think of all the women he'd had, all the women falling at his feet. As she was.

He laughed then. "If I had to force them then it wouldn't be any fun."

"Fun?" she echoed. "That's a strange term for it. I can't think of anything less like fun in the world."

"Then why are you here in my bed?"

"Because you dumped me here, tied up."

"So I did. Why did you take off your clothes when I asked you?"

For a moment she couldn't answer. But it was dark, and safe, and he was warm and strong and near. "Because I want you." It was only half the truth. She wanted him on so many levels she refused to think about it. But she would take what she could get.

"That's convenient, because I want you too. I've been burning for you, for days, weeks. Waiting for you."

"Waiting for me to do what?"

"To stop hating me for something I didn't do."

"I don't . . ." But he stopped her words, putting his fingers against her lips.

"You don't need to explain. I think we've put this off long enough."

It was time. She steeled herself. "All right," she said, and flopped back on the mattress, waiting.

Again he didn't move. And then she felt him lift up, move over her in the darkness, holding himself above her. "What are you doing?"

She'd made another mistake, she thought, some of the warmth that was filling her beginning to fade. "Getting in position. You said you were ready to take me, didn't you?"

"I'm not going to take you, Maddy. We're going to make love. And you're going to like it."

She could see his eyes even in the darkness, the intensity in them as he looked down at her. "I should warn you," she said. "I'm not a virgin."

He brushed his mouth against hers. "Neither am I." And before she knew what he planned he slid down her body, his mouth brushing against the curls between her legs.

"What are you doing?" she shrieked in real panic now.

"Making love to you. Whoever did it before didn't do a very good job. I'm going to do it right." And he put his mouth between her legs, holding her thighs apart.

Heat and shame washed over her. This was a horrible idea, what did he think he was . . . oh, my. A curl of sweet sensation seemed to spark from where his tongue was, and she found she was clutching the sheet beneath her, as he licked all her secret places, using his tongue to devastating effect before he touched her with his teeth, just the hint of a bite at the very moment he slid one long finger inside her, and she had to slam her hands over her mouth to keep from shrieking. The sensation was strange, frightening, and she wanted to beg him to stop.

"I don't like this," she said in a rattled voice, as stray shivers of reaction kept dancing across her body, a reaction she couldn't bring back under her iron control.

"Yes, you do," he said. "You're just not used to it." And he slid two fingers inside her as he put his mouth back down.

Her skin was burning up, a million pinpoints of tiny shocks, building, building, and she wanted to fight him, stop him, wanted to beg him to keep going. She wasn't sure what she wanted, but then he used his teeth again, moved his fingers inside her, pressing against the wall of her sex, and the ability to think shattered, along with her body. Even with her hands across her mouth she couldn't control her low, keening wail, or the way her body arched up against him as he pumped his fingers into her. When she fell back she was dazed, breathless, shocked beyond belief, and he slid back up her body, covering her in the darkness, heat blazing off him.

"What the hell was that?" she questioned weakly.

"I made you come. I'm going to do it again." He leaned down and casually licked the tight bud of her breast. It almost hurt. Almost, and she remembered him sucking at her, holding her. It was clear she knew absolutely nothing about this matter of making love, that it could feel so shocking, so life-altering, so . . . wonderful.

"Of course, we haven't gotten to the worst part yet," she muttered out loud, then could have slapped herself. He'd taken all her natural caution and ripped it away from her. God knew what she'd say next. Tell him that she loved him?

Because she didn't love him. Couldn't love him. She was going to marry an aristocrat and provide for her family. She had loved Tarkington and where had it gotten her?

She could sense his laughter in the darkness. "The worst part?" he echoed. "I wouldn't call it that."

"Well, it isn't," she said in a practical voice. "Not for you."

"I hate to bring someone else into our bed, Maddy, but exactly how many times have you done this before?" he asked gently.

"Once." Her voice left little doubt that she'd thought once was enough. And yet here she was, back again, so awash in sensation that she could barely speak.

"Then I've got just a little more experience. I'm very good at this, Maddy. Trust me."

She could feel him now, the blunt head of his cock at her entrance, and she started to brace herself for the assault, when he moved his mouth to her ear. "Breathe, Maddy Rose," he whispered. And he pushed, sliding partway into her.

"You lied," she accused him, holding herself terribly still. "It does hurt."

"That's because you're terrified," he said. "You need to let go. Put your hands on my shoulders. I won't let you fall."

For some reason she did what he told her, moving her hands from her mouth to rest on his hot skin. "I can't let go," she said in a tight voice.

"Poor darling," he murmured. And then he leaned forward and bit the lobe of her ear, hard.

She shrieked in shock more than pain, and he thrust into her, filling her so full she thought she might faint. It took her a moment and a deep, calming breath to realize that it didn't hurt, not the way it had the first time. "You're too big," she said with just a trace of grumpiness. "You won't fit."

"*Gracias,*" he said. "But I'll fit just fine, as long as you relax."

"What do you mean, you'll fit?" she echoed. "You mean there's more?"

"There's the harridan I know and love," he said with a laugh. "Yes, Maddy Rose, there's more. And you're going to take it all, and you're going to want it."

"You said I could stop," she said. "You said we wouldn't do anything I didn't want to do. I don't want to do this."

"Yes, you do. You're just frightened."

"I'm not afraid of anything," she shot back. She could feel her body softening, accepting him, and he pushed in further. She wanted to hit him.

"Of course you are. You're afraid of bats, and going out on the ocean, and losing yourself. You're afraid of lies, you're afraid of my body when all I want to do is make you feel good." He pushed in further, and unconsciously she shifted, accommodating him. "You're afraid of being vulnerable, you're afraid of me, and I'm willing to bet you're afraid of spiders." He cupped her face, and she almost thought she could see the faint glitter of his eyes in the darkness. "But you're not going to be afraid of this." And he pushed home, resting against her, and her fingers dug into his shoulder, so tightly they cramped. Holding on, not pushing him away.

"Don't worry, love," he said, brushing his mouth against hers. "It's going to be all right. I promise you." He rested his forehead against hers, breathing steadily, but she could feel the tension running through him, the sheer strength it was taking to hold still.

"Just get it over with," she said in a small voice. "I can stand it."

He laughed, and the sensation traveled through their bodies, and she felt the vibration of it deep inside her. "Such confidence in my skills. Tell you what, Maddy Rose. Lie back and let go, and let me know when you change your mind."

He began to pull out, and she almost panicked, thinking he was leaving, he'd changed his mind, when he pushed back in again, and she shifted once more.

He did it again, setting up a slow, almost lazy rhythm, and she gripped the sheets again, bracing herself. It took a moment before she realized this was different, this slow, sinuous slide of his body against hers, his cock inside her. She was no longer cold, she was hot, sweaty, moving her hips without conscious decision, letting the sensations move through her body, almost like a dance, as he slid his hands under her and pulled her up against him, and something sparked inside her, something so unexpected that she gasped. He didn't slow down, didn't stop—he knew her body better than she did. He knew what would give her pleasure before she did, she released her death grip on his shoulders and slid her arms around his waist, feeling the steady pounding of his hips, the flex of his muscles. She wanted more, more of him, more of everything. She arched up against him, and he thrust in deeper, deeper still, and the pleasure was so powerful she cried out, sliding her hands up to clutch his back, to hold on as he moved in a determined, endless rhythm. He slid his hands up her legs and wrapped them around his hips, and she kept them there, reveling in the new feelings it was evoking, and she was shaking in his arms and she didn't know why. This was like nothing she had ever imagined, and when he slid his hand between their bodies, touching the place where he'd licked and sucked and nibbled, something exploded within her, and she went rigid in his arms as everything hung suspended, breath and heartbeat and life itself. And then she collapsed against the bed, limp, complete. But he was still moving, faster now, and he hadn't moved his hand from between them, and when he touched her again she slammed her face against his shoulder to muffle her scream.

And then he was gone from her, spilling his seed on her stomach, hot liquid washing over her, and she wanted to cry at the loss of him. She wanted everything, even the danger of his seed, and instead he'd protected her. She waited for him to collapse against her, uncertain whether she had enough strength left in her body to hold him, when he dropped down beside her, taking her in his arms and rolling her over him, so that she lay sprawled across his body, his seed wet between them, joining them.

She was lost, broken, and yet somehow whole for the first time in what seemed like forever. She lay across him, boneless, as another stray convulsion swept through her body, and she drew her legs up to savor the sensation.

"Not enough for you, love?" he whispered in her ear, sounding lazy and satisfied. "If you want I can . . ." He began to move his hand down her hip, and she batted at it helplessly.

"Are you . . . trying to . . . kill me?" she gasped, trying to regain her steady breathing and totally failing.

"No."

She wanted to sleep, she wanted to curl up in his arms and stay that way. But he would leave her, she knew it. "Congratulations," she managed to say, as her heart rate began to slow.

"For what?" He was lazily stroking her back, twisting strands of her long hair between his fingers, rubbing it against her.

"You made your point. I liked it."

For a moment he said nothing. "You think that's what I was doing? Proving a point?"

She wanted words. Men didn't give words. Gypsy pirates especially didn't give words, when they had no words to say. "What else could it be? We both know this meant nothing to either of us."

"You mean because I'm a ship's captain and a former privateer and you're a lady? Or is it my gypsy blood that bothers you?"

He sounded as if the question was purely academic, but she was horrified. "Of course not. It's just . . ."

He moved, and she half expected him to leave the bed, leave her. But instead he rolled up against the wall, taking her with him, wrapping her in the safety of his arms. There must have been a blanket somewhere near their feet, because he pulled it up, tucking it around her. "Tell you what," he said in a steady voice. "When you figure it out, let me know."

"I don't . . ."

"Go to sleep, Maddy Rose. You can fight with me later."

She opened her mouth to tell him she wasn't going to fight. She was going to tell him what she should never, never say. She was going to tell him that she loved him.

But she was saved by the rocking of the ship, by his hand on the side of her face, gently pushing her head against his shoulder, by the sheer exhaustion, emotional and physical, that swept over her, and before she could say the damning words she'd fallen into a deep, dreamless sleep.

CHAPTER NINETEEN

WHEN MADDY AWOKE THE cabin was flooded with daylight, and she was alone. She immediately scrambled into a sitting position, dragging the blanket with her, moving to the far corner as she listened to the voices outside her door. A moment later she heard the peremptory knocking, and relief and disappointment flooded her. Luca wouldn't bother to knock; Luca would stride in without announcing himself.

"Come in," she said, hoping she sounded relatively serene, given that she was sitting naked in a man's bed.

It was Billy Quarrells filling the doorway, surveying her with profound disapproval. "Did I wake you?" he said, ignoring any social pleasantries.

She could do the same. "No. Where's Luca?"

If anything his look of disapproval deepened. "*The captain* is busy running the ship," he said, his emphasis correcting her. "I offered to look after you and he gratefully accepted."

"Look after me? You look as if you'd like to throw me overboard. Are you angry with me?" It probably wasn't the smartest thing to say.

Disapproval was coming off Billy Quarrells in waves, and he was both strong enough and ruthless enough to do just that.

"You're more trouble than I realized," he said shortly. "And if I think you're causing Luca any harm then there could always be a tragic accident. Things like that happen all the time aboard ship. I don't know as how anyone would miss you. And don't bother running to him, telling him I threatened you. He won't believe you, and even if he did he wouldn't give a damn. He wanted you, he had you, and now it's over."

It should come as no surprise—the captain wasn't a man for tender emotions or commitments. He'd been ruthless last night, demanding a response so bone-shakingly powerful it frightened her, but of course he didn't care about her, for all his calling her his "love." He probably didn't know the meaning of the word.

Though there were times when she thought neither did she. After all, she had given her body to the man she thought, until recently, as her worst enemy; she'd held nothing back. He'd taken her, given her the kind of scary pleasure she'd never imagined existed, and then left her, leaving Billy to do his dirty work. And now she sat huddled in the corner, feeling bereft.

"I won't cause him any harm," she said wearily.

"Nor make any untoward demands?"

"Like what? Marry me and save my reputation? That's already in tatters."

"Marriage to a gypsy would hardly save your reputation and you know it," he scoffed, eyeing her. "You'd be shunned worse than you are already."

So he knew who she was. Of course he did—he was Luca's oldest friend. Luca probably told him everything, including how pathetic she was. He'd taken her, stripped her down emotionally, and even if she tried to put a wall of words up between them afterwards he knew women well enough. He knew she was hopelessly besotted, and he was sending his best friend to end it rather than deal with it himself.

She wasn't going to dignify that with an answer. "So why are you here if you're not going to fling me overboard?"

"We'll be heading into a blow, and the cap'n told me to make sure you're settled before it hits. Since your ladyship has never bothered to set foot on your father's own ships before, you probably don't know this one has a bathing room. I'll take you there, then down to the galley for some food, and then you'll stay in your cabin, out of the captain's way, for the rest of the voyage."

She would have liked to tell him to go to hell, but for the sake of a bath she'd sell her soul to the devil. "And just how long is the rest of the voyage? Where are we going?"

"That'll be up to the captain. The first place we can safely dump you, if I know him. He said you were in too much danger in Devonport, though it seems to me you brought that on yourself with your snooping. I would have left you behind."

She gave him a wintry smile. "So where are we headed?"

He shrugged his massive shoulders, watching her beneath shaggy eyebrows. "Maybe London. Maybe the continent. You can find your way home, wherever that may be, from there."

With no money, no clothes—she didn't even know where her shoes were. When she'd woken up in the bed, trussed and gagged, they'd been gone. She glanced at the floor of the cabin. There was no sign of her discarded dress or the shift and pantalets she'd willingly pulled off. "And is there any plan for me to wear something, or am I spending the rest of the voyage wrapped in a blanket? Are you going to give me my clothes back?"

"There are clothes," he said briefly. "Do you want a bath or not?"

Keeping the blanket wrapped securely around her, she slid off the berth. It was higher up than she'd realized it, and her legs felt rubbery, and Quarrells caught her as she started to pitch forward, his big rough hands surprisingly gentle. "Haven't got your sea legs yet," he grumbled. "Why that man bothers with women is beyond me. You're nothing but trouble."

"So drown me," she muttered, trying to regain her equilibrium.

"Don't tempt me."

But she was no longer afraid of him. For all his bluster, Billy Quarrells wouldn't do a thing to hurt her. He was like a great shaggy dog—all bark and no bite, just wanting to protect his best friend. Angry as she was, she couldn't fault him for that.

The bathing room wasn't far—just a few doors down the narrow passageway, and to her surprise a bath had already been drawn. She glanced up at Billy, but his face was impassive, so impassive she knew he'd done this for her. "Thank you," she said as he released his supportive arm.

He shrugged. "There's clothes in the cupboard there, and the necessary behind the screen. I'll give you one bell and no more."

"One bell?"

He made an exasperated sound. "And you the daughter of a shipping magnate! Ought to be ashamed of yourself. One bell is half an hour."

"Then why didn't you say so?" she shot back.

"Because we're on board ship."

She rolled her eyes. All the nautical rules and terms were coming back to her, but she derived a perverse pleasure in playing ignorant. "Are you going to stay and watch me?" she said after a long moment, when he made no attempt at leaving.

He snorted. "Not my area of interest, dolly-mop. I just want to make sure you're not going to fall flat on your face or drown in the bathtub before I leave."

She ignored the insult. She wasn't quite sure what a dolly-mop was, but she knew it wasn't complimentary. "Wouldn't that solve a lot of problems?"

He appeared to consider it. "I hadn't thought of that. I don't think the captain would mind."

He was saying it to goad her, she knew it, but it still stabbed her to the heart. "Then go away."

Billy's eyes had narrowed. "Did he give you that bruise on your face?"

"What's it to you?"

"Did he?"

"No. That was the man who was trying to kill me. He gave me this one." She lifted her chin. She hadn't looked in a mirror since she'd left her room yesterday morning, but her chin was tender and she had to assume he'd left a mark.

Billy peered at her. "Don't see nothing. He always did have a light hand."

"You mean it doesn't tend to show when he beats women?"

"You're a sassy one, aren't you? No wonder he . . ."

"No wonder he what?"

"No wonder he thinks I ought to drown you. Wait for me and I'll be back." He was already gone before she could come up with an answer, and she heard the lock in the door. What had he said? A storm was coming? If the ship foundered and she was locked in a cabin she would drown with Mr. Quarrells's help.

She dropped the blanket and took care of things, refusing to even look down at her betraying body as she slid into the steaming water. It wasn't until she put her hands in that she let out an involuntary shriek of pain, and she drew them up, out of the stinging heat. She'd forgotten what she'd done to her wrists in the struggle against the ropes. They were red, raw bracelets of pain, and she forced herself to put them back into the water. She could hardly wash herself without using her hands, and the water would start the healing. Funny, now that she remembered they hurt like hell. Last night she hadn't even noticed. Last night in his arms.

She slid all the way under the water, soaking her hair. She'd washed it just a few days ago, in the large copper tub on Water Street, but she couldn't resist, and she held her breath, letting the water cover her, closing her eyes as she felt her hair drift around her. Maybe drowning wouldn't be that bad a way to die.

But she could only hold her breath for so long, and she surfaced with a gasp, dragging in the fresh air. All right, drowning wasn't the answer. And in fact it was just as well her night with Luca had been a singular event, one he had no interest in repeating. One night had almost demolished her will and her common sense—a second one would end her completely, and she'd be pathetic, begging for even a scrap of his attention. No, that would never happen. No matter how much in love with him she was, she would never . . .

She ducked under the water again. Bad thoughts, dangerous thoughts. She had to concentrate on what she could do. She had to make plans.

She should be happy. Finally she had proof that someone had been out to hurt her father, and now her. No one would have any reason to hurt her, and to have a hired killer show up and almost finish her off meant someone wanted her silenced. It would have made perfect sense if it were Luca.

The memory of Mr. Brown's limpid gaze came back to her. Luca didn't believe he was the one who'd hired the killer, but Luca hadn't looked into Mr. Brown's flat brown eyes.

Who the hell was he?

She knew she'd never met the man before, and her father had certainly never mentioned him. Then again, if his name was really Brown then she was Queen Victoria.

She needed to get back to London. She could insist on being paid for the days she'd toiled in the captain's household—she'd certainly earned it under Mrs. Crozier's direction. She could go to the police and make them listen. If she only knew of some way to get in touch with Bryony, she could ask her if she knew anything about the mystery man.

With enough money she could get back to Somerset and Renwick and figure out what to do next. Nanny Gruen was levelheaded and very wise—between the two of them they could come up with a plan. Even her airheaded younger sister might be able to help.

She climbed out of the tub, reaching for the length of thick Turkish toweling that had been laid out for her use. She was fine, she was perfectly fine. The best cure for a broken heart was to throw yourself into work. Not that she had a broken heart—that was clearly absurd. No, she'd had a setback, there was no denying that. But once away from Luca she would stop thinking about him. It was only natural that her body felt sensitized, attuned to his, that she could close her eyes and still feel him within her, moving, and her breasts would tighten and everything would cramp inside with longing.

She'd be over it in a trice.

The clothes were ridiculous. She stared at them in disbelief. Her petticoats were there, and to her astonishment they had been laundered, as well as her shift. There was no sign of her pantalets, and the only other article of clothing was an oversized white shirt that would doubtless reach to her knees. She shook it out, staring at it, and then brought it to her face. It was clean as well, smelling of soap and a sea breeze. And Luca.

She hadn't realized he was so much bigger than she was. His lean grace belied his actual size—the shirt was almost as long as her shift.

She dropped it, looking around the small cabin for anything, anything she could wear instead. Nothing. She had no choice. She pulled it over her head and let it drop down, ignoring the way it seemed to caress her body. At least she was decently covered, though the sleeves hung down below her hands. She started to roll them up, then stopped. To do so would expose her wrists, and that was the last thing she wanted.

What she wanted, needed, was to get off this blasted ship and get back to her original goal. So Luca wasn't guilty of sabotage—he'd merely taken advantage of the carrion left behind. She shouldn't be surprised—the man had been a pirate.

She heard the knock on the door—Billy must have returned. "I'm ready," she called out. The doorknob rattled but didn't open, and she sighed. "You locked it, remember? Don't you have the key?"

There was no answer. Just the quiet tread of someone moving away. Maybe not Billy—whoever had been at the door was too light, though not as silent as Luca. He had a faint hitch to his step as well—was it perhaps a peg-legged pirate? No, he'd probably clump along the deck. It had to have been Billy. "Can you let me out?" she called through the door, but whoever had been there had vanished.

It was probably close to ten minutes before the door opened, an impassive Billy Quarrells returning. "Why didn't you just leave the key in the door?" she demanded.

He frowned. "How do you know I didn't?"

"Because you tried to get in earlier, of course," she said impatiently.

"No, I didn't."

"Well, someone was rattling the doorknob. Was someone else planning a bath?"

"The bath is for the captain and any guests he might have, not for the able seamen," Billy said. "And both the captain and I were on deck. I told him you were ready to go."

That only hurt a little bit, she thought in relief. After all, it was only the truth, and she needed to accept it and move on. "Then who wanted to get in here?"

"Aye, that's the question. Come along, Miss Russell. Back to your prison."

For a moment she was afraid he really was going to put her in some kind of jail cell, and then she remembered they called it the brig on board a ship. Another one of those ridiculous terms, when the real words would do well enough.

Back to the captain's cabin, the wooden deck cool beneath her bare feet, and when she went inside it looked as if someone had cleaned the room. The berth was freshly made—no signs of what they'd done in it would remain. She turned to look at Billy. "I need to talk to Luca," she said abruptly.

"Anything you need to say to him you can say to me," Billy said. "He doesn't have time for you right now."

She could have clung to the "right now" if she were weak and addled. But she wasn't, she was a fighter. "Tell him I want to go home."

"You'll go where he takes you. Trust me, he wants to get rid of you as much as you want to be gone, and that's the Lord's truth."

There was an odd note in his voice, and she narrowed her gaze, staring at him. Did he look a little less disapproving, a little less grim? His next words confirmed it. "He's not for the likes of you, lass, and you know it. He's part gypsy, and he goes where he wants, when he wants."

"I'll have you know I'm planning to marry Lord Eastham. I have absolutely no interest in a pirate," she said stiffly. It wasn't a lie. She was planning to marry the old man. She just hadn't informed him of the fact yet.

"Privateer," Billy corrected. "And that's a good thing, then, for the both of you."

"How's she doing?" Luca didn't turn his gaze away from the sea, but he expected Billy could read him like a book.

There was a long silence. "She'll be fine," Billy said gruffly. "Just keep away from her and she'll get over you."

That caught his attention, and he jerked around. "What do you mean by that?"

"What do you think I mean? The girl's in love with you, like they all are. She's just another one of your conquests—don't give her another thought."

"I'm not," he said grimly, turning back to the ever-soothing balm of the sea. It was the calm before the storm, a time he knew well, and he was taking it in before all hell broke loose.

Billy followed his gaze. "We didn't outrun it, did we?"

"We'll find out. I think we'll miss the brunt of it, and the *Maddy Rose* is tough. She can withstand a lot."

"Like her namesake."

Luca whirled around. "What the bloody hell are you talking about? I thought you hated her."

"I've never hated her. I just thought she was bad for you. All upper crust and all that, and a liar to boot. I'll say one thing for her—she knows how to work hard. That old witch Mrs. C. near killed her."

But Luca was focusing on one thing. "You said you 'thought' she was bad for me. Past tense."

"Ah, don't go bothering me with your fancy English stuff. I should never have taught you to read," Billy said genially. "You prefer me to say that I think she's bad for you?"

"It depends on what you mean."

"Lord, boy-o, do you realize what a mess of trouble she is? I did what you told me to do. I told her you didn't want to see her again and you'd drop her off at the first port we come to."

"Good."

"You don't look happy about it."

"It's for the best. She's a grown woman. She knows better than to fall in love with a half gypsy who works for a living."

"Her father worked for a living."

"Whose side are you on?"

"Yours, laddie. Always yours." Billy put a heavy hand on his shoulder. "I just want you to make sure you know what you're doing."

Luca didn't answer. They'd ended the night at a standoff, even if she'd been curled up in his arms. They struck sparks off each other, and either or both of their lives could go up in flames. He knew what he wanted, and it didn't include an upper-class wife and a life in London. He didn't want her, damn it. Even if his body and something else inside him that he refused to recognize craved her.

"I'll take first watch," he said finally, changing the subject. "You're as good as I am in a storm . . ."

"Better," Billy said.

"Maybe," Luca said grudgingly. "Let's hope we don't have a chance to prove it."

The hold of the ship stank. It smelled of men living in close quarters, of rat shit and sour milk and grease and over everything else the strong stench of Chinese tea from previous voyages to the Orient. As the ship rolled back and forth beneath him, Rufus nestled into his spot behind the crates and decided he would never drink tea again.

They'd been out at sea for more than two days now, something he'd never expected. The cargo had been bound for Plymouth, not elsewhere, and yet that gypsy trash hadn't stayed long enough to have it unloaded before taking off again, and he should have been out for less than a day, just long enough for Rufus to finally finish what he'd started.

Rufus would have been astonished at his luck in being able to sneak aboard without being noticed, but he didn't consider such things luck. There had been signs all along—this was his path, his destiny. To wipe any trace of Eustace Russell and his spawn off the face of this earth, and it had been . . . not a mistake, exactly. He didn't make mistakes. But a miscalculation, a failure to understand his own importance in the scheme of things. Bringing down Madeleine Russell hadn't been a job for hired help, and the corpses of Parsons and the killer he'd hired were testament to that.

No, it had always been Rufus's lot in life to finish this, and he seized the opportunity as the gift and the duty that it was.

He just wished it hadn't required him to go to sea.

Really, there was no way a man like him should be trapped in the bulkhead of a clipper ship, feeling every dip and sway of the waves. He'd been sick at first, and the smell of that only added to the odors that surrounded him, even though he'd changed position several times to distance himself from the contents of his stomach. It was undignified but necessary, and he accepted it. The good news was that they couldn't possibly be at sea for long—they hadn't the supplies laid in, and he would escape the moment they reached land.

The bad news was they wouldn't be at sea for long, and he couldn't afford to wait. Madeleine Russell was going over the side of the boat, never to be seen again, and he would return to his hiding place until they landed, with no one the wiser.

He might have called it luck that he'd discovered in time where Morgan had taken her, but again, he knew this was simply one more sign that his path was true. That hulking idiot had locked her in the bathing room and taken the key! It would have been the perfect time to finish this—everyone was preparing for an upcoming storm. He'd heard the crew discussing it—their quarters weren't far from his hiding place—and he only hoped the captain would have the sense to bring them back in before it hit. In the meantime, though, no one would notice another sailor, albeit one with a slight limp, and the bundle he tossed over the side of the ship.

It had been easy to steal clothes, though they stank as well, making him shudder in disgust. He'd found a canvas bag large enough that he could stuff the girl inside if he were forced to dump her anywhere near witnesses, but he was hoping it would be easier than that. If the captain would just allow her to walk the decks for a bit, to get some fresh air, it could be child's play.

If the storm hit, he'd adapt. It would cover her death admirably, and no one would think to look beyond the simple tragedy of it. That is, if anyone considered it a tragedy. The gypsy didn't seem to have any use for her, for all that he spent the night shagging the hell out of her. The first mate was carrying out his orders, and he was a hard man.

It was easy enough to slip around the deck of the ship once the sun set. He looked like everyone else, with his cap pulled low about his ears. It had been a risk, creeping out to see if he could reach her, and he'd almost been caught. He was either going to have to get the key from Quarrells, that was the man's name, or figure out a reason for the captain to free her.

He wasn't worried. Things worked out as they were meant to, and he knew it was his task to kill Madeleine Russell and her sisters. He'd been . . . misguided to think other people might do it. It was for him and him alone.

The opportunity would present itself. All he needed to do was watch and listen. And wait.

CHAPTER TWENTY

Billy had brought her food, and Maddy had resisted the impulse to throw it at his head. There'd been a piece of rope left behind after someone cleaned the room and she'd wrapped it around her waist so she wouldn't feel as if she were in her nightdress. She didn't cry, she didn't rage. There was something in the air, a feeling of tension, a sense of danger that she couldn't explain, couldn't understand. It must be the storm that was coming—the very thought of it made her ill with fear. And yet . . . it seemed as if it was something else.

It didn't matter. If she were dead from the storm, that something else would probably cease to exist as well. The main thing she needed to do was get through it as calmly as possible. Which right now seemed unlikely.

She heard a quiet rapping on the door, but she stayed where she was, seated by the window watching the now choppy sea. "Yes?" she called out.

"It's Jones, miss. One of the kitchen hands. Just wanted to see if you needed anything else."

Jones must be from Wales, she thought absently. His accent sounded odd, and Jones was a Welsh name, wasn't it? "Get me a bottle of brandy so I can ride out this storm unconscious," she said flippantly.

"Yes, miss. Can you unlock the door?"

She laughed without humor. "Do you think I'd be spending my time stuck in this tiny cabin if I had a key? Your Mr. Quarrells has locked me in. If you want to bring me something you'll need to get the key from him."

There was no answer. How very odd. "Mr. Jones?" she called out. Still silence. He'd probably gone in search of Mr. Quarrells, who would promptly tell him to mind his own business.

But she didn't think so. It was just another patch of oddness in the strange afternoon. She stretched out on the bed. The water was getting a little rough, but everything in the cabin appeared to be bolted down except her. She vaguely wondered whether the added turbulence of the ocean would make her sick, but her stomach seemed made of cast iron. If anything she was still hungry.

Lying on the berth wasn't a terribly good idea either. It smelled like Luca—like clean skin and the ocean and something else indefinable. And all she could do was relive every moment from last night, every touch, every taste, every thrust, every shattering response that had destroyed her and brought her back again. She wanted him inside her again. She wanted his big, hard body covering hers, straining against hers, she wanted his hands, his mouth on her breasts, which had suddenly hardened, and she reached down to touch them, wondering if she could give herself any relief.

Nothing. They were simply her breasts, they'd been there forever and existed to be crushed by a corset or displayed by a low-cut dress. She'd never realized what a source of intense pleasure they could be.

But not from her. She squirmed on the bed, remembering, feeling him push inside her, his mouth on hers. She'd expected his pleasure, and her own happiness at holding him afterwards. Instead it had been all sky west and crooked—the pleasure he had given her had been astonishing, and in the aftermath he was the one who held her, stroked her hair, comforted her in her tears. This was all wrong.

She sat up, pushing her unbound hair behind her. There had been a comb but no hairpins to fasten the mass of dark hair, and if she'd still retained any when he'd brought her here they'd gotten lost in the bedclothes. Oh, God. She flopped back on the mattress. She wanted him. She wanted them together in this bed, naked again. She wanted to curl up in his lap, she wanted to tease him and talk about the books he read and sail with him to the ends of the earth.

It was obsession, pure and simple, stemming back to that childhood incident when she'd tried to run away with the gypsies. Those three days had been some of the happiest in her memory, though she'd regretted the grief it had given her father. But ever since then, whenever there were gypsies on the family land her father left them alone, in thanks for looking after her. And she would creep down and watch them, sometimes join them, listen to the stories they told at night.

But Luca wasn't a gypsy, he was a changeling in a staid world. He didn't belong, and yet he claimed a place there. It was little wonder she was fascinated by him, drawn to him.

She rolled over on her stomach, burying her face in the pillow. It smelled like his skin. She moaned, the feathers muffling the sound, and the ship gave a sudden lurch. She could hear the sound of the sails flapping in the wind, the creak of ropes as they were pulled down. Maybe they would all die in the storm. If they did, she only hoped they broke her out of this damned cabin and she went down in the water with Luca's arms wrapped around her. Because he was lying to himself just as she was. Last night had been no ordinary night, not even for him.

And if they survived this storm she would damned well tell him so.

The light had grown strange, a sort of greeny gray, as the ship rocked and jerked in the water. She curled up, facing the wall, the blanket wrapped tight around her, and she didn't even hear him come in.

••••••••••••••••••••••••••••••••

She seemed so small in the bed, Luca thought, looking at the figure huddled under the covers. Small and fragile, when she was anything but. He closed the door behind him, silently, and moved toward the berth, the ropes in his hands. He had to make sure he didn't listen to her. She'd argue, she'd fight him, and he had no choice.

"Maddy."

She froze—he could see her absolute stillness, like a wild animal scenting a wolf. She turned and looked at him, then down at the ropes in his hands. "Are you going to tie me up and throw me overboard to drown?"

He just looked at her. "Now why would I do that?"

She shrugged, trying to look unconcerned, but he could see the vulnerability in her mouth, and he wanted that mouth, so badly. "To get rid of me?" she suggested.

"I don't want to get rid of you. I want to save your life."

She gave him the most annoying look, one of deep distrust. "Why should I believe you?"

But he wasn't going to let her get to him, prod him into saying or doing something that he might regret. They could be dead in the next few hours. The storm was almost upon them, and it was bigger than he'd imagined. Everything was battened down, the sails were furled, and all they could do from now on was pray. And all he could do is come down here and protect Maddy. "I'm not arguing with you," he said. "I'm tying you down."

She gave a sharp laugh. "You don't need to tie me down. Don't you remember—I didn't put up any fight at all yesterday. All you have to do is touch me and my brain seems to melt."

"That's not why I'm tying you up, though I'd be very interested in playing those games with you once we make it to port. But for the time being the safest place for you is tied to your berth. Otherwise the rocking of the boat will throw you and you might be hurt, even killed."

She was looking unimpressed. "And what if the ship starts to sink? How am I to have even a fighting chance if I'm down in a cabin with my hands and wrists bound?"

She was wearing one of his shirts—Billy must have found it for her. The sleeves were so long they hung over her fingertips, and he caught her wrist and started to roll the sleeve upward when he was stopped by her involuntary hiss of pain.

"What's wrong?"

"Nothing," she said between gritted teeth. "Go right ahead."

He looked down at her, then at the long white sleeve that flowed over her arm. On impulse he reached for her other wrist, encircling it lightly before giving it a slight squeeze, and she hissed again. "Could you stop pawing me?" she snapped. "Just tie me up and get it over with."

He began to roll up her sleeve, and that was her signal to fight. It was over fast enough, he had her down on the bed, her arm trapped between their bodies.

"Damn it, Maddy," he said with an exasperated sigh. "Why do you fight me on everything? Be quiet and move over."

Her smart mouth was silenced for a brief, blessed moment, but she quickly regained her powers of speech. "Why?"

"Because I'm tying myself down with you, that's why. If we go down, we go down together."

She didn't move, staring at him as if he'd grown two heads, so he simply climbed onto the berth, nudging her out of the way while he tied one end of the rope through the grip on the far side of the bed. She still hadn't moved, crouched in the corner like a wounded falcon. "Don't you have to sail the ship?"

It wasn't a complete rejection, and he supposed he ought to be happy about that. "Billy's got the helm. There's no better man in a storm—if anyone can bring us through in one piece that would be Billy. Now lie down."

She was still looking at him uneasily. "I think I'd rather take my chances . . ."

He'd had enough. Catching her arms, he dragged her down onto the mattress, shoving up the absurdly long sleeves of the shirt she'd borrowed to wrap the rope around her wrists for extra security, when he froze, staring at the red weals. "Who did that to your wrists?"

"I did."

He cursed then, in Romany, for some reason sparing her his most profane utterances. Absurd, when she herself cursed like a sailor. "I shouldn't have tied them so tight," he said in a thin voice.

"You shouldn't have tied them so loose," she corrected him. "It gave me just enough room to try to wriggle out of them but not enough to actually do so. I did this to myself, trying to get free."

"Are you trying to make me feel better?"

"Oh, heavens no. I want you to feel as guilty as you possibly can," she said. "I just don't know why you would." She started to sit up, but he shoved her back again, muttering under his breath. She really was the most damnably obtuse woman.

He slid down beside her and began to weave the rope back and forth across them, around the frame and up again. He finished, then lay back beside her, breathing heavily.

She smelled wonderful, like soap and skin and sex, and it didn't matter how damned hard he was, he told himself to leave her alone. He didn't like the way he felt—obsessive, protective. He didn't need her complicating his life, even if he thought he wanted it. As for Maddy, she seemed convinced he thought she was nothing more than a problem. For a smart woman she was being an idiot, but it was better that way. He'd lie beside her, not saying a word, riding out the storm, and if by any bizarre chance they foundered he could make sure she'd at least make it to the surface, find her something to hold onto in the unlikely hope of a rescue.

She was lying rigid beside him, staring up at the ceiling as the ship bobbed up and down. He held still and realized her heart was hammering at twice its normal rate, so loud he could sense it, and he remembered her panic when she first knew she was on board ship. This could put her over the edge.

And there was another unpleasant thought. "Are you feeling seasick? This is the kind of weather that can turn the most experienced sailor green."

"Yes," she said promptly. "In fact, I'll probably throw up in the next few minutes. You really should get out of the room while you can."

"Cabin," he corrected absently. She sounded just fine to him. "I'll take my chances."

She muttered something uncomplimentary and fell silent. He was tired—he'd barely slept the night before, and even the violent rocking of the ship soothed him. As the presence of the angry woman beside him soothed him. He certainly was a perverse son of a bitch, he thought.

"You know, you don't have to stay here. I'll be fine on my own." She was doing her best to sound reasonable but he knew her too well.

"This is as good a place as any for me to ride out the storm."

"Maybe I'd rather be alone? I find this storm . . . unnerving, and I'd rather deal with it without an audience."

He let out a short bark of laughter. "I'm not your audience, I'm your lover."

He heard her outraged intake of breath. "You aren't my lover, you're my kidnapper."

"Technically both," he said. "And the man who saved your life once already, and is in the midst of doing his best to save it again. So be quiet and let me think."

"Think about what?"

"About what I'm going to do with you," he said in a cool voice.

"I thought you already made up your mind. You're going to dump me on the nearest piece of dry land and never see me again."

"That was the plan," he said wearily.

"Then what do you need to think about?"

"Whether I can let you go."

She didn't say a word. The ship was moving faster now, scudding through the violent waves even without benefit of the sails. The rain, which up till then had merely been a light drizzle, suddenly chose that moment to let loose, beating against the sides of the ship with a deadly ferocity. It was still daylight, but the cabin had grown dark, both from the blackness of the skies and the constant slap of waves against the porthole, and it was beginning to feel as if they were riding some massive, unbroken horse, bucking and kicking and tossing them about.

The rope holding them down was loose, just enough to keep them from being tossed about, and he could feel her beside him, positively vibrating with terror, clutching the mattress with a death grip as they were rocked back and forth. He did his best to lie still beside her—he hadn't decided whether she needed distraction or to be left the hell alone, when he felt something. It took him half a second to recognize it, because it was the last thing he expected. Her hand had released its grip on the sheet, and was reaching for his.

He immediately caught it, wrapping his fingers around her, careful to avoid the damaged wrists. She'd done it to herself, she was right about that, and yet he felt even worse about those injuries than he did about hitting her. He'd had no choice when he knocked her out—it was the only way to keep her safe, but he should have untied her when he left her in the cabin. She would be well rid of him.

A wave crashed against the side of the ship, slamming so hard the porthole smashed open and water sprayed into the room, and

Maddy screamed, turning and tunneling against him. There was enough room to pull her into his arms, placing his back to the sea spray that could just reach the berth, and he stroked her tangled hair, murmuring soft, comforting words as she trembled. They were still all right—Billy was steering a safe course through the storm, slicing into the huge waves instead of letting them hit them broadside, but Luca had no illusions. This was bad, so bad that even Billy might not be able to see them through.

He cupped Maddy's face, tilting it toward his, and kissed her. The ship jerked, her teeth slammed against his lower lip, and he laughed, wiping the blood away. "How can you think this is funny?" she cried, holding him so tightly he thought the tough fabric of his shirt might shred. "We're going to die."

"No, we're not." He kissed her again, a little more carefully, then gently wiped his blood from her mouth. "We're going to get out of here, and then we're going to . . ." The loud, cracking noise stopped him, and he knew the only thing that could make that kind of sound, and for a moment his blood ran cold.

"What was that?" she demanded in a terrified voice.

"One of the masts," he said, carefully prying her hands from his clothes and slipping out from beneath the ropes. "I have to go."

"No!" she shrieked over the noise of the storm.

"It's not going to make any difference whether I'm here or not," he said, tightening the ropes again.

"You could die!"

He leaned over and kissed her hard on the mouth, marking her with his blood. "You could only be so lucky. I've decided not to give you up, Maddy Rose. So unless I go overboard you're stuck."

He was at the door before the words sank home. She tried to sit up but the ropes held her in place. "What did you say?"

"I'll repeat it once we get through the storm. Stay put or I'll have to tie your wrists again and I don't want to do that. You hear me?"

"I hear you," she said dazedly.

A moment later he was gone.

Rufus couldn't stay belowdecks any longer. He couldn't stand the smell of his own sickness, the way his body was being smashed against the crates and the hull of the boat, the scream of the wind, the roar of the rain as it tried to pound the ship into a thousand splinters. The massive cracking sound finished him.

The ship was splitting in half, and he was damned if he was going to be drowned like the rats that were trapped down here, eyeing him out of glowing red eyes. They'd probably feast on his carcass if the ship survived and he didn't. Could someone die of seasickness?

He heard the pounding of footsteps overhead, up on the deck, and guessed that one of the main masts must have broken, leaving them adrift in the midst of a storm that seemed to have reached biblical proportions. How had he gotten it so wrong? He had finally listened to what his instincts had told him, he'd followed the bitch onto the namesake ship her wretched father had had built, and now he was facing death? It wasn't possible!

He straightened, brushing at the stinking, stolen clothes as if they were the finest wool. Of course it wasn't possible. How could he lose faith so easily? He'd been led to the ship—it would have been so easy to have missed it, missed his chance. Nothing worth doing was ever easy, and once he finished with the middle sister he could concentrate on the spoiled baby, back home safe on the grounds of Somerset, their stolen country home. It had been returned to its rightful owners, but that didn't mean the debt was wiped out.

The passageways were deserted as he made his way up from the bowels of the ship, clinging desperately to the ropes strung along the sides. He was almost at the top, ready to head out into the storm itself, when he realized that Madeleine would be alone. And this time they may have forgotten to take the key.

He fell twice making his way to the captain's quarters in the bow of the ship. Seawater had poured in through the hatch, and it was sloshing around his ankles, making things even more treacherous. It was dark down there, very little light coming from the portholes, and it wasn't until he was almost outside the door that he saw the key was gone. His fury was so powerful it temporarily washed away his nausea. Maybe he'd been wrong. Maybe she wasn't supposed to die by his hand, maybe she was simply going to go down with the ship, and it was up to him to survive. He had to make certain she was still trapped in there before he made his way topside.

He reached out and rattled the doorknob. To his momentary astonishment the door swung open, then slammed shut again as the ship lurched. "Who's there?" he heard her voice call out. "Luca? Is that you? Are you all right?"

Rufus chuckled to himself. This was the way it was supposed to be. He pushed the door open again, and waded into the cabin.

CHAPTER TWENTY-ONE

Hell was supposed to be flames and heat, but Luca knew better. Hell was howling winds and waves taller than a church spire and rain that lashed as hard as a whip. Hell was noise and pain, blindness, water everywhere, and no knowledge of where the next blow was coming from—the sea or the ship itself.

The mizzenmast was cracked, the crossways spar listing directly over the deck. Sailors were working, lashed safely, and Billy was wrestling with the wheel, a savage grin on his face. Billy had always laughed in the face of death.

So had he. But not today. Today Luca wanted to live with a fierceness he'd never known before. He wanted to make it through this bloody storm and come out the other side, limp his wounded ship to shore for repairs, and go downstairs and bring Maddy up into the sunshine. He'd take her off this blasted ship, to the first hotel or inn he could find, depending on where they washed up, and they wouldn't emerge for days, damn it.

If they made it through this he was going to marry her. He recognized that fact with a grim certainty. There was nothing like looking into the face of death to realize what mattered. Whether it was bad for her or not, he could no longer worry about that. He needed her. He needed her in his bed, he needed her to fight with, he needed to be around her and know she was safe. If no one had come to hurt her, if she were still pretending to be a maid in his household, he'd have gone in at night and stolen her away like his ancestors had done. She was his, and nobody else's, and he finally understood that fact with the certainty that impending doom made impossible to deny.

If they lived long enough he was going to have to convince her of that fact. She could do so much better than a half-breed sailor. But he no longer cared. She was his, and he'd kill before he let her go.

"How's it looking?" he shouted to Billy, making his voice heard over the devil's own wind. "Think the mizzen will go?"

"Aye," Billy shouted back. His face was covered with sheets of water, his grizzled gray hair plastered to his scalp. "The question is, where will she land? If she lands just right and the spar crashes through the sides then we're going down."

"No, we're not," Luca said. "When she starts to go you'll jerk the wheel in the right direction and it'll fall into the ocean. I've seen you do it half a dozen times. I have faith in you."

Billy snorted, then coughed as seawater went up his nose. "Sooner or later our luck is going to run out."

"Sooner or later," Luca agreed. "But not today. We'll . . ." His voice stopped, as he saw something emerge from the hatch he'd closed so carefully to keep more water from filling the lower decks. He blinked against the blinding rain, for a moment terrified that Maddy had ignored his orders and followed him up on deck. One good wave and she'd be overboard, and there'd be no way to save her.

But the figure was too bulky, though he couldn't make it out. And then a gust of wind blew the rain in another direction, and for a moment he was able to focus. It was a sailor, one he didn't recognize, and he had a struggling Maddy over his shoulder, and for the first time in his life Luca felt pure terror.

"Shite!" Billy cursed beside him. "Who the bloody hell is that?"

Everything inside him had coalesced into an icy, murderous rage. "Someone's got Maddy."

"Jayzus," Billy said. "Who? And why?"

"Concentrate on steering," Luca shouted over the noise of the storm, his voice grim. "I'll go for her."

He unfastened the rope he'd tied around his waist. Whoever was wrestling Maddy up onto the deck wasn't used to storms; he went down, sliding across the deck and slamming against the side, never releasing his grip on Maddy. She was fighting him, but the man had to have a grip of iron, and as Luca tried to make his way toward them he saw the man twist Maddy's arm behind her back in a cruel jerk that brought her to her knees. They were directly beneath the cracked mast, and he tried to shout out a warning, but the wind took his voice and whirled it away, and he watched the struggle as if from a great distance as he fought his way toward them.

The sea was a formidable enemy when she chose to be. More than once he'd lain, lashed to his bunk during storms like these, and he'd heard the voices of the drowned, a jumble of words swirling around his head. He'd seen visions, terrifying ones, beautiful ones, but right then he couldn't be sure of what he saw. Because if he blinked it looked as if Gwendolyn's tame friend, Rufus Brown, had Maddy in a death grip and was trying to haul her up and over the side.

She'd been right and he hadn't believed her. But how in hell had the man gotten aboard ship, and where had he been the last two days?

Luca shouted at them, but the wind took his words and whirled them away. Who the hell was the man, and why was he trying to kill Maddy?

Luca tried to move fast, but the water running across the deck was treacherous, and he went down, landing on his knees, as he saw Brown manage to haul Maddy up. In another moment he'd have her over the side, and it wouldn't matter that Luca would beat Brown to death with his bare hands. Maddy would be gone, taken by the other woman he loved, the sea.

He wasn't going to reach them in time. He heard the second crack overhead, as the mizzenmast began to topple, directly toward the area of the deck where Maddy was fighting for her life. Luca managed to scramble to his feet, but they were too far away, and the wind was blowing so hard he could barely move. It was pure impulse, but impulse had saved his life before. He managed a running leap against the wind, then dropped down and slid across the length of the deck, just as the mast began to fall, the deadly spar heading directly for Maddy and Brown.

There was no controlling his momentum, and he didn't care. He crashed into the struggling couple, the force of his impact wrenching Maddy away. The ship lurched, and he wrapped his arms around her as they slid backwards, away from Brown, who stood frozen in disbelief as the heavy mast crashed downwards, and the spar hit him squarely across the head. A moment later he was gone, with half the rail and a good portion of the mast.

Luca and Maddy had ended up against the pilothouse, and he held her, ducking his own head against the blowing rain. He'd heard the man's scream as he went overboard, and while the sound had brought him a vicious satisfaction he hoped Maddy hadn't heard it. It was the kind of sound that could haunt your dreams the first time you heard it.

He didn't dare move. With the railing gone it would be far too easy for the two of them to be swept after Brown, and he wasn't going to risk it. Every now and then the wind shifted and he could see Billy at the helm, fighting with everything he had inside him. The ship wasn't listing, and he could only hope the mast and spar had taken no more than the railing and a stowaway intent on murder, but he wasn't taking any chances. If there were a hole in the side the sailors would be doing their damnedest to bail and to patch it, but in this kind of storm it would be a lost cause. Right then there was nothing he could do but hold onto Maddy and wait to see if they survived.

The battle was endless. With her wet body plastered up against his, they slowly began to warm each other as they huddled against the rain. It was too chaotic to try to speak, and indeed, he didn't have the words right then. All he could do was hold her shaking body and try to shield her. And ignore the fact that, in the face of death, he was getting hard simply by being close to her.

He ducked his head down beside her, his mouth against her temple. He pushed the rain-matted hair away and whispered against the wet salt of her skin. "I'm not going to let you die."

She'd been coughing on and off. She must have swallowed some seawater at some point during her struggle, and he could barely make out the raw scratchiness of her voice. "You and what army?"

And he laughed. In the face of death he laughed, holding the woman he loved, the woman who never gave up without a fight. He hugged her close, folding her against him, and her hands were gripping his wet shirt, her head was buried against his shoulder, and he could feel her lips against him. Warm lips against his water-soaked skin. It was enough.

He barely noticed when the storm began to ebb. The rain was softer now, the rise and fall of the ship less violent, and the howl of the wind began to quiet. He didn't want to move from their protected spot on the hard deck; he didn't want to do anything but hold her.

"Storm's over, boy-o." Billy loomed overhead, and he turned to look at him, silhouetted against the angry sky, water still sluicing over him. "We made it through."

Maddy moved in his arms, her grip on his shirt loosening, but he held her tightly. "Who's got the helm?"

"Jeffries, who else? Only man I trust. Get up now. The girl needs dry clothes, and we're in sight of land."

He couldn't hesitate any longer. He released her, and sure enough she immediately scuttled away, sitting a fair distance from him, her face pale but determined. He resisted the need to haul her back, pulling himself up. The pitch and sway of the ship was definitely steadier. "Where are we?"

"Somewhere off the south coast of England or I miss my guess," Billy said. "The storm blew us all the way back. I'd been aiming for Normandy."

He reached down to her, but she ignored him, and he wondered if she was in shock. He leaned down and scooped her up, and she had the sense not to battle him in the still impressive wind.

She was shivering, and he was damned cold himself. He turned to look at Billy. "You need me?"

Billy shook his head. "It'll be easy enough to limp into port, even with one mast gone. Go warm up the lass before she turns into an icicle and I'll let you know when we dock."

"Any idea where along the coast?"

"I'm heading straight for the London docks. Best shipbuilders south of Liverpool there, and this fine lady is going to need some repairs. Who the hell was it who went over the side?"

"Gwendolyn's friend. Maddy was right after all," he said briefly, starting toward the hatch, Maddy tucked tightly in his arms.

Billy whistled. "Now that's a dangerously jealous woman."

Luca managed a laugh. He still couldn't believe how close he'd come to losing her. "I doubt that's why. I'm not worth killing over. Right now I've got better things to do than worry about a danger that's ended up at the bottom of the ocean."

Billy gave a meaningful look to the woman in his arms. "I'd say you do, boy-o. It should be smooth sailing from here on." As if in answer the ship gave a lurch, and Billy called an expressively obscene insult over his shoulder to the man at the helm.

Luca didn't answer. It was never going to be smooth sailing with the contrary woman in his arms. He was just going to have to figure out how to deal with her. Because he was damned if he was letting her go.

Maddy was so cold. Her mind refused to work—she couldn't make sense of what she'd seen, what had happened to her. That man . . . his scream . . . No, she couldn't think about that. All she could do was shake uncontrollably.

Luca carried her back to the cabin, and she could hear the water sloshing around his feet. He set her down in the middle of it, the water almost to her ankles, and her bare feet curled in protest, but she didn't move. Couldn't move. She stood there, swaying, watching him as he went to the porthole and slammed it shut again, locking it. The endless, horrible rocking of the ship had lessened, back almost to its normal, gentle movement, and she should have been shocked at how swiftly the storm had passed, how it had gone from certain death to almost calm. But she couldn't think.

Luca came to stand in front of her. "You're freezing," he said.

She wanted to come up with something clever, but her teeth were chattering too much. She didn't even want to look at him, so she closed her eyes, starting when she felt his hands on her. "You need to get out of these wet clothes," he said in a low voice. "Don't fight me on this."

As if she could. She trembled as he stripped the clothes from her, dropping them in the water at their feet, and when she was naked he picked her up and carried her to the berth. The ropes were still here, and he yanked them away, tossing them aside before setting her down on the mattress. It was still damp from the sea spray, and she shuddered against him.

"Bloody hell," he muttered, and somehow managed to rip the sheet off while he released her against the slightly itchy mattress. "Hold on."

Hold on for what, she thought. *For icicles to drip from my eyes? Damn, those were tears! There was no reason to cry.*

She closed her eyes, clamping her jaw shut so her teeth wouldn't rattle out of her head. In the distance she could hear the slap of more cloth hitting the water, and then he was on the bed with all six feet whatever of him, and there was nothing but his hot, silken skin against her, wrapped around her, his heat flowing into her.

Fighting him was out of the question, and she didn't want to. She wanted to sink into him, lose herself in him, and she slid her arms around him, pulling him closer.

He was hard. Of course he was. And as her shaking slowed to intermittent shivers she knew she was wet between her legs. Of course she was. She needed him, any way she could have him, for as long as she could have him. She needed him right now.

He must have felt when everything changed. He'd had her plastered up against him, his heat radiating into her, and he was rubbing her back, soothing her, when she began to relax, no longer rigid with cold, but melting, flowing, and without thinking she rubbed her face against his shoulder, an instinctive caress, as she tried to move her hips closer to his.

If he hesitated for even a moment she wasn't aware of it. His hand on her back slid up to cup her neck, pulling her back so that he could look down into her eyes. His deep, implacable black ones, that she could never read, looked into hers for an answer she didn't know how to give.

But he could read her better than she could read him, because he put his mouth against hers, soft and coaxing, breathing warmth and the taste of the sea into her. The sea that had killed a man, that had almost killed her. The sea that he loved.

And she kissed him back, loving the sea because he loved it, sliding down beneath him, accepting the ocean, accepting everything.

He ran his hand down her leg, then pulled her knee up over his hip. They were lying facing each other, but he made no effort to push her onto her back, he simply arranged her so that that he could slip his fingers between her legs, to that damp, secret place that sent spirals of warmth throughout her. He moved his mouth to the side of her face, kissing her lightly on her abraded cheekbone, and then she could feel his kiss against the tenderness in her jaw where he'd hit her. He kissed her throat, his tongue dancing across the swiftly hammering pulse at the base of her neck, and then he pulled each hand in front of him, kissing her injured wrists before setting them back around him.

But that wasn't good enough. Because she was no longer cold, she was a blazing coil of need, and she reached between them, sliding her hand down his chest, past the tight nipples she wanted inexplicably to put her mouth against. She moved her hand farther, down, down, to capture the iron-hard erection. He'd been hard when they'd been fighting death out there on the storm-lashed deck. And as she lay tight in his arms everything had boiled down to one essential thing, the one thing that mattered to her. Luca.

Luca. Who didn't love her, and certainly didn't need her. Except for this way, and in this moment of heat and desire it would have to be enough. Her hand slid along his length, fingers delicate, tracing each vein, and desires so shocking she could scarcely believe them shot through her.

"Lie back," she said, an order in a barely audible rasp of a voice. But he heard her—she had the illogical sense that he would always hear her, and he lay back on the mattress, watching her.

She moved to her knees, looking down at him in the shadowy light that had followed the storm. Even in the dusk he was beautiful, golden, muscled, perfect. And so hard for her. Waiting for her. She hesitated, unaccountably shy, and he lifted his hand to brush it against her lips. "Do anything you want," he said. "I'm yours."

She wanted to weep with his lie, but she didn't. Right then he might believe it. Right then maybe he did belong to her. She leaned over him and carefully ran her tongue across one beaded nipple.

He jumped, making an inaudible sound, and she looked up at him. "Again," he whispered, and she found she could still smile. She moved down and ran her tongue over him, then sucked the flat nub into her mouth as he had done to her, and he moaned in pleasure, and she felt his cock twitch in her gentle, soothing hand.

She moved to his other nipple, doing the same, but this time she let her teeth graze him, and his hips came up off the mattress. How strangely blissful, she thought. What else would she like to do?

She moved down, tasting the salt of the ocean on his skin, pressing her face against the thin line of hair reaching down from his belly. And then she put her mouth on him, tentatively, delicately, letting her tongue dance across the top of his cock before she enveloped it, sinking down and letting his hardness slide into her mouth.

She heard his muttered curse words, odd, because he seemed to like it. He put gentle hands on her head, cupping it, and showed her what to do, moving up and down on his erection, letting her tongue dance against it, sucking at it, accepting it completely. She wasn't doing this for him, she was doing it for her. It brought her an intense pleasure she hadn't imagined, and her hands grasped the base of it, as she took more of him into her hungry mouth.

And then he pulled her away. For a moment she fought him, until he covered her mouth with his, filling her with his tongue, his taste, as he rolled her beneath him. He was between her legs, the head of his mouth-damp cock pressed against her, and he slid in the first few inches easily, before she remembered to brace herself. "More," she whispered against his mouth. "Please. More."

He pushed all the way in, and a spasm of pure delight tightened her body around him, and he seemed to swell inside her. "Hurry," she whispered in clawing desperation, fighting for release.

"No. I want to savor this." His answering thrusts, slow and steady, made her want to scream in frustration. But he couldn't control her body, any more than she could, and he'd only thrust a half-dozen times before she climaxed, her body clenching down on his, her skin prickling in an endless contraction that left her breathless and panting. For some reason she expected him to follow, as he had last time. He'd held still inside her as her pleasure washed over her again, but the moment she'd fallen back he began thrusting again, at the same, steady rhythm, and she felt so full, so possessed, that another wave washed over her, tightening everything, and he held still once more.

When she fell back again, panting, he kissed her breathless mouth. "I can keep this up for hours."

"Why?" she gasped.

His laugh touched strange places inside her. "Because there's no where else I'd rather be. I want to stay inside you forever, I want to make you come so hard you can't even think, I want to forget where I end and you begin. I want everything from you, Maddy Rose. Everything."

Oh, God, she thought, as he slid his hands up to cover her breasts, his thumbs brushing across her nipples and he continued to . . . to . . . what was that word the stable hands had used when they thought she couldn't hear them? *Fuck*. Such a dirty, nasty, erotic little word. That was what he was doing to her. And she wanted more.

His hands on her breasts set off another paroxysm of pleasure, and this time when he moved again he was faster, his breathing a little more shallow. And then, to her shock and despair, he pulled out of her completely.

She cried out, reaching for him, but he simply turned her onto her knees, pushing her hands down on the mattress, her face into the pillow, as he pushed inside her from behind. It was different this way, he was even bigger, pushing against different places inside her, and she buried her cry of pleasure into the pillow, wrapping her arms over her head, as he moved, faster and faster, and just when she thought she couldn't stand any more pleasure he reached between them and touched her between her legs, above where they joined, and it was everything, death and madness, pain and joy, as she lost herself completely, drowning in waves of dark, saturnine delight.

He pulled out, and she felt the warmth of his release on her back, and if she'd had enough of her brain she would have wept, but she was still being racked by wave after wave of almost unbearable pleasure that followed her as he slowly pulled her down, wrapping his arms around her as the last bit of control drained from his body.

It was a long time before she could speak. A long time before she wanted to speak. But when she did, she still managed to come up with a challenge. "Hours?" she said in a hoarse whisper.

She felt his smile against her skin. He was lying with his head on her stomach, holding her. "The night is still young," he said.

And she shivered.

CHAPTER TWENTY-TWO

MADDY WOKE ALONE. OF course she did, she thought, shoving her hair out of her face. Luca had probably already left the boat and set sail for the Argentines, just like Tarkington.

The water was gone from the floor, as were her clothes. Instead there was a pile of clean linen, including a simple day dress and unadorned underclothing, though no corset. The ship was docked somewhere, but all she could see from the porthole was the great wooden side of the quay, and they could be anywhere from Gibraltar to the Orkney Islands as far as she was concerned.

There was even a pitcher of tepid water beside a washbowl. Apparently the bathing room wasn't working—either damaged in the storm or perhaps it didn't work when they were docked. It didn't matter. She washed her body as thoroughly as she could, washed off the saltwater and the rain, washed away the touch and taste of him from her skin. She couldn't reach the spot on her back where he'd spilled his seed the first time, and she was glad of it. What would have happened if he hadn't protected her from making a child? What if she'd conceived, and he'd been long out of her life, at sea somewhere, forgetting all about her? It would have been a total disaster.

A disaster she wanted so much she could weep with longing. But not now. She was made from sterner stuff than this.

During the evening and endless night they'd slept and awoken, made love in ways that still made her blush in the morning, and he'd made it clear he wanted her. Made it clear he'd come after her. She was a fool to expect words of love.

But then she was a fool. She didn't want to stay with a man who didn't love her, desperate for scraps of attention, signs of affection. Not when she was so desperately in love with him.

He'd done one odd thing. Her wrist had begun bleeding again, and he rose and went to look for bandages. When he'd come back to the bed he'd brought them, and a knife as well. She'd looked at it dubiously, still too languid to make a protest.

To her surprise he took the knife and scored his own wrist, just enough for a few drops of blood to well from his golden skin, and then he set it against hers. It reminded her of a childish ritual, and she said nothing, watching him out of slumberous eyes as he held their wrists together for an endless moment. And then he'd released her, bandaged both her hands, and made love to her all over again.

She looked down at her wrists. She wasn't a complete fool, just a besotted one. She'd never been in love before—her infatuation with Tarkington had been just that—but she imagined it didn't kill you, even though right at that moment she felt stabbed to the heart. If it didn't go away you had to learn to live with it, and she wasn't the sort of woman to mope and sulk. She'd move on, take Lord Eastham's offer, and live a happy life as a wealthy, titled woman. She supposed she should feel guilty that she looked forward to her impending widowhood so eagerly, but there was a limit to how cheerful she could be in the circumstances. You did what you had to do. What she had to do was get the hell away from Luca before she made an even bigger fool of herself.

What would happen if she told him she loved him? Nothing good. He was a gypsy, a wanderer, a man without ties.

Though he'd been planning to marry that whey-faced bitch, Gwendolyn Haviland, she reminded herself in a spurt of fiery jealousy. So why couldn't he marry her instead?

Because he hadn't asked her. It was that simple.

She had to leave, or end up weak and pathetic. Was her pride more important than love? She didn't know—she wasn't being given the choice. She only wished she had his baby to carry to Eastham with her.

It was a wicked thought, but it really shouldn't matter. Eastham already had an heir and two spares from his previous marriages, and if she were pregnant he'd preen at the sign of his virility. And she'd have something of Luca for the rest of her life.

But he'd been careful each time, pulling out, until she'd wanted him to stay inside her. He hadn't.

She had the dismal feeling that sometime last night, in the throes of something so bright and powerful she couldn't quite reconcile it, she might have said something damning. She might have told him she loved him.

If she did, he didn't notice. Because he hadn't stopped, in fact, he'd redoubled his efforts, until she had the very real fear that her heart might just explode from so much pleasure.

She wasn't sure she could face him. Not remembering what she'd done at his soft urging. Not remembering what he'd done to her.

She dressed. To her relief there was even a pair of soft leather slippers beneath the pile of clothing. Had they been put there to ensure she could leave? No money, however, which was a mixed blessing. There wasn't much she could do in a foreign city without a sou to her name, but money would have felt like a bribe, or even worse, payment for services rendered. She would make do as she was.

The door was unlocked. Of course it was—there was no need to hold her prisoner anymore. Stepping into the deserted passageway, she glanced toward the steps. That man had dragged her up them, and she'd been unable to break free. What would he have done if she'd agreed to go off with him when he'd asked her to? Would she have even made it out of Devonport and the surrounding area of Plymouth alive?

Why would he want to kill her? Affection for his new friend Gwendolyn was logical but far-fetched, and her instincts told her that wasn't it. He was the one behind her father's death, she knew it, just as she knew that Luca was innocent. The problem was, she had no idea why and now he was dead, as well as the people he'd hired, and she would never know the truth. Her sisters would be disgusted with her, but at this point she was no longer certain she cared. At least he was at the bottom of the ocean, never to hurt anyone again.

Her legs still felt weak as she pulled herself up the narrow stairs, though whether it was the aftermath of the storm or a night in Luca's bed was questionable. The day was overcast, and the deck of the ship was empty of everyone except a handful of sailors working on the broken mast. No sign of Luca. No sign even of Billy Quarrells.

She turned to look at the quayside, and blinked. Not at the docks themselves, but the city that stretched beyond them. At the unmistakable tower of the newly constructed clock near the city center. She was in London.

The gangplank was down, and no one cared enough to stop her. She didn't dawdle—moving down at a quick pace, but the moment she reached land she almost collapsed. Somehow she'd grown used to the relentless motion of the sea, and the sudden stillness of the land was disconcerting. She took a deep breath, trying to center herself, and looked around her. No sign of Luca anywhere. He was gone, vanished. Just as Tarkington had. But this wound was so much deeper, more devastating.

She knew the docks well, from the days when she used to visit at her father's side. She racked her brain, trying to think of someone, anyone in the area who didn't hate her father so much that he would lend her enough money to get back to the comfort and safety of Nanny Gruen's. She wanted to weep in her nurse's lap; she wanted to hide somewhere where she could start to heal.

The offices of Russell Shipping were closed and shuttered, and normally that would have made her furious. Not any longer—she had worse disasters on her mind. She turned, almost running into a short, stocky gentleman.

"Excuse me, miss . . ." he began, and then stopped in shock. "Miss Russell?"

It was Bottingly, one of the men who had worked for her father for almost twenty years, a sweet, well-fed man who always had the patience to explain anything she asked. "Mr. Bottingly," she said with a forced smile. "How good to see you. You look well."

And he did. Losing his employment didn't seem to have harmed him a bit. He flushed, looking almost guilty. "I've been working for some of the new owners, Miss Russell. One of your father's captains has been buying up the ships, and I expect he'll need help since I can't see him giving up the sea."

"Captain Morgan," she said quietly.

"Yes, miss!" Bottingly beamed at her. "Then you know about that. I wrote you when your father passed away, but I do want to say once more how sorry I am about what happened. I never believed he did anything wrong."

"Nor did I," she said, grateful. She was ridiculously close to tears, so she pinched herself, hard, to keep from disgracing herself.

"Miss Russell, is there any way I can be of assistance?" He was looking at her more closely now, and he'd probably realized she was out in public without a companion, a hat, or a reticule. "May I call a hackney for you?"

She shook her head. "No money to pay for it, I'm afraid. And no place to go."

A frown turned Bottingly's usually friendly face into one of deep concern. "You come with me, Miss Russell. There's no way I'll leave my dear employer's daughter stranded on the docks of London. I know just the thing."

She didn't, couldn't put up a protest. She had no other place to go. She let dear Mr. Bottingly settle her into his own, serviceable carriage and direct his driver to take her to Berkeley Square. "Don't you worry, Miss Russell. That's your sister's house now, even if she's not there, and you'll be welcomed."

She had her own doubts, as the driver set her down outside an elegant mansion on the square. She walked up the front steps slowly, prepared to be tossed into the street. She could always sleep in an alleyway. She could . . . she was out of options.

The door opened, revealing a gentleman's gentleman, perfectly groomed, looking at her blankly. "May I help you, miss?" He had just the touch of an Irish accent, and for some reason she felt oddly comforted.

"I am Madeleine Russell," she said, and he stared at her blankly. She took a deep breath and continued. "My sister is Bryony Russell, though I suppose she's . . ."

"Oh, I beg your pardon, Miss Russell!" he cried, clearly distressed. "Come in, please. We're so used to thinking of the new Lady Kilmartyn as Mrs. Greaves that I forgot her maiden name. We had no word you were coming, but it won't take but a moment to get a room ready for you. We've been waiting for his lordship's return any day now, but so far we've heard nothing."

She could have collapsed in relief, but she'd done too much collapsing, and the valet or butler or majordomo was smaller than she was. She didn't want him laboring under her weight. "Thank you, Mr. . . . ?"

"Collins, Miss Russell. I'm Collins." He ushered her into the house. The place gleamed, spotless and elegant, smelling of beeswax and lemon oil. Her sister had done a better job during her time in service than she had, Maddy thought with a trace of irony. "Would you like me to show you to your room? It'll be the work of a moment to air the sheets and start a little fire to take the chill off."

"That would be lovely."

"And maybe I bring you a tray? A light repast?"

She should have been starving. Indeed, in times of trouble and stress she often turned to food to distract her anxious mind. She should have been longing for a banquet given how bad things were and how long it had been since she'd had a decent meal. The very thought made her nauseated as the worst storm couldn't.

"Perhaps something later," she said faintly.

"And do you perhaps have luggage following, Miss Russell?" he said in a solicitous voice. That was the kind of butler to have, she thought blindly. The kind who looked out for you.

"I'm afraid not. My clothes were lost at sea." True enough, even if it had only been one dress and her undergarments.

"At sea, miss! How shocking. But not to worry. His lordship had your sister's closets filled with clothing he ordered from Paris, and I know she'd want you to use some. Just let me take care of everything. Is there anyone you wish me to inform that you're in town?"

She shook her head. Luca had left her without a word, and all she wanted to do was hide.

Seven days. Seven days without her, seven days to first get roaring drunk, get in a fight, argue with Billy, threaten to take the ship out again and run it aground, hire a private detective, give Wart a fortune, punch his fist into a wall, almost breaking his hand. Seven days without her and he was going mad. How was he going to live the rest of his life if he didn't find her?

Billy had been philosophical. "Clearly she don't want to be leg-shackled to a sailing man."

"Or a gypsy," he'd said bitterly.

"There's that," Billy had agreed, never one to spare his feelings. "Even if she didn't say no when you asked her, this is her answer."

"Asked her what?" he demanded, annoyed.

Billy had given him a long, measuring look. "Asked her to marry you?" he said in a careful voice. "Told her you were in love with her?"

"I didn't."

"You didn't," Billy echoed flatly. "And you expected her to sit around and wait until you said something?"

"I didn't think she needed a bunch of words. Words are easy."

"Not for you, apparently. Jayzus!" Billy exploded. "I know more about women than you do and I don't even like the creatures! They need those words, Luca. They don't guess, they don't live on hope. We took off to the harbormaster without a word and you thought she'd sit around and wait for you? They have their pride. You have to tell them. Fact is, the same is true of men. If you love someone you tell them."

"What makes you think I love her?" Luca snapped. He'd been a fool to even consider the possibility. The first chance she got she left him.

"Oh, maybe it's the way you're looking for a fight everywhere you go, or the way you've been drinking, or the fact that you're about to jump down my throat for even suggesting such a thing." He shook his head in disgust. "I've taught you everything I know, but I never thought I needed to explain something as simple as this. Didn't you tell that Haviland woman you loved her when you proposed?"

He glared at Billy. "Of course. It was a lie."

"And other women you bedded?"

"Yes."

"So what makes the difference?"

Luca had paused, wishing he had an excuse to punch Billy, knowing he only had the truth to offer. It was wrong, and inescapable. "You know the answer as well as I do. Because I really do love her."

Billy nodded. "Exactly. So go out and find her."

In the end it wasn't Wart, but Billy himself who found a trace of her. The newspaper had been three days old, but Billy had always had a fancy for reading the society posts, something Luca could never understand, and he'd found the notice buried in a paragraph of massive unimportance.

"Miss R. is in town, staying in Berkeley Square at her sister, the Countess of K.'s house while she and her husband, Lord K., enjoy a honeymoon abroad." With its refusal to name names it had taken Billy a while to make the connection.

"She's still in town, right under our noses," Billy had said. "And chances are she doesn't want a damned thing to do with you. But you'll never know unless you ask, eh?"

"She made her choice," Luca said flatly. "If she had feelings for me she would have stayed, not managed to sneak out the moment my back was turned."

"You didn't give her a choice, you moonling!" Billy snapped. "Listen to me. You're a pirate and a gypsy. You know how to get what you want. I've never known you to wait for permission. Unless you'd rather mope around like some moonstruck virgin, giving a bad name to pirates the world over."

Luca had glared at him. "Tomorrow," he said.

Billy glared back at him. "Right now," he said. "What's more important? Pride? Or love?"

"Pride," Luca said flatly. A moment later he was gone.

Maddy should have been feeling better. It had been a week of cosseting, of specially cooked meals and people looking out for her every need. It was a week living in a luxury she hadn't experienced since her father died, a week where she didn't have to clean, didn't have to work, didn't have to worry about anyone. She could sleep as late as she wanted, stay up as late, wander around in the back garden when no one was watching. She was safe and well cared for. Surely she should be feeling better by now.

If she ever saw Luca again she would spit in his face, kick him in the shins. No, she would be gay and cheerful, reminding him of all he had lost. And then she'd hire someone to kick him where she'd like to kick him. How could he have let her go? He said he'd always come for her. Where was he?

But days passed and Luca didn't show up. She wasn't sure how she expected him to find her, much less want to find her, but she wasn't feeling particularly reasonable. He had abandoned her the moment they reached London and never thought twice, while she couldn't think about anything else but him. So be it. There was always Lord Eastham.

Except that she couldn't bring herself to send the old man a note, informing him she was in town. Something kept stopping her—perhaps it was the memory of his liver spots or his tendency to drool. There was no hurry, she told herself, though Lord Eastham wasn't getting any younger. If she didn't do something soon she'd be a widow before she married.

Was the *Maddy Rose* still under repairs? Was he still here, ignoring her presence, or had he returned to Devonport and Gwendolyn Haviland? If so, he deserved her, and so she'd tell him. If she ever saw him again.

It was one of those rare sunny mornings in late spring as she sat reading in the garden, trying to ignore the hornets that were diving at her. She had found a number of salacious French novels, which she dearly hoped hadn't belonged to the villainous late countess, but by that time she was so desperate for distraction she couldn't afford to be too fastidious. Just because the woman had been a vicious, evil tramp didn't mean she couldn't have decent taste in wicked novels.

She set the novel down just as the wicked highwayman had captured the innocent damsel. The innocent damsel who was a watering pot, limp and pathetic.

Maddy's back stiffened. Had she been just as craven? Waiting around, sniveling, for Luca to appear and throw himself at her feet, begging forgiveness? He was a pirate, for God's sake. He wouldn't grovel for anyone.

Well, neither would she. But that didn't mean she had to accept defeat and slink away into the night.

Long ago she'd fantasized about grabbing him by the lapels and slamming his bigger, harder body up against a wall. And then kissing the hell out of him.

Maybe that was exactly what she needed to do. Right now, before he left London, assuming he was still in residence. And if he'd left?

Then she could board a train and go after him. Anything rather than continue on in this pitifully defeated misery. She was no victim, she was a heroine of her own love story, and she was going to make one last attempt at claiming what she wanted.

She was halfway toward the house when she heard the steps on the footpath, and she froze, her heart stopping for a moment before it lurched forward, rather like the *Maddy Rose* in the storm. The *Maddy Rose* had survived, so would she. Finally, *finally* he'd come for her.

She turned, joy bubbling within her as she expected Luca to round the corner. A feeling that died as Jasper Tarkington came into view.

"Darling!" he cried, throwing himself at her feet and grasping her hand, just as she'd hoped Luca would. "I was so afraid I wouldn't be able to find you! Can you ever forgive me?"

She stared down at his bent head in shock and disbelief. The days in South America had been kind to him. His sandy colored hair was now streaked with gold, his skin had turned a faintly darker color, though a far cry from the rich honey of Luca's skin. His sky blue eyes were looking up at her in such a beseeching manner that it was almost comical, and she stared at him, speechless.

"Jasper," she managed to say after a minute. "This is a shock."

He looked a little nonplussed, as if he had expected her to throw herself into his arms. A few months ago this had been what she had dreamed about, wept for, longed for. This was the man she had been planning to marry, the man she had given herself to. He had come back to her.

And she didn't give a bloody damn.

"I know I've been terrible, my darling," he was saying. "I was so confused when I left. You see, my family had been counting on your dowry, and you know people like us cannot simply marry for love, much as we might want to. I had to be practical and break it off."

She tried, unsuccessfully, to detach his clinging grip. What a botheration! She'd finally built up the courage to go after Luca and now Tarkington was in her way. "After you deflowered me," she said caustically.

He flinched. "Ah, but how could I resist you? You came to me, you were so sweet, so willing . . ."

All true enough. She'd been desperate, and he'd known it. So he was blaming her for that colossal mistake. "Why are you here, Jasper?"

"Why . . . because I love you, silly girl," he said with a laugh that was just this side of irritating. "I tried to make the wise decision, but I kept thinking about you, and I decided to hell with everything. Beg pardon," he added, suddenly realizing he'd used the word "hell" in a lady's presence. He had no idea who she was, or that *hell* was simply a pleasantry to her when she was properly riled. As she was quickly becoming. "It doesn't matter that your father was a depraved criminal. I'm willing to overlook it. I want us to get married."

"Why?" It was a simple question, but he looked taken aback.

"But I told you . . ."

"Not able to find a rich wife in the Argentines?"

He got up from his ridiculous pose by her feet, tugging down his waistcoat in an attempt at dignity. "In fact, there were a number of rich, beautiful women who would have made perfectly suitable wives. But I discovered that it was you I loved, Madeleine. I can't live without you." There were actual tears in his eyes, and she realized with a certain amount of shock that he meant it. He did love her. Of course, having a wealthy earl as a brand-new brother-in-law didn't hurt matters either, she thought cynically.

She opened her mouth to give him an answer when Collins appeared from around the hedge, followed by a short, slightly shuffling creature. "Oh, bloody hell," she said out loud when she recognized him, and Jasper drew back with a gasp of shock.

"My Lord Eastham," Collins announced with full pomp and ceremony.

"Dearest girl!" Eastham scuttled forward, reeking of scent. "I couldn't believe it when I read in the papers that you were back in town. I've missed you terribly! Tell me you're back in London to stay!"

It was difficult, but she managed to plaster a welcoming smile on her face. Damn the newspapers. She held out her ungloved hand and Lord Eastham promptly drooled on it. "How lovely to see you, my lord."

"But why didn't you send me a note telling me you were in town? I thought we had a special relationship?" he chided her. It was only then that he noticed Jasper standing off to one side, conflicting emotions washing over his handsome face.

"You know Mr. Tarkington, do you not, my lord Eastham?" she said with resignation. It appeared to be a question of feast or famine when it came to marriage, and at that point she was much preferring famine. She couldn't marry either of these men, no matter how wise it seemed.

She took a deep breath. "Gentlemen, I hate to be ungracious but I was just on my way out . . ."

"Nonsense, my dear," Eastham said. "What could be more important than your future?"

It was her future she was thinking of. She swallowed her instinctive retort.

Eastham reacted more quickly, turning his back on the interloper. "My dear, allow me to take you out to dinner this evening, and we can talk about the future."

"She can hardly go out alone and unchaperoned!" Tarkington snapped.

Eastham turned on him, a venal little toad up against youth and propriety. "We all know just how alone and unchaperoned she was right before you left for South America, young man. You were the one who ruined her for marriage, not I!"

"Ruined me for marriage?" Maddy said blankly.

Eastham turned back to her, an uneasy expression in his faded eyes. "My dear, you can't have expected me to offer marriage? I have my family name to protect. You're soiled goods, but lovely and charming for all that, and I was planning to settle a house in Mayfair on you, as well as a generous allowance . . ."

"You bloody son of a bitch!" a voice roared, and Maddy wondered if now was a good time to faint. All she'd needed to make this comedy of errors complete was the arrival of the pirate captain.

She was aware of a number of things, all observed as if from a great distance. First, that Lord Eastham sailed through the air quite gracefully for a squat, toad-like figure, landing in the rose bush with a comically high-pitched scream. Dismissing him, she turned back to see Luca confronting Jasper, another shock. She'd always thought

Jasper was so tall, so handsome. He looked pale and weedy next to Luca, with a weak chin, a pale mustache, narrow shoulders, and an expression of almost pathetic fear.

"Who the hell are you?" he demanded, his voice quavering just the slightest bit.

"Her husband."

Maddy jerked her head toward him in shock. Husband? What the bloody hell was he talking about? He hadn't even asked her, much less actually gone ahead and married her.

Tarkington was looking at him in disdain. "Don't be absurd. She'd never marry a filthy gypsy."

She was at last beginning to enjoy herself, despite what lies Luca was spinning. In the background she could hear Collins extricate Eastham from the rose bush, with the old man muttering threats and imprecations towards all and sundry as Collins steered him away from the garden.

"Actually he's a very clean gypsy," she pointed out, feeling devilish. "And he's also a pirate."

Luca didn't turn to look at her—all his attention was concentrated on the trembling Tarkington. "So you're the man who decided to seduce her and then run off. Quite the gentleman, aren't you?"

"It's none of your . . ."

"I told you, she's my wife."

"Excuse me," she broke in, more interested in Luca's claim than Tarkington's reaction, "but I don't remember getting married."

"I'll refresh your memory," he snarled, his eyes still boring into Tarkington's. Maddy had experienced the full force of that black gaze, and she was surprised Tarkington's knees weren't knocking together. "Now I can't decide," he continued to Jasper, "whether I should kill you or simply beat you to a pulp."

"You can h-h-have her," Jasper stammered. "Not w-w-worth the trouble."

In the next moment he was on the ground, having been the recipient of Luca's fist. Maddy walked over to Tarkington's motionless form. She gave him a sharp little kick. "You're very good at rendering people unconscious, aren't you?"

Finally he turned to look at her, the fury slowly fading, and for the first time since she'd known him the devilish pirate captain looked almost uncertain. "You have truly terrible taste in men," he said flatly.

"I know," she agreed, giving him a speaking look. "When did we get married? I don't happen to recall it."

"When I stole you away and took you to bed, and then later we were joined by blood. Among gypsies that constitutes a wedding twice over, and you're now a runaway bride." He was watching her closely. "And there's no such thing as a gypsy divorce."

"Give me one good reason why I should pay any attention to all this. We're nothing alike."

His slow grin melted her, like butter under the hot sun. "No, not alike at all. Neither of us is ruthless, stubborn, deceptive, adventurous. I despise clever, forceful women who can give as good as they get. And we're terrible in bed together. I can hardly stand to kiss you."

"True enough," she said solemnly. "I see another problem."

"You don't love me?" he suggested, clearly believing such a thing was impossible, the conceited jackass.

She didn't answer that one. "You're only half gypsy. You're going to have to marry me in an Anglican church as well."

For a moment he looked stunned. "Are you proposing?"

"I'm countering your proposal." God, she'd missed him. God, how she loved him. "I was about to come and find you, you know, if these two hadn't gotten in my way." She stepped over Tarkington's prostrate body without a second glance, coming up to him, knowing he could see the love in her eyes. There was no way she could hide it. "And there's one more thing."

Before she could ask he'd pulled her into his arms, his mouth on hers, and she wanted to weep with joy. But the time for tears was past. When he finally lifted his head he gave her that glorious, wonderful smile that made her heart melt.

"Yes," he said, before she could ask the question. "Of course I'm in love with you. Why else would I be here?"

"Maybe you missed my sweet nature?" she suggested.

He laughed, and kissed her again, lifting her feet off the ground and swinging her around. "You're going to make my life a holy hell, aren't you?" he said when he set her down again.

"I'll do my best," she promised sweetly. "And I love you so much I'm willing to sail back on a boat with you."

"Ship," he said automatically, even his dark eyes were smiling. "That's true love indeed."

"Yes," she said, "it is."

ABOUT THE AUTHOR

ANNE STUART is a grand master of the genre, winner of Romance Writers of America's prestigious Lifetime Achievement Award, survivor of more than thirty-five years in the romance business, and still just keeps getting better.

Her first novel was *Barrett's Hill*, a gothic romance published by Ballantine in 1974 when Anne had just turned twenty-five. Since then she's written more gothics, regencies, romantic suspense, romantic adventure, series romance, suspense, historical romance, paranormal, and mainstream contemporary romance.

She's won numerous awards, appeared on most bestseller lists, and speaks all over the country. Her general outrageousness has gotten her on *Entertainment Tonight*, as well as in *Vogue, People, USA Today, Women's Day*, and countless other national newspapers and magazines.

When she's not traveling, she's at home in northern Vermont with her luscious husband of thirty-six years, an empty nest, three cats, four sewing machines, and one Springer Spaniel, and when she's not working she's watching movies, listening to rock and roll (preferably Japanese), and spending far too much time quilting.